RULES IN RESCUE

NICHOLE SEVERN

MARKED BY THE MARSHAL

JULIE ANNE LINDSEY

MILLS & BOON

First Published in Great Britain 2019
by Mills & Boon, an imprint of HarperCollins*Publishers*
1 London Bridge Street, London, SE1 9GF

Rules in Rescue © 2019 Natascha Jaffa
Marked by the Marshal © 2019 Julie Anne Lindsey

ISBN: 978-0-263-27402-8

0219

MIX
**Paper from
responsible sources**
FSC
www.fsc.org
FSC™ C007454

Printed and bound in Spain
by CPI, Barcelona

RULES IN
RESCUE

NICHOLE SEVERN

For my readers.

I finished this book a month before I gave birth to my second demon spawn.

It was nice knowing you while I was still sane.

Chapter One

"I need your help," she said.

Four simple words had ripped weapons expert Anthony Harris away from his current surveillance assignment and into downtown Anchorage at three in the morning.

And there she was. Glennon Chase—his ex-fiancée—needed him after all this time.

"I haven't heard from you in almost five years and now you need my help?" The weight of the Beretta M9 in his shoulder holster kept him focused on the situation at hand and not on the shadows under those hazel-specked green eyes. He shouldn't have come. Too much history between them. Too easy to get wrapped up in her again. "Don't you have an entire team of soldiers to help you with whatever investigation you're working?"

The muted beam from her flashlight streaked across the pitted hardwood floors of the abandoned house. She'd given him the address over the phone, insisted he couldn't be followed. Because she wasn't supposed to be there. According to his contact, the Military Police Corps had assigned her to investigate the theft of a weapons shipment out of Joint Base Elmendorf Richardson. So why had Glennon told her superior officer she was on base when, in reality, she was about to be charged with breaking and entering downtown?

"I'm not here on an official investigation." Her gaze darted out the front window, her fingers visibly tightening around the flashlight. Nervous? That wasn't like her. At least, not the Glennon he knew. Correction: had known. A lot had changed over the last five years. Her dirty-blond hair, now darker than he remembered, had been pulled back in a loose ponytail. Nothing like the polished, professional way she used to wear it. Long, lean muscle peeked out from under her thin T-shirt, a far cry from the soft features he'd loved all those years ago. She'd always been strong, but she'd obviously been pushing herself physically since the last time they'd been in the same room together. And damn, she looked good.

"My partner, Bennett Spencer…he's missing. You're the only one who can help me find him," she said.

"A missing persons case." Tension flooded through the tendons along his shoulders, pulling his Kevlar vest tighter. Blackhawk Security's CEO, Sullivan Bishop, had hired him as a weapons expert, using his knowledge from over a decade with the 75th Ranger Regiment to the team's advantage. War, death, murder. He'd seen it all. But this…this was different. He'd been trained in recovery and rescue, but every cell in his body screamed he shouldn't have come. Partnering with his ex? Flat-out dangerous. "You need the police. Not me."

"The police can't help me." She took a single step toward him, hesitant. Desperation seeped into her movements, in the way she held so tightly onto the flashlight in one hand and her Glock in the other. Something had scared her—or someone. And while the idea she'd been rattled didn't sit well, this wasn't the assignment for him. The past had to stay in the past. He'd moved on. She had to do the same.

Her voice dipped into a whisper. "You're the only one I can trust."

He held back a laugh. Trust? That word meant nothing to her. Anthony shortened the distance between them, the hairs on the back of his neck rising. Heat simmered under his sternum. "What would you know about trust?"

Her brows drew inward, her one and only tell when things didn't go her way. Nice to see he could still get to her.

"I know what you must think of me, but I wouldn't have called unless I was absolutely sure about getting you involved. I can't do this alone," she said. "There's no one else who can help me. Please."

What the hell had she gotten herself into here? He scanned the rest of the street out the dirt-covered front window. The cul-de-sac looked like any other neighborhood downtown. Snow piled up in yards and on flat roofs, white brick with a few scattered trees clinging to the structures. The Kevlar weighed him down as he scanned the rest of their surroundings. No movement on the street, no shifting of shadows.

Taking a deep breath, he forced himself back into the moment. "Sorry. You've got the wrong guy. I'm sure the army can help you find the right one."

Anthony turned back the way he'd come. The dilapidated floorboards creaked under his steps.

"I have a son," she said.

Ice ran through his veins and he stopped cold. Heart

thundering in his chest, he tried to wrap his head around her words. A son? He turned around slowly, the house protesting his shifting weight. He ran the numbers. They hadn't seen each other in five years, not since she'd walked out on him while he'd been on tour. A slight tremor shook his hand.

"How…" How old? He clenched his jaw. No. It wasn't possible. She wouldn't have left if she'd been pregnant. She would've told him. Which meant she had moved on. Just without him. "Why are you telling me this?"

"I'm going after my partner with or without your help." Moonlight crawled across her features as she moved toward him. The shadow along one side of her face shifted as she widened her stance. "My son has a better chance of his mother coming home if you have my back."

That was how she was going to play this? Putting the blame on him if something happened to her. As if blame hadn't already eaten him from the inside. He faced her completely, a hint of the rage he'd held back when she'd left bubbling to the surface. "You have some nerve—"

A laser sight crawled across Glennon's T-shirt.

Anthony lunged. The front window exploded as the echo of a single rifle shot rang through his ears. He crushed her into the floor then rolled them both near the wall. The world spun, but adrenaline kept him focused and alert as it had in far too many situations just like this. Single shooter armed with a sniper rifle. The echo of the shot died fast, but not before he'd pinpointed the shooter's location: the trees south of the house.

Anthony raised his head above the windowsill, his

knees on either side of Glennon's waist, and scanned the tree line. The Beretta found its way into his hand. Wood exploded to his left as another bullet ripped through the darkness. He ducked below the window to avoid losing his head.

Glennon had clamped a hand over her left shoulder, both her gun and flashlight discarded on the floor where he'd tackled her. The small amount of moonlight reaching them showed something dark and wet spreading through her fingers. Blood. She'd been shot. Squinting, she let a small groan vibrate through her.

Peeling her hand back, Anthony scanned her shoulder. "Can you move?"

A scream escaped her control, singeing his nerve endings. She rolled onto her side and pushed herself upright. "I'm fine. Just get us out of here."

He aimed for the now motionless trees and fired. Three rounds. Four. The gun kicked back in his hand with each pull of the trigger. No movement. No return fire. The shooter had done what he'd come to do and disappeared. Or maybe not.

Hell. Pulse pounding hard in his throat, Anthony holstered his gun then reached for her. Wrapping one arm around her back and the other in her hand, he wrenched Glennon off the floor and into his side. Her roselike scent—a scent that seemed to cling to him—claimed his attention as they moved through the house. He couldn't focus on that now. There were no guarantees the shooter had vanished or that he'd come alone, but they weren't going to sit around and wait to find out.

Mentally alert. Physically strong. Morally straight,

he reminded himself. The words had been drilled into his mind at boot camp.

Glennon picked up her discarded weapon. Moving when he moved, turning when he turned, she followed his lead, not missing a beat. "Do you want to help me now?"

Want to? Hell, no. Need to? Apparently.

"Do you really want to have this conversation while you're bleeding?" He steered them toward the north end of the house, opposite the shooter's last known position. If they had any chance of making it to his SUV without being shot, this was it. One hundred yards. That was all they had before they reached the vehicle, but that distance could feel like a mile when under fire. Pulling up short of the slashed screen door at the back of the house, Anthony scanned her from head to toe. "Ready?"

She nodded, blood coating her gun hand.

"Keep low, move fast and use me as cover if you have to." He didn't give her a chance to respond as he kicked the screen door aside and rushed them onto the covered back porch. A gust of freezing December air took the breath from his lungs. Hiking the Beretta shoulder-level, he sidestepped along the side of the house, making them as small a target as possible in case the shooter decided to come around the corner.

Snow crunched under their steps. Once they reached the corner of the house, they could make a run for it. Until then, the snow would only slow them down. Instincts on high alert, he listened for movement—anything—that pointed to an ambush.

"On my count." He had the SUV in his sights and Glennon glued to his side. "One." He studied the fast-spreading pattern of blood across her T-shirt. "Two." There were no other options at this point. They had to run. Now. He slowed his breathing, wrapped his free hand around her upper arm. A rush of electricity shot through him at the contact. "Three."

They raced toward the open white-picket-fence gate. A third shot exploded from the trees. Then a fourth. Anthony maneuvered Glennon to his opposite side, using his body as a shield, and emptied the Beretta's magazine toward the trees.

Alaska winters were some of the darkest on the planet. He couldn't see a damn thing, let alone narrow down the shooter's location in a patch of thick trees without stopping. Getting Glennon to safety had to be his priority. Pocketing the empty gun as they crossed the cul-de-sac, he unholstered another weapon and fired.

"Go, go, go!" Fifty feet. Thirty. The SUV came to life at the press of a button and, within seconds, he'd shoved Glennon into the back seat. He ripped open the driver's door, hiked himself behind the wheel and rammed the vehicle into Reverse. The houses that lined the street blurred as he leveraged his arm against the passenger's headrest and slammed his foot against the accelerator. One last bullet fought to penetrate the windshield as he maneuvered the SUV out of the neighborhood, tires screaming in protest, but didn't make it through. One of the perks of working for a heavily resourced security company: bulletproof glass. He'd never been more grateful for it than right that second.

He spun the vehicle around and sped away from the abandoned house and the single shadowed figure standing in the middle of the street. The gunfire died, his fight-or-flight response returning to normal. The SUV's engine roared as he pushed it faster. One glance at Glennon in the rearview mirror and he white-knuckled the steering wheel. He inhaled deeply to slow his racing heart rate. "You still alive?"

"I'm alive. Thanks to you." She refused to look at him, staring out one of the back windows. Pretending the last few minutes hadn't happened—that she hadn't just been shot—wouldn't get her out of answering his questions.

He relaxed against the seat, finally able to take a full breath since setting foot in that house. "Good, then you can tell me who the hell tried to kill you."

SEVENTY-TWO HOURS. That was how long her partner, Sergeant Bennett Spencer, had been missing.

Criminal Investigations Special Agent Glennon Chase read his last text message on her phone's screen for the hundredth time as the SUV plowed through the snow-covered streets of her hometown.

I found proof.

What did it mean? She hadn't been able to locate him since. He wouldn't return her calls, hadn't been seen anywhere near his army barracks or shown up at the temporary office they'd been assigned to complete their investigation. On top of that, the GPS on his phone had gone offline. Or been destroyed.

But Bennett was alive. She had to believe that. Otherwise...

"Your guess is as good as mine at this point." Glennon pressed her palm against the bullet wound in her left shoulder as she shifted in the back seat. Pain flooded through her but it kept her focused. In the moment. Her attention slid to the wall of pure muscle in the driver's seat. Because letting her guard down around Sergeant Major Anthony Harris would be a mistake she couldn't afford. Not again.

The former Ranger hadn't changed a bit. Aviator sunglasses hanging from his T-shirt, sandy-brown hair, full beard, thick muscles strapped inside that familiar Kevlar vest adorned with a patch of the Grim Reaper. Gun at his side. He was attractive, intelligent, protective—everything she'd imagined she'd needed when they'd first gotten together after basic training. He'd still been in the army then, her weapons instructor out of Fort Benning. And those eyes...the darkest blue she'd ever encountered. Dark and deadly.

"Hope a bullet in the shoulder was worth it." Anthony kept his focus on the road, but the dangerous sinking of his tone meant his focus rested one hundred percent on what had happened back at that house. She didn't blame him. An ambush had been the last thing on her mind when she'd tracked Bennett's GPS to that location. "Did you at least find what you were looking for?"

Right. Focus. She swallowed the rush of warmth spreading through her chest and stared out the passenger-side window into the cold. "You mean aside from proof someone doesn't want me to find my partner?" She inhaled through another round of pain and pressed her shoulders into the leather seat as a distraction. "No."

The house had been abandoned long before she'd gotten there, but Bennett's GPS hadn't lied. He'd been there for close to an entire day before his phone had been turned off. Or died. Which didn't make sense.

They'd been assigned by the provost marshal general to investigate a stolen shipment of military hardware out of JBER here in Anchorage. Guns, ammunition, rocket launchers. At no point in their investigation had an abandoned house located downtown come into the equation. Bennett shouldn't have been there.

"One-word answers aren't going to help me keep you alive." The rough edge to Anthony's voice added to the weight in her stomach.

Relief flooded through her, however fleeting. She shouldn't have called him, but after two days of no leads and running into dead ends, she'd run out of options. Going to the police, even involving the army in her partner's disappearance, could put her son in danger. Because while she didn't know exactly what'd happened to Bennett, her gut said he hadn't walked away. In the end, Anthony was the only person she could trust not to get himself killed and to protect her in the process. "Does that mean you've decided to help me?"

Anthony pressed a button hidden beneath the driver's sun visor and swung the SUV down into an underground parking garage. The building wasn't familiar. At least, she didn't recognize it. Several SUVs, exactly like his, lined the parking stalls. No other personnel were visible in the cement fortress. No security guards. No employees. The place was empty.

"We're here," he said.

She caught sight of four cameras mounted to the ceiling, all with small red lights beneath the lenses. That, coupled with the Batcave entrance, gave her an idea of where they'd ended up.

Blackhawk Security. His new employer.

Anthony shouldered his way out of the vehicle and

rounded back to open her door for her, weapon in hand. Always the gentleman, always prepared for the worst.

"I've got to say, I never imagined you working in the private sector." He certainly hadn't been willing to change careers when they'd been a couple.

She slid out of the SUV, but fell into him when another round of pain shot across her shoulder. With one hand on his chest to keep from face-planting on the cement, she tried to ignore the seductive heat snaking through her. Being shot at, taking a bullet—that she could handle. It'd been part of her job since the day she'd been promoted to special agent within CID. But being this close to him, his clean, masculine scent resurrecting countless nights spent wrapped in each other's arms... Glennon added another foot of space between them.

No. Despite her need for Anthony's help, that was as far as it'd go between them. Nothing more. She pulled away. Her voice wavered as she forced her gaze from his. Or was it from the blood loss? "What finally made you decide to leave the wars behind?"

"We need to take a look at that wound." He slammed the door closed behind her and headed for the single elevator on the north side of the parking garage. Studying their surroundings, he adjusted his vest. Ready for anything.

A rush of warmth crawled into her neck and face as she kept on his heels. The elevator doors closed behind them, her stomach dropping as they ascended to the top floor. Whether it was from the change in elevation or being caged in a small container with the one man she thought she'd never see again, she didn't know. Didn't matter. She had a job to do and the bullet tearing through her left shoulder should've kept reminding her of that.

With a muted ding, the elevator doors parted and they stepped onto a darkened floor. It was after hours. Most Blackhawk Security personnel had obviously gone home for the day, but Anthony led her to a single lit room at the end of the hall.

A breathtaking view of the Chugach Mountain range took up the entire east side of the floor, and her insides ached. This had been her home for most of her life. She'd loved it. The wildlife, the snow, the sunsets and beautiful lakes. Leaving this city—she glanced at Anthony—leaving *him* had been one of the hardest decisions she'd ever made. Even if it had been the only option at the time.

"I've already called in the rest of the team." Anthony diverted her to a hallway to his left, bypassing an occupied conference room, and motioned her inside the first door. "But I'm going to check out that wound first."

"Like I said back at the scene, I'm fine." She'd taken a bullet before. And lived. But he didn't need to know the details of that particular investigation. "I came to you to keep me alive, and so far, you've done a bang-up job. Now, let me do mine."

She made her way back to their original route and swung the floor-to-ceiling oak door open with her uninjured arm. The large conference room was dominated by men and women she assumed made up the founding core of Blackhawk Security. One stood immediately, striding toward her with his hand extended. He was muscular, although not quite as big as Anthony. Dark hair and a five-o'clock shadow were eclipsed by his sharp sea-blue eyes. "Sullivan Bishop, CEO of Blackhawk Security. You must be Ms. Chase. We've heard a lot about you."

"Sergeant Chase." Probably nothing good, considering how things had ended between her and Anthony. She wrapped her blood-free hand around Sullivan's calloused grip. "But as much as I love the chitchat, I don't have a lot time. My partner is missing and the longer I'm here, the less likely I'll find him alive. So I need Anthony to help in the recovery. I'll pay whatever fee you set. There's just one condition—you can't involve the authorities or the army."

"All right. Then let's get to the point, Sergeant." Sullivan threw Anthony an amused smile before dropping her hand and folding his arms across his chest. His stance screamed military—wide legs, impossible to push over if she tried. A SEAL, if she had to guess. She could tell by the haircut. "Who put that bullet in your shoulder and why?"

Anthony threaded his fingers around her uninjured arm, hiking her into his side. "She needs to get this wound checked before we get into this."

Hadn't they already covered this?

"I have no idea." Stinging pain worked through her as she wrenched out of his hold to take a seat. As much as she appreciated his concern, they didn't have time for this. Flashes of the night's events were fresh in her mind and she needed to remember every detail. Talking it through was the only way to do that. The shooter could be anywhere by now.

Collapsing back into one of the leather chairs, she exhaled hard, checking her wound. No major damage. She'd live, but she'd need a good cleaning, and stitches front and back. "But I'm positive it has to do with my partner's disappearance. I tracked Sergeant Spencer's phone GPS to that location. Obviously someone doesn't want me following in his footsteps."

Anthony took a seat two chairs down, her awareness of him at an all-time high.

"Could it have been your partner who pulled that trigger?" Another member of the team leaned forward in his chair, fingers laced on the dark reflective wood. His expression seemed to light up at the idea.

She'd done research on the people in this room before dialing Anthony's number. Sullivan Bishop: CEO. Elizabeth Dawson: network security. Kate Monroe: profiler. Vincent Kalani: forensics. She'd had to know what kind of support—if any—she'd have access to during her off-the-books investigation. But something about Elliot Dunham, Blackhawk Security's con-artist-turned-private-investigator, made her hope the firm had a whole lot of hazard insurance to keep him on their payroll. "It's not him. I know Bennett. He'd never take a shot at me."

"It's amazing what some people will do to keep their secrets safe." Elliot smiled. "And going to the police is a bad idea because…?"

All eyes landed on her, a physical pressure holding Glennon in her chair. "The fewer people involved, the better."

She had her own secrets. Granted they wouldn't stay buried forever, but she wasn't about to reveal them right here, right now. And not to these people. She glanced toward her ex-fiancé, every muscle in her body strung tight. A rush of dizziness crashed through her and she checked her stained shirt. Too much blood loss. Damn it. Maybe she should've listened to him after all. She couldn't go on like this much longer.

Gripping the table hard, Glennon tried to breathe through the darkness closing around the edges of her vision. "On second thought, I think I'll take you up on that patch job now."

Chapter Two

Memories could only get a man so far.

Having Glennon here, his hands on her skin, resurrected those irrational feelings he thought he'd buried
a long time ago. He wiped the excess blood from her
wound, doing everything in his power not to crowd
her as he worked. That was the thing about Glennon.
She urged him to get closer, pulling him in with her
scent, the brightness in her gaze and her smile. But
she'd made herself perfectly clear when she'd tugged
her arm out of his hold in the conference room. Calling him tonight had been strictly business.

"How bad is it?" A hiss escaped from between her
teeth as he inspected the wound for shrapnel, but she
turned her head away to hide her reaction. Exhaustion wreaked havoc under her eyes, but she wouldn't
admit she needed sleep. Wouldn't admit she needed
anything. Always insisted on taking care of herself.
Which made her asking for his help in the middle of
the night...suspicious.

"Could've been worse. Looks like a through-and-
through. Just the one piece of shrapnel." He'd seen
plenty of bullet wounds on tour. Not for the faint of
heart, but she held her own.

Anthony discarded the sliver of metal and bloody gauze into the biohazard bin then reached for the needle and thread he'd already prepped. Crude, but she'd asked for a fast patch job. No anesthetic. No doctor consult.

"Good." Glennon tugged at her T-shirt and sports bra to give him better access. All that perfect, creamy skin exposed only for him. "Let's get this over with."

Pinching the wound with sanitized hands, he sutured the sides closed. The rise and fall of her lean shoulders set his heart rate at an easy rhythm. As much as he'd wanted to hunt down that shooter on his own to make the bastard pay for putting a bullet in her, relief spread through him. She was alive. That was all that mattered. She'd asked him to protect her, and he'd done his job. But pulling bullet fragments from her shoulder wouldn't be the end of it. Not in the least.

Silence descended in a physical pressure against his chest. He'd imagined this day, the one where he'd be face-to-face with her again. He'd demand a reason for her leaving, try to explain why he'd gone on yet another tour. The conversations had played through his head on a near constant loop since the day he'd come home to the empty house they'd shared. But none of his fantasies had included a bullet in her shoulder or Glennon centered in a sniper's crosshairs. He swallowed back violent ideas of revenge sprinting through his head. He had to focus on something else. Anything else but her. "How old is your son?"

The idea she'd been with other men since leaving—had had a child with one of them—tightened the muscles down his spine. It shouldn't have. They hadn't been together in five years. So why did the thought of her moving on make him tighten his grip around the needle?

Her rough exhale cooled the overheated skin down his forearm. "I think it'd be better for both of us if we stick to talking about Bennett's disappearance, don't you?"

"All right." Anthony tied off the suture and used the scissors from the first-aid kit to clip it short. He taped a piece of gauze over her wound to keep the stitches dry then disinfected and packed up the medical supplies. The patch job disappeared as she maneuvered her clothing back into place.

Focus on her missing partner? No problem. Compartmentalization had become one of his best skills. He exhaled to rid his system of her intoxicating scent, the one that kept pulling him in closer. "Our forensics guy, Vincent, pulled the bullet from the windshield of the SUV, but we won't know where it came from for a few more hours. You can grab a change of clothes from Elizabeth and crash in one of the empty offices until then."

"No." Glennon shook her head as she hiked her jacket over her shoulder, wincing. "I'll take the change of clothes, but I'm going back to that house as soon as possible."

He faced her. Go *back*? Was she insane? Before he knew it, he was in front of her, forcing her to look up at him. An icy feeling crashed through him. He'd almost lost her back at that house. Now she wanted to put her life in danger a second time in less than two hours? His six-foot-four-inch frame towered over her but Glennon held her ground. "Because one bullet wound wasn't enough? Are you going for a shot in the head this time?"

"I came here to find my partner and that's exactly what I'm going to do," she said. "Sergeant Spencer's GPS put him in that house for over twenty-four hours. And since I didn't have a chance to search the place properly before someone tried to shoot me, I'm going back. You can either come with me to make sure it doesn't happen again or give me a set of car keys. Your choice."

"You could've died back there, Glennon." Right in front of him, no less. And that wasn't an option. He'd seen enough death in combat to last him two lifetimes. He wasn't going for three. Her natural warmth worked through his T-shirt, raising his awareness of how close he'd gotten to her. Or maybe it was the flat-out fear of her taking another bullet that put him on edge. "You're not stepping out of this building without protection."

"Good. Then we have a deal. Now let's get to work." She stepped away from him, slowly this time, but the pressure in his lungs refused to let up. That seemed to happen a lot since she'd come back into his life a few hours ago.

Despite the size of the medical suite, Glennon took her original seat beside him. She extracted her phone from her jacket pocket and handed it to him. "Bennett sent me a message right before he disappeared."

"'I found proof.'" Anthony noted the edge of the photo behind the message, a boy with buzzed blond hair and the hint of a wide smile, but nothing more. Had to be her son. Maybe four years old. "What did he mean by that?"

"I don't know. He won't answer my calls and hasn't

been seen since for me to ask him." She took the phone and shut off the screen. "I called in a favor from a friend stationed on base and downloaded the GPS data from Bennett's phone. His last reported location was that house."

"Family? Friends? Girlfriend? Kids?" Despite his gut instincts, her partner's disappearance might not have anything to with the assignment that'd brought them to Anchorage at all. Could've been a breakdown, a piece of Sergeant Spencer's past his partner or the army knew nothing about. Elliot Dunham's earlier observation soured on his tongue. This whole disappearing act might've been set up by Bennett himself, a way to get him out of trouble. Wouldn't be the first time he'd seen enlisted soldiers leave their post.

"No. He didn't have anyone as far as I know, but he hasn't been acting like himself since we got here. Closed off. Showing up late to work if he shows up at all." Glennon shook her head as she leaned back in the chair. "Unfortunately, our assignments don't really let us keep in contact with many people outside of work."

That meant Sergeant Spencer had no one to come looking for him. Except Glennon.

"I'm out of leads." Disappointment clouded her normally bright gaze. "I'm worried he's gotten in over his head with something."

"You want to go back to that house to find the shooter who put a bullet in you." Not a question. He could read her intentions in the way she rubbed at the hole in her shoulder. The plan made sense. Despite the fact that the idea of her stepping foot in that house hiked his pulse higher, it was their best lead to finding her partner.

Then again, Anthony wanted—no, *needed*—to hunt down the bastard who'd ambushed them, too. One way or another, he'd even the score.

"I don't think someone taking shots at me tonight was a coincidence, and I don't think you do, either." She had that right, but chances of the shooter staying behind after they'd high-tailed it out of there were slim.

"I know things—" she laced her fingers together and set her elbows against her knees "—didn't end well… But I'm hoping we can move past this awkwardness—or whatever it is—between us. I can only imagine how much you hate me for leaving, but I appreciate your help." A half-smile pulled at one corner of her mouth. "Truce?"

"I don't hate you, Glennon. Trust me, I've tried." The words were out of his mouth before he had a chance to think about their meaning. But it was the truth. Anthony leaned back in the office chair, his shoulder holster and Beretta within reach on the countertop. "Tell me about the work you two have been doing. Is there a chance someone—a suspect—might be looking for payback from one of your investigations?"

"Bennett and I have been partners for over three years. We've worked a lot of investigations together. If one of those is the starting-off point, I couldn't tell you which one." Glennon wiped her palms down the legs of her blood-spotted jeans. "And I've been through them all. Several times. Nothing has stuck out."

"Then tell me about your current investigation," he said.

"For the past year we've been looking into dozens of individual thefts of military weapons off army bases around the country. Most recently, a shipment of hardware has disappeared right here out of Anchorage. Usually, within a couple weeks, the weapons turn up on the black market or in the hands of our enemies, but not this time. Not a single weapon registered as stolen has turned up, which made us think whoever took them might be sticking around."

Glennon swiped the tip of her tongue across her bottom lip, running one hand through her hair before sitting forward again. "So, about two months ago, Bennett had the idea of mapping the locations of each theft, and checking those locations against enlisted soldiers stationed there at the same time. Only one name kept coming up. Staff Sergeant Nicholas Mascaro. It was a huge win for the army. After Bennett and I turned in our report and handed over all the evidence we'd collected, Nicholas Mascaro was court-martialed and convicted."

"I heard about the investigation against Mascaro." Even after leaving the military, he still had contacts. Although, he hadn't known she'd been involved so closely in the staff sergeant's arrest. A swell of pride rushed through him and he straightened a bit more. She was a damn fine investigator, no doubt about it. But something didn't sit right. Anthony thought back to his source. "But there's no way one man could run that kind of operation on his own."

"You're right." Glennon sat back in her chair. "Despite what Bennett and I wrote in our report, the army couldn't definitively tie anyone else to the staff sergeant, let alone place him at the head of the entire operation. And he's not giving up any names. So Mascaro made a deal and the investigation was officially closed."

Confusion furrowed his brow. "Then why are you and your partner here?"

"A second shipment of weapons was stolen from JBER three days ago. After Nicholas Mascaro was arrested. Bennett believed someone took control of the operation while their patsy took the fall." Glennon stood. Collecting his weapon and holster from the countertop to her right, she offered it to him, grip first. "And I think he was trying to tell me he found the proof."

THE HOUSE HADN'T changed in the last two hours, aside from the extra bullet holes peppering the walls. Fresh blood spatters added to the stains on the west side of the living room. Her blood. The hole in her shoulder ached as if to remind her of the last time she'd stood in this spot. Her attention slid to Anthony as he riffled through a stack of old newspapers, the muscles along his back hardening with every move. If he hadn't been there…

Memories of her four-year-old flashed across her mind like lightning. His blond hair, his perfect smile, the way he'd held on to her so tight before she'd left.

Hunter was fine. He was safe. She'd made sure of it. And if anything did happen to her, he'd be cared for. Arranging his future in case something happened to her had been the only way she could track down Bennett without the army at her disposal.

Glennon ignored the tightness in her throat as she wiped at her face with the back of her hand. He was fine.

Focus. There had to be some kind of evidence pointing to the reason Bennett had come here. She kicked at a loose floorboard, but the space underneath had either never been used or been emptied out. They'd been here an hour and come up with nothing. No bullet casings. No new skid marks on the road aside from theirs. Nothing from the neighbors. Whoever had taken those shots had been either a professional or a soldier.

Glennon laughed to herself. She was getting ahead of herself. They had nothing tying Bennett's disappearance to her current investigation or the military. For all she knew, he'd needed a couple days away from the pressure of the marshal breathing down their necks for results. Her gut instincts said they were connected, but the courts didn't prosecute based off something that couldn't be proved.

"Anything on your side?" she asked.

"Not yet." Straightening, Anthony stretched to his full, muscular height. The beginnings of sunrise glinted off a thin sheen of sweat across his forehead as he ran a hand down his face. He'd come prepared. Well, more prepared than usual. The Beretta in his shoulder holster had a couple new friends hidden in his cargo pants, his Kevlar vest, even the holster strapped around his thigh. He wasn't about to be taken by surprise again. "You?"

She studied him from the safe distance she'd decided to put between them back in the medical suite. At least three feet of space separating them at all times. That'd be the only way she could think straight during their time together. Although, now that she watched him, her body urged her to close that space. Five tours in extreme conditions ranging from jungle to desert hadn't taken away from his overall attractiveness. Hardened him, yes, but not in a bad way. And damn if that didn't resurrect some of those feelings she'd buried. But she hadn't come back here to make the same mistakes. She hadn't even planned on seeing him at all during her assignment on JBER.

"Glennon?" The weight of those dark blue eyes pinned her to the spot.

"No. Nothing." Glennon sank against one wall, exhaustion pulling at her. She wiped a bead of sweat off her neck. What were they supposed to do now? She had zero jurisdiction off base as long as Bennett's disappearance was considered a simple missing persons case. And she couldn't bring in the local police. Not yet. Not until she could guarantee her name would be left out of the reports. "Has your computer expert come back with a history on this place yet? Who owns it?"

"Last time I checked in, Elizabeth was working her way through an entire network of shell corporations without any end in sight," he said.

Defeat spread fast. Her partner had been here. How could he disappear without anything to show for it? This couldn't be it. She'd been trained for this. She couldn't have failed him already. Stalking across the empty living room, she picked up an old two-by-four covered in spider webs. "There has to be something here."

She shoved every ounce of energy into her swing. The board vibrated in her hands with each strike, pain exploding through her shoulder. She didn't care. Pins and needles crawled up her arms as mildewed drywall peeled away from the wall, but she wouldn't stop. Not until she found a clue.

"Glennon." The concern in Anthony's tone tunneled deep into her bones, but she only pushed herself harder.

She wasn't leaving this house until she had proof Bennett had been here. It was the only lead she had. He was the only person who could help her bring down the rest of Staff Sergeant Mascaro's team. Another streak of sweat slipped from her hairline and down her neck. Why was it so damn hot in here? Shouldn't the gas company have turned off the furnace when the house was abandoned?

A calloused grip encased her hands from behind, his arms caging her against a wall of muscle. Anthony turned her into him and Glennon froze. The lines at the edges of his eyes creased as he stared down at her. His grip still wrapped around hers, he studied her with determination etched into his features. "We're going to find your partner. I promise."

Promises. What good were they when nobody lived up to them? Glennon nodded, her attention wandering to the condensation building on the large front window. "It's twenty degrees outside. Nobody has lived in this house for years." The two-by-four grew heavy in her hold. She dropped it to her side but didn't let go. "Why is it so hot in here?"

"Because someone turned on the furnace." The revelation hardened Anthony's expression. He stepped away, surveying the rest of the room before unholstering the Beretta at his side. Checking the magazine, he chambered a round into the barrel. The action, so simple, forced her to swallow the tightness in her throat. This was what he did best, what she'd tracked him down for, but the sudden change consuming him from head to toe urged her to take a step back. She'd read his classified files. She understood what the "Grim

Reaper" was capable of and a shiver ran through her.
"Stay behind me."

"What makes you think you get to have all the fun?"
Setting the two-by-four on the moldy carpeting as quietly as she could, Glennon took his left side as she
withdrew her service weapon. One bullet. That was
all it'd take to seal her and her partner's fates. The
army would court-martial Bennett for going MIA, no
matter what his reason, and drag her through the mud
alongside him. She shifted her finger off the safety.
Couldn't happen.

They moved as one, just as they had when he'd gotten her out of the house the first time, her steps in sync
with his. Nervous energy skittered up her spine. She'd
gone into plenty of dangerous situations like this before. Soldiers-turned-criminals, bullets, blood. Every
investigation she'd worked had left its own mark. It
was part of the job. But moving along this hallway,
with *him* by her side, sent a tingling sensation down
her spine that she hadn't felt in a long time.

Moonlight filtered through broken windows and
bullet holes the shooter had added to the walls, playing across Anthony's face as he stalked through the
house. For such a large man, he barely made a sound.
He motioned with two fingers to their right. The signal was clear. They'd reached the stairs leading to the
basement. And whoever had turned on the furnace
after the shootout could still be down there.

Anticipation hummed through her veins. Glock
raised to eye level, she fought off the shot of pain
spreading through her shoulder. She was ready. This
was it. With a single nod, Glennon took the first step.
The unfinished wood groaned under her weight, and

she paused to listen. No movement below. Nothing to suggest they were in for another ambush, but she wouldn't relax just yet. She'd had too many close calls already. Her mouth dried up; her breathing became shallow.

She paused on the last step, nothing but darkness ahead. Something brushed across her right side. Anthony. His clean, masculine scent filled her lungs, and she surveyed the full unfinished basement before they made their next move. But something charred and rotten replaced his scent within a few seconds of her hitting the bottom stair. She covered her mouth and nose in the crook of her elbow. "I recognize that smell."

She'd come across it only once since she'd been with the Military Police. An arson investigation at Pope Army Airfield in North Carolina, one of her first for the army. The fire had consumed an entire C-130J Hercules plane right before takeoff. The pilot had been sealed in the cockpit after an altercation with another airman. The smell. That was what she remembered most. "Charred remains."

Reaching for the flashlight strapped into her Kevlar vest, she brought it to life and swept the beam across the floor. Large boot prints had been preserved in a thin layer of dust. Fresh, from the look of it. But the uneven lines beside them? Those were drag marks.

A groan interrupted the heavy silence and they swung their weapons to the left in tandem. Anthony's boots hit solid cement. Weapon aimed high, he moved farther into the darkness.

Dread sank like a stone to the bottom of Glennon's stomach as she followed suit.

A click of his flashlight expanded their visibility,

but only slightly. There were still three other corners of the room they couldn't see, but her gut told her whoever had turned on the furnace had disappeared long before they'd showed up. Still, she couldn't shake the vein of ice working its way up her throat. Whatever was down here—whatever they found—would make or break her investigation into Bennett's disappearance.

They reached the furnace as it kicked on for another round, the struggling mechanical groan raising the hairs on the back of Glennon's neck.

Holstering his weapon, Anthony ran his fingers over the side of the unit then lowered his flashlight beam to the floor. Four screws had fallen into the dust building up around the furnace. Glennon holstered her own gun as he handed her the flashlight. The reverberation of metal on cement as he set the panel down vibrated through her. A rush of foul air hit her hard and she buried her mouth and nose into her elbow. Anthony did the same, reaching into the unit with his free hand.

His mountainous physique blocked her view into the blackened depths. "Can you see anything?"

"Yep." A hiss escaped from between his teeth. He turned toward her, the burned remnants of a rifle highlighted by the flashlight beam. "What's left of a Heckler & Koch G28 sniper rifle. Still hot, too. Safe to assume it's the same model used to put a bullet in your shoulder three hours ago."

"The shooter tried to clean up his mess by destroying the gun in the furnace." Not a bad idea. But that left them no closer to recovering her partner. Unless... Hope spread through her chest as she stepped closer to him. "You're the weapons expert. Do you think any fingerprints survived to track down the owner?"

Leaving the rifle inside, Anthony shifted out of her way so she could see the rest of the furnace, both flashlights highlighting what else had been stuffed inside. "Looks like we already found him."

Chapter Three

Red-and-blue patrol lights deepened the shadows under Glennon's eyes as she watched the scene from the SUV. When was the last time she'd slept? Twenty-four hours ago? More? He couldn't imagine the thoughts running through her head as the remains of her best lead were loaded into the back of the coroner's van.

Anthony had kept her name out of his statement to Anchorage PD after he'd put in the initial call about an incinerated body in the furnace. Whatever was going on here—whoever had killed the shooter who'd ambushed them—it had obviously been to keep Glennon off the investigation into her missing partner. His gaze drifted back to her. She'd been right from the start. Sergeant Spencer's disappearance had something to do with the missing shipment of weapons. Why else would a shooter try to take her out, too?

"We're done here," he told the officer. "You know how to contact me at Blackhawk Security if you have any other questions."

He had to get her to safety, someplace off-the-grid where nobody—not even his team—could find her. Where he could protect her. Anthony maneuvered around the officer and headed for the SUV.

Glennon followed his movements slowly.

Wrenching the vehicle door open, he dropped into the driver's seat. Her sweet scent hit him hard, but he didn't try to fight it off this time. After the night they'd had, he needed that piece of her with him. He breathed her in a bit deeper. Anything to ease the tension of nearly losing her all over again tonight. Spots of blood seeped through her bandage.

"What did you tell them?" she asked.

He turned the key in the ignition. The engine growled to life and he forced his eyes to focus on the road. "That we were looking to spice things up in our sex life."

She smoothed her expression. "And they believed you?" Motioning to his clothing, she leaned against the passenger-side door. "You, in all this Kevlar, with at least three weapons strapped to your chest? They believed you?"

"Don't worry. I didn't give them your real name." In reality, Anchorage PD hadn't asked too many questions about what he'd been doing in the house at all. After what had happened back in November, they recognized him and understood what kind of work he did on a regular basis. And who he did it for. Blackhawk Security had become a company the police could rely on after its CEO, Sullivan Bishop, had taken down one of the worst stalkers in city history, a case the department had moved to the bottom of their priority list. Anthony shoved the vehicle into Drive.

"Very funny." She crossed her arms over her chest, accentuating the lean muscles through her forearms. "What are you doing? We can't leave." She surveyed the cul-de-sac as he swung the SUV around, spinning her upper body toward him from the passenger seat. Her icy glare shot through him, but he wasn't about to stop. "That body is our only lead to finding my partner. Do you trust the police to fill us in if they find something?"

"We searched every inch of that house tonight, sweetheart. What exactly are you hoping they're going to find that we couldn't?" Anthony pressed his foot down on the accelerator when they hit Spenard Thruway. "Besides, you're beat. We need to take a look at that wound again, then you're going to get some sleep while we wait for the ballistics report on that bullet to come in."

"I'm fine." She settled back into her seat. "And don't call me sweetheart. You're here to protect me while I search for Bennett. Nothing more."

"Yes, ma'am." Tightening his grip around the steering wheel, Anthony studied Westchester Lagoon as they headed south. Nothing but blackness and the hint of lapping waves stared back at him. Wasn't that just the perfect metaphor for the growing silence between him and Glennon? Damn, he'd screwed things up with her to hell and back. He should've been there for her while he'd still had the chance, should've been satisfied with what he'd done for his country the first four times instead of hopping on the next transport. Maybe then she wouldn't treat him as though he were a stranger now.

He headed farther south, out of the city. Miles of nothing but trees and starlit sky stretched out before them. It was the best place to hide. No one would be able to track them out here. And even if they did, he'd be ready. The familiar rise and fall of the south end of the Chugach Mountains indicated they were close. A few more minutes and he could relax in his own territory.

"Where are you taking me?" Her voice barely overrode the sound of the heater, and he chanced a quick glance toward her. Adrenaline could only take the human body so far, and Glennon's supply had run out. Lids closing, she fought to stay awake, but wouldn't last much longer.

"Where no one can find us." Within a few minutes, gravel crunched under the SUV's tires as he pulled into a long driveway. The cabin was dark. Isolated. And, after discovering the shooter's body in that furnace, it was the best chance they had of recovering in peace.

He pulled to a stop beside the small lakeside cabin and then unloaded his gear as she made her way inside.

Dropping everything on the floor, Anthony turned on the nearest light switch. "The place isn't much, but it's fully stocked and secure." He studied her expression, trying to read any sign of what she had planned for their next move, but she'd always kept a good handle on the thoughts running through her head. "You can take the guest room at the back. Bathroom is right next door to it. Just the one, unfortunately, so we'll have to share. I never bring anyone up here."

"Never?" She surveyed the two-bedroom, one-bathroom space then moved to the front window. "It's perfect. Suits you."

"Thanks." He liked his solitude, but liked it better with her here. Hoisting his bags over his shoulder, he felt the first effects of having gone over twenty-four hours without sleep. Her call had pulled him off another assignment, but he couldn't fault her for that. "Let me unpack my gear while you settle in, and I'll bring you something to eat in about ten minutes."

"Thank you." She forced a smile but the exhaustion weighing her down didn't let it reach her eyes. She headed for the back of the cabin empty-handed, taking nearly every ounce of his control with her. Damn, he'd missed her, and no matter how many times she reminded him nothing would happen between them again, he couldn't help but imagine what they could've been together. Stopping shy of the hallway, Glennon turned back. "For everything."

Ten minutes later her voice stopped him just outside her cracked door, only a sliver of light spilling into the hallway. He pushed it open a few inches.

"I know what I said." Her back was to him where she sat on the bed, but her words registered crystal-clear. "Things are…more complicated than I thought they'd be here. It'll be a couple more days. Can you please put him on the phone? I just need to hear his voice." Dressed in a set of his oversize T-shirt and sweats, Glennon shifted on the guest bed, head down, legs stretched in front of her and ran her hand through her hair. The sight rocketed his pulse into dangerous territory. "Hey, baby." Her voice lightened in an instant, a beautiful smile spreading across her expression. "I know. I'm sorry I woke you. I just missed you so much. Are you being good for Grandma?"

Anthony settled against the door frame, entranced by the sudden shift in her mood. The plate grew heavy in his hand, but he'd stand there all night if there was a chance he'd get a glimpse of that smile again.

"You went to the zoo without me? That sounds fun. Can I call you again tomorrow so you can tell me more about it?" Those mesmerizing green eyes brighter than he'd ever seen, she leaned back against the headboard and crossed her legs over the pillow top. A laugh escaped from between her perfectly pink lips, tightening his insides. "Okay. Go back to sleep, my love. I'll see you soon."

He couldn't move. Couldn't think. In the few seconds she'd spoken to her son, he'd felt her undeniable love, and something inside him splintered. He gripped the plate hard. She would've made an amazing mother to their kids. Hell, she was obviously an amazing mother already. Couldn't even keep herself from calling her son so early in the morning. Anthony ignored the tightness in his throat and straightened. Didn't matter. She'd made it clear how their relationship would proceed. As partners. Nothing more.

With three knocks, he shouldered his way into the room with everything on a plate. "Hungry? I made your favorite. Aspirin, clean gauze and my special egg salad sandwich."

"Yeah." Glennon shot off the mattress, wiping at her face. A split second later she turned toward him again, locking down any hint of emotion. She sniffed as she maneuvered around the bed. "I'm starving. Thanks."

His stomach sank. She was getting far too skilled at hiding those emotions of hers, to the point he questioned whether he'd really seen her smile a few minutes ago. "Was it something I said?"

"What? No. It's not you. I appreciate you letting me stay here." She shook her head, a flush of pink rising in her cheeks. Her long fingers brushed against his as she reached for the plate. Heat seared through him as

she took a step back and raised the plate in acknowledgment. "And for the food. I—"

"You miss your son." He'd read it in the way her skin had paled in the few short moments after she'd disconnected the call, in the way her tears had dried a path down her cheeks.

"Stupid, right? I mean, he's safe. That's all that matters. Nobody knows about him. Not the army. Not his father. I shouldn't have anything to worry about." A weak smile played across her mouth. Shoulders rising on a deep inhale, she glanced up at him, signs of her apparent misery wiped clean from her expression. "I can't tell you how much I've missed your egg salad. Every time I've tried to re-create the recipe, it turns out wrong. I finally gave up trying."

"I add hot sauce at the end." Okay. He'd pretend she hadn't let a piece of herself out into the open.

Anthony backed toward the hallway, reaching for the doorknob to close it behind him. "Get some rest, change your gauze. The ballistics report should be here soon. We'll figure out our next move then."

"Listen, I know things are different between us now, but I've had a hell of a day." Her lips parted as she took a single step forward and, for the first time, he noted the dark swirl of purple nail polish on her bare feet. She glanced at her cell phone on the nightstand. "Hunter usually sleeps in my bed, and I won't be able to sleep unless…"

Grip tight on the doorknob, Anthony froze. Pressure built in his lungs.

She locked her gaze on him, determined, sincere. "Will you stay with me until I fall asleep?"

WHAT HAD SHE been thinking?

She hadn't. That had been one of the problems whenever Glennon was around him. She couldn't think straight. And here, in a small lakeside cabin filled with his scent, with *him* mere inches from her, she'd must've lost her damn mind. She ran her free hand through her hair, a nervous habit she'd used to try to relieve some tension over the past few years. Without success.

"You think that's a good idea?" Anthony released the door handle, his tone registering exactly how much she'd already asked of him in the last four hours. *Too much.* Especially for a man she'd walked out on while he was in the middle of serving his country, a decision she'd regret for the rest of her life.

"No." Heat rose up her neck and flooded her face. She shook her head, forcing another smile she didn't feel. Her fingers tingled, urging her to run her hand through her hair one more time, but she rolled them into a fist at her side instead. Taking another step toward him, she focused on the raised outline of a chain hidden under his shirt. Dog tags? "And I don't have any right to ask after everything you've done for me already. But the past couple days have been a nightmare and I need… I need you to stay."

Anthony swayed on his feet as though he intended to back toward the door. His full beard kept her from reading his expression entirely, but his eyes had always been the window to his thoughts. Gorgeous, dark blue eyes she'd tried for years to forget. And right now, the battle swirling in their depths was spreading across his features. His brows drew inward as he ran a hand down his beard. "Glennon—"

"Please." She fought the urge to grip his shirt to

keep him from leaving. Notching her chin higher, she studied the face she'd missed since the day she'd left. "If it helps, I promise to keep my hands to myself."

"It's not your hands I'm worried about." He moved into her. A rush of his reinvigorated, clean, masculine scent filled her lungs as her brain fought to catch up. Had he showered while she'd been on the phone with Hunter? Only the thin fabric of a T-shirt she'd found in one of the dresser drawers separated them. He kept his touch light, giving her enough room to escape if she wanted to. Which she should. Because she'd most definitely violated her three-foot rule. "Do you ever think of what might've happened if you hadn't left?"

Glennon swallowed hard, her pulse pounding behind her ears as she set the plate of food, the painkillers and gauze on the bed. No point in lying. He knew her too well. She passed her tongue across her too-dry lips as he stared down at her as though she were the only woman in the world who mattered to him. "Sometimes."

All the time. The only way she'd been able to give those thoughts a break over the last five years was by throwing herself into her work and into being there for her son. Throwing herself into everything that didn't include Anthony Harris. She'd made her choice then and she stood by it now. She'd suffer the consequences, no matter how many times she'd thought of coming home. She stared at the open door behind him for a moment, into the darkness of the cabin.

"Sometimes I think I could've changed your mind, convinced you I was enough for you to stay home." The comforting warmth rolling off him in waves urged her to stay put. It'd been a long time since she'd gotten

lost in somebody's touch, relied on someone other than herself. She'd almost forgotten what intimacy felt like since becoming a single mother. It'd be easy to give in to him. Right here, right now. Forget about her missing partner, forget how lonely she'd been over the last few years, and just do something for herself for a change. But extricating herself from a romantic relationship with this man had been one of the hardest things she'd ever done. Something she wasn't interested in doing again, not with Hunter involved.

"But that was a long time ago. Things have changed." Glennon stepped out of his hold, the rough calluses on his palms catching on the cotton shirt she'd borrowed. "And it finally took me leaving to realize changing your mind was one case I'd never have closure to."

Disappointment darkened his features. "You were always enough for me, Glennon. More than enough." His tone dipped into dangerous territory, raising tiny goose bumps on her arms. He countered the step she'd taken to the point where she had to stare up at him. "You were the only person who could help me forget what I'd seen every time I came home. You were the one I trusted to keep my head on straight, to bring me back to who I really was. Not the soldier. Me. You were everything."

Her knees shook, the blood drained from her face. As Military Police, she'd walked into dozens of situations more confident than she felt in this moment. This wasn't the plan. The rules had been plain. No matter how many times the past came back to haunt her, she'd keep herself in check. But now… "I didn't know that."

The muted ding from his phone released the pres-

sure building behind her sternum. Saved by the bell. She took the opportunity to distance herself from his reach as Anthony checked the screen. Sitting on the bed, she stared down at her hands as her stomach flipped. From hunger or from the sincerity in his voice, she had no idea. Didn't matter. She could only fix one of those things at the moment. The other? Couldn't happen again. Nothing could happen between them again.

"The ballistics report came in early," he said. "Vincent's contacts in forensics were able to lift a print from the homemade bullet recovered from the windshield."

So much for getting a couple hours of sleep. Glennon shoved off from the bed, a strike of pain spreading across her shoulder. She massaged the area around the wound as she moved to view the screen. He flipped through the report too fast for her to see specifics, but one line stood out among the rest, highlighted on the phone's screen.

"Private First Class Gani Miller." The name sounded familiar on her lips. But where had she read it before?

"Left the army because of a dishonorable discharge, now makes his living as a gun for hire. Paid to take you out." Anthony swiped his thumb across the screen to the next page. "I'll have Elizabeth look into his financials to find out who hired him."

Glennon stayed put as he called the former NSA consultant. Mentally sifting through her investigations for the army, she studied the recliner tucked into the corner of the room, but couldn't really focus on anything in particular. Where had she heard that name before? A shooter for hire had most likely made his way to the top of her Most Wanted list, but that wasn't it. She reviewed the list every morning before heading

onto the base, and Private Gani Miller's name hadn't been on there as of yesterday. "Do you have a laptop here?"

Anthony spun toward her. "I packed one in my gear. Gray duffel bag in the hallway."

In less than two minutes she'd powered the laptop up and logged in with the username and password Anthony had written down for her while on the phone with Elizabeth. The screen came to life as she settled back on the bed.

Her heart skipped a beat.

There, in the center of the black desktop background, was a photo of…her. Smiling, arms wrapped around her brand-new fiancé. The memories of that day interrupted her concentration as she zeroed in on the yellow-gold engagement ring he'd slipped onto her finger moments before the photo had been taken. She'd set that same ring on the kitchen counter as she'd walked out the door for the last time five years ago. What had he done with it?

"All right." Anthony disconnected his call. "Elizabeth is pulling everything she can find on Gani Miller as we speak. Still nothing leading back to who owns that house, though."

Panic flooded through her. Glennon rushed to bring up the backup of her investigation files. The mattress dipped as he sat beside her. She swallowed hard then typed the shooter's name into the search bar. No point in bringing up the past. They had more important things to worry about now. "I know I've heard that name before. If Private Miller has been at this for a while, he might be linked to one of my investigations."

The fact the sniper had been military couldn't have been a coincidence.

The search of her files came up blank.

Her eyebrows drew together. She checked that she'd spelled the shooter's name correctly and pushed Enter a second time. Nothing. There had to be some connection. "That's weird. I know I've come across that name before."

"Are you remembering it from somewhere else?" Anthony leaned into her to get a clear shot of the screen. His powerful, muscled thigh brushed against her, and she licked her lips.

"I don't know where else…" A single image of handwritten notes flashed across her mind. "That's it." Glennon checked another file, one she'd been compiling since her partner had gone missing.

"After Bennett disappeared, I searched his barracks and found a bunch of notes he'd scribbled on napkins he'd left in the trash bin. Most of it was nonsense, but that name—Gani Miller—was on one of the napkins with a few others." She reentered her username and password to access the secure files. "I took pictures of them in case something led to Bennett's whereabouts, and uploaded the photos to my online storage."

A new rush of hope blossomed in the center of her chest. They had a name, a lead. She could find Bennett and get back to her life. Back to her son. Double clicking the track pad, Glennon leaned away from the laptop. No. No, no, no, no. Her throat tightened. "That's not possible."

"What's not possible?" Anthony shifted the computer out of her lap and onto his own. With a few clicks

of the track pad, he stroked his beard. Confusion swept across his features. "Where are the files?"

"They were there. I backed up my files from my laptop to this drive in case something happened and I couldn't get to my computer." Which probably meant... Glennon stood, crossing the room to the pile of clothing she'd discarded on the floor.

"And now they're gone," he said. "How?"

"Someone accessed my backup and deleted them." She stripped out of the borrowed sweats then pushed her legs into her jeans, all thoughts of privacy retreating to the back of her mind. Nobody knew about those files. How had evidence catalogs, Bennett's investigation notes, witness statements and photographs of the napkins all disappeared overnight?

"And I think I know where they're going next."

Chapter Four

"Where the hell do you think you're going?" He wasn't about to let her walk into another ambush, even with the possibility of finding her partner. "You haven't slept in who knows how long, you're running on empty, and there's blood dripping down your shirt. You're going to crash any second. You need—"

"What I need is to find Bennett." Glennon turned her back to him while she crossed her arms under the oversize T-shirt and brought it over her head. Shadows played across her lean back as she bent for her clothing. Blood spotted the gauze taped across the backside of her wound, but his attention shot to the raised lump of scar tissue over her ribs, the one paler than the rest of her skin. The one that looked strangely like another bullet wound. She'd been shot before?

Glennon faced him, pulling the shirt she'd borrowed from Elizabeth over her head. "Everything I had in those backups came from Bennett. He's the only one who can prove Staff Sergeant Mascaro's operation has been taken over by a new leader. And there's only one place someone could've accessed those files to delete them."

"What is that?" He nodded toward her, each word

tearing from him. "That scar on your back. Where did it come from?"

She froze, spine a bit straighter. She placed her boots on the bed carefully, slowly. "Thought you'd recognize an old bullet wound when you saw one, Ranger. Don't you have a few of these yourself?"

"When?" Anthony didn't blink, didn't move. Any second now his control would shatter. Someone had shot her and she hadn't said a word, hadn't reached out to him before now? He wanted details. A name. Whoever had pulled that trigger would wish they hadn't. "Who?"

"Doesn't matter. Reliving old investigations isn't going to help me find my partner any faster, and that's what I hired you to do." She reached for her boots and sat on the edge of the bed, lacing them quickly. The blazing determination in her expression said she wasn't going to see reason. In the end, it didn't matter what he said to convince her otherwise. It wouldn't work. Once she set her sights on something, the devil himself couldn't stop her. That was one of the things he'd loved about her. Glennon headed to the door, wiping a strand of hair out of her face without glancing back at him.

But she wasn't getting away that easily. Anthony crossed the room in three strides and wrapped a hand around her arm. Spinning her into him, he filled the door frame. She wanted to leave? She'd have to go through him, and he wasn't moving until she told him the truth. "What's so damn important about this case that you're willing to put your own well-being at risk?"

"Because it's my last." She visibly flinched at the words, something he'd never witnessed before. Her sudden reaction lightened his grasp on her arm. Either

her words had hit a sore spot or Glennon was far more exhausted than she wanted to admit.

He released his hold as pressure built in his gut. "What do you mean?"

"When this is over—" she pulled back her shoulders "—after I recover Bennett, I'm putting in my papers for discharge."

"You love your job." Anthony gave her another foot of space. He'd followed her career from the start. Processing crime scenes on bases, illegal dealings across state lines, all those soldiers she'd helped. She'd spent the last decade studying, working for a cause she believed in. And she was damn good at it. What could've possibly changed? "You've made a difference. Why would you want to leave?"

The answer sat on the tip of his tongue before she even said a word.

"Hunter." The glassy haze over her eyes revealed she wasn't really seeing him in front of her. "When I was shot last year..." She shifted on her feet. "He's four years old. He's already had to live without a father in his life. He deserves to grow up with a mother who isn't risking her life on the job or who might not come home at all." A thin smile curved one side of her mouth as she lifted her eyes to his. "I love my job, and I think I'm good at it, but I love him more. And I want to see him grow up. I want to see school pictures, watch him fall in love for the first time, get married. Have a family of his own someday."

She rolled her lips between her teeth and turned her face away. As if she needed to hide from him. "Sounds silly when I say it out loud. Me, giving up the past ten years of my life. But sacrifice is part of the job, right?

That's what I agreed to when I decided to keep him after I found out I was pregnant. I just honestly didn't think this day would come."

"It's not silly." Anthony slid his hands around to her lower back, drawing her into him. Surprisingly, she let him. The muscles down her spine stiffened, but inch by inch they released as he held her. Her rosy scent drifted from her hair as she closed her eyes. Rose oil had always been one of her favorite natural perfumes.

She pressed her cheek into his chest, right over his heart. Still a perfect fit. Then again, he'd always believed she'd been created just for him. "But as much as you want to finish this investigation, you're not going anywhere until you've had a couple hours of sleep."

"What?" She stepped back.

"You hired me to protect you." He framed her face between his calloused hands. Rough against smooth perfection. Dark versus light. "If my legacy is to step in front of a bullet for you, so be it. That's my job. But I can't do that job if you're determined to destroy yourself first."

Her lips parted. She was beautiful. Absolutely, gut-wrenchingly beautiful. Always had been. Always would be, to him. But the small burst of a smile didn't reach her eyes; rather, it merely accentuated the hollowness and exhaustion etched into her features.

She pointed at the window and stepped out of his hold, one hand on his chest. "You want me to catch up on my sleep while Bennett's out there, possibly dead?"

"You aren't good to anyone in your current condition, especially your partner, and we aren't going to solve anything unless you have a clear head." Anthony countered her escape, his voice dropping as he backed

her to the end of the bed. "So to answer your question, yes. Right now, the most useful thing you can do for your partner is get some rest."

Her knees hit the bed frame and she collapsed onto the mattress. Pink flared in her cheeks. She rubbed at her left temple. "You're probably right. I can barely see straight. But the files—"

"Will still be deleted when you wake up." He leaned forward, boxing her in with his arms as he gripped a pillow behind her. His mouth mere centimeters from hers, he shoved the memory of her taste, the feel of her lips on his, down deep. No matter how much he wanted to close that small space between them, he wouldn't violate her request to keep their relationship professional.

Heat spread through his chest as her sharp exhale slid across his throat. He should go. Peeling himself away from her, away from her raw, warm energy, he handed her the pillow. "Don't worry. I'll watch over you."

"I have no doubt." She settled back against the mattress, fully dressed, as he took a seat in the recliner across the room.

Within minutes her breathing slowed, barely audible over the pounding behind his ears. Her expression was relaxed, no longer hollow and controlled, the stress all but gone.

The nightstand lamp reflected off a hint of metal protruding from under the edge of her pillow, right near her hand. Anthony crossed the room, his mouth pulling tight to one side. A blade. But not just any blade. A combat blade he'd brought home from Iraq. The one he'd given her for their two-year anniversary. He studied the angles of her cheekbones, his fingers tingling

to brush away a strand of stray hair that'd fallen across her face. As much as she'd made it clear she wouldn't acknowledge their past, the blade proved she'd obviously had a hard time cutting those emotional ties.

His hand trailed to the chain stashed under his shirt collar. Then again, so had he. He moved back to the recliner, the Beretta in his shoulder holster digging into his side.

It had already started, his getting wrapped up in her again. And it hadn't even taken a full day. He'd invested hundreds of hours into his training. Weapons and explosives, interrogation, recovery, extraction, capture. All of it had been for nothing when it came to her. She'd blown past his defenses—circumvented the walls he'd built—with four simple words. *I need your help.* Damn, he was a sucker for pain. Because that was the only way this could go. In the end, whether they found her partner or not, Glennon would go back to her life when this was over. She'd move on. Again. And he'd be left to pick up the pieces. Again.

Exhaustion pulled him deeper into the chair. He'd been trained to sleep with one eye open—never knew when or where an attack would come. The intel he'd requested from Elizabeth about the shooter who'd tried to kill Glennon wouldn't be in for a few more hours. He'd set the security system and restocked his ammunition before bringing her the sandwich. If anyone came after her again, he'd be more than ready.

She was safe. He'd made her a promise and he'd be damned sure he kept it.

"Good night, sweetheart." He might be a sucker for pain, but for him, any small amount of Glennon would be worth a thousand bullet wounds.

A soft creak reached his ears. Anthony unholstered his gun automatically as he flipped his watch for the time. He'd taken position in the chair two hours ago. Pinks and oranges bled through the thick curtains. Sunrise. His heart pounded hard in his chest as he surveyed the room. Glennon hadn't moved from the bed, but had rolled onto her side sometime while he'd been asleep. He slid out of the chair, cocking his ear toward the door. Nothing.

But it hadn't been nothing. That creak. He'd heard it. And the only spot in the cabin where the floorboards protested like that was right in front of the bathroom, mere feet from this room.

Someone had broken into the house.

With one last glance at Glennon, Anthony gripped the doorknob. He slipped into the hallway and closed the door behind him. His eyes adjusted to the darkness fast, every instinct on high alert.

From the center of the hallway, the shadowed intruder widened his stance. "You can't protect her from what's coming."

Anthony raised his gun and took aim. "Watch me."

Two gunshots exploded through the darkness.

Glennon rocketed out of bed, wrapping one hand around the combat blade she'd stashed under her pillow and the other around her service weapon on the nightstand. The room was empty, her panicked breathing blocking any hint of sound outside her closed bedroom door. "Anthony?"

He wasn't there.

She rushed into the hallway. Swinging her weapon

up to shoulder height, she forced her heartbeat to slow as her eyes adjusted to the darkness. Listen. Breathe.

Glennon hugged the wall as she moved, one foot in front of the other. The floorboard in front of the bathroom protested under her weight with a groan, and she froze. Nothing. No sign of movement anywhere in the house. No other shots fired. Had she dreamed the whole thing?

Glennon cleared the cabin room by room, the hairs on the back of her neck standing on end. No. Those shots had been all too real, and the fact that Anthony wasn't in the cabin screamed something had gone wrong.

Morning streams of sunrise intensified a shadow as it rushed past the largest window in the front room.

She swung the Glock around, finger beside the trigger. A rush of freezing Alaskan air caught in her throat. The front door was open. She ran her tongue across her dry lips. She'd taken a killing shot once before. If something had happened to Anthony...

No. She had to focus. He could take care of himself. Hell, the Rangers had given him a nickname that only brushed the surface of his capabilities. The blade she'd stuffed into the waistband of her jeans cut against her skin as she forced herself out onto the porch. Pink-and-orange rays of sunrise highlighted the short expanse from the cabin to Campbell Lake, but nothing more. Nobody on the pier, nothing but fishing boats docked at the edge of the water. A thin line of trees surrounded the property, but nothing moved.

Damn it. Where was he?

"Anthony!" She took a single step off the porch. Her ears strained for a hint of what might be waiting

for her, only the lapping of soft waves fighting for her attention. The gun grew heavy in her grasp. Something was wrong. He wouldn't just leave. He wouldn't abandon her.

A roughened palm clamped over her mouth, another around the barrel of the Glock. Ripping it from her grasp, her attacker tossed the gun to the ground, out of reach.

Her head slammed back into his shoulder as he lifted her off her feet. A scream worked up her throat. She swung her momentum forward to unbalance him, but his hold wouldn't loosen. His hand slipped from her mouth. *The knife.* If she could get to the blade...

"You're going to stop looking for your partner, Sergeant Chase." His rough growl vibrated through her. "Before you get yourself and the people you care about killed."

Her spine seized. The people she cared about... Hunter.

"If you go near him, I will kill you." Glennon rammed her elbow into her attacker's solar plexus, and went for the knife stuffed inside the waistband of her jeans. In a single movement, she arced the blade up and back over her shoulder. His hand disappeared from around her waist as she swung at his collar. But missed. He'd jumped back from her and she dived for the gun. Landing hard, she knocked the icy breath from her lungs and slid her finger over the trigger. She hiked the gun over her shoulder and fired. The gun kicked back in her hand.

But he was gone.

The corner of the cabin ruptured in splinters from her shot. The bullet had missed its mark. Glennon sur-

veyed the rest of the porch, the pier, the thin line of trees surrounding the property. He'd disappeared.

"Glennon!" Anthony's concern carried across the property as he ran out of the tree line toward her. He darted past the corner of the house, gun in hand, after her attacker.

Her breath sawed in and out of her lungs. Shoving to her feet, she gripped her weapon and gave chase. She pumped her legs hard. The bastard had threatened her son. He wasn't getting away.

More than thirty yards ahead, the figure dressed in head-to-toe black and a ski mask ripped open the door to a waiting pickup. They were going to lose him. Desperation dumped another round of adrenaline into her blood.

Her attacker raised his weapon. In a split second both she and Anthony had been placed on the wrong side of the gun. But Anthony didn't stop. Two shots kicked up dirt and snow at his feet, but he kept advancing.

"Anthony, no!" Rushing forward, she put herself between him and the chance of high-speed lead poisoning, just as he'd done for her back at the abandoned house. She shot her hands up, her gun pointed at the brightening sky in surrender. She wouldn't risk Anthony taking a bullet for her, no matter how used to the idea he'd become. Puffs of air crystalized in front of her lips, but she couldn't move—couldn't think—as her attacker climbed into the truck and turned over the engine. Anthony's chest pressed into her uninjured shoulder, as though she was the only barrier holding him back.

Within seconds the truck tires kicked up gravel at the end of the property, and her attacker disappeared.

Her hands ached from gripping her weapon so damn tight. A rush of defeat flooded through her. She collapsed onto her knees, every ounce of energy draining from her. It'd been a warning. Despite hitting dead end after dead end, she'd somehow gotten close. Why else would someone break in? The intruder's words registered as her nervous system returned to normal. *You're going to stop looking for your partner.*

She wasn't the hiding type. She'd fight. She'd find Bennett, and she'd protect her son. Snow worked its way through her socks, but the sharp pain in one knee pulled at her focus. She'd hit something. Moving her knee, Glennon focused on the small metal pin reflecting the final stages of purple-and-blue Alaskan sunrise.

An American flag pin.

"You okay?" Anthony's boots appeared in her peripheral vision as he closed in on her. "Did he hurt you?"

A chill swept across her back the longer she studied the pin. "No. I'm…fine."

"Bastard disabled my security system. He ran into the tree line and doubled back." Rage darkened Anthony's voice as he crouched beside her. He lowered his voice. "I heard another gunshot."

"I shot at him." Glennon curled her fingers into her palm, the sharp edge of the pin digging into her skin. She'd taken the shot. Shoving off the ground, she took a full breath of cold morning air to clear her head. Didn't work. Nothing but tracking down her partner would. "We need to get to my barracks."

"Someone just attacked you. Every second you're

out in the open, you're at risk." Anthony raised the Beretta he'd relied on for so long, using it to point to the location the pickup—and their attacker—had disappeared. The furrow between his brows deepened as anger sparked in his eyes. "That sniper who put a bullet in your shoulder was a professional, sweetheart. That bastard who just bypassed my security system? A professional. These guys aren't messing around. You're not safe, and I will not lose you a second time."

Shock beat through her and Glennon swallowed hard. The swooping of a bald eagle along the tree line pulled her back into the moment. Her missing partner. The fact someone had broken into the cabin to threaten her. The shot she'd taken. "Then it's a good thing I hired a Ranger to protect me."

"Glennon..." he said.

No. They weren't doing this. She couldn't.

"I hid the hard copies of the files that were deleted off my backup in my barracks." She leveled her chin with the ground. Wood splintered off the spot where her bullet had penetrated the corner of the cabin. Her attacker was gone, his warning crystal-clear in her head. She tucked the combat blade into her left boot. Her hands shook, even with one wrapped around the grip of her gun, and before she understood what was happening, Anthony had encased them in his grasp. His heat penetrated the thick haze of her last few minutes.

If she was being honest with herself, she'd missed this. Missed him. Because even though Anthony Harris had been nicknamed the Grim Reaper by his superiors, he'd always held the skills to bring her to life. Even after she wasn't his anymore. She might've needed a

bit of that warmth right now, but she slid her hands out of his. "We should get going."

Stepping away from her, Anthony extended his hand toward the cabin. It was hard to read his expression. Tight. Hollow. Jaw clenched. As though he were locking down the emotions burning through him as she had so many times around him. "Lead the way, Sergeant."

Sergeant. Not sweetheart.

Glennon brushed past him, her stomach heavy. Her attacker had threatened her son. Wrong choice. He'd known who she was, knew of the people she cared about. He should've killed her when he'd had the chance. If anything happened to her son now, she wouldn't hesitate like he had. A threat to back off the investigation and a single warning shot. That'd been it. He was lucky that was as far as it'd gotten. Still, none of it made sense.

She froze.

"He's been watching me." How else could her attacker have found her so quickly? The dull ache in her wrists from the gun's kickback intensified as a shudder raced through her. The thought of being watched—stalked—tightened every muscle she had. What else had the intruder compiled on her? Her memory drifted to the conversation with her son. What was this guy willing to use against her to back off the search for her partner?

She spun into Anthony. "Watching us."

"I will find him, Glennon." The rage tightening the tendons between his neck and shoulders disintegrated the second he set sights on her, the growl from his voice disappearing. "You don't have to be afraid."

"I'm not afraid. He warned me to back off. He

threatened me and the people I care about. If anybody is going to find him, it's me." The American flag pin in her pocket demanded attention. She rolled back her injured shoulder. Pain zinged through the wound like lightning, but it only solidified her determination and cleared her head. "I don't care what that bastard said. Those files are the only lead to finding Bennett and putting an end to this nightmare. And I'm going to see this through to the end."

Chapter Five

Her attacker had gotten close to her. Touched her.

Pain radiated through Anthony's knuckles and into his shoulders from his clenching his fists so hard. He didn't care. He could've lost her this morning. Again.

Rolling his head back onto his shoulders, he mentally counted to ten. Two attempts on her life in two days. So far he'd done a bang-up job of keeping her safe. He ran a hand through his beard. How had that bastard gotten past his security system in the first place?

The soldier stationed at the entrance to the base reviewed their credentials.

"Welcome to JBER, Sergeant Major Harris, Sergeant Chase." The soldier handed back their ID. "Weapons, please. You can retrieve them when you leave."

Glennon and Anthony both handed over their handguns, saluted and then drove straight for the barracks. Pulling into the lot, she shoved the SUV into Park, but didn't move to get out. "All right. You haven't said a word since we left the cabin, and I'm starting to think it has something to do with what happened this morning."

Her sarcasm wouldn't lighten his mood.

"You could've been killed." The words ripped from his throat. How could he have been so careless as to follow those tracks? The second her attacker had taken off for the trees, he should've known the bastard would double back to get to his target: Glennon. Anthony locked his jaw, the ache at the base of his skull intensifying as they stepped from the vehicle.

"But I wasn't." She closed the self-imposed distance between them as she rounded the front of the SUV, slipping her hand across his arm. A rush of electricity shot through him. After all these years apart, how could she still affect him like this? "If you hadn't been there to head that guy off in the hallway, who knows what would've happened. You saved my life whether you want to see it that way or not."

He wasn't sure about that. Her attacker had had her within his reach, could've ended it right then, yet he'd run for the pickup. Glennon's relayed warning had echoed through his mind since leaving the cabin. What if they were coming at Sergeant Bennett's disappearance all wrong?

She dropped her hold, heading inside, and he inhaled sharply to steady himself. Tan paint, white tile, an endless hallway and heavy steel doors. Just as he remembered, although he'd only been stationed here a few weeks before shipping out. Anthony missed the weight of his Beretta as they moved toward her room. Chances of needing it on base were slim, but the thought of someone gunning for her grated on his nerve endings.

"Home sweet home." She dangled the key between her index finger and thumb then handed it off. No

physical contact this time. "Try not to make a mess. I have inspections when my leave ends in three days."

He slid the key into the door and twisted, shouldering his way inside. After flipping the light switch, he stepped back into the hallway. "Whoever searched your room before we got here obviously didn't get the memo."

"What?" Glennon pushed past him.

Her room had been trashed. Feathers from slashed pillows nearly covered the floor, while holes in walls crumbled drywall onto the ripped sheets. Whoever had broken into Glennon's room had been searching for something. Anthony focused the lingering rage climbing up his throat into searching for the files. It'd been a damn good thing she hadn't been anywhere near here.

He hugged the wall, moving through the room one step at a time. No movement. No intruders hiding under the twin-size bed or in the wood cabinets where her uniforms and civilian clothing spilled out onto the tile. His instincts said whoever had caused this mess had taken off a while ago. Could've been the same person who'd taken care of the shooter back at the abandoned house. The same person who'd broken into the cabin? That gave them at least a two-hour head start.

Every cabinet had been opened, every couch cushion destroyed. No stone left unturned. But Anthony read no real organization in the search. It had been disorganized, frenzied. The shooter who'd put a bullet in her shoulder had been a professional. The man at the cabin? Also a professional. This was…something else. Desperation.

"Well, I think I'm definitely going to fail inspection." Glennon ran a hand through her hair, collapsing

onto the edge of her mattress. The small muscles along her jaw tightened. She tried to hide her reaction, but hints of disbelief bled through her stony features—the slight widening of her eyes, the way she rolled her fingers into the center of her palm. She kicked personal items out of her way. Some clothing, a toothbrush, a broken compact mirror. "The only reason someone would've done this was to look for the hard copies of those files deleted off my backup."

And it had to be someone enlisted. There was no other way they could've gotten on base.

"Where are they?" Anthony nodded at the hole in the back of the cabinet, the perfect size and shape for a wall safe. Although, the safe had clearly been taken by the intruder in a quick getaway. Interrupted during their search? Before they left he'd get in touch with base security to check the security footage. Not a whole lot of places a soldier could disappear with a wall safe in tow.

She stood, making a beeline for the bathroom. Within ten seconds Glennon reemerged, an empty manila file folder in one hand and a black laptop in the other. She tossed the folder onto the floor. "They got the hard copies I taped under the bathroom sink." Hiking her thumb over her shoulder, she leaned against the doorjamb. "And they destroyed my laptop. Unless your computer expert can recover a damaged hard drive, everything I had on Bennett's disappearance is gone."

"I'll have Sullivan call in Captain Reise to start processing the scene with the base's investigative unit. She's a prosecutor stationed here at JBER, but she should have a few favors to call in." Anthony gripped

his cell phone. "She might be able to tell us what our next move is."

"Do you honestly think it'll do any good? Seems like every time we get a lead, it's a dead end." Glennon tossed the battered laptop onto the bed and studied the room once more. "Whoever did this is military. And they obviously don't want me to recover Bennett. So either they have something to do with his disappearance or they're covering someone's ass. Maybe both."

Covering someone's ass. The furrow between his brows deepened. "You think this is linked to the stolen weapons shipments."

"That's my reigning theory. Bennett is smart and he's trained. He wouldn't go down easily. He sent me a message saying he had proof. Most likely proof someone had taken Staff Sergeant Mascaro's place at the head of the theft operation. Intel like that could be enough to kill for." She nodded at the shared door on the other side of the room. "Bennett's barracks are— were—right next to mine. Probably looks as good as mine does right now, too, unless the marshal has gotten to it."

"The marshal." The attacker at the cabin had known he was a Ranger, had known where to find them, had had the ability to bypass highly secure alarm systems. There were only so many people in the world who had access to that kind of intel and training. "I'd say he's a good place to start."

"You think the Provost Marshal General, a man who reports directly to the Chief of Staff of the US Army, has something to do with Bennett's disappearance?" She turned away fast, a burst of laughter escaping up her throat before she faced him again. "That's ridicu-

lous. The marshal sent us here to investigate the stolen weapons. Why bring us here at all if he didn't want us to find the soldiers responsible?"

"To keep an eye on your work, to see what you and Bennett uncovered. And if you found something he didn't like...he could get rid of the evidence." And the investigators themselves. The pieces were falling into place. Anthony didn't have the proof, but there was too much opportunity to not at least talk to the man.

"And when Bennett found proof Mascaro's operation was still going strong under new leadership, the marshal contracted a hit on both of us to tie up the loose ends." Glennon sank against the bathroom doorjamb again, her gaze locked on the laptop. She rubbed at the hole in her shoulder. Shaking her head, she shoved away from the doorway, a new shade of determination coloring her features. "Still doesn't tell us where Bennett is. If we're going to accuse the Marshal General of being involved, we need hard evidence to prove it. Irrefutable."

"Agreed." Anthony's phone buzzed in his hand. Sullivan Bishop, CEO and founder of Blackhawk Security, had gotten his significant other to agree to process the scene off the books. But he and Glennon weren't going to wait around. He'd promised to protect her during this investigation, and that was exactly what he'd do. Even if it cost him everything. "Tell me how we find him."

Glennon extracted her phone from her jacket pocket and swiped her finger across the screen. "Lieutenant General Samuel Sykes is usually stationed at CID command in Quantico, but he's decided on a more hands-on approach with this investigation. Just so happens, he's right here on base. I even have a picture." She shuffled

around the bed through the debris, her boot catching on the corner of the frame. She fell forward.

Anthony moved fast, catching her before she hit the floor. He wrapped his hand around her wrist, her strong pulse beating under his touch. A flood of light pink burned into her cheeks. A rough exhale escaped from between her lips as he righted her, but he didn't let go. Her sweet rosy scent surrounded him, drawing him closer. Another bolt of electricity—stronger than before—surged through him. Damn, what her touch could do to him. Her attention drifted farther down. To the chain around his neck that had dislodged from under his T-shirt when she fell.

The one with her yellow-gold engagement ring strung through it.

HE'D KEPT IT all this time. Her ring. Not just kept it, but wore it around his neck. Glennon swallowed hard. Close to his chest.

She straightened, taking a step back. He couldn't still have feelings for her after all these years. He'd moved on. They both had. He'd gone into private security; she'd put everything she had into her career to forget him. There'd been other women for him and other men for her. Although, as she ran through the short list of dates over the past few years, she couldn't deny she'd held Sergeant Major Anthony Harris on a pedestal. He'd been her first love. Always would be. Her throat dried. "Why do you have my engagement ring?"

"I never intended for you to see that." He fisted the ring and shoved it back down his shirt. Turning away from her, Anthony moved with predatory power. He closed down his expression the same way she closed

down hers when she didn't want to surrender the upper hand. Pure stone.

"That's not an answer." Her heart drummed too hard and too fast in her chest. She didn't let her expression change, but couldn't control the tingling sensation spreading down her body. A single step forward was all it took for him to face her again. "Do you...?" She licked her lips. "Have you been wearing that all this time?"

"The most important people in my life are my team." Sadness swirled in those dark blue eyes, rocketing her heart into her throat. She knew that. While on tour in Afghanistan, his entire team had been killed right in front of him. He hadn't ever given her the details, but a few calls up the chain of command had filled in the blanks. Forty-eight hours without support in enemy territory. And he'd made it out alive. Done things that would most certainly haunt him for the rest of his life. For his team.

But that had been when things had changed. That had been when his commanding officers had given him his nickname. The thin, white scar that disappeared into his beard became more pronounced.

"You're still on that team, Glennon. You have been since the day I met you," he said.

"Anthony..." She didn't know what to say to that. What *could* she say? Glennon backed toward the bed, the soft part of her knees hitting the mattress. This was a mistake. Had she known asking for Anthony's help would put him in this position, she never would've dialed his number.

She studied the mess around her. They were standing in the middle of a crime scene. She had a job to

do. She hadn't come back to Anchorage to tear open past wounds, but she wasn't about to give him false hope, either. Notching her chin parallel to the floor, she stood. One step. Two. Debris parted as she closed the space between them. His masculine scent washed over her as she reached up, framing his strong jaw between her hands. "I…can't."

She'd promised herself not to get involved with any partner she'd been assigned. For the Military Police. With the army. First rule in rescue: keep emotional distance. She couldn't get involved, couldn't risk her emotions taking over a case. And she couldn't do personal relationships anymore. Not since…him. And not since her son had come along. Because a relationship didn't just involve her anymore. It would affect Hunter's life, too.

But Anthony tested that boundary as he stared down at her. She traced the small white scar that cut across the left side of his face with the pad of her thumb, one she'd never noticed before, hidden beneath his soft facial hair. Sliding his palms over the back of her hands, he leaned into her touch. He gave a single, quick nod. "I know."

Her hands slipped from his but she couldn't move—couldn't think—as he backed away. The outline of her engagement ring was still visible through his shirt. How had she not recognized it for what it was before now?

"We should go." He started walking toward the door, taking every ounce of heat from her body with him. "The marshal isn't going to wait around all day for us to ambush him."

"Anthony." She fisted her grip around the hem of

her jacket to keep from reaching out for him. Seconds passed. Ten. Maybe more. What was she supposed to say? The ring, his confession… She hadn't been prepared for any of it. "I'm sorry. I wish I could—"

"Don't do that." Hand on the doorknob, he cocked his head over his shoulder. "You got exactly what you wanted, Glennon. And it didn't matter who you left behind in the process."

She schooled her expression as his words shot straight through her.

He wrenched open the door.

"I wasn't finished." Her voice turned to ice while every cell in her body caught fire. "You might think you have me figured out, that I left because of some pathetic fear of commitment. But you're wrong." Her feet sank into the floor as though they'd been buried in cement. "What I was going to say was that I wish I could tell you the truth."

"What do you mean?" Anthony turned to her. The lines between his eyebrows deepened as the heavy door automatically closed behind him. His voice dropped, deep, dark and sexy, and a shiver slid through her. "What truth?"

How could he possibly still affect her like this? Like they hadn't been apart the last five years. Like her entire world hadn't flipped the second she'd set eyes on him. Like she was still the rookie in basic training who'd fallen head over heels for the Ranger she'd met during weapons training.

She bit the side of her tongue. She couldn't do it. Couldn't tell him. Because no matter how much Anthony deserved to know, she couldn't stand the possibility of him hating her more than he already did. She

needed his help to find Bennett—plain and simple—
and she couldn't risk him walking away.

Pressure built in her lungs the longer he stared at
her, expecting answers. Only there was nothing simple about their situation, was there? "That I'm sorry
for leaving the way I did. I shouldn't have disappeared
while you were on tour. Doesn't change my reasons
for leaving. But after I heard what happened to you in
Afghanistan, I realized too late I should've done a lot
of things differently."

Anthony didn't flinch. Not so much as a muscle-
twitch. His pulse beat steadily at the base of his throat
as he studied her, always in control. Always assessing.
But he couldn't possibly know what she was hiding.
He nodded. "You know you clench your fingers into a
fist when you lie, right?"

"I do not." She glanced down at her hands. Uncurl-
ing her fingers, Glennon rubbed her palms down the
sides of her thighs. She'd had that specific tell under
control for years. What had changed? She raised her
gaze to his. Hell. Didn't she already know the answer
to that?

She cleared her throat. "I called in a few favors after
I left. I know you spent two days in enemy territory
alone, out of ammunition, out of provisions, and that
the only way you made it back alive was by shooting
your way out."

He closed in on her, fire, rage—everything he kept
caged from her—bleeding to the surface of his tightly
held control. Not to intimidate her but to get her attention, to let her know he wasn't about to back down.

She was forced to look up at him. Didn't he realize
she hadn't been able to focus on anything but him the

last two days? That it took every ounce of her remaining strength to keep her distance?

"I'm trained to read people, Glennon. That means I can read you." He traced the length of her neck with his fingertips, catching her off guard. An explosion of need filled her. She held her breath.

Leveling those dark blue eyes with hers, he leaned in close. So close all she had to do was shift forward to meet his lips if she wanted to. "Just answer me about one thing. Honestly."

Her heart beat loud behind her ears.

"Is whatever you're hiding going to get us killed?" he asked.

She shook her head. "No."

"Then that's all I need to know." He slid his hand to the back of her neck and pulled her into him. Crushing her against him, Anthony kissed her with a punishing desire she'd never felt before. He surrounded her, controlled her, slid his mouth over hers as though he'd been waiting for this moment since the day she left.

And she let him.

She'd wanted—no, *needed*—this release, needed *him*, more than anything else at the moment. Forget Bennett. Forget the investigation. Forget she'd landed in the crosshairs of a sniper and could take another bullet at any moment. Right now, there was only Anthony. Her strong, reliable, loyal Ranger. If only for a few seconds, she'd give up control. She'd let the feelings she'd buried for the last five years take over. Her insides caught fire as she melted against him. Had it always been like this between them? So freeing? Roaring electricity shot up her spine. Hell, she was an idiot

for kissing him back, but how long had it been since she'd trusted someone this completely?

His fingertips pressed into the back of her skull, refusing to let her budge as he swept his tongue past her lips. He worked to claim her from the inside and—right in the middle of her destroyed barracks, with her peers on the other side of the door—she didn't care. No hesitation.

Passion and familiarity spread through her as his full beard tickled the oversensitized skin along her jaw. The sensation only spurred her further. She kissed him back, kissed him with everything she had. Shoving years of loneliness, of pain and self-doubt into the near-forgotten connection between them, Glennon surrendered for the first time in years. To him. Always to him.

Anthony pulled back first and she swayed on her feet. His masculine scent drove through her system, determined to mark her from the inside. Staring down at her, he shifted on his feet, but kept her close. "I've wanted to do that since the moment I saw you in that abandoned house."

Abandoned house? She blinked to clear her head. Right. The investigation. Her partner.

Glennon maneuvered out of his grasp. His pupils grew smaller as she ran a hand through her hair. Air. She needed air. She'd gotten so lost in him, she'd completely forgotten why she'd called him in the first place. To find Bennett. Rolling her lips between her teeth, she bit down to get her head back in the game. It'd felt good to let go for those countless seconds, to give up her control for a moment, but it couldn't happen again. Not with him. Not with anyone.

Glennon moved to the door. "You're right. The marshal isn't going to wait around all day for us to interrogate him. Let's go."

Chapter Six

She'd lied to him.

While she'd claimed whatever she was hiding wouldn't ultimately get them killed, Anthony had read the distress in her expression. He slid his finger along the side of his Beretta as they waited outside the downtown office building. Civilian turf. Nothing to tie back to Glennon if this went south. According to the lieutenant general's administrative assistant, the marshal had a meeting scheduled here in ten minutes. Enough time to get some answers.

Glennon hadn't said a word since they'd left the barracks, but the uneven tension straining her jawline as she watched out the passenger-side window for their target revealed the truth: he shouldn't have kissed her.

Anthony wouldn't apologize. He wasn't sorry. But the silence that had filled the inside of the tinted SUV pressurized the air in his lungs. "Want to talk about it?"

"There's nothing to talk about." She kept her eyes on the side mirror. "You kissed me. I kissed you back. Won't happen again. The end."

He tapped the back of his head against his headrest, his grip light on the Beretta in his lap. As much as he wanted to believe she meant every word, he'd been part

of that kiss, too. She'd surrendered to him. For those few brief moments she'd given up her tight control, had reverted to the woman he'd fallen in love with during her basic training. And damn, what he wouldn't give to feel that release again. To see her let go. "How can you be sure it won't happen again?"

"There's our target." Glennon sat forward in her seat, unholstering her service weapon as the marshal's nontactical vehicle pulled up to the underground parking garage of the building with two armed military escorts. She unlocked the door and shouldered her weight into it. "Let's go see if the marshal wants me dead."

Anthony was right behind her. His boots hit the asphalt, instincts on high alert. They'd lost the advantage of ambushing Lieutenant General Sykes under the cover of darkness, but he wasn't about to open fire in the middle of a public street, either. They had to be smart about this or risk involving Anchorage PD, the army and any other interested parties—the last thing Glennon wanted in this investigation.

She jogged across the street, gun at her side.

Anthony surveyed the area in case Sykes was being watched. Tall, with a slight build, headed into his seventies with a full head of white hair and deep wrinkles, the marshal didn't scream suspected traitor, but Anthony wasn't taking any chances. Not with Glennon in the crosshairs. The rooftops were clear. No civilians took more of an interest in their movements than normal. So far, so good.

Glennon picked up the pace when the tail end of Sykes's vehicle cleared the entrance to the garage, but she pulled up short once she approached the corner. Back pressed against the wall, she closed her eyes for

a split second then turned to Anthony. She locked on him, determined, controlled. One hundred percent the special agent he'd imagined she'd become. "If this goes sideways, we'll be court-martialed. You can still back out."

No. He couldn't.

"I've got your back." His pulse beat steadily in his chest. This was what he did for a living, what he'd been born to do. Adrenaline dumped into his blood. Primary objective: protect Glennon. If her interrogation with the marshal went south, he'd get her out of there. No matter what. Giving up wasn't in her personality, but her life was far more important than this investigation. He pulled back the slide on his weapon, ensuring he'd loaded a round into the chamber. He nodded once. "On your signal."

"Go." Glennon swung her Glock up as she rounded the corner.

A rush of icy air slammed into him as they descended into the darkness. His senses adjusted slowly. Glennon's outline was straight ahead of him. She moved with quick, sure movements toward Sykes's NTV parked in the second row at the back of the garage. No sign of the marshal or his armed escorts. Anthony listened for movement. The start of a car, footsteps—anything to give them an idea where their target had gone. He gripped the Berretta tighter.

Nothing. The garage was too quiet for this time of day.

As they neared the NTV, he caught sight of two bodies. Two soldiers. His instincts prickled a warning. Damn it. Sykes had known they were coming.

Anthony lunged for Glennon up ahead, wrapping

his hand around her arm. He tugged her into him a split second before a bullet ripped through the darkness. Cement exploded to their left as a column absorbed the shot. Her breath slammed out of her chest and across his neck with the impact. Shuffling sounds echoed off the asphalt, but not long enough for Anthony to pin down their target's location. Her fingers gripped his Kevlar vest, keeping him pressed against her. His fight-or-flight instinct sharpened his senses. He sure as hell wouldn't take flight. The son of a bitch had taken a shot at her. Wouldn't happen again.

"You shouldn't have come here, Sergeant Chase," a deep, drawling accented voice called out. "You're in over your head."

Glennon's chin notched higher, her shoulders stiffening. She rolled off him. *Follow the plan.* She'd distract Sykes while Anthony closed in on the target. "Is that the same warning you gave Sergeant Spencer when he confronted you about your ties to Mascaro's operation?"

A low rumble of a laugh vibrated through the garage as Anthony maneuvered along the south wall of the garage, gun in hand. The marshal's voice barely reached him. "You have no idea what you're talking about, little girl. The operation you and your partner have been investigating is more than you can take on. Hell, it's more than the US Army can take on. Sergeant Spencer understood that."

The outline of a man about Sykes's height and build moved from around a white van thirty feet ahead. Toward Glennon's position.

Anthony focused on the four cars between him and the marshal. She could take care of herself, he had

no doubt about that, but he picked up his pace all the same. He heel-toed it across the cement, ensuring he kept his weight evenly distributed so the lieutenant general wouldn't know what hit him. The muscles in his shoulders ached the longer he held the gun up, deprived of oxygen as he held his breath.

"Did you kill him?" Glennon's voice wavered.

Three cars between him and the target. Anthony kept low and moved fast. Two cars. The scent of spicy aftershave clouded his head.

"I barely escaped with my life after Sergeant Spencer came looking for me." Sykes's outline sharpened as Anthony closed in. The marshal raised his weapon and took aim. A quick glance in Glennon's position revealed how close she'd gotten. Too close. And directly into Sykes's sights. "I won't make the same mistake with you, Sergeant."

Anthony pulled the trigger.

The bullet ripped through his target's shoulder, an almost identical wound to Glennon's. The marshal crumbled to the pavement, a rich groan filling the garage. But to Sykes's credit, he didn't scream.

Dim overhead lighting chased the shadows from Glennon's features as she moved in, weapon aimed at her commanding officer. Even with a bullet in his shoulder, Sykes was a highly trained military operative in his glory days. A threat.

Anthony kicked the marshal's gun across the pavement, out of reach. Metal scraped against asphalt as the weapon disappeared under a parked car a few spaces down.

"The mistake you made was assuming I'd come

without backup." Glennon crouched low as the marshal clamped a hand over the hole in his shoulder.

Blood seeped from between the lieutenant general's fingers, but Sykes would live to tell his tale. As long as they got their answers. Someone had sent a professional shooter after Glennon, then another man to break into his cabin. Anthony wasn't leaving until he found out who would be on the wrong end of his weapon next time.

"Where is Sergeant Spencer?" Glennon's voice promised a not-too-happy ending for the marshal.

Anthony's phone vibrated in his pocket. One look at Captain Reise's email and the forwarded scene report from Glennon's barracks said they had the right guy. "Your fingerprints were all over Sergeant Chase's barracks." He nodded toward the marshal, but Glennon only had attention for her commanding officer. Not a hint of surprise on those beautiful, stone-like features. "He destroyed the files you gathered on Bennett and Sergeant Mascaro's operation. Should've been more careful, sir."

The marshal didn't respond. No surprise there. Trained operatives spent hundreds of hours counteracting interrogation tactics. Sykes wouldn't admit guilt, but the small twitch of his white beard gave way to another almost inaudible groan.

"Tell me where Sergeant Spencer is, and you might be able to call an ambulance in time," she said.

"You don't scare me, Sergeant Chase. You're not a killer." The marshal's chapped lips thinned into a smile. He checked back over his shoulder, toward Anthony. "As for the company you keep, that's a different story."

Glennon blinked. "You don't know anything about us."

"Oh, I know plenty, darlin'." A thick Texan accent bubbled to the surface. Sweat across Sykes's forehead reflected the dim overhead lighting. Blood loss tended to have that effect—it drained color from the face, forced the hands to shake. "I know you're from Anchorage. That your daddy walked out on you and your mama at a young age. That you were engaged to Sergeant Major Harris here before you transferred to the Quantico office. And that you, my dear, are not prepared for what's about to happen."

"You killed your escort," she said. "Why?"

Anthony searched the garage. They weren't getting anywhere with this guy. The marshal wouldn't tell them anything about her missing partner. He caught sight of the elevators at the north end of the building, the panel above the doors counting down. Level three. Level two. The hairs on the back of his neck stood on end. "Glennon."

"And I know your secret," Lieutenant General Sykes said. "The one you've been keeping from the army and your bodyguard here."

Anthony homed in on the marshal.

Straightening, Glennon lowered the Glock to her side. If the garage hadn't been so dark, Anthony would've sworn the blood had drained from her face. Her gun hand shook briefly, but she stilled so fast, he could've been mistaken. "You're lying."

Level one.

"Glennon, he's baiting you so he can stall." Anthony maneuvered around the marshal. Someone was about to step off that elevator and, from their current position fewer than fifty feet from the doors, blow their entire operation. "We've got to get out of here."

Bright red lines across the elevator's electric panel said they were out of time.

"Your partner had a secret, too, Sergeant Chase." The lines around Sykes's eyes deepened—to counteract the pain in his shoulder, most likely. "Don't suppose the fact Sergeant Spencer is a lieutenant in Nicholas Mascaro's operation is the reason he's gone missing, do you?"

The elevator doors parted.

HER WORLD SLOWED.

Anthony raised his weapon in her peripheral vision. Thumping vibrations shot through her as sparks exploded off two cars nearby, but Glennon couldn't move. It wasn't possible. The marshal was lying. Bennett wouldn't have gotten himself involved with a criminal organization. Everything they'd done the last six months had been to bring down Mascaro's operation... He wasn't a lieutenant.

"Glennon!" Anthony shoved her down. "Get out of here!"

The dimly lit garage blurred as she hit the ground. Reality caught up as Lieutenant General Sykes army-crawled away from her. Bullets ricocheted off the vehicle at her back, and she shook her head clear. The Glock remained heavy in her grip as she lunged. Catching his arm with one hand, Glennon ripped her commanding officer from the asphalt and ran. Sykes wasn't going anywhere. Not until she had what she came for.

Anthony fired two shots—three—as he followed close on her heels. "Go, go, go!"

Who the hell was shooting at them?

She pumped her legs hard, dragging the marshal

behind her with everything she had. The bullet in his shoulder slowed them down, but she wasn't about to leave him behind. He jerked forward—trying to rip away—but Glennon kept a tight hold on his arm.

They dove behind a white commercial van at the back of the garage. The rhythmic firing of automatic gunfire echoed loudly in her ears. The van would give them enough cover for the next few minutes, but they couldn't afford to be pinned down much longer. Every second she wasted trying to get answers out of Sykes limited her and Anthony's chance of escape.

She fought to catch her breath, turning on her commanding officer. She fisted his three-star-decorated uniform and wrenched him toward her. Asphalt bit into her knees with his added weight. "You're involved in Mascaro's operation. Tell me about Bennett. Now."

Something wet and sticky dripped down her T-shirt.

"Seems like we're both running out of time, Sergeant Chase." The marshal's coffee-brown eyes glassed over.

Blood. He'd been shot in the chest. No, no, no, no. "Come on. Stay with me, Marshal. Tell me where my partner is."

"We're pinned down." Maneuvering around the van, Anthony crouched low and switched his magazine for a fresh reload.

Relief flooded through her, but didn't last long. He'd get them out of here. Whatever it took, she believed in him. But the provost marshal general was losing blood fast and the chances of getting information out of him were quickly dwindling. Hell burned in Anthony's cold blue eyes, locked on Sykes, and a shiver chased down

her spine. This had been exactly why she'd come to him for help.

Focusing on the blood spreading across the asphalt, Anthony shook his head. "He took a bullet to his left lung. He'll suffocate before we have a chance to even move him." His voice was flat.

"That's not good enough." The gunfire pounded through her head, never ceasing. How were they going to get out of here? "Please—" she leveraged both palms against Sykes's wound to stop the bleeding, in vain "—tell me about Sergeant Spencer. What happened to him? Where can I find him?"

"Mascaro…paid me…will kill… Sergeant Spen—" Blood stained the corners of Lieutenant General Sykes's mouth as he sagged back against the pavement. A rough exhale escaped him as the life drained from his aged features.

"No. You're not allowed to die on me! Tell me where Bennett is." Glennon leveraged her weight and pumped eight quick pulses to get his heart started. Counting another eight, she barely registered the strong grip trying to pull her back. Wrenching out of Anthony's hold, she slid her blood-covered fingertips to her commanding officer's neck. No pulse. Frustration climbed up her throat.

The marshal stared at the ceiling, unmoving.

He was dead. And any information he'd had about recovering Bennett had died with him.

"Glennon, we need to get out of here!" Anthony's voice barely registered over the gunfire that seemed so much louder than a few minutes ago. Strong hands ripped her from beside the marshal's body and thrust her toward the back of the van.

"The only way we're getting out of here is through the main entrance." Another round of bullets ricocheted off the vehicle. Three shots? Four? Glennon couldn't think. Her best chance of putting an end to this investigation had just bled out on the asphalt six feet away. Anthony unloaded the rest of his magazine at the shooters then took cover once again to switch weapons. "We need a plan here, sweetheart."

Blood coated her palms, but she gripped her Glock hard nonetheless. A dull ringing filled her ears. Glennon shook the last few minutes of the lieutenant general's life from her memory. Sykes might've held the answers to her investigation, but she wasn't giving up. It wasn't in her personality. Dead or alive, she'd find Bennett and put an end to this nightmare. Even if she had to break a few of the very laws she'd upheld to do it.

She turned on Anthony. This wasn't over. "Mascaro's operatives want me." She counted the rounds left in her magazine and slammed it back into her weapon. "They're going to have to come get me."

"You hired me to protect you." Anthony took position at the corner of the van. Locking his eyes on her, he resurrected heated flashes of the gut-wrenching kiss they'd shared in her barracks. When he'd kissed her, she'd been lost. His fingers had threaded up the back of her neck and into her hair, and the rest of the world had fallen away for the briefest of moments. The scar disappearing into his full beard combined with tanned, weathered skin had turned him rough, but the way he'd held her, the way he'd touched her, revealed just how much he cared. He'd get them out of here. He'd take

care of her. "And I'll be damned if I let you get your-self killed."

She swayed toward him. She nodded to focus. She couldn't think about that right now, couldn't think about him. Whoever these guys were—whoever had sent them—they weren't interested in talking. Pro-fessionals only wanted one thing: the target. Glennon glanced at her former commanding officer. If there were casualties in the process, that didn't matter. She'd get her answers one way or another. "I want to know what the marshal meant about Bennett being part of Mascaro's operation. I'll take the shooter on the left. You take the right. We need these guys alive."

"You got it, sweetheart." He rounded the van, weapon aimed, and fired.

Glennon followed close behind, taking the low ground. The two shooters had taken position across the aisle, each using a vehicle for cover. Gripping her Glock in both hands, she dropped to one knee and pulled the trigger. The gun kicked back in her hand, but she barely registered the pain in her shoulder this time around. Adrenaline pumped into her veins, focus-ing her senses on the single shooter to her left.

Kevlar and a bulletproof face mask absorbed her direct hits. Damn it. These two had come in full tacti-cal gear. Army-level gear. She couldn't get a read on the man behind the lieutenant general's NTV. Had the shooters come on orders from Staff Sergeant Mascaro himself? Or had they been waiting to ambush the mar-shal? She redirected her aim, the air in her lungs pres-surizing the longer their targets stayed upright. Only one way to find out.

Sinking to the pavement, Glennon flattened her-

self against the asphalt. Ice worked through her veins. Two shots was all it took to sweep the shooter's legs out from under him. He hit the hood of the NTV face-first and collapsed, dropping his weapon in the process. A deep groan hit her ears as she pushed to her feet.

Anthony closed in on his own target. The second shooter clamped down tight on a bullet wound that had skimmed his neck with one hand, but kept firing with the other. The gun clicked empty as Anthony charged. He slammed the shooter into the pavement, disappearing behind the car.

Heart in her throat, Glennon waited. One breath. Two. Shuffling teased her ears, but not from the shooter she'd taken down. Her jaw hardened. She gripped her gun tight. If one of those bullets had gotten through his gear... No. She couldn't think like that. Anthony was a Ranger. He'd taken plenty of hits over the years and delivered thousands more. Even with all those battle scars, he was the strongest, most loyal man she'd ever known. With calculated, slow steps, Glennon edged around the front of the vehicle.

Anthony wrenched the shooter to his feet, unbalanced.

"Damn it, don't do that to me again." She ran a hand through her hair. Sweat coated her palm. She wiped it down her pants, the tension pulling her shoulders tight then releasing in small increments. She breathed a bit easier. He was okay.

Until she noticed the dark, wet stain of blood spreading across the front of his thigh.

Anthony swayed on his feet, his eyelids heavy.

"You've been hit." The garage blurred in her peripheral vision as her blood pressure skyrocketed. Color

drained from his face and Glennon rushed forward, ready to catch him if he collapsed.

Stinging pain spread across her skull as she was ripped back into a wall of Kevlar. "You're not going anywhere."

She twisted against her attacker's grip on her hair, hoping to plant her knee straight in his groin... But the hot metal of a gun barrel pressed to her forehead froze her to the spot. Deep brown eyes stared back at her but she couldn't make out any other features beneath his bulletproof face mask. He swung her around again, bracing her back to his vested chest as his free hand gripped her throat. A single glance at the back of the vehicle where she'd thought she'd taken out the first shooter said it all. She'd been played. He hadn't been injured, hadn't even been knocked unconscious.

"Sergeant Chase—" his deep voice echoed from under the mask "—I've been waiting to get my hands on you."

Chapter Seven

Anthony's grip tightened around the unconscious shooter in his grasp while the second pointed a gun at Glennon's head. Pain splintered his racing thoughts. He couldn't see her face, but the deep reserve of rage he'd buried over the years took control all the same. It had started with losing every member of his team behind enemy lines and it had ended when Glennon had walked out the door. He wasn't about to lose another teammate. He wasn't about to lose her.

"Break a single hair on her head and it'll be the last mistake you ever make," he said.

Sweat beaded under his jawline, his vision blurring for a split second. His heart jolted in his chest. Fury built in him, a deadly rage that wouldn't be controlled. He let the bastard's partner collapse, the body hitting the pavement hard with fifty-plus pounds of gear. His fingers curled into his palm, tingling with the urge to wrap his hands around his Beretta. Or the bastard's throat. He wasn't picky. If it came right down to it, he'd beat the life out of any man who dared threaten her. No matter how much blood he lost. Which, by looking at the puddle under his left boot, had been quite a bit.

"Big words coming from a man bleeding out in the

middle of a parking garage." The shooter's voice lacked any distinct accent, his face hidden beneath layers of gear. Anthony could barely make out anything clearly other than brown—almost black—eyes. Six feet, about two hundred pounds of pure muscle. No visible tattoos or birthmarks. The only way they'd get a clue to this guy's ID and whoever had hired him would be with an autopsy. And as the seconds passed, Anthony was becoming more comfortable with that route.

The shooter was playing it safe, positioning Glennon fully in front of him, using her as a shield as he moved the gun barrel to her temple. "What do you think, Sergeant Chase?" He pressed his face mask against her ear and the muscles down Anthony's spine jerked. "Should I finish him off now or let him go out the hard way? My orders never said anything about bringing *him* back alive. I was only paid to get intel out of you. By whatever means necessary."

Sergeant Chase. Orders. The way the guy talked spoke volumes. They were dealing with soldiers. Nothing he hadn't handled before, but the bullet in his thigh might be a problem. He had to stay conscious. Keep her alive. With his veiled admission to needing to bring Glennon back alive, the shooter had given away more intel than he'd probably meant to. The bastard had been sent by Mascaro. And with Lieutenant General Sykes's involvement, they now had proof—her and Bennett's investigation for the army had been compromised after all.

"What makes you think he's going to let you walk out of this alive?" she asked the shooter. Glennon nodded to Anthony, her expression steady. Not an ounce of fear darkened those mesmerizing green eyes, but he

read her uncertainty in the way her knuckles whitened as she held on to the shooter's wrist at her throat. She swallowed hard.

"Should we test that theory?" The shooter pressed the barrel of the gun harder into her temple, throwing Glennon off balance. "If I'm not walking out of here alive, neither are you."

Not going to happen.

Rage exploded from behind Anthony's rib cage and spread fast. The edges of his vision darkened, putting the bastard in the middle of his own personal crosshairs. Adrenaline dimmed the pain in his leg as he rushed forward. Screw the Beretta. He'd tear this SOB apart with his bare hands.

Understanding exactly what he intended to do, Glennon twisted and threw her elbow back into the shooter's face mask. Her captor dropped his hold from her throat, giving her an out. Anthony closed the distance between him and the shooter as she dove for the ground.

"She's not going anywhere with you." Fisting the Kevlar vest in his grasp, Anthony ripped the face mask and underlying ski mask from the shooter's head and tossed them at the nearest car door. The vehicle's alarm and flashing headlights kept rhythm with his racing heartbeat. He pulled back his arm, ready to end this once and for all. For Glennon.

Black hair and tanned skin were all he registered as a fist slammed into the right side of his face. The world tilted on its axis, but Anthony refused to let go of the man in his grip. Another hit landed home and he collapsed to one knee. Pavement cut into him. Copper and salt filled his mouth as the wound in his leg bled faster.

But the pain—the dizziness—was nothing compared to what he'd endured for his country.

"Come on now, Ranger," the shooter said. "I've read your file. Give me a challenge."

Anthony spat salty blood onto the asphalt. This guy wanted a fight? All right. He'd give him everything he had. He straightened, but with the amount of blood pooling on the asphalt, quickly sank. He caught sight of Glennon reaching for her weapon a split second before the shooter planted his boot in the middle of her back.

A small gasp wheezed from her mouth.

"Don't worry, Sergeant Chase. I haven't forgotten about you." The bastard kicked her gun underneath the nearest car then fell to one knee beside her rib cage as he lowered his voice. Blood from the raw wound along his neck dripped onto her flawless features. "Before this is over, you're going to give me what I want or die in the process."

A growl exploded from his chest as Anthony came up swinging. His fist connected with the shooter's bullet wound—shocking his opponent—but the guy wouldn't stop there. He lost the Kevlar, the protective gear that was only weighing him down.

Sweat slid underneath the collar of Anthony's shirt as Glennon scrambled for her weapon. "Take care of him." He nodded at the first shooter who still lay unconscious at the back of the car. "I've got this."

She disappeared behind the car, blood smeared across her expression.

His attacker charged. Catching the bastard at the neck and waistband, Anthony flipped him and slammed him into the pavement. The smell of cigarettes drifted up from the shooter's clothing as he landed a boot in

the center of Anthony's chest. Anthony staggered back, but went in for another strike. The shooter rolled off the pavement, hands up, and blocked the hit. Legs staggered, knees bent, shoulders squared, elbows in. This guy was definitely military. Green Beret, if Anthony had to guess. And the only way to take down a Green Beret was death.

"There's the Ranger I've heard so much about." The shooter pulled a blade from his ankle. "Show me what you've got."

Combatives training took control. Anthony wrapped his fingers around the guy's wrist and pulled him closer. Rotating the blade away and up, he drove his elbow into the shooter's twisted arm. The crunch of bone breaking quaked down his spine as the clash of steel and asphalt echoed throughout the garage. His knuckles met his assailant's jawbone and he quickly followed through with his elbow to the same spot.

The guy fell hard. A deep growl filled the silence. "That's more like it."

A combination of sweat and blood loss blurred Anthony's vision. He swayed on his feet. He didn't have long before he blacked out. Fisting the bastard's shirtfront, he wrenched the Green Beret to his feet. Pain surged through his thigh with the additional weight. "You tell Nicholas Mascaro as long as I'm around, Glennon Chase is off-limits. Understand?"

Swelling consumed one deep brown eye, an uneven smile curling the shooter's mouth. "You can't protect her forever, Ranger. Even if you kill me now, they'll send someone to take my place." A deep rumble of a laugh worked up the SOB's throat. "One way or an-

other, your woman and her partner are dead. You're just extending the date they'll carve on their gravestones."

His woman. Anthony's grip tightened.

Overhead lighting glinted off a flash of metal in his peripheral vision. But he wasn't fast enough. The Green Beret swung another small blade fast, and it landed home. The breath rushed from Anthony's lungs, agony ripping through him. He'd taken bullets, sustained stab wounds. None had taken him out of commission before, but he doubled forward now. Glennon's engagement ring fell from under his shirt collar. The edges of his vision darkened.

"No!" Her shadowed outline rushed toward him. "Anthony!"

"Don't worry, Sergeant Major Harris." The blade slid from between his ribs as a strong grip squeezed his shoulder. The shooter set his mouth against Anthony's ear. "I'm going to take real good care of her."

Two distinct gunshots exploded. From a Glock. Glennon's service weapon? He couldn't be sure. The shooter jerked against him but didn't go down, spinning toward the source. Anthony shook his head to clear the fuzziness closing in fast, but strength drained from his muscles every second he wasted trying to get his bearings.

The grip on his shoulder vanished. He couldn't breathe. Couldn't think. Where was she? He blinked to restart his system. Blood and sweat drenched his clothing. He had to get up. Had to get Glennon out of here. Fisting his hands, Anthony shoved to his feet. He'd lost a lot of blood, but he had enough left pumping through his veins to finish this.

The shooter closed in on her. Her gun clicked empty

and she took two steps back, that beautiful green gaze searching for something—anything—to fight back with. She widened her stance, fists up. Blocking the first hit, Glennon knocked the Green Beret's weapon from his hand but wasn't fast enough to counter the second hit. His fingers wrapped around her neck as he sandwiched her between his body and the hood of the nearest car. She bowed against the metal, one hand on his wrist, another hitting her attacker as hard as she could—but the hit barely fazed him. He was too strong.

"Let her go." Every cell in Anthony's body propelled him forward. No thought. Only Glennon. In a split second he secured the shooter's head between both hands and wrenched as hard as he could. The body collapsed to the asphalt. He stared down at the single brown eye that hadn't swollen shut from the fight, his breath sawing in and out of his lungs.

It was over. For now. He sank his weight into his uninjured leg, clamping a hand over the stab wound in his side.

"On second thought, I'll tell Staff Sergeant Mascaro myself," he said.

THE GRIM REAPER had arrived. And her attacker had most certainly pissed him off.

Glennon rubbed at her throat, swallowing back the last twenty minutes. She leveraged her weight against the hood of the car to keep from collapsing. Bodies littered the ground. The marshal's escorts, the marshal himself, the two shooters sent to retrieve her. So much blood. What the hell had Bennett gotten himself into?

"Anthony," she said.

His name left her lips as a whisper. That was all she

could manage right now. She locked her attention on the engagement ring around his neck, the one smeared with crusted blood. She closed the distance between them slowly but he never focused on her. A pool of dark liquid collected under his left boot. Bullet to the thigh. Stab wound to the rib cage. Had there been more damage? Framing her fingers along his jawline, she forced him to look her in the eye. "Talk to me."

Sirens reached her ears. She glanced toward the garage entrance. Ambushing the marshal, capturing one of the shooters in the hope of doing their own interrogation...this whole thing had been a mistake. And all to find a missing partner who might be involved in the very operation she'd been trying to bring to justice. She had to get Anthony out of there before local police showed up. "Okay, come on."

Glennon stopped cold. Guns. Where were their guns? Hell, she couldn't leave them behind. Their prints would put them in the center of a manhunt once Anchorage PD collected them as evidence. And the army would follow. She couldn't have her name on those reports. Couldn't put her son at risk.

Swinging Anthony's arm over her shoulders, she maneuvered him against the side of the nearest car. And she couldn't do that to Anthony. Not after everything he'd done for her the past two days. Her stress response drained from her system as she crawled beneath both parked cars. One Beretta, one Glock.

Anthony pushed away from the vehicle, trying to stand. How he was still conscious, she had no idea, but she couldn't do this by herself.

The sirens grew louder. She didn't have time to collect bullet casings, and there were far too many scat-

tered across the entire garage for her to get them all. Exhaustion dragged her down as she hefted Anthony into her side again. His solid weight unbalanced her. "You can do this, baby. I'm going to get you help. We just have to get to the SUV."

Baby? Heat crawled into her cheeks. Where the hell had that come from? Glennon shoved the thought to the back of her mind. She had more important things to worry about right now. And, with any luck, he wouldn't remember any of this later.

He mumbled something unintelligible as she hauled him up the garage entrance ramp. Sunlight blinded her for a split second. She guarded her eyes against the blazing sun, but quickly leveraged her hand into his chest to hold Anthony upright as his legs started giving out. He'd parked the SUV a little over a block away on the other side of the street. They would make it. She had to believe that. Her throat ached. "Come on. You got this."

Head down, she dragged him across the road. Pressure of civilian stares as they passed built in her chest. Two people, both covered in blood, walking down the street. Nothing to be alarmed about. The first patrol car swung around the corner at the end of the block and she rammed herself into Anthony's uninjured side to take cover behind a car parked along the road. The street was about to be shut down and when Anchorage PD identified the bodies, the army would take over. They had to move. Her previous experience with local PD told her they had about three minutes. Another patrol car rounded the block, lights and sirens blaring. Make that one minute. Shoving her hands in his cargo pants'

pockets, she searched for the SUV's keys. "Don't get any bright ideas. I'm trying to save your life."

"At least take me to dinner first." His words slurred, his eyes heavy. Was he even coherent?

"It's a date." A smile pulled at one edge of her mouth as her fingers closed around the key fob. Even in life-or-death situations, he could make her laugh. That'd been one of the reasons she'd fallen in love with him all those years ago. His unyielding determination to put her first. No matter how hard the situation. The smile vanished. Had she ever really fallen out of love? She liked to think she hadn't been holding on to him all this time, but after what he'd done back in that garage for her, after he'd saved her life… No. Now wasn't the time.

Glennon pressed the button to start the SUV. "But let's make sure you don't bleed out on the sidewalk first."

She hauled the passenger-side door open.

The door's side mirror exploded. She flinched away, gripping Anthony's shoulder and shoving him inside the vehicle. "Get down!"

Return fire from at least three police officers reached her ears, but didn't stop another bullet from whizzing past her head. Heart trying to pump out of her chest, she reached for one of the many guns Anthony had installed inside the SUV and took position at the back quarter panel.

The second shooter, the one she'd zip-tied after Anthony had knocked him unconscious, fired back at police. One officer went down. Then another. The shooter fell as a bullet hit his Kevlar dead center from the third, but was already straightening. What the hell

were these guys made of? Steel? He raised his gun, and Glennon pulled back. A third shot ricocheted off the SUV's bumper. One glance in the shattered side mirror revealed Anthony had passed out. Too much blood loss. "Damn it."

Should she try to take down the shooter with orders to capture her, or get Anthony to the hospital?

Her thumb released the gun's safety mechanism. No question. She had to get him out of here. And a quick check over her shoulder said she didn't have much time. The shooter was closing in on them. Fast.

She dove into the back seat, climbing behind the steering wheel as fast as she could. Reaching for Anthony's seat belt, she strapped him in but didn't bother with her own as the back window shattered. Apparently this Blackhawk vehicle's windows weren't bulletproof.

She started the engine, ducked down in the driver's seat, hauled the vehicle into Drive and slammed on the accelerator. The SUV launched away from the scene. In the rearview mirror, she saw the shooter climb into a waiting car.

"I thought you said this thing was bulletproof." Her breathing hitched as the SUV fishtailed at the end of the block. She couldn't go straight to the hospital. Not with a psychopath who was willing to take down civilians right behind them. Couldn't lead him to Blackhawk Security. Although a welcoming party wasn't a bad idea… No. She couldn't risk anyone else taking a bullet for her or becoming Nicholas Mascaro's next target. The uneven thump of her heart beat hard behind her ears. Glennon tapped her palm against the steering wheel. "Anthony, come on. Stay with me."

He'd know what to do. But one look at his color-

less, slackened features said he wouldn't be waking up anytime soon. They had nowhere to go. And they'd run out of time.

Daytime headlights blazed directly behind the SUV as she accelerated onto Seward Highway. Snow-crusted mountains and dried pine trees hugged one side of the road. Turnagain Arm waterway was on the other as they sped out of the city. Hints of pink and orange, reflected on the icy water, were already turning the sky to fire. She could lose the shooter once the sun went down, but her instincts said they didn't have that long.

"We're going to get you help." She didn't have any other choice. She'd have to try to escape them now. At least long enough to get Anthony stable. Wrapping her fingers around his lifeless hand in his lap, she squeezed. Her lower eyelids stung. "Hang on for a little bit longer. Please."

She couldn't lose him. Not now. There hadn't been a chance to tell him everything. About why she'd left, how often she regretted her decision, how many times she'd thought about picking up that phone. But it was more than that. He was Anthony. Her first love, her biggest supporter, the first glimpse of her future, the man who, in the past forty-eight hours, had dedicated himself to her survival. The man she'd missed. The man who altered her breathing every time he touched her…

Glennon took a deep, calming breath. She'd get him out of this one way or another. She owed him that much.

Slush and chunks of ice kicked up around the vehicle, the SUV's tires spinning out as she turned around one smooth corner of highway. She'd learned to drive in Anchorage winters as a teenager. She could handle it.

Glancing in the rearview mirror, she kept tabs on the shooter's vehicle as it closed the distance between them. Freezing Alaskan air worked its way inside through the webbed back window as the sound of a growling engine reached her ears from behind. Through the shooter's windshield, she spotted the gun in his hand as he rolled down his window. She forced her attention back to the road ahead. Just a bit farther.

Two shots echoed off the cliffs.

She ducked lower in her seat, knuckles white on the steering wheel. They were going to make it. No matter what. She'd get Anthony the help he needed. Another glance in the rearview mirror—

A forty-ton Mack truck pulled onto the highway directly in front of her.

The breath rushed out of her. Glennon hit the brakes, tires locking as she pressed her spine into the seat. She gripped the steering wheel with both hands and swerved to avoid the truck, throwing herself into Anthony's shoulder.

The front end of the SUV missed the truck by mere inches as she cut across the highway and through a wooden guardrail. Weeds and mud covered the windshield as she slammed on the brakes again. The tires slipped on the thick ice clinging to Turnagain Arm's shoreline. They were going too fast. The lip of the shore catapulted the SUV into the air and they dove headfirst. Gravity crushed her into her seat as she reached for Anthony. "I've got you. Just hang—"

Chapter Eight

The collision of metal meeting ice thrust Anthony forward in his seat. The seat belt cut into his chest as crystal-clear water rushed across the windshield. His head slammed back into the passenger seat. Vision blurred, he blinked to clear his head as pain rushed through his system. The front of the SUV pitched engine-first into deep water, a steady horizon of water climbing up the length of the windshield. His heels automatically dug against the floor. They were going under.

Deadly calm slid over him. He'd survived worse. And under fire. But Glennon…damn it. Where was Glennon?

He caught sight of her slumped against the steering wheel, her face angled away from him. She hadn't buckled her seat belt.

"Glennon." His throat threatened to close with his next breath. Releasing his seat belt, Anthony dove for her as freezing Alaskan water rushed across his boots. They had two minutes, maybe three, before the interior of the SUV would be submerged completely. He pulled her from the steering wheel. Her head snapped back, but no response. A thin line of blood highlighted the angles of her features as it ran under her shirt.

He brushed a strand of hair from her wound as water climbed up his shins. "Open your eyes, sweetheart."

Nothing. Color had drained from her normally flawless skin but a thready pulse beat against his fingers. He had to get her out. At these temperatures, and with the water soaking through their clothing, hypothermia would set in a lot faster than normal.

"Okay." He ducked to see through the now-broken rear windshield. The SUV had landed approximately twenty feet from shore. They didn't have any other choice. "We're going to have to swim for it."

After that? He'd have to go for the survival supplies Blackhawk Security operatives were required to carry in their vehicles. And hope the lake didn't swallow them first. Water rose up his thighs, gushing into the bullet wound in the thickest part of his muscle. Pain zinged through him.

Anthony hauled her to him. His instincts screamed for him to get Glennon out of the vehicle—*now*—but they couldn't swim for the shore yet. Not until the lake had engulfed them completely.

"Stay with me, sweetheart." Seconds stretched into minutes. The last bit of daylight through the front windshield vanished. Ten more seconds. The water kept rising along the side windows. Five. He secured her against his side with one arm and reached for the door handle with his free hand. Ice pumped through his veins from the waist down. Setting his lips against her ear, he closed his eyes for a split second. "Stay with me, sweetheart. I'll get you out of here."

And he always kept his promises.

The SUV had sunk low enough that the driver's-side door was completely submerged. He used every

ounce of his remaining strength against the door as his side of the SUV tipped toward the lake floor. A scream ripped up his throat as pain and thousands of pounds of water fought against him. Water no longer seeped through the floor into the vehicle's interior but rushed to fill the unoccupied space. No time to think. He filled his lungs with her rosy scent. And dove into the ice-cold depths.

Chunks of ice and thick weeds clouded his vision as he pulled Glennon from the SUV. Pressure built through his system. He'd get her to the shore. No matter what.

Twenty feet. That was all they had. Twenty feet until she was safe.

His muscles burned. Below-freezing temperatures slowed his movements. Every cell in his body screamed for release. Sunlight broke through the blackness and he kicked with everything he had toward it. Thin strands of blood floated ahead of him, almost racing him to the surface. Whether from his wounds or Glennon's, he didn't know. Did it matter?

His pulse pounded loud in his ears but slowed the more he struggled to the surface. Air pressurized in his lungs. His system was using oxygen reserves faster than he'd expected. He'd lost too much blood. He couldn't keep up this pace. He estimated five more feet until they broke through the surface. He blinked against the exhaustion weighing him down. With every push forward, both Glennon and his wounds pulled him down. At his current rate, they wouldn't have to worry about hypothermia. They'd both drown before it had a chance to take over.

No.

He wouldn't give up that easily. He'd failed his team-mates once. He wouldn't fail her.

Bubbles rushed from his mouth and nose as he kicked harder. Two feet. One. Anthony broke through the surface first, shattered pieces of ice scratching against his neck as he hauled Glennon above water. His lungs seized. He fought for air but couldn't seem to get enough. His body's defenses were already suc-cumbing to the low temperatures. Soon his heart rate would drop so low, he wouldn't be able to function. Then his organs would start shutting down.

And Glennon...she shook in his hold. Good. Her body was still trying to warm itself, but the dark tint of blue to her lips said she wasn't getting enough oxy-gen. He hugged her into his side but his body heat had dropped too low to do her any good.

Damn it. Focus. Get her to the shore. Get the water out of her lungs. "I've...got you...sweetheart. Almost... there."

Reaching for the closest grouping of weeds, he pulled them closer to the shoreline. Numbness worked through his fingers and up his arms. He had mere min-utes. Three. Maybe four. He couldn't breathe. Couldn't think. Gurgling sounds reached his ears. The lake had consumed the SUV. And their supplies had gone down with it.

His boots hit land. Anthony dragged Glennon through the remaining wall of weeds and onto the snow-covered rocks. Setting her head against the ground, he lowered his ear to her mouth. She wasn't breathing. Her pulse beat unevenly against his fin-gers. Panic flooded through him. Covering her mouth with his, he plugged her nose and pushed air into her

lungs. He found the spot over her breastbone and put all his strength into forcing the water from her lungs. The fuzziness surrounding his thoughts cleared but the numbness in his extremities would take a hell of a lot longer to shake. "Come on, baby."

Darkness circled the edges of his vision, but he wouldn't stop. Not until she opened her eyes.

She jerked beneath him with each compression, her skin pale. But still no response.

"Open your eyes, damn it." His control shattered. Precious air his organs needed rushed from his lungs. He bit the inside of his mouth to keep from screaming. He'd already lost too many people in his life. His parents when he was nineteen. His Ranger team in Afghanistan. Her.

He hadn't thought about the future since Glennon had walked out on him all those years ago, but now… that future included Glennon. His Glennon. She wasn't walking away from him. Not again. And not like this. "Glennon, breathe!"

Water sputtered from between her lips as she coughed. Her chest contracted beneath his hands as he turned her onto her side. She scratched at the rocks beside her.

"That's it, sweetheart. Just breathe." The pressure that had built in his chest released. Anthony rubbed small circles into her back, struggling to stay conscious. He blinked against the wave of dizziness gripping him from head to toe. Spots of red stained the snow on his left side. His stab wound… His fingers closed around her Kevlar vest in a last attempt to stay upright. "I've…got you."

Anthony collapsed. His head hit the rocks, the lake's

horizon at the wrong angle. Glennon didn't move, her expression peaceful but full of color. She'd survived. That was all that mattered. He'd done his job. She was safe. Ringing filled his ears. "Glennon…"

The growl of an engine echoed off the nearby mountain. A car door slammed. Footsteps crunched through the thin crust of snow from behind, but he couldn't move. They'd been run off the road, he remembered now. He'd passed out from blood loss, but the shooter, the one who'd shot at them as they fled down the highway, must've survived. His hand ignored his brain's commands to reach for the gun strapped to his thigh. Chances the weapon would fire after taking a swim in below-freezing water were low. But if the bastard had come to finish the job, Anthony would fight until the end.

"You know, we were ordered to bring Sergeant Chase back alive, but it looks like the problem has taken care of itself." The shooter he'd knocked unconscious stood above him. He pulled his mask over his head, green eyes and facial scars twisting with a thin smile. Dog tags swung from around the man's neck. Planting a steel-toed tactical boot across Anthony's chest, he pointed the barrel of a Smith & Wesson handgun center-mass. "As for you, you're just the icing on the cake."

The onset of hypothermia had already started shutting down Anthony's system. He fought against the weight pressing him into the ground. He'd lost too much blood. He focused on the slow rise and fall of Glennon's chest. He'd lost everything. "Stay away from her—"

Three gunshots exploded across the shore.

The shooter hit the ground, unmoving. Another set of footsteps broke through the thin layer of ice clinging to the rocks around them. Stepping into the stream of sunlight, gun in hand, the figure crouched beside Anthony but didn't move to take another shot. Recognition flared.

"I warned her to back off." Sharp, angled features blurred in Anthony's vision as darkness closed in. Gravel coated the soldier's voice, exactly as Anthony remembered from the morning the intruder had broken into the cabin. The soldier holstered his weapon then reached for Anthony. "She should've listened."

"You're both lucky to be alive," an unfamiliar female voice said.

Glennon cracked her eyelids. Fluorescent lighting blinded her for a split second as she blinked to adjust. The machines a few feet away registered her stats. The last memories before they'd gone into the lake flashed across her mind. She homed in on the woman seated near the door and licked the dryness from her lips. Elizabeth Dawson. Blackhawk's network security expert. Her throat burned. Exhaustion pulled at her, but she forced herself to focus.

"How did I get here?" Five simple words. So much energy to get them out. She rubbed at her throat and blinked against the onslaught of fluorescent lighting. What the hell had happened on that highway? How had she gotten to the hospital? The last thing she remembered was screaming Anthony's name before they'd gone into the lake.

Didn't matter. She'd survived. And if the army had discovered she had a son as the marshal had said, then

Mascaro's operatives undoubtedly knew about him, too. She had to get out of here. She had to see Hunter.

"An anonymous Good Samaritan saw the whole thing," Elizabeth said. "He drove you both to the hospital himself. Said Anthony pulled you out of the SUV and onto the shore."

Glennon pushed back against the bed to sit up. Pain shot through her shoulder and she locked her jaw to keep a moan at bay. How long did it take for a bullet wound to heal anyway?

"Where is Anthony?" Her words were thick, heavy.

"Resting. He'll live. Sullivan's with him now." Amusement played across Elizabeth's mouth as she studied Glennon from her position. The butt of a Glock peeked out from beneath her leather jacket. Apparently network security was more dangerous than sitting in front of a computer screen. Or had Elizabeth been assigned guard duty?

The former NSA consultant tapped her black-painted fingernails against the chair railing. "He's the most guarded man I've ever met, but if there's one thing I know about Anthony Harris, it's that a knife wound to the ribs and a bullet to the leg won't stop him from doing his job."

Glennon's spine tingled. She'd gotten that right. That'd been one of the two reasons she'd called him for help in the first place. The man had been sculpted from steel and infused with a determination like no other. Like the good Ranger he was supposed to be. As for the other reason... Heat crawled up her neck. She ran her hand through her hair as a distraction.

"But I should tell you, he's not going to be very happy when he wakes up," Elizabeth said.

"What do you mean?" Glennon straightened in the bed. Had he changed his mind? Would she have to find Bennett on her own now that they'd discovered Mascaro's involvement in her partner's disappearance? She swallowed hard. If the past two days revealed anything about this investigation, it was that she couldn't do this on her own.

"During the firefight downtown, something happened." Elizabeth reached into her jacket pocket, her expression guarded. She extracted a tangle of titanium. Shoving to her feet, she crossed the room and offered the mess to Glennon. Short dark hair hid her expression. "And I'm not sure what he'll do when he finds out about it."

Recognition flared. Anthony's favorite pair of aviator sunglasses. The exact pair she'd gifted him once upon a time had been destroyed. Lenses cracked, one earpiece missing completely. A laugh bubbled up Glennon's throat. "I can't believe he still has these." Well, had. She ran the pad of her thumb over the tinted glass. "I bought them for him right after I graduated basic training."

He'd kept them after all this time. Just as he'd kept her engagement ring around his neck. Her head pounded. Damn it. This was supposed to be easy. She'd had a plan. Find Bennett. Resign from the Military Police. Put in her discharge papers and get on with her life. Her and Hunter. The two of them against the world. That was it.

But now... Anthony was there. Protecting her. Risking his life for her. Resurrecting a part of her she hadn't expected to feel ever again.

And now he'd been centered in crosshairs meant for her.

Because of her.

"What about the shooter?" she asked.

The lighting from behind the bed sharpened the edges of the Elizabeth's jawline. "What shooter?"

Her throat tightened. Glennon struggled to swallow and she could only imagine how bad the bruises on her neck looked. "We were ambushed. He ran us off the road."

"The team has been scouring that scene for the past eight hours with Anchorage PD," Elizabeth said. "There wasn't any evidence of a shooter."

Air rushed from her lungs. He'd gotten away?

"Then I need to get out of here." Glennon set the sunglasses on the bedside table and threw back the sheets. She pulled the catheters and monitors from her skin. Rushing to collect her clothes from the nook under the window, she spun toward the bathroom. "I've wasted enough time when I should be out there looking for my partner."

"I can see why Anthony's broken Sullivan's number one rule for you." Elizabeth's voice stopped her cold. "You're as stubborn as he is."

Glennon turned. "What rule?"

"We're warned about falling for our clients or co-workers." Elizabeth stood, crossing her arms across her middle. The gun inhibited some of her movement, but the network analyst didn't seem to mind. Might've even been used to it. "Causes too many problems with our assignments. Once emotions get involved, makes it hard for us to focus on the job. Leads to risks that might've been avoided in the first place."

Elizabeth wanted to talk about risks? The tiny muscles along Glennon's jaw jerked. She'd risked everything—her job, her partner, her life—in going to Anthony for help. If she hadn't? The price would've been far greater. Not just for her but for everyone in her life.

"Sounds like you've learned from personal experience." Besides, Anthony wasn't falling for her. Couldn't be. Not after what she'd done to him. Not after dragging him into this mess, after putting his life in danger. Glennon shook her head, thankful the rapid flutter of her heart rate couldn't register on the screens anymore. None of this had been part of the plan. A blast of cold air from the vent above reminded her how exposed she was standing there in only a thin sheet of a gown. How vulnerable. She hugged her still damp clothing—and her empty shoulder holster—tighter. "I thought you were the computer expert. Not the profiler."

"I don't need to get inside Anthony's head to see something clearly staring me in the face." Elizabeth headed for the door. Wrenching the thick door open, she turned back, frozen in the doorway. "Be careful, Glennon. If anybody on this team is compromised, we're all at risk. And so are our clients."

Elizabeth disappeared into the hallway.

She was right. Glennon clutched her clothing tighter. Letting old feelings come between her and Anthony, letting him in again, would endanger them both. The investigation. That was all that mattered. All that *could* matter.

She pushed her legs into her jeans and finished dressing as fast as she could. Her army credentials had been set on the table beside the bed. Hospital adminis-

tration had most likely registered her into the system using her ID. The army would know she'd been here, had probably already sent someone for her. The marshal wasn't the only compromised operative in Nicholas Mascaro's unit. The two shooters from the garage had been military. So she didn't have much time.

Where was her service weapon?

Palming her credentials into her hand, Glennon paused as she reached for Anthony's broken sunglasses. Every second she wasted in this room stacked against her chances of recovering Bennett, but she didn't move. Couldn't. Anthony had broken Blackhawk Security's number one rule. For her.

Her forehead throbbed as she backed toward the door, leaving the sunglasses behind. If she left now—

The door swung inward. "Going somewhere?"

Anxiety flooded the muscles down her spine. That voice… She closed her eyes, committing it to memory all over again. Glennon tamped down the need to hear his heart beat against her ear, to confirm for herself he was okay. "Elizabeth told you I was leaving."

"You hired me to protect you." He stood directly behind her. How had he moved so quietly? So quickly? Anthony's voice dipped into dangerous territory. "I don't stop when I'm tired or injured. I only stop when the job is done. And I'm not done with you."

A tremor chased across her back, loosening the small muscles down her spine. She automatically leaned toward him, her weight shifting onto her heels. That pull he had on her… She'd always been weak when he'd gotten so close. Tendrils of his controlled exhalations raised the hairs on the back of her neck. All she had to do was fall. And he'd catch her. He'd al-

ready proved as much over the last few days. So why did the thought of taking that final leap paralyze her to the core?

Elizabeth's claims echoed through her mind. Emotional attachment brought risk, could compromise the entire team. And no matter how much she wanted—no, *needed*—that human connection right now, Glennon couldn't risk the fall. He'd left her without a net once. She wouldn't let it happen again. "Is that all you see me as? A job?"

That would make moving on after the investigation a lot easier.

"I want you, Glennon. Always have." The words were nearly a growl from between his lips. He moved into her, his chest pressed against her spine. Predatory. Dangerous. But at his core, Anthony was a man who'd fight desperately for his clients. Fight for her. His body heat tunneled beneath her clothing, chasing away the myriad aches and pains. "We're in this together. Until the end. And I'll be damned if I let you walk out of my life again."

Chapter Nine

Hypothermia. Stab wound. Bullet wound in his thigh. It would've been a hell of a way to die.

But all of that vanished with Glennon turning into him, her rosy scent spreading through his system. He'd meant every word. Every cell in his body, every thought, wanted her. Always had. What that meant for their future—if they even had a future—he didn't know. But he wasn't about to lose her all over again. Not without a fight.

The bruise on her forehead had faded slightly, but guilt ate at him. He framed her jawline, running the pad of his thumb across the lump where her head had hit the steering wheel. To her credit, she didn't flinch. First the bullet in her shoulder then the head wound. Some kind of bodyguard she'd hired. "I'm sorry I didn't take better care of you."

"I'm alive, aren't I? That's what I hired you to do." Brilliant green eyes locked on him. A small curl of one side of her mouth brought his attention to her lips. How in the world could she stand there as though they hadn't just been through hell and back? "But in the future, not dying while we're trying to escape a pair of corrupt soldiers would help your cause."

A laugh rumbled through his chest. Right. She'd saved his life, too, hadn't she? Dragging his ass out of that garage while dodging an onslaught of bullets couldn't have been easy. Her determination to get the job done had saved his life. No matter the risk. "Guess that makes us even."

"Not even close, Ranger. You…" She dropped her hand, her smile disappearing, but didn't move away. Her shoulders rose on a strong inhale, color draining from her features. "I thought you were going to die. All that blood—"

"I owe you my life." He closed the slight distance between them.

She lifted her gaze to his. Her expression said she didn't believe him.

Anthony set his hands on her hips, locking her against him. He understood. All too easily, those agonizing seconds of panic, the memories of almost losing her as he'd fought to expel the water from her lungs rushed to the front of his mind. And he never wanted to think about them again.

He moved slowly, giving her a chance to escape. Planting his mouth below her earlobe, he inhaled as much of her as he could, making her a part of him. Forever. "We survived. Together. That's all that matters."

Glennon nodded into his chest but hesitation stiffened the muscles along her back. "I just… Not knowing if you were going to make it out of that garage alive, if I could get you the help you needed, were the worst seconds of my life. I never want to go through that again."

"Keep talking like that and I'll think you care about me, sweetheart." The steady thump of his heart pulsed into his left ribs and thigh. Nearly sixty stitches ached

as they stood there in the middle of her hospital room, but Anthony didn't dare move. He'd stay in this moment forever if she'd let him, hold on to her as long as he could. Pretend nothing bad waited outside those hospital doors. Pain be damned. She was worth every agonizing second. He slid his fingers beneath her jaw, notching her chin higher. "I'm not going anywhere."

"Good. Because I can't do this by myself. I don't want to do this by myself." She passed her tongue across the small cut in her lower lip. "I need you."

"You have me. You always have." The control he'd held on to so tightly since that first kiss in her barracks drained from his veins. Anthony crushed her against his chest, his mouth on hers, his fingertips digging into her lower back. Careful of each and every wound, he memorized the one woman who could break him inch by slow, agonizing inch. The remnants of spearmint exploded across his tongue as he explored her mouth. Fresh. Invigorating.

Damn, he'd missed this. Missed her. Desire barreled through him, tightening the muscles down his back and across his shoulders. He kissed her slowly, carefully, savoring every move of her mouth against his as he threaded his fingers through the base of her ponytail. Forget her missing partner. Forget Nicholas Mascaro. Forget the past. All he needed was Glennon. Here. Now. Forever. His lungs worked overtime to keep up with his racing heartbeat. He'd let her slip away once, but the truth rang clear as he broke the kiss. He'd kill to keep her by his side.

Hell, he already had. And he'd pull that trigger all over again if it meant she stayed here.

"This is a bad idea." Stiffening, she pulled away,

running one hand through her hair. She did that a lot. Used that single action to distance herself from him. Emotionally. Physically. But she wouldn't get away that easily. Not this time. "It's not part of the plan."

"And at exactly what point in your plan did you expect to be shot, get run off the road by a contracted soldier, and drown in Turnagain Arm?" he asked.

"You make a valid point." A laugh burst from between her lips and she pressed her fingertips to the cut at one corner. "Do you remember anything after the crash? I hit my head pretty hard. It's still all a bit fuzzy."

Anthony let her take a step back. His skin cooled at the loss of her natural heat, but he'd remember the feel of her pressed against him. Forever. "Bits and pieces."

The memories of those final moments before his body had finally shut down had replayed in his head over and over since he'd woken in his room a few hours ago. How could he possibly tell her the truth? This entire investigation—her investigation—depended on her partner's innocence. On Sergeant Bennett Spencer being Mascaro's target, as Glennon had become.

Only they'd been wrong from the start.

"Elizabeth said the police couldn't find any evidence of the shooter that followed us out of the garage. How is that possible?" she asked. "Some Good Samaritan witnessed the whole thing but he never saw the shooter and his accomplice in the Mack truck run us off the road in the first place?"

Good Samaritan? That wasn't how Anthony remembered it. He curled his fingers into his palm. Damn it. He couldn't hide this from her. If they were going to find Bennett and put an end to this investigation, he

had to tell her the truth. "There is no Good Samaritan. The driver of the truck isn't working with the shooter. He *killed* the shooter."

Glennon froze for a split second, one hand fastened around the back of her neck. "How do you know that?"

"After I resuscitated you on the shoreline, the shooter came to finish the job." Pressure built behind his sternum. He'd fought like hell to get to his weapon, but he'd been helpless. Worthless. Now that he thought about it, Anthony supposed he owed the driver a thank-you. "He didn't get the chance."

"Why would the driver do that?" She sank onto the edge of the hospital bed, her gaze distant, questioning. "If they weren't working together, why run us off the road in the first place? Why drive us to the hospital? It doesn't make sense."

No. It didn't. But in a missing persons investigation, there were no easy answers. And she wasn't about to like his next one, either. "Bennett Spencer was driving the Mack truck, Glennon. *He* ran us off the highway. He killed the shooter before the bastard had a chance to abduct you."

Her attention snapped to him, lips parting on a strong exhale, features smooth. Her white-knuckled grip tightened on the edge of the mattress. "That son of a bitch. I knew it."

She knew what, exactly? "I just told you I recognized your partner as the man driving the truck who ran us off the road, and that he killed one of Mascaro's operatives. And that makes sense to you?"

"I was going to wait until I was sure…" She pushed to her feet, one hand diving into her jacket pocket then out again. Her fingers uncurled and centered in her

palm was a small American flag pin. It wasn't anything special, available at any drugstore, but it obviously held some kind of significance. She wouldn't have kept it otherwise. "I found this at your cabin. After the operative broke in."

"Is this supposed to mean something to me?" Anthony took the pin, his fingertips sliding against her palm. A surge of awareness shot up his arm, resurrecting only a sliver of the desire burning through his veins, but Glennon didn't seem to notice. Or was she focused on the pin to avoid looking at him?

"No, but it means something to me. It's Bennett's." She nodded toward the evidence—evidence she'd kept secret from him for two days. "He's kept it in his desk drawer as long as I can remember. It was his sister's. Never wore it, never told me why he'd held on to it after all these years, but it was important to him." Glennon crossed her arms over her chest. Shaking her head, she turned away from him as a hint of pink colored her face and neck. "I couldn't find it after he went missing. Now I know why."

"Because the marshal was telling the truth." Anthony's stomach dropped. Hell. Things were about to get bloodier and messier. With Glennon centered in the middle of it all. "Bennett is part of Mascaro's crew."

"Looks that way. So you have a choice. You can return to your surveillance assignments and get back the life you had before I added you to Mascaro's hit list. Or you can help me bring the bastards down. All of them. Bennett included." Red tinged her cheeks. "Either way, I have to go. What's it going to be, Ranger?"

"When have you ever known me to shy away from a fight?" He handed the pin back to her and patted him-

self for weapons. The staff had confiscated everything when Sergeant Spencer had dumped them at the hospital's front door. They were going to have to make a pit stop. "Just tell me where we're going."

"At the moment, to get my gun back." Glennon rushed past him, her shoulder clipping his arm. She ripped open the door. Half turning her face toward him, she froze. "Then to protect my son."

How could Bennett do this to her? Two years as partners. She'd trusted him with her life, trusted him with her secret. She'd let him inside her house, made him part of her son's life. Uncle Bennett. What was she supposed to tell Hunter now? Pressure built in her chest as she ground her back teeth together. Bennett had known everything about her. Obviously she couldn't say the same for him. She was an investigator, for crying out loud. How could she not have seen the truth?

Glennon kept her footsteps light as she approached the house, weapon in hand. Fanning her fingers over the gun's grip, she exhaled hard. Her pulse beat loudly in her ears. Mascaro had already sent hit men after her and Anthony. But she'd kill every last one of them before they laid a finger on her son.

"You're blaming yourself." The mountain of muscle close on her heels had her back, even with the slight limp he fought to hide from her.

"Did the Rangers train you to read minds or is that a new skill of yours?" Anthony had had a choice back at the hospital and he'd chosen to follow her into battle. She should've been relieved. She had a better chance of bringing down the crew responsible for putting that bullet in his leg with him at her side, but... The but-

terflies in her stomach spread through her entire system. She hadn't prepared for this day. Imagined it? Sure. But those had only been fantasies. This...this was real. She swallowed hard, took a deep breath. Anthony was about to meet her son. Holstering her weapon, Glennon knocked on the faded red door, her muscles strung tight.

"I don't need to be able to read minds to know what's going through your head. I know exactly what you're thinking, sweetheart." His deep, rumbling laugh vibrated through her, he was so close. The scent of soap and man clouded her senses over the freezing air around them, but she couldn't help but breathe a bit deeper. Wisps of his breath tickled the back of her neck. "There was no way you could've known about your partner. Bennett is a double agent. And he's obviously very good at his job."

From inside, footsteps echoed off the house's original hardwood floors.

A gust of blistering cold brushed against her as she turned into him. He didn't understand. She wasn't blaming herself. "I'm not ashamed I didn't see him for what he really was. I'm pissed off."

The door swung open, the racking of a shotgun shell loud in her ears.

Glennon froze but didn't raise her weapon. Physical tension radiated off Anthony as he moved to her side. Holstering her Glock, she smiled at the woman on the other end of the gun. "Hi, Mom."

Green eyes, nearly the exact same color as hers, narrowed on her then widened. The older woman lowered the shotgun an inch but kept her wrinkled grip tight around the weapon. While other moms were teaching

their daughters how to braid their hair or how to put together the perfect outfit for the first day of school, Helen Chase had been teaching her daughter how to assemble and disassemble that same shotgun on the kitchen table. Blindfolded. Of the few good memories Glennon had of her childhood, those were her favorite. Just her and her mom. The two of them against the world. "You forget something? You're not supposed to show up here unannounced, girl. That was part of our deal."

Helen's thick East Kentucky accent warmed Glennon through and through. Damn, it felt good to be home. She dropped her hands to her sides as another gust of cold uprooted a corner of her mother's signature flannel long-sleeved shirt. "I came to make sure my son is safe. You can put the gun down now."

"I told you I'd protect him with my life and I meant it," Helen said.

Another deep laugh vibrated through Anthony's chest. He nodded at the older woman, a mixture of respect and amusement etched into his expression. "Helen. Been a while."

The shotgun found a new target as her mother swung it toward him. Helen's gaze never left his as she cocked her head. "*This* is who you hired to help you bring down those bastards who came after you and my grandson? Girl, I thought I taught you more sense than that. Didn't what happened between me and your daddy teach you anything?"

"Excuse me?" Anthony's voice dipped into dangerous territory. The weight of his gaze pressed the air from Glennon's lungs as he spun on her. "I'm going to forget the part where Helen compared me to your

deadbeat asshole father. Mascaro's men came after you and Hunter *before* you hired me?"

Damn it. Glennon stiffened.

"Wasn't important at the time." The sound of broken glass hitting tile, her reaching for the combat knife she kept under her pillow and extracting her service weapon from the gun safe under her bed slid through her mind. She and Hunter had made it out of the house just fine. They'd holed up in a hotel room the rest of the night after she'd called the police. She'd then informed the marshal she and Bennett would be looking into a missing shipment of weapons at JBER and left for Anchorage the second her CO had approved. "I didn't know who broke into my house or if it had anything to do with our investigation. I still don't."

"How about you let me decide what's important to this investigation from now on?" Anthony gripped his beard, pulling at the hair. He had a point. First, Bennett's American flag pin. Now this. He had every right not to trust her right now. "Anything else you're not telling me?"

She flushed as Helen's attention drifted from Anthony straight to her. She silently screamed for her mother to keep her mouth shut. Now wasn't the time. Not here. Not yet.

"Well, hell. Looks like you two still have a few things to work out. But it's best not to make yourselves easy targets standing out here in the cold." Helen lowered the shotgun barrel toward the floor and cleared the doorway. "Come on then. Get inside."

A wall of hot air slammed against Glennon as they walked through the door. The cold had never bothered her, but the blistering ice in Anthony's eyes froze her

to the core. Her throat tightened. This day kept getting better and better.

A familiar combination of her mother's perfume and the lingering scent of home-fried chicken sank deep into her lungs. She hadn't set foot in this house in years, but the living room, dining room, kitchen—all had remained the same. No family photos hung on the walls, destroyed years ago in a fire. Barely any personal effects adorned the space. The only thing that had changed? The shelf of countless liquor bottles her father had kept stocked was empty. Glennon glanced at her mother.

No. Helen shouldn't have compared Anthony to her father. Their situations weren't the same. The man at her side would never drink himself into a rage and take it out on his family. In fact, given the chance, she'd bet the former Ranger would have more than a few words for the man who'd left his wife's and daughter's lives in ruins. She'd always known a part of her—some small, distant part—had urged her to join the Military Police so she could track the deadbeat down for what he'd done. But the past was better left buried. She studied the Ranger at her side, then spun on the edge of the worn area rug.

"Can't remember the last time you were in this house." Her mother's fierce green eyes landed on her and an understanding passed between them.

Glennon nodded. They both knew why she hadn't come home. Too many bad memories. "Where's Hunter?"

"Asleep in your old room. He likes it in there. Hardly ever leaves." Her mother set the gun upright against the wall beside the front door. Wasn't the only one,

either. Over the years, Helen Chase had collected an entire arsenal to protect her home and her family. She secured the front door and armed the alarm. Although she hadn't smoked in years, deep lines creased the edges of Helen's mouth. "He's been asking about you, wants to know when you're coming to take him home."

Home. Hell, Glennon didn't even know where that was anymore. Back in Stafford, Virginia? Here, in Anchorage? Anthony turned as he surveyed the rest of the house in her peripheral vision, her awareness of him at an all-time high. She'd promised to keep her emotions in check before hiring him.to protect her—for her son's sake—but after what had happened back in the garage, almost losing him... Her stomach sank. Truth was, he was more than a bodyguard. Always had been.

"This thing that we're doing... These people." Bennett's features flashed across her mind. "It's more complicated than I thought."

"So you said over the phone two nights ago." Helen fisted her hands on her hips, her weight shifting onto one side. "I told you I'd protect Hunter with everything I got so you can do what you gotta do, but I need to know. What exactly have you gotten yourself into, girl?"

"I can't tell you. Not yet, anyway." She swallowed the urge to reveal everything. The dead sniper, Bennett's involvement in Nicholas Mascaro's operation, how very close she was to losing her tightly held control. She glanced at Anthony and rolled her fingers into her palms. A couple more days. That was all she needed to end this nightmare. "But I promise, it's almost over. I just wanted to make sure he was okay."

Anthony lowered his chin to his chest, glancing back at her over his shoulder. "Hallway."

"Grandma—" small footsteps scuffed against the hardwood floor down the hall "—I need water and ice in my cup, please."

Warmth shot through Glennon as a head of short blond hair came into sight. A familiar pair of worn Batman pajamas and bright green eyes cleared the adrenalized haze of the last few days. Air rushed from her lungs. Her eyes burned. "Hey, baby."

Hunter's attention snapped to her, his eyes widening, mouth dropping open. "Mommy!"

The living room blurred in her vision as she closed the distance between them. Landing hard on her knees, Glennon wrapped Hunter in her arms. The pain in her shoulder pulled at her but she pushed it to the back of her mind. "I missed you."

"I missed you, too." His thin, four-year-old arms tightened around her neck.

An invisible weight of relief bore into her. She lifted her gaze to Anthony, surprised to find the rough edges that had sharpened his features for so long had softened. Pulling back slightly, she framed Hunter's small face between her hands. The butterflies in her gut rebelled in full force. She exhaled to expel the burning sensation exploding in her chest. This was it. This was her chance to tell the truth. "Hunter, baby, I have a friend here I want you to meet."

Chapter Ten

He'd never stood a chance.

Years of intense training, combat operations, losing trusted friends and facing off with death more times than he could count hadn't done him a damn bit of good. Glennon Chase had always been the one war he couldn't fight.

And he didn't want to. Not anymore.

A smile brightened the darkness that had been permanently etched on her features since he'd set sights on her. Chasing her son around the coffee table, Glennon roared at the top of her lungs. For the past hour, she and Hunter had taken turns succumbing to the tickle monster. Their combined laughter had even reached him outside while he'd conducted a perimeter check, and he couldn't keep from smiling. They were perfect together—a family—but an imagined vice tightened his chest nonetheless.

"They make quite the pair, don't they?" Helen handed him a fresh cup of coffee then pushed her shoulder into the wall beside him. She shifted her weight from one leg to the other. Must be one of her old injuries from her married days acting up. "I was surprised to find you standing next to her out there on

my porch. So how'd she do it? How'd she convince you to help her after what she did?"

He straightened, the coffee swishing against the side of his mug. "Hunter."

"She tell you who his daddy is?" she asked.

"No." Did it matter?

Helen nodded in his peripheral vision. "You know, I'd never met my grandson until a couple of weeks ago." She took a sip of her coffee, her swallow audible. "Glennon wouldn't come back here after growing up the way she did. Couldn't even step foot in this house until tonight. Can't say I blame her." Helen shifted again, her long, grayish-blond hair swinging forward. "But you didn't come back here to listen to me ramble on about the past. It's the future that matters, don't it?"

Damn straight. And his entire future had just started running around the couches for another game of tickle monster. Heat worked into his hand as he stared into the watery black reflection of the coffee. He forced the small muscles around his eyes to relax and sipped from his mug, the dark, rich liquid burning his throat on the way down. The taste escaped him as Glennon and her son collapsed into a pile of giggles on the living room floor. He'd already experienced as much evil in the world as he could tolerate. This right here? This perfect little family? That was what he'd wanted since the moment he'd set eyes on her back in his teaching days. It was everything. She was everything.

"She's strong. Stronger than I was at her age." Helen's lips thinned into a hard line, the wrinkles around her mouth growing deeper. "She's a big-time investigator now, but whatever this is she's wrapped up in—" she nodded toward Glennon "—I need you to get her

out of it, Anthony. I need you to do what you've got
to do to make sure my daughter comes home to that
boy, understand?"

No question. While he'd initially fought against getting wrapped up in the one woman he never thought
he'd see again, he'd made his decision the second he'd
recognized her voice over the phone. He'd never given
up on her. Never intended to let her go, but he'd kept
his distance. Hadn't looked for her. Out of respect.

The weight of her engagement ring against his skin
pulled at his attention. No. He wasn't about to lose her
again. And as for Mascaro's crew? They could have
her over his dead body. Glennon was his. Forever. "You
have my word."

"Anthony, save me!" Hunter's call was drowned in a
flood of laughter as his mother clamped her hand over
his mouth from behind.

Hesitation gripped him hard. His drumming heartbeat was too loud behind his ears. Haiti, Bosnia,
Kosovo. None of those operations had trained him for
this. What was he supposed to do? The little boy he'd
met not an hour ago wanted him to join in his game.

"Go on now." Helen took the cup from his hand.
"He's promised me he's not biting people anymore.
But I'd keep your fingers out of his mouth just in case."

What was one more scar?

"Understood." All right then. This was it. Anthony
nodded as he stripped out of his shoulder holster and
set it on top of a bookcase to his right. Next, the blades
he kept strapped at his ankle and thigh. After unloading his entire arsenal, he was ready. Advancing onto
the battlefield, he dove straight into action. His entire
body heated as Glennon smiled up at him from her po-

sition on the floor. Screw the stitches. Seeing these two so happy when everything in his life centered around guns, blood and betrayal was all that mattered. His control crumbled as another round of laughs exploded around him. "I never leave a man behind."

Hunter fought against his mother's hold, his small, crooked smile wide. "Get her!"

"And get on your mom's bad side? I don't think so." Anthony went in for the attack, aiming straight for Hunter's underarms.

A high-pitched scream nearly burst his eardrums as the four-year-old lifted his feet to kick out. Anthony dodged the first attempt but caught a hit to the gut the second time around. Hunter fell onto his back, sandwiching Glennon between her son and the floor. Right where he wanted her. Crooking his finger, Anthony whispered the plan in Hunter's ear. "Got it?"

Hunter nodded, spinning into his mother. In two seconds flat the boy pinned her wrists against the floor. Faux screams filled the living room as Glennon fought against her son's strength. "Got you!"

"Wait! You weren't supposed to go until three." Anthony shrugged. "Tickle her!"

The four-year-old didn't have to be told twice, consumed with the need to make his mother laugh.

Tucking her chin against her chest, Glennon curled into a fetal position, but that wouldn't save her. Not from him.

Anthony maneuvered around the other side of the fight. Wrapping his grip around one wrist, he hauled her off the floor and against him, her back to his chest. Her rosy scent filled the living room as he lifted her

uninjured arm above her head. She was exposed. Vulnerable. "Now, Hunter! Go, go, go!"

"No!" Her spine tensed as her son took advantage. She fought to pull her arm down, to get away from him, her laugh smooth and addictive in every sense of the word. "This isn't fair. There are two of you and only one of me."

He committed the sound to memory. Lowering his mouth to her ear, Anthony inhaled her scent deep into his system. No matter what happened at the end of the investigation, he would have this. If only for a night, he'd made her smile, made her laugh. She'd been happy. "Haven't you heard, all is fair in love and war?"

"Oh, it is on." She kicked at the floor and launched them backward. The maneuver broke his hold on her wrists and she spun into him. Wrapping her arms around his middle, Glennon rolled them across the worn rug with a lightness he'd never seen in her before. The living room blurred in his vision then vanished altogether, his entire focus centered on her. The danger that awaited them outside that front door, the betrayal of the past three days, had vanished the second she'd laid eyes on her son.

The ache in his chest lessened as he pinned her beneath his weight, her expression bright and full of something he hadn't seen in a long time. Hope. Her chest rose and fell against his as she fought to catch her breath. A fleeting smile burst across her features as she brushed away a stray piece of hair that had caught in her long lashes. "You two might've won this round, but this isn't over. We're not finished."

"You got that right, sweetheart." Seconds slipped by as he stared down at her, but the sudden onslaught of

forty pounds of deadweight crushing him into Glennon cleared his head. Reaching back, he rolled away from her as he maneuvered the laughing four-year-old into his arms. He fell back against the nearest couch, fought to catch his breath. Pain surged through the wound in his side. "Oh, man. You got me."

"All right, boy." Helen rounded the corner from the kitchen, securing the lid on Hunter's cup into place. She hiked one hand onto her hip and offered him the drink. "I filled up your water. Time to get your tiny butt back in bed."

Hunter's drawn-out groan pulled a laugh from Anthony's chest.

"Listen to Grandma, baby." Glennon shoved to her feet. "It's way past your bedtime."

"Okay." Eyes downcast, feet dragging across the rug, Hunter closed the distance between him and his mother, giving her a tight hug good-night. "When will we be going home?"

Anthony's stomach sank.

Glennon raised her gaze to his from over her son's shoulder. The light speckling of freckles across her nose darkened as color drained from her face. "Soon, baby. Mommy just has one more thing she needs to do."

"Okay. Be careful. Don't get hurt again." Hunter released his hold, turning toward Anthony with one hand raised. "Bye."

"Bye, buddy." Anthony offered a high-five as he caught Glennon wipe her hand across her cheek. "I had fun playing with you. We'll do it again, okay?"

With an overexaggerated nod and a quick pit stop to grab his drink from Helen, the four-year-old Caped

Crusader disappeared down the hallway with his grandmother close behind.

"That's the second time I've had to leave him here. He doesn't understand why." Glennon sank onto the floor, devastation etched into her expression as she stared after her son. Sniffling, she shook her head. "Not sure you're cut out for playing with my son again." She nodded at his wound. "You're bleeding."

Anthony pulled his shirt away from his skin, the spreading red stain across his T-shirt registering. Damn it. He must've torn a few stitches wrestling across the floor. A rough laugh shook through him. "He's definitely stronger than he looks."

"That, he is. Come on. My mom has a sewing kit around here somewhere." Glennon offered him her hand. "We'll get you stitched back up then go over our next move to find Bennett."

"There won't be much to go over. I've already worked it out." Sliding his hand into hers, Anthony ignored the sting in his side and stood. "Your partner started this war. We're going to end it."

A SKY FULL of pinks, greens and oranges—and Anthony was staring at her.

Puffs of air crystallized in front of her mouth as they took position in the tree line surrounding the cabin. A chill swept up her spine, but not from the dropping temperature. Not even from the anticipation of their target walking into Anthony's crosshairs. Because, after all these years, her heart still skipped a beat at the sight of him.

She swallowed hard, lying on the tarp and blanket they'd brought to protect them from the snow. Aurora

borealis danced above them, providing a minuscule amount of light, but Anthony had trained for operations exactly like this as a Ranger. He didn't need daylight to locate his target. He'd get the job done, even with a brand-new set of stitches in his side. "It's going to be hard to spot our target if you keep staring at me."

"I'm good at multitasking." One edge of his mouth turned upward. He'd armed himself with his favored Beretta, set up a sniper rifle and strapped on a combat knife, but the most fearsome weapon he held was that minefield of a smile. He pressed his left eye against the scope, relieving a bit of the pressure that had built in her chest.

"If you say so. Just remember you've already used up the saving-your-life coupon from me, so I'd focus if I were you." Glennon forced herself to study the span of property between them and the cabin. To prove she could. The trap was set. All she'd had to do was turn on her army-issued phone after coming back to the cabin and wait. With Campbell Lake to their right and a wide expanse of nothing but snow in front of them, they had the best view of anyone coming to collect on Staff Sergeant Mascaro's contract on her head. Whoever that might be.

Danger edged closer; she could feel it. Cold worked through her thick coat, down into her bones. She scanned the woods surrounding them for movement.

"Hell, I've missed you." The words were rough, rumbly and so low she hadn't been entirely sure she'd heard him right.

She jerked her gaze back to his face. "What?"

Anthony shifted his trigger finger alongside the rifle. "You know me better than anyone, Glennon, even

my team. And I don't believe in giving up." He kept his eye pressed to the scope. "Especially not when it comes to us."

She didn't know what to say to that. He wanted to have this discussion now? In the middle of the wilderness as they waited for Mascaro's men? She surveyed the landscape for signs of another soldier coming to collect the price on her head. "And you think now is the time to have this conversation?"

"When else are we going to find a time we're not being shot at or hunted down?"

Okay. He had a point.

Dark blue eyes centered on her, compressing the frigid air locked in her lungs. "You're the best investigator I've ever met. You're insanely smart, you'll do anything for the people who matter most to you and you're not afraid to stand up for what's right."

Her insides warmed, counteracting the numbness taking root in her fingers and toes.

"Why are you telling me this?" She licked her dry lips, a minor mistake out here in below-freezing temperatures, but she couldn't think. Couldn't breathe. Anxiety clawed an ugly path up her throat. "What do you want from me?"

"Everything, sweetheart." The tendons along the line of his neck flexed. "When this investigation is over, I want you and Hunter to stay here, in Anchorage, with me. I don't care what you're hiding. I can handle every single secret you have."

Her heart iced, her lips tingling with numbness. No. He couldn't. Because the second she revealed the truth, he'd walk away. He'd hate her. Nausea rolled in her stomach. And then who would she have? Everyone

else in her life had already betrayed her. Her heart-beat drummed too loud in her ears as she pushed to her feet. She curled her fingers into the palms of her thick gloves in an attempt to bring some blood flow back. She couldn't risk losing him. Not Anthony. Not yet.

Space. She needed to put space between them. "I have to go."

"Glennon, wait." His brows drew inward a split second before she cleared the tree line.

The sound of crunching snow followed close on her heels as she waded through the brush. A strong grip wrapped around her biceps. The world blurred as he spun her around. Anthony pressed her into his chest, held her up as her knees shook. He'd left the rifle in position behind him, abandoning his post. "You left me once. I'll be damned if I let it happen again without good reason."

He still had his fingers wrapped around her arm, and her breath hitched. Even through her winter gear, he could make her feel too much. Her body's response to Anthony had always been off the charts. She was too attuned to him. Too sensitive. And that was a very dangerous thing.

"I left because you weren't there when I needed you the most." The gut-wrenching shift in his expression filled her with dread. His hold lightened. She swallowed hard, the words much sharper than she'd intended, but she had to make one thing clear. This wasn't just about the two of them. "And if it happened again, it wouldn't only affect me. Do you understand?"

The dimple almost completely hidden beneath his beard deepened. "I would never do *anything* to hurt Hunter."

"I believe you. Now. And I think you believe that,

too." A blast of Arctic chill swept through her, hammering at her already exhausted defenses. Physically. Emotionally. "But what's to stop you from re-upping for another tour or deciding your assignments with Blackhawk Security are more important than us?"

The blue in his eyes dimmed. He seemed so much… bigger in that moment. Dangerous, even. But Anthony would never hurt her. Hell, he'd taken a bullet for her. Luck had nothing to do with her standing there. She'd cheated death. Because of the Grim Reaper. But still, he didn't answer.

Glennon nodded. "I barely kept my head above water when I left Anchorage, Anthony. I won't put my son through that. And if this means you can't help me anymore, I won't hold it against you."

Her boots sank into soft powder as she turned away, slowing her escape. But she wouldn't stop. Couldn't. No matter how much she wanted to go back, to slip into his hold, they didn't have a future together. Soon, the investigation into Mascaro would be over and she'd go back to CID headquarters in Quantico. Where she belonged.

The weight of his gaze drilled into her from behind as she climbed the cabin's front steps. He hadn't followed her. She should've been relieved, but the tingling in her arm—where he'd touched her—spread fast.

Shouldering her way inside, Glennon exhaled the remnants of his clean, masculine scent from her system. She pressed her spine into the thick wooden door. Sweat built underneath her clothing, but it had nothing to do with the flames simmering in the fireplace a few feet away. She'd done the right thing. Pain shot

through the back of her skull as her head hit the door. She closed her eyes. "I did the right thing."

Swiping a glove under her nose, she tossed her winter gear over the back of the couch and escaped to the guest bedroom. Having another door between them wouldn't erase the past ten minutes from her memory, but it would help to relieve the urge to march back out there in below-freezing conditions. That wouldn't do any good. What more was there to discuss?

Stay with me.

Why did that idea feel so…right? Whatever she felt for him now wasn't real. At least, not anymore. She'd fallen in love with him years ago. Her feelings—however clouded—were an echo of that time. Had nothing to do with the last three days. Had nothing to do with the fact he'd stood by her side, protected her, saved her life. Had nothing to do with the way he'd gotten Hunter to laugh or given her son a pass on tearing open his stitches. Floorboards groaned under her weight as she paced to the curtained window. Did it?

A laugh burst up her throat. She was Military Police, for crying out loud. Yet here she was, hiding. Hiding from the truth. Glennon ran a hand through her hair, turning at the sound of heavy boot steps coming down the hallway. Soft beeping reached her ears. Anthony had set the alarm. A door closed softly, followed by the sound of running water. The shower. She was kidding herself. Of course she'd started falling back in love with him. How could she not?

Anthony Harris was the kind of man any soldier would be lucky to have by her side, the kind of man who loved fiercely and protected loyally. She exhaled hard. Hell, she couldn't believe she was doing this.

Glennon ripped open the bedroom door. He was the kind of man who could make her forget the nightmare around her, if only for a night.

Steam worked its way from underneath the bathroom door. The bright red light on Anthony's new security alarm panel said the cabin was secure. Mascaro's crew wouldn't get in without her knowing, but hesitation still gripped her hard, her hand positioned over the doorknob. One twist. That was all it would take. She could have everything she'd ever wanted. The chance to have a real family. One breath. Two. Shouldering her way inside, Glennon froze.

Standing outside the shower, stripped down to nothing but a pair of dark cargo pants, Anthony stood as though he'd expected her. Ridges and valleys shifted across his bare abdomen as he tossed his shirt to the tile floor. The tattoo she'd traced countless times twisted up his arm. Death Before Dishonor. And wasn't that the perfect representation of a Ranger. "Glennon, I—"

"I don't want to talk." A slow exhale escaped her control as she met his gaze. Unflinching. Bare. Vulnerable. Taking a single step forward, she gripped the edge of her T-shirt, lifting it over her head. Her hair fell in loose strands around her face. Discarding her shirt, she removed her boots using her heels. "Tonight, I only want you."

Chapter Eleven

Silence woke him.

Sliding his hand over the sheets, Anthony reached out for her. Glimmers of green and pink illuminated the edges of the single window in his room. He rubbed his eyes with the ball of his palm. Damn, how long had he been asleep? Two hours? Three, tops? Time had lost all meaning once they'd finally climbed out of the shower. And he didn't regret a single moment, the feel of her wrapped around him still fresh in his mind. Her scent still clung to him. Being with her again… Hearing his name on her lips had been everything and so much more. He'd never forget tonight. And couldn't wait for so many others.

He rolled onto his side and scanned the bed with what minimal light came through the curtains. Empty. He narrowed his gaze to see through the dark. She couldn't have climbed out of bed that long ago. The sheets were still warm. "Glennon?"

A tingling sensation climbed up his spine.

The pressure of a gun barrel dug into his back. "Where is she?"

Anthony shot up and swung hard, knocking the

weapon out of his assailant's hand. The thud of the gun hitting the floor resonated loudly in his ears.

Pain exploded across the right side of his head with a direct hit, but didn't slow him down. Grabbing his masked assailant by the back of the neck, he launched his knee into the attacker's stomach as hard as he could. No way in hell this bastard would get to her. He wouldn't fail her. Not again.

The intruder rammed his shoulder into Anthony's middle, shoving his bare feet across the cold hardwood floor. He slammed his elbow down into his opponent's spine. Once. Twice. His heart beat loudly behind his ears as the operative dropped—hard—but Anthony wasn't finished. Straddling his attacker, he rocketed his fist into the man's face. A knee caught him in the back and he launched forward, his head hitting the nightstand.

The intruder swung down, every move, every strike, militaristic.

Blocking the punch with one hand, Anthony rammed his fist into his assailant's rib cage. He shoved to his feet. A growl—predatory and full of rage—ripped from his throat as he closed in. These people just didn't get the message. Glennon Chase was off-limits. She was his. And he'd put a bullet in every single one of them to keep her safe.

A solid kick to the man's chest sent his opponent straight into the bedroom window. Broken glass rained down around them as his attacker slumped to the floor. But the fight was far from over. They'd already broken into his house twice, somehow bypassing his security. There wouldn't be a next time.

The bedroom light blinded him for a split second and he swung around, prepared for another fight.

Glennon stood in the doorway. Wearing nothing but one of his large T-shirts that covered her from mid-thigh up and her unlaced boots, her service weapon was firmly gripped between both hands. Standing there, unashamed and determined to do the job. And damn if that wasn't the sexiest thing he'd ever seen. Broken glass crunched under his attacker's boots as the bastard got to his feet. Glennon closed in on her target. Her gaze shifted to Anthony then back. Was that hesitation he read across her expression? "You know the drill, Bennett. Put your hands on your head and drop to your knees."

"You going to arrest me, Glennon?" The mask hid the intruder's features but that voice… Anthony recognized it straight off the bat. First from the break-in, then from the docks.

With slow movements, the attacker gripped the black ski mask in his hand and pulled it from his head. Brown hair and a sharp, shadowed jawline stood out against the hollowness that had consumed the sergeant's features. Running from the authorities had obviously taken a toll. "Here I thought we could still be friends after everything I've done for you."

Son of a bitch. They'd recovered Bennett Spencer. The investigation was over. His gaze cut back to Glennon. Anthony curled his fingers into his palms as a wall of heat rushed against him from the vent above his head. He'd gone to bed—and fought Bennett—in nothing but his boxers, but he wouldn't move a damn inch to get dressed as long as the bastard was free of cuffs.

"Done for me?" A rough laugh worked up her throat

as Glennon shifted her weight to her back foot, widening her stance and making herself a smaller target, exactly as he'd taught her in basic. "You've got to be kidding. For two years, all you've done for me is lie. What you should be saying is, 'Thank you for not putting a bullet in me, Glennon.' Or 'Hey, partner, by the way, I'm part of the operation we've been tasked to investigate. Thought you should know.'"

"Well, I thought taking care of that sniper who put a bullet in your shoulder or saving your life at the side of the road was awful nice of me. I guess I could've let those assholes kill you." Bennett shrugged. The muscles along his jawline sharpened. Brown eyes—darker than coffee—locked on her, sending the controlled rage Anthony held on to close to the surface. "And, hey, partner, by the way, I'm not part of Mascaro's operation. At least…not anymore."

"What? Did they revoke your membership once they found out you've been moonlighting as CID?" Glennon adjusted her grip on the gun. "And you're the one who ran us off the road in the first place. How am I supposed to trust anything you say?"

"You killed the sniper and that shooter on the shoreline." Anthony crossed to the closet and scanned his thumbprint for access to his gun safe. In another two, maybe three minutes, Glennon's arms would start to ache from holding her weapon up so long, but Bennett wouldn't get the drop on them. He loaded a magazine into his Beretta and secured a round in the chamber. Not again. This time he'd put the traitor down if forced. "If you were with Mascaro and his crew, why bother?"

"No offense, Ranger—" Bennett interlaced his hands behind his head "—but I think I'd be more com-

fortable having this conversation with all of us wearing clothes."

"No, we're doing this now, *partner*." The last word sneered from Glennon's lips. She lowered her weapon but the rage etched into her features intensified. The safety on her gun remained off. She didn't trust Bennett. And with good reason. The sergeant had successfully infiltrated the Military Police—background checks, polygraph tests, multiple interviews. He'd lived a double life for years. Hell, if Bennett weren't part of the crew trying to kill the woman he loved, Anthony would have half a mind to recruit him into Blackhawk Security. "You betrayed the army. And me. In fact, I wouldn't be surprised if you're the one who deleted my files off my backup drive."

"Didn't I warn you not to come after me?" Bennett lowered his hands.

Anthony tightened his grip around the Beretta as the sergeant rose. One small move. That was all it would take and this entire recovery would be a thing of the past.

"Damn it, Bennett. Did you really think a warning would stop me from coming after you?" Tension tightened the tendon in Glennon's neck as she straightened. "Give me one good reason why I shouldn't arrest you right here, right now."

"You mean aside from the fact you don't have any proof I was part of Mascaro's operation? Come on, Glennon. You and I both know you'd be wasting your time. I'm a lot smarter than I look. Besides, we're on the same side. Mascaro's organization wants me dead as much as they want you. Maybe even more." Bennett studied her from head to toe, his expression cold. Cal-

culating. Danger beneath smooth waters. A man who'd chosen treason over his country always had an escape plan in case things went south. So what was Bennett's? "What I can do is help you bring down Mascaro's crew for good. Interested?"

Confusion cracked Glennon's stone-cold control. "Why would you help us?"

"He's trying to avoid prison time." Anthony maneuvered between Glennon and her partner. He'd stand between her and any threat. Always. Not because they were partners in this investigation. But because it was her. "He wants to strike a deal with the new marshal when the investigation is over."

Couldn't blame him. If the army could connect Bennett with any of the crimes Mascaro and his operatives had been accused of, he'd never see the light of day again. A large part of Anthony reveled in that idea. Bennett had dragged Glennon—and her son—into this mess, had put her in the crosshairs. Then again, the sergeant had also saved her life. Twice.

A rumbling laugh escaped Bennett's throat. "I'm not going to prison, Ranger. Like I said, I'm smarter than I look." He crossed his muscled arms over his chest, shifting his weight between his feet. "Actually, I just plan to systematically kill every last one of those bastards. From the bottom hit man to the woman giving orders at the top."

Anthony's gaze focused on Bennett. Woman?

Glennon took a single step forward. Grip still wrapped around her weapon, she narrowed her gaze. "What woman?"

"Jamie Mascaro," Bennett said.

Anthony ran through Glennon's investigation notes in his head. "Staff Sergeant Mascaro's wife?"

"Bingo." Bennett uncrossed his arms, one hand facing toward Glennon and the other reaching for something in his leather jacket pocket. "And I've got the proof. Turns out she set her husband up from the beginning. She tipped the marshal off to the crew's extracurricular activities and put her husband front and center in our investigation. But then our CO decided to take a cut himself, but that's a story for another day." The sergeant offered Anthony a piece of paper, his attention cutting to Glennon as she maneuvered beside him. "She's a piece of work if you ask me. Kind of reminds me of you, Glennon. Only you're not evil."

"Let's say I believe you about being on Jamie Mascaro's bad side. You found out who'd taken Nicholas Mascaro's place at the head of the operation." Glennon studied the evidence as Anthony unfolded the beaten sheet of paper. "And that's the only reason they're hunting us down? Why you disappeared?"

A photo of a blonde woman—maybe thirty-five, forty years old—standing beside a military-marked crate, surrounded by soldiers, stared up at him. In her hands? An M4 assault rifle, same make and model of the shipment of missing weapons Glennon and Bennett had gone chasing in the first place. Jamie Mascaro. The woman most certainly knew of her husband's criminal activities, despite what her testimony had revealed during the staff sergeant's trial.

"Not exactly." Bennett tugged a hand through the gelled brown hair at the back of his neck. "That would be because I was one of Nicholas Mascaro's lieuten-

ants. And Jamie there—" he nodded at the photo "—is cleaning house."

HER PARTNER HAD been one of Staff Sergeant Mascaro's men. Just as the marshal had claimed. Bennett had told them everything. How he'd faked his GPS data to draw out Jamie Mascaro to the abandoned house that belonged to her husband, how he'd waited there for the sniper who'd put a bullet in Glennon's shoulder then taken him out, and how he'd gotten through Anthony's security system at the cabin. Twice. All of it. Felony after felony stacked against the man she'd once considered her closest friend. Because this investigation couldn't get any worse.

Sweat lessened her grip on her Glock before she finally clicked on the safety and tossed it onto the bed. She'd just needed a minute to herself. Alone, Glennon dropped her head back against the bedroom door. Dark, rumpled sheets claimed her attention. She'd broken her only rule. She'd lost her emotional distance and fallen into bed with the one man she'd sworn to keep at arm's length. Yet at the same time Anthony had given her a glimpse of everything she'd ever wanted: a real family. A second chance.

Then Bennett had to ruin her short reprieve and everything else she'd believed the last few days. He was involved with the very people trying to kill her, but she couldn't prove it. Other than his admission, which she hadn't gotten on tape, he'd covered his tracks too well. But did she really want to? Bennett was the one man who could bring down Mascaro's crew for good. An insider. With his intel, they could disassemble the entire operation and secure weapons shipments all over

the country. The investigation would be over. She could put in her discharge papers. She could move on with her life.

Glennon shoved away from the door, throwing her discarded clothing onto the bed.

A soft knock spun her around. "You okay?"

Anthony.

Her feet dragged as she headed to the door. Twisting the knob, she faced off with a wall of pure, seductive muscle. Dressed in a pair of low-hanging jeans and a black T-shirt, he was far sexier with his hair out of place and a little frightening with his hard, determined expression. She straightened a bit more, pressed her lips together and nodded once. "I'm fine."

A lie. What about the past three days had been fine? Hell, the last two hours had turned her entire world upside down. But he didn't need to know that. Her partner going missing hadn't broken her. Leaving her son hadn't broken her. Bennett's flat-out betrayal hadn't broken her. This thing with Anthony? That wouldn't break her, either.

Those deep, dark eyes narrowed on her. What did he see when he looked at her like that? How close she was to splintering apart? Could he see the cracks in her defenses widening? "You think I can't see it when you lie to me, but I do."

Heat climbed up her neck and into her face. Goose bumps rose on her arms as a blast of warm air descended from the vent in the ceiling. She cleared her throat. "What are you talking abou—?"

"You're already pulling away," he said.

"I meant what I said outside." Glennon swallowed hard as she leveled her chin parallel with the floor. "I

won't have you come into my life—into my son's life—
then disappear when you decide your duty is more important than we are."

"Is that what you think of me? That you're temporary? That I'll get bored? That this doesn't mean anything?" Growling, he closed in on her, fire replacing
the cold depths in his eyes. "I took you to bed. No other
woman can say the same. That means everything to
me, Glennon. It means...you're mine."

His? Her breath caught. She forced her fingers to un-
curl from her palms. He hadn't taken any other woman
to bed? Ever? Warmth flooded her. She fought to think.
To breathe. He was right. That did mean something.
Her focus shifted to her engagement ring hanging
around his neck. He'd never stopped believing they
could be happy together.

"It meant something to me, too." The words left
her mouth in a mere whisper as pain knifed through
her. She'd learned a long time ago that those closest
could turn on her in an instant. Her father. Bennett.
Even Anthony had played an important role in building her defenses. And she wasn't sure she could survive that devastation again. She forced herself to take
a step back when all she wanted was for him to wrap
his arms around her. "But did you forget we've been
through this before?"

His brows drew inward, tugging at the scrape across
his forehead. His pulse beat unevenly at the base of his
throat, eyelids heavier than a moment ago. Exhaustion
pulled at his expression. Dirt still clung to his hairline.
"We're not the same people we were back then. There's
more at risk now. More reason to give us a shot."

Because of Hunter. Glennon exhaled hard. Her son

had gone four years without a father in his life, someone other than her to count on. Anthony was right. They had a lot more to lose now. Maybe that was all they needed to finally make this work between them. She could, at last, give Hunter the real family he deserved. "Hunter and I... We're not some mission you can complete." She dragged her tongue across her lips, her mouth dry. "We need someone in it for the long haul."

"Have you ever known me as anything other than dedicated?" He lowered his mouth to hers but paused. "I dare you to find someone who loves you more than I do, sweetheart."

Her army-issue phone vibrated on the nightstand a few feet away.

The breath she'd been holding rushed from her lungs. Saved by the bell. Crossing the room, Glennon caught the number before one last ring. Blocked. She hit the green button and brought the phone to her ear. "Special Agent Chase—"

"I assume you know who I am," a female voice said.

Glennon turned to Anthony. Dropping the phone from her ear, she tapped the speaker button.

Confusion deepened the lines across his forehead as he inched closer.

"Jamie Mascaro." Glennon stared at the phone, ticking off the seconds on the screen. Thirty seconds. That was all she needed for Blackhawk Security to trace the call. Thirty seconds and she could end this nightmare. "Unless you're calling to apologize for sending three soldiers to kill me, I'm afraid we don't have a lot to talk about."

"Oh, I don't think that's true, Sergeant Chase." A

light tapping sound echoed through the line. Fingernails on a desk? "See, you have something I want, a
certain lieutenant from my husband's command who
knows too much and puts my entire operation at risk.
I was hoping you and I could make a deal. You turn
Sergeant Spencer over to me and I'll call off the contract I put on your head."

Shadowed movement caught Glennon's attention
in her peripheral vision. Bennett. Inhaling slow and
deep, she motioned him inside. He was part of this,
too. And while she could give him up—put an end to
this investigation and move on with her life—there
were still lines she wasn't willing to cross. Giving up
her partner was one of them. No matter how much he
might deserve it.

Tense moments ticked past. This was it. They could
do this. Together. "Sorry to disappoint you, Mrs. Mascaro, but I don't make deals with crim—"

Laughter cut through her words. Sinister. Dominat-
ing. "Please, Sergeant Chase. Call me Jamie. Because,
despite what you might think, we're about to become
very well acquainted with one another. In fact, I'm
willing to bet you'll do just about anything I ask once
you uncover the small insurance policy I took out to
secure your cooperation."

Insurance policy? Glennon searched Anthony's features. That full bottom lip, his dark blue eyes. Dread
pooled at the base of her spine. Insurance—

"Mommy?" Hunter's voice crossed the line, draining the blood from her face.

Anthony swore, the small muscles lining his jaw
rock-hard.

Her heart skipped a beat, the breath rushing from

her lungs. Every muscle in her body threatened to fail. No. No, no, no, no. Her grip on the phone loosened as her knees buckled. The bedroom—and everyone in it—blurred. Rough hands caught her before she hit the floor, leading her to the edge of the bed. The mattress dipped with Anthony's added weight. Her throat tightened. "Hunter?" She swallowed hard, closing her eyes. "Is that you?"

"Mommy, I want to go home." The desperation in her son's small voice gutted her.

Rage, white and hot, flooded through her. She opened her eyes. Her vision sharpened. She clung to the phone. Fifteen more seconds. Fifteen more seconds and she'd have a location. Forget bringing Anthony as backup. Glennon would rip the woman apart with her bare hands. "I'm coming, baby. I promise. Mommy is coming for you."

No answer.

"Hunter?" Panic threatened to set in. Had Mascaro hung up? The timer on the screen read twenty seconds. Not enough time to trace the call. Glennon nearly shattered the phone, her pulse too loud in her ears.

"Such a sweet little boy. It'd be a shame if he didn't come home," Jamie Mascaro said. "You know what I want, Sergeant Chase, and I know you're tracing this call. All you have to do is bring me Sergeant Spencer and I will disclose your son's location. You have my word."

The word of a criminal, a woman who'd turned on her own husband to take over his operation.

Glennon studied Bennett. Deep brown eyes, darker than a few minutes ago, softened. His nod released the pressure in her chest. He'd turn himself over to Jamie

Mascaro. For her. For Hunter. "If I find a single bruise on him when I find him, I will kill you."

"That will be entirely up to you, Sergeant," Jamie Mascaro said. "Two hours. Come alone with Sergeant Spencer or your son pays the price."

The line went dead.

"Well, this seems like a good time to give you two some privacy. And, you know, get my affairs in order before that woman puts a bullet in my head." Bennett headed into the hallway, the jokes, the witty banter, his sarcasm, draining from his expression.

Glennon tossed the phone onto the bed, numb. Jamie Mascaro had her son. Her hands shook, blood pressure dropping fast. Tears burned on her lower eyelashes a split second before another rush of fury swept through her. She ripped the bedside lamp off the table and hurled it at the wall. This was why she'd kept her son a secret. Why she hadn't told his father about him. She forced her focus to Anthony. Helplessness threatened to consume her. She had to stay in the moment, stay in control. The second she gave in to those thoughts, Jamie Mascaro—and her organization of traitorous thieves—won. Running her palms down her bare thighs, Glennon rolled her lips between her teeth to keep from screaming. "She's not going to hold up her end of the deal."

She was sure of it.

"Then we've got two hours to find Hunter before the meeting." The words came as a growl from Anthony's throat. The veins in his arms swelled. Pure ice squelched the fire that had simmered in his gaze a moment ago, all evidence of the man she'd started falling in love with gone. The Grim Reaper had arrived, but

this time, she wouldn't try to hold him back. "I swear to you, I'll get your son back."

"Good." Glennon straightened. She had to tell him. If they were going to risk it all—if they were going to recover Hunter—she couldn't lie to him anymore. She cleared her throat. "Because Hunter is your son, too."

Chapter Twelve

There were only two things in life a person couldn't take back. Bullets and words. The latter stuck with him now. *Because Hunter is your son, too.* She'd kept his son from him for four damn years. The little boy with the bright green eyes and wide smile. She'd kept his family from him. Rage exploded in his chest. But he couldn't think about that right now. Not with Hunter out there. Afraid. In danger. Alone.

"Don't think we're finished talking about this." Anthony strode across the street toward her childhood home for the second time in twenty-four hours. No way in hell were they finished. In fact, they were just getting started.

"Fine. You want to talk about this right now, with our son missing?" Glennon spun on her heel, shoving a hand against his chest in the middle of the street. Arctic temperatures formed crystalized puffs of air in front of her mouth, but the cold barely seemed to slow her down. "Yes, I kept him from you, just like I kept him from everyone else. I didn't want the people I hunted for the military to ever have leverage over me, but apparently, everything I've done to keep him safe has all been for nothing. They found him. He's out there—"

tears welled in her eyes as she motioned toward the street "—all alone. Because of me."

"I could've protected him, Glennon. I could've prevented this from happening if you'd just told me the truth." Devastation deepened the lines forged between her eyebrows, and his gut tightened. She blamed herself for this mess, but she wasn't innocent. His fury burned hot and deep. First, she'd kept evidence crucial to identifying a suspect to herself. Second, kept the break in at her apartment back east from him. Now this. Jamie Mascaro would pay for what she'd done, but how was he supposed to trust Glennon now? Closing his fingers around her arms, Anthony forced her to look at him. "I'm only going to say this once, and I want you to believe every word. None of this—Bennett disappearing, the bullet in your shoulder, the accident, Hunter being kidnapped—is your fault. That's on Jamie Mascaro, and she's going to pay for the rest of her life. I'm going to make sure of it, but I can't do my damn job when you're keeping things from me."

"I should've been there for him." The words were whispered from between her paling lips as though she hadn't heard a single word he'd said. "I should've been the one keeping him safe. Maybe then, this wouldn't have happened."

"You were. You did everything in your power to make sure he couldn't be connected to you." He couldn't keep this space between them any longer. Wrapping her in his arms, Anthony rested his chin on the crown of her head. She fit perfectly, almost as though they were two pieces of the same puzzle.

Alaskan temperatures battled with her natural heat. He memorized the feel of her pressed against him all

over again. The rise and fall of her shoulders intensified the friction between them. He had to concentrate on the operation—on getting his son back—and
not the fact she'd lied to him for close to five years.
"Jamie Mascaro outmaneuvered us this time. It won't
happen again."

"Well, I wish that made me feel better." Pulling back
slightly, she wiped at her eyes. Strands of hair escaped
from the tight braid at the back of her head, all evidence of the controlled, emotionally distant investigator a distant memory. Love did that sometimes, had a
way of breaking even the strongest person in two, and
he had no doubt in that moment: Glennon was breaking. "The meeting is in a couple hours, and I doubt
Bennett will wait back at the cabin much longer. We
need to get moving."

"We're going to get our son back, Glennon, and,
after we do, you and I are going to finish this conversation," he said.

She nodded. Twisting around, she headed toward
the house. Then froze. She drew her service weapon
at the sight of the busted front door, rushing forward.
"Mom?"

"No." Anthony caught her by the arm and pulled her
back, then unholstered his Beretta. He trusted his instincts. Jamie Mascaro already had what she wanted:
leverage. The new head of her husband's operation
didn't have any reason to leave operatives behind, but
he wasn't going to risk Glennon going inside without
him surveying the property first. He nodded to the
west side of the house. There'd always been a chance
Helen Chase would become a target, but he honestly

prayed for the operatives who tried to take her out. "Get behind me."

She maneuvered into position, gun in hand, close on his heels.

He led them around the back of the house, senses on high alert. Snow crunched under his boots as he spotted a path of three distinct sets of footprints. Anthony raised his left hand, signaling for Glennon to stop. Three-man team. Their tracks headed toward the front of the house, originating from the tree line. The perfect approach, seeing as how there weren't any windows on this side of the house. Helen never would've seen them coming. However, one set had deviated from formation, forging a path to the breaker box. He crouched near the box and picked up a severed padlock.

"What is it?" Moonlight cast Glennon's shadow over his shoulder.

"They cut the power to the house." He tossed the padlock back into the snow. "And to Helen's alarm system." He straightened. These bastards had taken his son. Orders be damned, he'd make them pay. But first, they had to get to Helen. She was the only one who might be able to give them a lead on where Mascaro had taken his son. "Let's go."

They cleared the backyard. No movement. No sign of an impending ambush. Testing the back-door screen, Anthony reached for one of the blades tucked into his arsenal and cut through the aluminum mesh. The door was secure. If they played their cards right, there wouldn't be reason for anyone still inside to think it wasn't secure. They could surprise these bastards, finally gain the upper hand. And maybe secure some leverage of their own.

"Wait." Glennon reached over him and into the light fixture to his right. A moment later she handed him a key. He stared down at her but she only shrugged. "My mother hid a spare key out here in case one of my friends needed a place to stay. Guess she forgot about it."

Anthony inserted the key into the lock and twisted the doorknob. Letting his Beretta lead, he shouldered his way inside. He fought to adjust to the darkness. One. Two. Three seconds was all the time he needed before ice ran through his veins. The house had been destroyed, every inch littered with debris, bullet casings, glass. And blood.

A sharp gasp reached his ears from behind. Glennon.

His grip tightened on the gun. Damn it, he shouldn't have brought her in here. She'd already lost her son. Who knew what else they were about to find. If Mascaro's people had laid a hand on Helen, they'd wish they had killed him back in that parking garage. They had to find her. Fast. Anthony nodded toward the living room. The team had come through the front door, straight into the living room. If they were going to find anything—anyone—it'd be there.

Following the trail of debris through the kitchen, he slowed his movements so as not to shift the evidence. The second they secured Helen, he'd call in Vincent Kalani. Blackhawk's forensic expert would lead them to the men responsible for this mess, and Anthony would take it from there.

Moonlight highlighted the origin of the battle. Bookcases overturned. Sofas losing their cushioning through bullet holes. The coffee table tipped on its side. The

space had transformed into the complete opposite of his last memories in this room. Memories of Hunter.

Movement claimed his attention on the left.

A shotgun blast exploded from the darkness. Arcing wide, it barely missed his right arm.

Anthony pulled Glennon to the floor with him, ready for another shot. Hiking his weapon up and over his head, he aimed for the shooter taking cover behind the last remaining bookcase. His ears rang. His heart beat hard at the back of his skull. Next chance he got, he'd take the shot.

"No, don't shoot!" Glennon climbed over his legs and wrapped one hand around his wrist. Her breath fanned across his neck, raising goose bumps along his overheated skin. "Mom, it's okay. It's me. It's Glennon."

Shadows shifted behind the bookcase. "They took him." Flat, strained words. "I did everything I could. I shot one of them. But the other two…they…took him right out of my arms."

Relief flooded through him. Helen was alive. Shoving to his feet, Anthony lowered his weapon as Glennon rushed to her mother. He scanned the rest of the living room. Television destroyed. Area rug covered in glass and…a blue blanket decorated with monsters. Stained with blood.

The sound of glass shifting across the hardwood floor broke through the silence from behind him. Every muscle in his body tensed. They weren't alone. One of Mascaro's operatives had stayed behind after all. His fingers tightened around the gun. He spun on his heel.

"Anthony?" Glennon helped her mother into a nearby chair.

Closing the distance, Anthony caught sight of one of the intruders fighting to crawl to the safety of the front door. Not a chance in hell. He lunged for the operative. Gripping the man's Kevlar, Anthony forced the bastard to his feet and slammed him into the nearest wall. A groan escaped the guy's throat. Rage boiled beneath Anthony's skin. The edges of his vision darkened, focusing on his prey. "Where did they take him?"

A white smile disrupted the smear of blood across the soldier's face. No answer.

Pulling the intruder toward him, he placed the barrel of his gun under the guy's chin and clicked off the Beretta's safety. "Where?"

"Anthony." Glennon rushed into his peripheral vision. But she wouldn't be able to talk him down. Not this time.

Blood dripped onto his boots. Helen had been right. She'd hit the bastard all right. And Anthony would let him bleed out in the middle of the entryway if the son of a bitch didn't start talking soon.

Glennon approached slowly, her service weapon aimed. "This one's mine."

ONE SHOT. That was all it had taken to get Hunter's location out of the shooter. And with a single call to Bennett, they finally had the upper hand. They were going to end this nightmare once and for all.

Anthony shoved the SUV into Park along the dirt road. "We're here."

"Good." This was it. Up ahead, a small wooden shed sat in the middle of dried weeds and tall dead trees off to the left. The sun had gone down, but clear tire

tracks dug uneven paths along the road. For an abandoned water shed, the area had obviously been used recently. Anticipation surged through her. According to Mascaro's man, her son was being held in that shed until further instruction. This could all be over in a few minutes.

But…

She checked the burner phone Anthony had supplied, rolling her lips between her teeth.

"No word from Bennett. He should've been here by now." Had he changed his mind about turning himself over to Mascaro? Her rib cage tightened. Glennon leaned forward in her seat, fingernails digging into the soft leather. They'd parked a few hundred feet from the shed, but even from this distance there should've been some evidence Hunter was in that building. Lights. Guards. Cameras. Vehicles. And where the hell was Bennett? Dread pooled in her stomach. This was wrong. It was too quiet. "This doesn't feel right. Bennett should be here by now."

"It's a trap." Anthony's voice dipped an octave. Gaze cutting to the rearview mirror, he reached for his weapon. "Get down!"

The back window shattered.

Glennon launched forward. A flash grenade landed in the back seat and she rushed to cover her ears. In vain. Her vision brightened into nothing but white as an explosion robbed her of her hearing. Pings of sound registered through the ringing in her ears. Gunshots? She couldn't be sure, feeling blindly for the weapon she'd dropped onto the floor.

A blast of Alaskan air rushed against her a split

second before rough hands pulled her from the SUV. Snow and dead weeds crunched beneath her as she hit the ground. Muted voices echoed around her as she was wrenched to her feet and pushed forward. She tumbled into the side of the SUV, the grenade affecting her balance. She blinked to clear her vision. Two seconds. Three. Shadows shifted in front of her but she couldn't make them out. "Where is my son?"

Another push.

She landed on all fours, rocks and ice cutting into her palms. Her vision cleared in small increments, revealing five armed operatives in front of her, but a flash of headlights kept their identities shadowed. The ringing in her ears lessened as another soldier zip-tied her wrists behind her back. Pain splintered across her wounded shoulder, eliciting a groan from her throat, and she clamped down hard on her back teeth.

Anthony landed on his knees beside her, the stain of blood thick in his hairline.

She fought against the zip ties. "Anthony—"

"Grab Hunter as soon as you can and run. Don't worry about me." His voice leveled out. Deep. Dark. Dangerous. Where fire usually blazed in his blue eyes, coldness stared back at her and her breath caught.

"Sergeant Chase, I thought I made myself perfectly clear." A woman, presumably Jamie Mascaro, stepped around one of the vehicles and in front of the headlights. Her heeled boots wobbled on the uneven terrain, long hair shifting over her shoulder. "You were to bring me Sergeant Spencer at the designated meeting point alone."

"Where is he? Where is my son?" Plastic cut deep

into her wrists the more she struggled, but she wouldn't stop. Wouldn't give in.

Jamie Mascaro stepped forward. "You broke our deal—"

"Where is he!" Glennon lunged to her feet, but a hand on her injured shoulder shoved her back to her knees.

A predatory growl reached her ears a split second before Anthony twisted around. A flash of metal caught her eye as the operative holding him collapsed. Unconscious or dead, she didn't know. Did it matter? Headlights highlighted the thin layer of sweat on Anthony's cheeks, his expression perfectly cold. Perfectly dangerous. A single step toward her raised goose bumps along her neck and arms. "Get your damn hands off her or wind up like your friend here."

The soldier backed off.

Her throat dried on her next inhale. Wrenching away from the grip on her shoulder, she left the soldier at her back to fend for himself as Jamie Mascaro signaled for the other four armed men to stand down. The zip ties fell to the ground with a swipe of Anthony's blade. Glennon fought the urge to rub at the raw skin, collected the assault rifle at her feet and aimed for Jamie Mascaro. "You have five seconds to bring me my son, or I give the signal for Sergeant Spencer to put a bullet in your head."

Such a lie. Bennett wasn't a sniper and she still hadn't heard from him, but she had to try something. She had no doubt Anthony could take down a couple of Jamie Mascaro's operatives, but the two of them against five armed men with assault rifles? Not a

chance. She needed to see Hunter. Make sure he was okay. She could figure out the rest later.

"You think I didn't know about your little reconnaissance mission?" A high-pitched laugh drifted across the dirt. Jamie Mascaro angled her head over her shoulder, nodding once. A soldier to her left circled around one of the vehicles and reached inside, extracting a zip-tied man from the back seat.

Glennon narrowed her gaze, her fingers tightening around the gun's stock. The man's size, stature, even his walk, revealed his identity before the headlights did. Restrained, bruised and bloodied, he stared straight at her through swollen eyelids as her stomach flipped. "Bennett."

They'd captured him. The investigation against Mascaro's operation, the evidence, all of it depended on him. Without Bennett, she couldn't close this case. Without him…she had nothing. Jamie Mascaro was going to kill him, and the army would be forced to drop the investigation. She'd walk free. But then why was Jamie Mascaro still here? She had what she wanted.

The gunman shoved Bennett down onto his knees.

"Move." Anthony pushed the operative behind her forward. Dust clouded the streak of headlights shining on them, but she caught sight of the blade at the soldier's throat clearly. "You have three seconds to bring out the boy or I start gutting your men one by one."

Another laugh reached her ears. Jamie Mascaro hiked a hand to her waist. "Oh, I like you. Need a job, Ranger? The pay is phenomenal."

Glennon shifted her weight between her feet. Coldness worked down into her bones. The snake already had what she wanted. What more could she—

The realization hit hard, the air rushing from her lungs as though she'd taken a punch to the stomach. Ice worked through her. Jamie Mascaro wasn't just after Bennett Spencer. The new head of the operation wanted more. "We had a deal."

"One," Anthony said.

"A deal that you broke, Sergeant Chase. Granted, I planned on breaking it to begin with, but you beat me to the punch. Now we're going to strike a new deal. One you won't be able to back out of." The woman came closer, balancing on those impractical heeled boots. High-arched eyebrows, thin lips and piercing eyes came into focus. "Bring out the boy."

Every muscle along Glennon's spine tensed. She swallowed back the tightness in her throat. Seconds passed. A full minute. She scanned the ring of vehicles, covering the glare of headlights with one hand as she squinted past the brightness. Where was he?

Anthony stilled, waiting, with the soldier still struggling in his grip. But the bastard was no match for her Ranger. No one was.

A small outline rushed from between the vehicles but was held back by one of Jamie Mascaro's men. "Mommy!"

"Hunter." Glennon took a step forward, ready to risk going up against assault rifles and the men carrying them to get to him. She dropped the gun to her side. He didn't need to see her holding a weapon. He was scared enough. "I'm here, baby. This will all be over soon."

"Let go!" The four-year-old swiped at the soldier holding on to him, but the hits didn't faze Mascaro's man.

Hers would. And the second she had the chance, she'd take every single one of them out.

"You're right. This will all be over soon." Jamie Mascaro raised a gun of her own, a small Ruger she'd hidden in her coat pocket, and aimed. At Anthony. "But not for you, Sergeant Chase. I want to get to know you better."

With a direct hit to the soldier in his hold, Anthony knocked the operative unconscious.

Glennon's heart worked to explode out of her chest.

Anthony discarded his hostage into the snow, and stepped between her and Jamie Mascaro. Always the protector. Always putting her first. "You're out of your damn mind if you think a bullet from you will stop me from getting to that boy."

Nausea rolled through her. Then rage. Hell no, it wouldn't. Anthony would fight until the job was finished, bullet wounds be damned. But... She couldn't lose him. Not again. "You want Sergeant Spencer in exchange for my son—" she took a deep, cleansing breath, Mascaro's intentions crystal-clear now "—and you want me in exchange for Sergeant Major Harris."

The weight of Anthony's wide gaze compressed the air in her lungs. "Not happening."

"You're one of the few people who know who I am." Jamie Mascaro held the Ruger steady. "And I can't have you running around revealing my identity. If word got out who was running my husband's operation..." She cocked her head to one side. "Let's just say I worked too long and too hard to overthrow Nicholas to lose allies because I'm a woman."

Sweat dripped down Glennon's spine. Her mouth dried. "The deal you made. It was a setup from the

beginning. You weren't ever planning on letting me go home with my son."

"Well, I am a criminal, Sergeant Chase. You had to see it coming," Mascaro said.

Hunter for Bennett. Anthony for her. Glennon straightened a bit more. Judging by the way the woman's hand shook holding the gun up for this long, she could take out Jamie Mascaro, no problem. The woman wasn't a soldier. She'd just taken control of her husband's criminal organization. Glennon would be cutting off the head of the snake. But... Her shoulders sank. There was no guarantee Mascaro's men wouldn't follow through with their orders. That left Anthony, Bennett and Hunter all at risk. A risk she couldn't afford.

"Glennon," Anthony said, "don't even think about it. We'll find another way."

He could always read her. That was what made him so damn good at his job. She focused on Hunter struggling to get free of the armed soldier behind him, then memorized everything she could about the operative. When she had the chance, she'd make him pay for putting his hands on her son.

There was no other way. At least, not one that would get Hunter home tonight. And as for Anthony... Glennon tossed the weapon she'd lifted off the soldier into the snow. She wouldn't lose him again. Not like this. "You've done the job I hired you for, sweetheart, but I'm assigning you a new one." A faint smile curled her lips. When would be the next time he called her that? Her throat threatened to close as she raised her hands over her head in surrender to Jamie Mascaro.

"Take care of our son."

Chapter Thirteen

She was tearing him apart.

"You're not doing this." Anthony wrapped his hand around her arm, jerking her into him. Like hell his job was finished. Did she honestly think he'd let her walk away again? After everything they'd been through? They had a son together. His muscles ached from tension, every cell in his body ready to rip these bastards apart with his bare hands. Only he couldn't. Not with a chance of Hunter getting caught in the crosshairs. He unclenched his jaw. "I won't lose you again."

"You're running out of time, Sergeant Chase," Jamie Mascaro said.

Four operatives left, each armed with an M4 assault rifle. Plus Jamie Mascaro and her Ruger. Any one of those bullets could rip apart his life. Anthony tightened his grip on the gun he'd taken from the bastard who'd dared put his hands on Glennon. The knife wouldn't do a damn bit of good. Six rounds. Five targets. His attention slid to Hunter. One innocent, perfect, four-year-old boy. Didn't leave a whole lot of room for error.

"You're not losing me." She framed his jawline with her hands, brilliant green eyes locked on him. A rush of her rosy scent drove straight into his lungs. "Besides,

you're not the only one trained in combat, Ranger. I know how to take care of myself."

Yet she'd offered herself up as the perfect hostage.

Rage rode him hard, but he tried to hold it back. For her. For Hunter. "I can do this. Say the word and I'll—"

Glennon fastened her hands behind his neck and pulled him against her. His mouth crashed onto hers. Ferocious desire exploded through him, igniting his strongest protective instincts. Having her to himself these last three days... It wasn't enough. It would never be enough. She had worked herself under his skin, and he had no idea how to get her out. Didn't want to know how. Her hands slid against his cheek. So soft. So...final.

Pulling away from him, Glennon set her forehead against his. "Protect Hunter. No matter what."

"Enough." Jamie Mascaro's voice penetrated the haze clouding his mind. Two soldiers came forward and ripped Glennon out of his hold. "I'm running out of patience."

His fingers burned against the dropping temperatures and the freezing steel of the rifle in his hand. Anthony took a single step forward, fire raging in his veins, but two more assault rifle barrels promised to cut him down if given the chance. He couldn't help her. Couldn't save her. But he could save their son. "This isn't over, Mascaro. Doesn't matter where you hide, I'm coming for you."

"I look forward to it, Ranger. But remember. I saved your life today. I could've killed you anytime and you wouldn't have seen it coming." Jamie Mascaro turned her back on him with a nod to the operative holding onto his son. "Shoot Sergeant Major Harris if he

moves an inch." She paused. "Better yet. Shoot *her* if he moves an inch."

"Mommy!" Hunter ran through the snow, wrapping his arms around his mother's legs, and Anthony's gut clenched. "Where are you going?"

"Stay with Anthony, baby." Glennon didn't have the chance to stop as the two operatives at her side pulled her toward the waiting vehicles, leaving Hunter in the snow. Alone.

Anthony fanned his grip over the gun in his hand. He couldn't take a step. Not without igniting an all-out war. Her footsteps wavered as they led her to one of the SUVs. December flakes disrupted the blinding light coming from the headlights, but the heartbreak in her last words was clear. She didn't believe she was coming home. Her voice strained as she looked back over her shoulder. "He's going to watch over you until I can come home, okay?"

Another soldier wrenched Bennett to his feet and hurled him back inside one of the waiting vehicles. Separate from his partner.

Anthony tried to get his control back, but Glennon had been the only one who could talk him down from the brink of rage. Always had been. His heart beat too loud, the rush of adrenaline too strong. He gripped the gun hard. He had to focus. Breathe. But every breath pressurized in his lungs.

He had to get her back. He *would* get her back. But not right now.

He watched as Glennon ripped herself out of the soldiers' holds, determined to walk on her own. She'd let this play out, but on her terms. Despite the fact she was walking away from him—again—Anthony had

to respect her for that. Two gunmen collected their unconscious soldiers from the snow a few feet away, loading them into one of the SUVs.

Engines growled to life as Glennon paused, her gaze locking on his. A single nod was all she gave him before ducking inside the waiting vehicle, Jamie Mascaro close behind. In thirty seconds, the road was clear, snowflakes dimming distant taillights.

She was gone.

"Hunter." Anthony dropped the rifle and rushed forward, sliding onto his knees as he wrapped his arms around the boy. Cold worked through his clothing and deep into his bones. He lifted Hunter against him. "It's okay. I've got you. You're safe."

His son shook in his arms. "Where's Mommy going?"

"She'll be right back." Anthony stared after the disappearing convoy. Spinning back toward his SUV, he hung on to Hunter with everything he had. "I promise."

He wrenched the back door open, tossing the remains of the flash grenade into the snow. After securing his son in the seat, he pulled his emergency kit from the hidden compartment in the floor.

Anthony exhaled hard. His son. Hell, he had a son. He still couldn't believe Glennon had kept Hunter from him.

He wrapped his son in the blanket from his kit, pure green eyes—the same shade as Glennon's—staring up at him. Running his hand through the boy's short blond hair, he curled his hand around the back of Hunter's neck. No more mistakes. No distractions. Glennon was coming home. But first he had to get Hunter to safety. He extracted the burner phone stashed under

the extra ammunition and hit the speed dial for Blackhawk Security.

The line rang only once.

"Oh, good. You're alive." Sullivan Bishop's voice pulled the logistical side of his mind onto the next operation: recovering Glennon Chase. "I was beginning to wonder."

"Glennon's been taken," he said.

"Give me the details." Two snapping sounds crossed the line. Sullivan most likely trying to get the team's attention. "Location?"

"Five operators, plus the leader, all armed with M4s. All military. I'm one mile southwest outside Far North Bicentennial Park. Track my vehicle's GPS for an exact location." He checked his watch. Anthony studied the small shed off the side of the road. "Bogies on the move two minutes and counting, headed north. One civilian left behind." His gaze cut to Hunter huddled in the blanket, drifting off to sleep. His son was safe. That was all that mattered. His jaw hung open, heart rate dropping as adrenaline drained from his veins. "Send whoever you've got. Now."

"We have your location. Elizabeth, Vincent and Elliot are wheels-up in two," Sullivan said. "ETA fifteen minutes."

His grip tightened around the phone, the plastic protesting. Fifteen minutes. Too long. Every minute he wasted waiting around for backup, the greater the chance he'd lose the convoy's tracks. Anthony forced his tongue from the top of his mouth. But he wasn't about to put Hunter in danger. The boy had been through enough. First being taken from his grandmother by force, then losing his mother.

He didn't have a choice. He had to wait.

"Hold on a second." Sullivan's end of the line went silent. Two seconds. Three. In less than two minutes, Glennon could be anywhere in Anchorage. Jamie Mascaro had the resources and the contacts to get a private plane out of the state in under an hour. They had to make a move. Now. "Vincent had his contact in Anchorage PD forward the forensics report from the scene at Helen Chase's home."

Anticipation flooded through him. "And?"

"The shooter's boots had a specific gravel stuck in the treads, and we were able to track it to a stretch of warehouses near Tina Lake. The system matched it instantly to the manufacturer, thanks to an unsolved robbery from last year. Could be a lead on your girl," Sullivan said. "And don't think we aren't going to talk about the bullet in that guy's leg. It's only a matter of time before Anchorage PD gets a hit on the ballistics."

The bastard was lucky one bullet was all Glennon had had the stomach for, considering he'd helped Jamie Mascaro kidnap her son.

"Is the shooter talking?" The warehouse theory was all they had, but he wasn't about to go in blind. Too many risks. Too many ways the entire operation could go sideways. Too many ways he could lose Glennon for good. "Anything I can use?"

"No." Sullivan lowered his voice. "Listen, Anchorage PD is collecting a lot of bodies linked to this investigation. They can't charge you with anything yet, but, Anthony, I've been there. I know exactly what you're thinking."

Sullivan had been there. One month ago when his own brother had come back from the dead to target

Captain Jane Reise, Sullivan's then-client and now the love of his life. The former SEAL had shot his own flesh and blood to save the woman he loved. Something Anthony was more than prepared to do for Glennon. "So promise me whatever happens when the Grim Reaper comes calling, it'll be clean. For your own good and mine."

Anthony stared into the fresh tracks at his feet. If it hadn't been for Sullivan, he would've been left for dead in Afghanistan during his last mission for the Rangers. He owed the former SEAL his life. But no matter how much he wanted to give his word, to promise this wouldn't come back onto Blackhawk Security and his team, he couldn't. Jamie Mascaro was about to find out exactly what kind of monster Anthony had caged all these years.

"Redirect the team. Have them meet me at Tina Lake." He hung up then dropped the phone into the snow, crushing it under his boot. Wrenching open the driver's-side door, he hurried in behind the wheel. The engine growled to life and he shoved the SUV into Drive. He hiked himself higher in the seat to get a better view of the back seat, of his son. The boy stared sleepily back at him. Anthony took a deep breath. No question. Just as Sullivan had been given the choice, he'd do whatever it took to recover the love of his life. Forget duty. Forget why she'd hired him in the first place. He wasn't going anywhere. Not without Glennon.

"Let's go get your mom, buddy."

GLENNON OPENED HER EYES, gasping. Clarity came in a sudden, sharp rush. Ice squeezed her body as she

fought against the zip ties at her wrists and ankles. Her head pounded. What the hell had Mascaro drugged her with? She brought her bound hands to her neck, wincing, cold seeping into her clothing. The injection site burned. The convoy had gone maybe a mile from the abandoned water shed when she'd been drugged. She could be anywhere right now. Shaking off the gripping effects of the drug, she focused on the only source of warmth pressed against one side of her.

Bennett?

His shoulders rose and fell in even currents. He was alive—breathing—but had most likely been drugged with the same cocktail. She blinked against the pain tightening the muscles down the back of her neck. She had to focus. Make a plan. Because she wasn't dying today. Not when she'd gotten her son back. Not when she'd gotten Anthony back. She shifted on the cold cement floor. They had to get out of here. Glennon studied the massive empty space. Wherever here was. "Bennett, wake up."

Shoving against her partner, she sat up. A wave of dizziness closed in fast, but she kept her balance. Barely. She uncurled her stiff fingers. Had Jamie Mascaro really stripped them of their coats? Reaching for her boots, she untied her shoelaces then tied them together through the ties at her wrists. She'd never had to saw her way through zip ties before, but there was a first time for everything. Seesawing her feet back and forth, she worked through the plastic. The muscles down her thighs burned, her body heavy.

Movement registered to her left. Lights flared from around a closed door. Someone was coming. She worked faster, harder. Mascaro had made her inten-

tions perfectly clear. She and Bennett were to be interrogated then dealt with. Killed.

The ties at her wrists snapped, but she still had to deal with her ankles. And her partner. "Bennett."

A deep groan reached her ears. "Why does it feel like someone hit me over the head?"

"If you don't get yourself out of those zip ties, you're going to have a much bigger headache when Jamie Mascaro puts a bullet between your eyes." She inhaled long and deep, forcing her heart rate to slow. Concentrate.

"Why, Glennon, is that you?" Pain roughened his voice. Bennett struggled to sit up, his boots scraping against the cold cement floor. The light from around the door reflected off the whites of his eyes, but it was still too dark to make out anything other than a few old haul trucks. "Last thing I remember is someone sticking a needle in my neck while I was scouting out the location. Did we win?"

"Not yet." Her hands shook. She balled them into fists and stretched her knees out to opposite sides. With one strong push on either knee, the zip tie around her ankles snapped. She bit back a moan as the plastic cut into her briefly, then pushed to her feet. "Mascaro changed the rules. She exchanged Hunter for you. Then Anthony's life for mine."

A laugh rumbled from Bennett's chest as she crouched beside him to help him sit straight. "And here I thought the woman who wants me dead would stick to her word. Shame on me."

"And here I thought I could trust my partner. Shame on me." The words left her mouth much sharper than

she'd intended. But there were some sins that couldn't be wiped clean with a joint abduction.

Glennon unlaced his boots and retied them as she'd done with hers. The ties snapped after a full minute of silence. He could take care of his ankles himself. Standing, she surveyed the space. A warehouse of some kind. Moisture clung to the air, dampening her clothing more than the sweat working down her collarbone. A warehouse near water. Lake or Pacific Ocean? Only one way to find out.

"Glennon, wait." Bennett straightened, his dark outline wobbling toward her before his strength returned. The dizziness. Whatever Jamie Mascaro had drugged them with clung tight to their nervous systems. Who knew how long it would pull them down? "I need you to know why I did it. Why I joined Nicholas Mascaro's crew. It wasn't for the money, although it was a nice perk."

"I don't think now is a good time." She ran her sweaty palms down her jeans, searching for another door in the barren space. Too dark. They'd have to spread out. Fast. Before the guys with guns came back.

"We're not being shot at yet," Bennett said. "I think now is the perfect time."

Something in her snapped. What was it with the men in her life determined to talk things through at the most inconvenient times? He wanted to talk about this now? With Jamie Mascaro and her traitorous soldiers right outside the door? Fine. Her face heated then went ice-cold. "It doesn't matter why you did it, Bennett. You lied to me. You betrayed me and this country. I let you into my life, into my son's life. I trusted you and you threw it in my face—"

"Nicholas Mascaro was a witness in my sister's disappearance." Bennett ran a shadowed hand over his face. "He saw the suspect two minutes before she vanished off base."

What? Her stomach sank. The American flag pin. She'd known it had belonged to his sister, but the reason he'd held on to it… Damn. Losing someone that close, someone you loved more than anything, would change anyone. For better or for worse. Anthony's pale features as he lost blood due to his wounds in the parking garage flashed across her mind. She couldn't imagine that pain. Didn't want to imagine it.

Glennon swallowed hard, her throat closing. "I'm sorry. I didn't… You never said anything."

"Well, it's not exactly something I advertise, seeing as how she's the reason I chose to betray my country. And my partner." He tapped his knuckles into her arm. "Nicholas brought me into the operation to help find her abductor. Made me a lieutenant to gain the trust of his contacts and use them to track down the man who…". A shaky inhale reached her ears through the darkness. "The guy might've been the head of a criminal organization, but he was the only lead I had. In return, I got him access to the big guns on base. Before I knew it, I was embedded deeper than I intended. Guess his wife doesn't like that."

"Did you find him? The man who took your sister?" Glennon ran her hands along the nearest wall, searching for anything that could get them outside. Ten seconds passed. Twenty. The hairs on the back of her neck stood on end. Every cell in her body waited in anticipation as Bennett searched the other side of the room.

"No, I never found him." His voice lightened as he

maneuvered past her toward another wall. "And I never will if we don't get the hell out of here."

Right. Glennon shook off the tightness in her chest, staring after his retreating form. Jamie Mascaro wasn't going to wait around for them to make up before she put a bullet in their heads. But one thing was clear. "I would've done the same thing, you know."

Bennett froze mid-escape. "Done what, exactly?"

"If I'd lost the one person I loved more than anyone in the world like that, I would've done whatever I had to, to find whoever had taken them from me." She took a step forward. The image of Anthony rushing toward her son out the back window of the SUV—their son—after she'd surrendered herself had burned itself into her mind. It was that exact moment when she'd realized what she was losing by getting into the back seat of the SUV with Jamie Mascaro: her family.

No matter how hard she'd fought to keep him at arm's length, no matter how many times she'd tried to convince herself he'd leave when duty called, her Ranger had worked his way back into her heart. She'd fallen in love with him again. Probably had never fallen out of it in the first place. And hell, she wanted nothing more than to feel his massive arms around her right now. At least then she'd feel safe. Secure. And not alone. "The only difference is I would've trusted my partner."

Bennett didn't have a chance to answer.

"Over here." Her fingers grazed over a door frame in the darkness. She slid her palm across the freezing metal. Knocking once, she set her ear against the steel. There was nothing on the other side as far as she could tell. Hopefully no one waiting to put a handful

of bullets in their chests. Maybe they were going to escape this nightmare after all. She ran her hands along the metal. What kind of door didn't have a doorknob? "Okay, maybe not."

"Let me see." Heavy footsteps approached from behind. Bennett's hands collided with hers as he inspected the door by feel, and she drew back. He launched his shoulder into the steel. Once. Twice.

It wouldn't budge. A rough exhale feathered against her chilled skin and she ran her hands up and down her arms for warmth. If Jamie Mascaro planned on leaving them in here to freeze to death, she had a good start. "Is it still considered a door if there's no way to open it?"

Glennon faced the rest of the space. "There has to be another way out of here. Isn't it against code to only have one exit?"

"Do you honestly believe Mascaro is concerned with the building code?" Bennett's voice shook, whether from the drugs or the dropping temperatures, she didn't know. Either way, they didn't have much time. Jamie Mascaro was going to kill her and Bennett, or else the warehouse would. "I ran with Nicholas and his crew for over a year. I know every property he acquired to store the stolen weapons. This isn't one of them."

"I don't think knowing the property would make any difference against a team of armed infantrymen." Movement from under the lit doorway rocketed her pulse into dangerous territory. A weapon. She patted herself down then rushed toward one of the trucks a few feet away. They needed something to fight off Mascaro and her operatives.

Glennon pulled herself up the single step to the passenger-side door. There. The broken shifter. She

wrenched the door open, the hinges screaming in protest. Bringing a metal pipe to a gunfight wasn't the best idea, but it was the only shot they had. She traced a path back to the spot they'd been bound, then to the door.

Bennett took up the other side. Waiting.

The door opened. Yellow light spilled across the floor, outlining two distinct shadows.

Glennon swung as hard as she could. Metal connected with bone, the crunch sickening and loud. The soldier hit the ground as another rushed forward. Bennett collided with the operative, taking him to the ground. Two more surged through the door, both armed with assault rifles, and took aim.

She tossed the pipe and backed away from the door, hands raised in surrender. Fear thickened in her veins. This was it. These men were going to kill her. She'd never get the chance to tell Anthony why she'd left Anchorage in the first place. Never see her son again. Her throat tightened as she fought to breathe evenly. This couldn't be it. Not yet. He deserved to know she loved him.

The echo of heels on cement grew louder. Then stopped. Overhead lighting highlighted Jamie Mascaro's thin lips and stone-cold expression. The skintight black leather dress accentuated the woman's curves, but it was the hatred in her expression that raised the hairs on the back of Glennon's neck.

"Bring them with us as collateral." Mascaro closed in, studying Glennon's features from forehead to chin before turning away. "We've got company."

Chapter Fourteen

The Grim Reaper wasn't supposed to fall in love, but that rule had gone out the window a long time ago. Jamie Mascaro could beat him, take his life or break his soul, but he'd be damned if he let her take Glennon.

He crouched along the shoreline of Tina Lake, the MK 17 SCAR assault rifle from his trunk resting across his thighs. Abandoned vehicles, semi-trailers, mountains of dirt and greenery all held potential for an ambush. Too many possibilities. At this time of night, the entire area had been vacated. Perfect for a militarized criminal organization to operate undetected. Gravel—the same color Vincent had matched to their shooter from Helen Chase's home—slid through his fingers easily. No movement. But that didn't mean they weren't alone. Four warehouses, any of which could hold two Military Police investigators.

And time was running out.

"I counted five operatives at the exchange, all armed with M4s, plus the leader, but I'm not taking any chances." And with his son handed off into Vincent's care after the team had met him on location, he could focus on getting Glennon back. Standing, Anthony brushed dirt off his hand along his pants, his

Kevlar vest pressing on his shoulders. He faced off with Elizabeth Dawson and Elliot Dunham, their features and choice of weapons highlighted by construction spotlights surrounding the area.

A former NSA consultant and a con artist. Not soldiers, but just as reliable and just as dangerous under the right circumstances. And these were the right circumstances. "We'll search this first building then move on to the next until we find Jamie Mascaro's hideout. Liz, you're at the north entrance." He pointed straight ahead. "Elliot, at the east. I'll take the south. Your earpieces have GPS if you're taken. Meet back here in five to search the next building. We good?"

He tapped the small earbud in his left ear. Both teammates cringed from the sound.

"Good." Elizabeth unholstered her weapon from beneath her black leather jacket, both hands tight on the grip.

"I'm thinking I should've brought a bigger gun." Elliot raised one hand. "Can I switch with you?"

"How about I ignore your GPS if you're taken? Let's move. Mascaro won't keep our targets alive long." If she hadn't tied up the loose ends already. No. He couldn't think like that. The second he gave in to that line of thinking, there was no telling what he might do. Or who he might kill. Anthony kept low and moved fast to the south end of the first warehouse, gravel crunching under his boots.

"Do you think he'll really ignore my GPS if I'm kidnapped?" Elliot's whispers died as he and Elizabeth moved around the east side of the building.

Setting one shoulder into the door, Anthony pressed his ear to the steel. Nothing. The breeze rustled the

weeds lining the lake a few hundred yards away, a couple red foxes wrestling along the shore. But no sound of movement from behind the door, as far as he could tell.

He tested the lock then hiked the rifle into his shoulder. His instincts screamed in warning. Who left a warehouse like this unlocked in the middle of the night? Maneuvering in front of the entrance, Anthony wrenched the door open and slapped his hand into position on the rifle. The answer came easily enough: a criminal mastermind who expected company.

Darkness consumed him as he heel-toed it into the building. His heart beat steadily in his chest, the rest of his senses on high alert. He didn't need to see in the dark to find Glennon. This was what he'd trained for, what he'd been hired for. This was what he did best. Steel reverberated underneath him as he stepped onto an overhead walkway. He scanned the space below with what little light reached across the warehouse floor. Oil barrels, haul trucks, a couple forklifts. Alaska was known for its oil exports. This place had obviously been one of the six oil refinery storage warehouses in the state.

He moved down the center walkway. His thigh holster ricocheted off one of the handrails, the ping of metal loud in his ears. Anthony tightened his hold on the rifle's grip. So much for the element of surprise.

The walkway sparked as gunfire erupted off to his right.

He hit the walkway hard. The raised metal edges cut into his cheek, but didn't distract from the shooter below. Shoving to his feet, Anthony swung his rifle over the handrail and down toward the shooter. One pull of the trigger. Two. The rifle kicked back into his

shoulder. He released the breath he'd been holding. No return fire. Either he'd hit the soldier or the shooter had started searching for a better shot.

Keeping aim, he moved across the walkway, deeper into the warehouse. Adrenaline rushed through his veins. Light from an open door spilled across the cement floor. And there, right at the edge of darkness, was a pair of boots. He tapped his earpiece, moving to the other side of the warehouse. "I've got one down. Report."

"Two down for me," Elizabeth said. "Looks like we're in the right place after all."

"Oh, man. You guys got to shoot people already?" Elliot's heavy breathing crackled over the line. "I've got nothing but offices on this side of the building. And they're all empty so far."

"That makes three. We're missing at least two more, plus Jamie Mascaro." Anthony took the stairs two at a time. Swinging the rifle across the large space, he kicked at the downed operative's boots. He'd been shot all right. Two bullets. One to the soldier's vest, the other to his throat. He wasn't getting up anytime soon. "The warehouse is clear."

"The offices are clear," Elliot said in his ear.

"I'm clear here, too," Elizabeth said. "There's no one else here."

"Mascaro wouldn't have left three men behind for nothing. We're missing something." Anthony searched the rest of the space. Dark spots interrupted the muted gray color of the cement floor about ten feet away. His footsteps echoed off the oil barrels as he followed the pattern to the west side of the building, toward the lake. Could be oil. Could be… He locked onto the

wide roll-top door. Blood. He tapped the earpiece. "Oil warehouses like this would need access to the water to load barrels onto ships for distribution." He pulled his shoulders back. "They're on the docks."

Sliding his finger along the trigger, Anthony took a single step toward the door. Something crunched under his boot. Four distinct zip ties littered the floor. Fury burned through him. Two for Glennon and two for Bennett? He kicked them out of the way. They'd been broken. Maybe she and her partner had gotten loose? Didn't explain the blood, but at least that line of thought interrupted the rage threatening to rip him apart from the inside. He took a deep, cleansing breath. Glennon had always been the one to bring him back from the edge when he'd come home from tour, and he prayed like hell she could do it when this was over.

"I want everyone on the west side of the building in thirty seconds."

"Copy that," Elizabeth said. "On my way."

Elliot reported in next. "You got it, man."

He kicked the padlock that secured the roll-top door out of the way, pulling at the chains along the wall, forgoing the element of surprise. A rush of Alaskan air raised the goose bumps at the back of his neck—clean, crisp. With a hint of rose. He held on to that scent with everything he had. Glennon. She was close. He stepped out into the open. "I'm coming, sweetheart."

Pain splintered across the right side of his head. He jerked away from the hit, swinging the rifle toward his assailant. A kick to the chest knocked Anthony to the ground, his head hitting hard, and the gun slid across the asphalt. Vision blurred, he fought to focus. Damn it. Groping for his nearest weapon, Anthony shoved to

his feet, blade in hand. One target. He ran full-force, swinging his arm out wide.

His attacker ducked under his arm then came around and wrapped both arms under his shoulders and around his neck. Pressure built in his chest the longer the soldier cut off his air, grip tight over his trachea. Rookie move. His head pounded in rhythm with his heartbeat, the stitches in his thigh and rib cage protesting, but all it took was one shift in weight and Anthony heaved his assailant into the ground. He slammed his elbow back into the attacker's face. Once. Twice. Blood splattered against his long-sleeved shirt. The rifle was close, but by the time he got to it, the soldier would have the advantage. Not going to happen.

The unsheathing of a blade forced Anthony to roll. Rock and ice cut into him as he returned to his feet. He wrenched backward at a swing of his opponent's blade. Blocking the second swing, he caught the attacker's wrist and nearly snapped the damn thing in two. Metal on asphalt rang in his ears a split second before a scream broke the steady lapping of water nearby.

Hiking the bastard into him, he growled, "Where is she?"

Two spotlights blazed to life over the docks, spilling light across the wide-open expanse of gravel.

"We've been expecting you, Sergeant Major Harris." Jamie Mascaro stood in front of a dumpster centered between two docks, high heels sinking into the dirt. "Time to finish this."

Shoving the heel of his boot into the soldier's knee, he took the fighter out of commission. Another scream penetrated his haze of rage. He released his hold as he turned to face the newest threat. His opponent col-

lapsed. He wasn't even sorry for the lifelong pain and discomfort the man would have to endure.

Elizabeth and Elliot rounded from the east side of the building, weapons up, waiting on his order.

"I couldn't agree more." He took two steps forward. "Give me what I came for and you might make it out of here alive."

"You're not exactly in a position to make demands, Ranger." Jamie Mascaro snapped her fingers. A second set of spotlights flickered, illuminating the last two soldiers positioned at the end of each dock. One guarding Bennett, the other with Glennon. They were alive. Relief spread a burning sensation across Anthony's chest, but not for long. Each was tied to a chair on the end of the separate docks. Gagged, vulnerable, the military investigators fought to get free.

The setup was simple. If he went for one, Mascaro would order the opposite soldier to push the other into the lake. Would let them drown. "Tell me, Anthony, what's more important to you. Love?" Jamie Mascaro swung her arm out, toward Glennon. "Or duty?"

THERE WAS NO WAY Anthony could save them both in time.

Glennon glanced at the soldier watching over her, the one with blood dried across his face from a pipe to the nose. She fought back a smile. The one who'd put his hands on her son. Tasked with making sure she didn't get loose again, he'd zip-tied her wrists behind her back this time, but he'd been in a rush. Enough of a rush that she'd been able to work her knuckles against each other in an attempt to snap the plastic. The flood of relief at seeing Anthony drained her. How could it

not? There was no way both she and Bennett would get out of this alive. It was one or the other. Use Bennett to take down Jamie Mascaro and the rest of her operation or save Glennon. And if the teammates he'd recruited as backup interfered? Mascaro was sure to get rid of both her and Bennett simultaneously.

That had been the beauty of her plan.

But… Her gaze cut to the sidearm strapped to her guard's leg. There was more than one way to break a zip tie. Curling her fingers into her palms, she closed her eyes. She hadn't died in that warehouse. She wasn't going to die out here on the dock.

"What's it going to be, Ranger? Use Sergeant Spencer to bring me and my operation to justice or save the woman you love?" Jamie Mascaro wagged her red-tipped index finger from side to side. "Ticktock, ticktock."

Anthony curled his fingers into a fist. Even from this distance, Glennon noted the hard shift in his expression and her heart pumped a frenzied beat in her chest. Air rushed from her lungs and the gag in her mouth warmed. She recognized that look. Anthony Harris no longer stared out through the dark blue eyes she hadn't been able to get out of her mind the last five years. He'd been replaced by the man who'd had to shoot his way out of Afghanistan to survive, the man who blamed himself for his team's deaths.

The man who'd slowly taken pieces of the Ranger she'd loved every time he'd come home from tour. She couldn't lose another piece of him. She wouldn't.

"Who said anything about justice?" Anthony fanned his grip over his firearm.

A shiver chased down her spine, the chair protest-

ing with the slight shake of her body. But the creak
of wood wasn't enough to draw her guard's attention.
She needed something more—anything—before it was
too late.

"Time's up." Jamie Mascaro angled her head over
her shoulder. Toward Glennon.

Planting her knuckles against each other, Glennon
forced them together with everything she had. Pain
bolted into her wrists and forearms, but she ignored it.
The zip tie snapped and she reached for the soldier's
sidearm. She wrapped her fingers around the grip but
wasn't fast enough.

A rough hand clamped on top of hers a split second before agony exploded across the right side of her
head. She hit the dock hard, splinters working their way
under her fingers. A predatory growl ripped through
the haze closing in on her. Her vision blurred. Gunfire
echoed off the lake. The operative fisted a chunk of her
hair, wrenching Glennon to her feet. She grabbed at
his hand to relieve the spread of pain, her jaw locked
against the groan working up her throat.

A bullet clipped her attacker's shoulder and he spun
fast, taking her to the ground with him.

A splash of water reached her ears.

Dread sank like a stone in her stomach. Bennett.
The soldier assigned to guard him had pushed him into
the water and had started firing on Anthony and his
team. She rammed the heel of her hand into her guard's
bullet wound as hard as she could, but the grip in her
hair refused to let up. Raising her hands, she slammed
her forearms into his. His hold dropped and she ducked
as the soldier reached to secure her again. She planted
her hands against his chest and shoved him only mere

inches. She went for the gun in his thigh holster again, barely unholstering the Glock before he kicked it out of her hand. It hit the dock, out of reach. She dove for the weapon as two more gunshots cut through the silence from the other dock. Her fingertips skimmed the metal as her guard pulled her back to him by her boot.

"Elliot, no!" Elizabeth Dawson's warning pierced through the gunfire.

"I'm hit!" Elliot said.

Oh, no. One of Anthony's team had been taken down. The soldier flipped her onto her back, pinning her beneath him. They had to get to Bennett. Without him, Jamie Mascaro's operation would live. Millions more military weapons would reach the country's enemies.

Long fingers wrapped around her throat. She tried prying her guard's grip loose. But he was too strong. Too heavy. She kicked against him, but he wouldn't let up. Darkness closed in. Pressure built in her chest— there was no way for her to get the oxygen out. Glennon bucked again.

Wrenching her off the dock, the soldier slammed her head back against the old wood.

Her body wouldn't respond to her brain's commands. Get up. She had to get up. Stars in the night sky blurred, her attacker's face losing definition. Ringing filled her ears.

Low, fast-paced vibrations reverberated along the dock. A gun barrel slid into her vision, aimed between the operative's eyes. Then *he* slid into her vision. Her heart stopped. Stopped then started racing. The man staring out through those dark blue eyes was blood and

death and war, but in that moment he was everything she needed him to be. "I've been looking for you."

The operative released her, raising his hands over his head as he stood.

She swallowed against the bruising tightness in her throat. Rolling onto her side, Glennon clawed out from under her attacker and coughed to restart her lungs. Her vision cleared, her throat raw. She wrapped her hand around the Glock she'd taken from the soldier and disengaged the safety. Hiking the gun over her shoulder, she used Anthony for balance and climbed to her feet.

"You put your hands on my son," Anthony said over Elizabeth and Elliot's gunshots on the other dock.

The operative's attention slid to Anthony then back to her. "Better hope your bodyguard is a good shot. One bullet isn't going to stop me from carrying out my orders, sweetheart."

"She's not your sweetheart." Anthony fired. Once. Twice. The man assigned to toss her into the lake collapsed. One bullet to the cheek. One to the head. "She's mine."

Exhaustion pulled at her muscles, but it wasn't over yet. Bennett. They had to get to Bennett. A wave of dizziness messed with her balance and she overcorrected. Strong hands righted her. Glennon adjusted her grip on the gun. Her breath heaved in and out of her lungs. She blinked to clear her head. Movement from across the lake drew her attention to the second dock, where Bennett had gone into the water.

Elizabeth and Elliot worked together and hauled her unconscious partner from the depths.

Relief flooded through her. "We've got him—"

A bullet to the shoulder twisted Anthony around,

two more sinking home in his thigh and hip as he raised his Beretta. His boot slipped at the edge of the dock and he plunged backward into the lake.

"No!" The water consumed him, beads spraying across her face. Glennon lunged as rough hands wrenched her backward. She gripped her attacker's wrist and hiked it around and up, flattening out the last soldier's arm. One hit with her elbow broke the bone and she used the space between her index finger and thumb to jam his trachea.

He clamped a hand over his throat and hit the dock hard, his wrist still in her grasp.

A gunshot from behind spun Glennon around, fists up.

"You've surprised me, Sergeant Chase. But now, it's just you and me." Jamie Mascaro's heels thudded across the dock. Motioning the injured soldier up with her Ruger, the weapons dealer nodded at Glennon's discarded Glock. He collected it then pushed Glennon forward. One shot. That was all it would take for Jamie Mascaro to get away with kidnapping and murder, to disappear to some non-extradition country while pocketing millions of dollars in profit from the stolen weapons. "You had your suspect. I served my husband up on a silver platter. You arrested Nicholas, but you couldn't let me have this, could you? Couldn't let me show that bastard I wasn't something he owned, that I was strong enough without him."

The gun wobbled in Jamie Mascaro's hand, the lines around the woman's mouth deeper than Glennon remembered.

"It's over, Mascaro. Sergeant Spencer has all the evidence we need to court-martial the soldiers you re-

cruited, and send you to prison for the rest of your
life." The ache in her chest refused to dissipate. It grew
stronger every second Anthony stayed beneath the surface. Every second she didn't know whether he'd survived. "There've been too many lives taken already.
This doesn't have to end with more blood."

"You took everything from me!" Jamie Mascaro
gripped both hands around the Ruger's grip. "And now
you're going to pay."

Water splashed from the surface of the lake and the
soldier positioned behind Glennon disappeared.

A growl ripped from Anthony's throat, streams of
water running down his face. The veins in his arms
struggled from beneath his skin as blood dripped to
the dock. "Not if I have anything to say about that."

"It's not possible." Jamie Mascaro backed up a step.
Her bottom lip quivered as she aimed the Ruger at the
Ranger. "Why won't you just die?"

"Anthony!" Glennon shoved him out of the way
and lunged. Wrapping her arms around Mascaro, she
wrenched the woman to one side, but the edge of the
dock was much closer than she'd originally estimated.
The world tilted on its axis as they fell into the lake.
Water worked into her mouth and nose, freezing her
from the inside. Pressure built in her lungs, but she refused to release her grip.

Jamie Mascaro fought, clawing toward the surface,
kicking at her with those ridiculous heels. No. She
didn't get to take Anthony from her. Glennon tightened her hand around a bare ankle. Mascaro kicked at
her again. Shadows passed above them, highlighted by
the spotlights. Ten seconds. That was all she needed.
Jamie Mascaro would pass out and they could end this

nightmare. Her heart pounded hard in her chest. Bubbles escaped her nose and mouth.

A wave of disturbed water rushed against her.

She was running out of air. Her grip on Mascaro's ankle began to slip as darkness closed in.

Chapter Fifteen

He had her.

Anthony tightened his hold on the dripping wet woman in his arms. The horrible clawing in his chest had finally subsided. She'd come too close to death. He'd nearly lost her, but he'd be damn certain he never would again.

Perched at the back of the ambulance, they had a clear view of the scene. He set his chin on the crown of Glennon's head as the EMT ripped the blood pressure cuff from her arm. Her hair had frozen in long, stringy strands, her skin was paler than normal, the hollowness in her features deeper, but Glennon had never been more beautiful to him than in that moment. She'd survived. "Are you in pain?"

"Every inch of me aches." She watched as Jamie Mascaro was led to the back of a police cruiser, a faint smile curling one corner of her mouth. "But I guess that means I'm alive, doesn't it?"

He didn't return her smile. Her partner had been recovered. Mascaro's operation had been destroyed. Their jobs were done. But every cell in his body raged. "You shouldn't have risked your life like that."

"After everything we've been through, I wasn't

about to let that woman put a bullet in you." Her shoulders rose on a strong inhale, her gaze distant. In an instant she focused on him. "Isn't that what love is? Wanting to keep the person you love most in this world safe? It's a choice. And I choose to love you, Ranger. Forever."

A growl vibrated up his throat as he stared down at her. "Say that again."

"What?" she asked. "That I love you?"

"Yes." Heat counteracted the ice working through his veins. "Say it again."

Her eyes brightened, as though she knew exactly what kind of power she held over him. "All right, but on one condition."

"Anything." Whatever she wanted, he'd give it to her. Right now. Right then. Forever. "Anything you need or want from me, it's yours."

"It's time to let it go. That guilt you carry." The light in her expression dimmed. She framed his face with one hand, her fingers driving through his beard. Glennon scanned his features. "I see it in your eyes every time I'm in danger. I see it in the way you don't hesitate to pull that trigger. Or in the way you put your life at risk time and again to protect me. You believe you could've done more for your team on tour, but I'm here to tell you, you couldn't have saved them. You did everything you could and I'm proud of you."

How could she possibly know that? Heat climbed up his spine. Anthony dropped his arm from around her, flashes of that battle to survive fresh in his mind. But Glennon fisted her fingers around his soaked Kevlar vest to keep him from retreating. She pulled him close, grounding him, keeping him in the moment.

"Glennon—"

"You're scared to lose anyone else. I've understood that more in the last three days than you'll ever know, but you're not the man I fell in love with when that guilt turns you into the Grim Reaper. You're not mine and you can't be a father with it hanging over your head." Dropping her hold, Glennon started to back away, and his pulse rocketed into his throat. "You have a new team—" she nodded toward Elliot and Elizabeth stitching up their wounds "—and now you have a family. We need *you*. Here. Now. Not a ghost of you."

Anthony engulfed her hands in his, studying the small freckles across the backs. He'd lived on that guilt, pushed himself harder, survived. Now he was supposed to let it go? How? "Is that why you left? Why you kept my son from me?"

Remnants of fury coated his words. How could he forgive her for that?

Running her thumb over the patch on his vest with one hand, she notched his chin higher with the other. "Every time you came home, you were different— lost—and I didn't understand. I didn't know what to do or how to help you. And after the last time… I left.

"I was pregnant and scared. I didn't know how much of you would come home or if you'd stay after I told you. But I was wrong." Glennon sniffled, crystalized beads of water sticking to her eyelashes. "I'm sorry. I'm sorry we wasted so much time, that I lied to you—"

Anthony pulled her into him, crushing his mouth down on hers. Because he had to. Because not kissing her had been eating at him since he'd pulled her out of that water. His fingers tangled in the frozen hair at the back of her neck as a groan escaped up his throat.

A shiver rocked through her. From the desperation in his hold on her or from the dropping temperatures, he didn't know. Either way, he'd never let go of her again. And he'd be the man she needed. He'd do whatever it took. If that meant taking himself out of the protection game or going to support meetings, he'd do it. For her. For Hunter. For their family.

Anthony pulled away first.

"I want you more than any job, more than the breath in my lungs and more than anything else in this world. I'm here, sweetheart. One hundred percent." He set his forehead against hers but kept her close, pressed into him. Her rose scent, buried under a layer of lake smells, worked down into his lungs. "You never have to worry about that side of me again. He's gone. And I'm not going anywhere."

"Good. Neither am I." Wrapping long fingers around his wrists, she closed her eyes and huddled deeper into the blanket the EMT had wrapped around her, a puddle pooling at her feet. Excess water from the lake seeped into his own clothing, freezing him to the core, but Anthony wasn't going anywhere. Not without her. "I need to get out of these clothes."

"I can help with that." He bent his mouth to hers, savoring her for another few short seconds before reality set in. Reports. Following up with Anchorage PD. Filling in the army. Reporting to Sullivan for his next assignment.

"First, take me to our son," she said, "then you can take us home."

"To the cabin?" Even on the verge of hypothermia, Glennon Chase was determined to put their son first. And he loved her for it.

He stood, with effort. Threading his fingers through hers, Anthony pulled her to him. Desire raked down his spine at her touch as he fit her against him. Right where she belonged. A quick nod solidified his plans for the future. Her and Hunter. His family. Everything he'd ever wanted. A smile curled his mouth as he planted a quick kiss to her lips. "Absolutely, sweetheart."

Red-and-blue lights illuminated the scene. The coroner's van was parked at the far end of the parking lot. Anchorage PD would want a full report, but that could wait. Glennon was his priority. She was all that mattered.

Medics wheeled Bennett Spencer past them to a second ambulance. Hypothermia. A bullet in the shoulder, another in the rib cage. He'd live. The bastard was too stubborn to die.

"Hey, hold up," Anthony called to the EMTs, motioning to the gurney with his chin. They slowed. An oxygen mask blocked most of Bennett's face. The guy looked like he'd been to hell and back. Barely conscious, blood staining his shirt, eyes sagging closed. But this couldn't wait. "Glennon wouldn't be here if it wasn't for you. I owe you."

Bennett blinked slowly at him, every breath a rasp. "Is…th-that appreciation I…h-hear?"

"Don't flatter yourself." Glancing down at Glennon, he tightened his hold on the only woman who'd been able to break him. If it hadn't been for Bennett, he wouldn't be standing there. And Glennon… He'd have lost her all over again. He'd have lost everything. "I know a good JAG Corp prosecutor. Call the office and ask for Jane Reise. Tell her I sent you. Then, when you're clear of all the charges the army will level

against you, come work for us. Blackhawk Security could use an operative like you."

Laugh lines deepened around Bennett's eyes. "Tall, dark…and hand…some?"

A laugh burst from between Glennon's pale lips.

"I take it back. You're obviously delusional from loss of blood." Squeezing her into his side, Anthony nodded at the EMTs on either side of the gurney. "Get him out of here before I change my mind."

The gurney bounced over uneven ground before the EMTs loaded Bennett into the back of the ambulance.

Steering Glennon toward his waiting SUV, Anthony studied the scene one last time. The investigation was over. Jamie Mascaro would serve the rest of her life behind bars in a women's correctional facility, within a stone's throw of the husband she'd betrayed. Glennon could put in for discharge and they could finally start their lives together. But not until—

"Mommy!" Hunter's excited voice carried over the noise of one ambulance siren and the ongoing conversations between officers. The four-year-old rushed across the gravel, leaving Vincent in the slush. Three seconds. That was all it took him to reach his mother.

Dropping to her knees, Glennon wrapped him in an all-consuming hug, planting her face into the space between his neck and shoulder. Her fingers moved along his back and dug into his shoulders. Nothing in the world would be able to part them, and Anthony would kill anyone who tried. "I missed you. Are you okay?"

Hunter nodded as the Blackhawk Security's forensics expert trod across the scene. The crooked smile Anthony couldn't get out of his mind flashed wide. "Vincent showed me how to dial 9-1-1!"

"Yeah, you were supposed to leave that part out." A big smile, surrounded by a full beard, creased the laugh lines around Vincent Kalani's brown eyes, and something significant shifted. The ex-cop never smiled. He was too serious. Too hell-bent on revenge. In the year or so Anthony had known the forensics expert, he'd never seen those pearly whites. Seemed Hunter had that effect on a lot of people.

"How very thoughtful." Glennon lightened her hold on her son long enough to throw an amused glance in Anthony's direction, and he couldn't help but laugh. "Laugh all you want, Ranger. You're going to be the one to wake up when Anchorage PD shows up at our door at three in the morning."

His laugh died as he narrowed his gaze on Vincent. "You're a dead man."

Something—no, someone—tugged on the bottom of his T-shirt. Hunter stared up at him, green eyes bright. He pulled Anthony to his knees and reached into his jacket pocket. Cupping his hand alongside his mouth, he looked over his shoulder toward his mother. The boy kept his voice low, but not low enough that Glennon couldn't hear. "Can we give Mommy her present now?"

With a single nod and a faint salute, Vincent backed toward his waiting SUV.

"Sure, buddy." Anthony held out his hand, careful to hide the gift from prying eyes. "Do you want to help?"

An enthusiastic nod curled Hunter's mouth into a smile. Anthony moved his son into position beside him. "Okay. Come here."

"When did you guys have time to get me a present?" Standing, Glennon cut her gaze to Hunter, a smile

overwhelming the paleness in her features. Confusion deepened the three distinct lines between her eyebrows.

"Down on one knee, buddy." Curling one arm around their son, Anthony mimicked Hunter's position, groaning through the new stitches in his thigh, then raised his focus to Glennon. Every muscle in his body caught fire at the sight of her. This was it. Now or never. He lowered his mouth to his son's ear. "Here we go. Say, 'Sergeant Glennon Chase.'"

"Sergeant Glennon Chase." Hunter's small voice grew louder with each word.

"What's going on?" Glennon dropped her hands to her sides, shifting her weight between both feet. Her attention ping-ponged between him and her son. "What are you doing?"

"We love you with all our heart." Anthony waited as the boy repeated every word, anticipation spreading through his chest. Every officer, Blackhawk Security operative and even the medicolegal investigator watched in silence. "We want you to be ours forever."

"We want you to be ours forever." Hunter spun from side to side, clasping his hands.

Anthony focused on the woman he'd never fallen out of love with—this beautiful, intelligent, caring, badass woman of his—offering her the gift in his hand. Slush worked through his pants as he tightened his hold around Hunter, but he didn't give a damn. He'd kneel here all night if it meant spending forever with her. With the chain looped around his middle finger, he let go. Flickering patrol lights reflected off her engagement ring as it twisted at the end of the chain. "So will you make us a family?"

One month later...

DAWN BROKE OVER the Chugach Mountain range. Perfect and cleansing.

Glennon reached out, a line of tears burning in her lower lash line as she squeezed her mother's hand. She blinked the moisture back. Her engagement band spun around the oversensitized skin of her ring finger. She couldn't breathe. Couldn't think. Was this really happening? The two most important people in the world waited for her near Campbell Lake's shoreline, but all she could do was stand there.

"Are you ready?" Helen asked.

"Hell yes." With both Mascaros behind bars, she'd submitted her discharge papers and left the army behind. She'd sold her house and moved her and her son across the country to a city she'd been determined never to step foot in again. All to be with Anthony. This was just the next step in that plan. She couldn't wait to start a life with her weapons expert. Everything she'd ever wanted waited down the aisle lined with dozens of pinecones from the nearby tree line. Her future. Her family.

The entire Blackhawk Security team rose as she got into position. Everyone except Bennett, who she wouldn't see for twelve to eighteen months after his sentencing. She raised her toes to hit the inside top of her black rain boots. "I'm ready."

Music reached her ears as she and her mother passed a stack of fresh firewood lined with white candles. Tightening her hand around the collection of wildflowers, she set sights on the man she planned to spend the rest of her life with.

Four days of stolen moments. Four days of near-death experiences. Four days of rediscovering why she'd fallen in love with Anthony Harris in the first place. That was all it had taken. Her fear of losing him to his overachieving sense of duty had vanished the second he'd dove into the lake to save her rather than take down Jamie Mascaro. The rules had gone out the window then. Hell, they might've gone out the window the moment she'd dialed his number for help. They seemed so…worthless now.

He was a protector, and a damn good one at that. He'd done his job while she'd barely held things together. And wasn't that what she needed most in the man she wanted to raise her child with? Someone she could rely on, trust? Someone who would protect her and their son with every fiber of his being?

Glennon sucked in a deep breath. She'd never had a chance when it came to him. He was hers from the minute he'd walked in to teach her firearms class in basic training all those years ago. And she'd always been his.

She studied Hunter, his expression full of anticipation. Her lips spread into a smile. Dressed in a black suit and shirt with a bright red tie, the exact same color as his father's, her son held on to Anthony with everything he had. Her Ranger—their protector—held on just as tight.

Gravel crunched under her boots as she headed down the aisle, Helen at her side. Sullivan, his significant other, Jane, Elizabeth, Vincent, Kate, even Elliot in his sling smiled and nodded as she passed. She fought to keep time with the music, but impatience tightened her fingers around the bouquet of wildflowers. The shoot-out with Jamie Mascaro hadn't taken

this long. She rolled her numb lips between her teeth. This was it. This was what forever felt like.

Getting married in the middle of January had seemed ridiculous when Anthony had suggested it. But now? Glennon couldn't wait another second without being married to her man.

"Pick up the pace, Mom." Tugging Helen along with her, she closed the distance between her and Anthony, the quartet scrambling to keep up with the change in pace. Laughter echoed off the pines surrounding them, but she pushed it to the back of her mind.

A wide smile flashed across Anthony's features, his beard speckled with fresh snowflakes.

"Here we go." Spinning into her mother, she kissed each side of Helen's face. "Thanks, Mom. For protecting me. For giving me a safe haven." She clasped both hands in hers. "For teaching me how to shoot a gun." A laugh broke through the sudden burst of emotion bubbling to the surface. "And for being there for me when I needed you the most."

"Come on, girl, I ain't dying. Not until I see my daughter married anyway." A single tear raced down Helen's wrinkled cheek. She wiped a strand of hair out of Glennon's face. "But I will say one thing. I'm proud of you, baby girl. You turned out exactly as I hoped, and I'm gonna take full credit for that." Laughter filled the clearing again as Helen turned her attention to Anthony. "And you. Don't make me use my shotgun on you, you hear?"

"Yes, ma'am." Anthony clasped his hands in front of him and nodded. Laughter glittered in his eyes and Glennon's heart skipped a beat. Even after all these

years, he affected her in new ways every second she laid eyes on him. "You have my word."

Helen took her seat, leaving Glennon with her Ranger. Sliding his calloused hands into hers, he helped maneuver her opposite him. Blue eyes, the same color as the sky above them, settled on her, and the world faded. Everything—the flickering candles off to her right, the temperature—disappeared. Only she, Hunter and Anthony remained.

"We gather here today to finally unite Glennon and Anthony in holy matrimony. And what a journey it's been, from what I understand." The minister's words died on the slight Alaskan breeze coiling through the trees as she studied the man across from her. What seemed like mere seconds later, the priest turned to her weapons expert. "Do you, Anthony, take Glennon as your lawfully wedded wife, in sickness and in health, until death do you part?"

"Before I answer, there are a few things I need to say. But not to you, sweetheart. At least, not yet."

Anthony squeezed her hand then quickly let her go. Suspicion rose the hairs on the back of her neck as he twisted to his left and knelt beside their son. "Hunter, I promise to protect you with my life. I promise to take you fishing even though I don't know how to fish, to tell you funny jokes, to help you with your homework, to give you tips on girls when you're eighteen and I can't stop you from dating, and to watch any show you want to watch, however many times."

Glennon couldn't stop the laugh rising up her throat. He was going to regret that last promise as soon as Hunter got home and forced him to watch every epi-

sode of *Mickey Mouse Clubhouse*. Her heart threatened to burst.

"You deserve a dad who can always be there for you, the best dad you could ever ask for." Anthony braced his hands on Hunter's shoulders. "And I'm going to be that guy for you, okay?"

Hunter nodded, biting his bottom lip with all his small upper teeth. Wait. She narrowed her gaze. Was that chocolate around his mouth?

"Do I have your permission to marry your mom now?" he asked.

"Yeah." Hunter crumpled his tie in one hand and gave his father a high-five with the other.

"Thanks, buddy." A single kiss to their son's forehead sealed the deal. This was the man she wanted to spend the rest of her life with.

Anthony straightened, taking her hands in his. "Okay. We're good to go."

The minister started over. "Do you, Anthony, take Glennon as your lawfully wedded wife, in sickness and in health, until death do you part?"

"Not yet," Anthony said. "I have two conditions."

Her shoulders sank. He had to be kidding.

"Let me get this straight. You want me to marry you, but you're negotiating conditions in the middle of our wedding." She forced the tension to drain from her muscles, but even in the middle of the most perfect day, the day she'd been looking forward to for over a month, he was determined to make that impossible. "Don't you think this discussion should've happened *before* the actual wedding?"

"Where's the fun in that?" Anthony winked. "Glennon, I will never choose any job or anyone, except our

son, over you ever again. You are my priority. You are my future. I will never do anything to put that at risk, and I will do anything to keep you safe. The first condition I'm setting is that we're honest with each other for the rest of our lives. No secrets. And you'll tell me you're pregnant the next time."

She swallowed at the tightening in her throat as he winked. In vain. A smile pulled at her mouth as she adjusted her hands in his. He wanted more babies with her. "Okay. Second condition?"

His quick glance at Hunter raised the hairs on the back of her neck. With a single nod, her son—*their* son—coaxed Anthony to go on. What were these two up to? "Second condition. You need to come work for Blackhawk Security. As one of our lead investigators."

"What?" Shock exploded through her. Her mouth dropped open. The entire reason she'd decided to quit the army was to spend more time with her son. Working for Blackhawk Security, starting a brand-new career... None of that would let her make up for the long nights and missed weekends. For four years, she'd relied on someone else showing up at his bedside when the nightmares came, making his favorite breakfast in the morning, taking him to the zoo when one of her and Bennett's cases got too intense. Hunter deserved a parent at home, one who could be there for him to kiss the scratches and scrapes.

Anthony didn't get to take that away from her. Didn't matter that they were having this conversation in front of the entire Blackhawk Security team.

"Your timing sucks, Ranger." Glennon lowered her voice, too many prying ears waiting for her an-

swer. "I told you why I was resigning from the army. Hunter deserves—"

"A parent at home. I know," Anthony said. "Which is why I told Sullivan a few minutes before the ceremony that I will only be taking assignments when you're home to be with our son."

The air rushed from her lungs. What?

"I know for a fact you love your job, Glennon, and you're damn good at it." Rough fingers wrapped around her wrist then slid across the back of her hand. His body heat battled with the ice setting up residence under her skin as he took her hand in both of his. Goose bumps pimpled down her arms as he studied her, jaw slack, lips parted. "I've seen the way you work, the way you care about the victims in your cases. And I never want you to have to give that up. Not when you can help so many more people."

Truth resonated through her. She loved her job, everything about it. And he was right. She was damn good at it. But she loved Hunter more. She slid her hand over her son's small chest, pressing his spine into her leg. His heart beat steadily under her palm as Anthony's hand warmed her to the bone. "I don't know what to say."

"Say yes, Glennon," Anthony said. "Then I'll marry you."

Blood rushed from her head. She shifted to keep her balance, her black rain boots squishing along the shoreline. Too much. This was all too much. And he…he was willing to sacrifice his career so she could keep hers. How the hell had she gotten so lucky? She scanned the faces in the audience. "You don't have to do this. I don't need my job. I have savings. I have—"

"I told you I would do anything to make you happy."
Diving into his pocket, Anthony extracted a second
band, this one embedded with diamonds. "And I meant
every word."

Her hand shook as he slid the wedding band onto
her finger. She ignored the rush of excitement radiating
from the center of her core. She wouldn't have to give
up her career. Because of him. A smile consumed the
seemingly permanent darkness in his features, and her
heart rocketed into her throat. "All right. Then, yes."

"Then it's a deal." He wrapped his hands in hers.
Addressing the minister, he kept his attention locked
on her. As though she were the only woman in the entire world. "Good to go."

"All right then." The minister leaned in. "Do you,
Anthony, take Glennon as your lawfully wedded wife,
in sickness and in health, until death do you part?"

"Hell yes, I do," he said.

The minister turned to her. "And do you, Glennon,
take Anthony as your lawfully wedded husband, in
sickness and in health, until death do you part?"

"Hell yes, I do." Forget the dropping temperatures.
With the way her Ranger looked at her now, her blood
had started boiling. If he kept this up, she wouldn't
need her fur-lined coat during the reception.

"Then I now pronounce you husband and wife," the
minister said.

Hollers and clapping echoed off the surrounding
trees, but Glennon only had attention for her husband
and son. Her heart started beating again.

Hunter clapped along with the guests, jumping up
and down.

"And you said you'd never get involved with one of

your partners." Anthony kissed her then. The deep, desperate kind of kiss she'd been craving. The kind that told her he'd never choose his job over her or their son, that she was alive because of him and that fear wouldn't stop them from being happy. Never again. "Any other rules I need to know about?"

"Yeah." She shivered as his beard tickled against her lips. "Don't give my mother a reason to shoot you."

* * * * *

MARKED BY
THE MARSHAL

JULIE ANNE LINDSEY

Dedicated to red wine and coffee.
I couldn't do it without you.

Chapter One

Kara tilted her face away from the scalding July sun. It was the hottest, driest summer on record in Shadow Point, Kentucky, and she was eternally grateful for the misty breeze blowing off the fountain at Memorial Park. Her sleeping infant, Casey, on the other hand, seemed utterly unaware that her mother was slowly melting in the afternoon heat. Casey was like that. Naturally content, perpetually at ease. Not at all like the other moms had warned Kara babies could be. Casey had slept through the night by eight weeks and continued to be as lovely and charming as ever at four months.

Kara wiped the back of one sweaty arm across her forehead. A year ago, she'd run three miles before dawn. These days she was lucky to power walk half that before dinner. The heat wasn't helping. She parked the three-wheeled jogging stroller in a berth of shade from an ancient oak and checked her step counter for time and distance. Already 10:00 a.m., and she was a thousand steps shy of her goal. She'd have to make them up indoors. The temperature was rising, and Casey would soon be ready for lunch.

Kara inhaled the sweet scent of blooming flower beds and the busy vendor carts positioned throughout Me-

morial Park. She eased her backside onto the fountain's wide marble edge and waited for her heart rate to fizzle back to a steady thrum before making the final trek to her car. She gulped the dregs of warm water from her bottle and let her eyes slide shut.

"Beautiful day." A man's voice sprung her lids open. The brim of his dark ball cap was pulled low over his forehead, casting shadows over his wide, deep-set eyes. His dark blue jeans and shirt clung to his bulky frame, likely applied there by a dewy coat of sweat. He clasped his hands behind him and peered into Casey's stroller. "Pretty lady you've got there."

"Thank you." Kara set a protective hand on the stroller's side. She concentrated on Casey's sleeping face instead of keeping eye contact with the man, hoping he'd take the hint. Kara wasn't interested in a conversation or anything else he had to offer. What she needed was to go home and take a shower. Maybe change into something that wasn't soaked in sweat.

"She looks like you," he marveled. "Is her daddy at work? He must be missing her fiercely."

Kara's gut clenched at the thought of Casey's father. A man she'd thought was good and decent, one who'd claimed to love her until a small pink cross appeared on the pregnancy test. Suddenly, he wasn't ready for a life with her. Certainly not prepared for fatherhood. He was sorry, but he just couldn't do it, and how did this happen anyway?

Kara forced the hard rock of emotion down her throat. *This* had happened because she'd allowed herself to let him in, when she knew full well there was only one man in the world meant for her, and it wasn't the man making excuses about commitment.

"No," she answered with more bite than intended.

Casey's father wasn't at work, as far as she knew, and he wasn't missing Casey at all, but that was his loss and Kara's gain. Casey was a gift. Kara knew that now, but for months she'd thought the pregnancy was her punishment for naively letting another man into her life. She figured this was what happened when women were gullible and stupid. The idea, of course, was laughable now. Her pregnancy had been a blessing that changed the shape of her world, and for the first time since the real love of her life had left her, Kara was profoundly at peace.

Except for this guy, contentedly pursuing a conversation, despite the fact that she'd barely looked in his direction. "I'm sorry," she said, looking pointedly at her wrist. "I really should get going. It's time for her bottle, and I want to get her out of this heat." She stood on tired noodle legs and set her hand firmly on the stroller handle. Kara leaned forward, but the carriage didn't budge.

The man had moved his hand to the stroller's opposite side, curling meaty fingers over the edge and effectively holding it in place. "Must you go so soon?" He hitched one side of his mouth into a sinister half smile.

"Yes."

Something dark flashed in his eyes. "May I hold her before you go? Just for a moment?"

"No." The word leapt off Kara's tongue with venomous warning. Adrenaline rushed through her veins, stiffening her posture and renewing her strength. "Please remove your hand from my baby's stroller," she seethed. Her stance widened on instinct and her muscles tensed to fight. It was a new and semi-frightening sensation, but in that moment she was sure she could flatten this man

if needed. If he attempted to lay a finger on her daughter, they'd soon find out if she was right.

He stared, unmoving.

"Now," she ground out the word.

Slowly, his fingers pulled away from the stroller. He slid the offending hand into his pocket. The other hung limply at his side. The oily smile she longed to knock off his face had morphed into something like disappointment or distaste. A silver lighter appeared in his hand, pulled swiftly from his pocket. He flicked it to life and watched with the same menacing expression he'd just given her. The flame sputtered, then died with a closing snap of the lid. He tugged the brim of his hat and lifted his gaze back to Kara. "Watch yourself," he warned. "I hear it's going to be an inferno."

With that, he strode away, angling deftly through throngs of parents and caregivers gathered at the little water park nearby. The musical sounds of children's laughter sent a shiver down her spine. The contrast of their happiness to her own fear was unnerving. She watched raptly until he was out of sight, just in case he decided he'd like to hold one of those splashing children the way he'd wanted to hold Casey.

Kara's lungs filled suddenly on a deep intake of air. "Time to go, baby doll."

Casey squirmed at the sound of her mama's voice. A small complaint fell from her tiny rosebud lips. Eyes still pinched shut, she flailed her arms before going limp once more. Someone was due for a feeding.

Kara whirled the stroller away from the fountain, thankful to have left her car parked in the opposite direction from the water park where the man was last seen. If she never saw him again, it would be too soon. In fact,

the way her skin was crawling right now, never returning to Memorial Park would be fine by her. Matter of fact, she wouldn't be able to live with herself if that guy harassed anyone else today because she hadn't spoken up. Heaven forbid he lay a hand on any child. The minute they were safely locked inside her car, Kara would call the local sheriff and file a report.

US MARSHAL RYDER GARRETT listened with slow burning fury as his brother West, the Cade County sheriff, relayed a report made by Kara Noble about a strange man at Memorial Park. The fact that someone had upset Ryder's former fiancée was enough to tighten his jaw. The fact that her description of the man in question matched fugitive Timothy Sand had Ryder packing his bags. Even the remote possibility that Sand was anywhere near Kara was enough to send Ryder back to Shadow Point. He hadn't been home in three years, but he was already making plans to obliterate the speed limit on his way.

"She said that?" Ryder asked for the third time, shoving clothes haphazardly into a duffel. "She told you the man said it was going to be an inferno?"

"Yep," West answered. "I remember you saying something like that once when you still lived in town. Your fugitive liked to say it. Any chance he's free again?"

Ryder recognized the leaden weight of failure cooling on his shoulders. "Yes." The word was a knife to his chest. Sand was never put away for what he'd done, and now Kara was in danger because of it.

"I didn't mention it to her," West said. "Didn't want to upset her any more than she already was, but I figured it was worth a phone call to see what you thought."

"To see what I thought?" Ryder snapped. "I think a

damn fugitive threatened my—" He stopped short. His what? She was nothing to him anymore, and he'd allowed it to be that way. *Caused it to be*. "Kara."

"All right. So, what happened with Sand? I thought he was arrested."

"He was. Another marshal took over my cases while I relocated a family for witness protection. He caught Sand on a lark. A call to the tip line actually paid off, but the marshal was new and overzealous. He didn't have the right evidence to make his case, and Sand's weasel of a lawyer got the whole thing whittled down to parole and time served." Ryder had been sick when he came back to town and heard they'd had Sand and didn't lock him up. He couldn't eat. Couldn't sleep. Ryder got busy preparing a watertight case against Sand for the murder of Sand's first wife. The crime that started it all. He was darn close to having everything he needed to make sure Sand never saw sunlight. Then Sand's parole had ended, the ankle bracelet had come off and Sand had gone MIA. Until now. "I won't let him get away this time," Ryder promised.

"Well, let's hope that's true. Meanwhile, I can't ignore the possibility there's a murdering arsonist in my county. I put Cole on patrol in Kara's neighborhood and added a deputy to Memorial Park. What are you going to do?"

A low swear slid off Ryder's tongue. He gave his forehead a rough scrub. Kara had unequivocally expelled him from her life. She'd packed his bags and set them on the porch with a note telling him he had to go. Her heart couldn't take watching him waste away any longer in pursuit of one fugitive. It wasn't worth it to her. Was it worth it to him?

Sadly, yes. It had been. Putting Sand behind bars had

become symbolic of Ryder's ability to be a marshal, to protect his family, fiancée and anyone else in his charge. He'd bound his self-worth to the apprehension of this man, and he couldn't catch him.

Ryder yanked the zipper on his duffel and slung it over one shoulder. Now he had to go back and protect Kara from a danger he'd inadvertently caused her. West wanted to know what he was going to do? There was only one answer. "I'm coming home, brother."

"Good," West agreed. "For what it's worth, and at the risk of sounding like Mom, it's long past time for the two of you to talk. I hate that Sand is the reason you finally will, but I'm glad anyway. Kara will be, too."

Ryder barked a humorless laugh. Yeah. Kara would be thrilled to see him. He'd stewed in his losses every day, but she'd gone on to find love with someone else, apparently. "Did you say she has a baby?"

West didn't respond. They both knew that was exactly what he'd said.

Did he have to protect the new man in her life as well? His gut fisted at the thought. "How old's the kid?"

"Only a few months. A girl."

Ryder let his eyes drift shut, momentarily frozen in remorse. "She's married, then?"

"Nope. Rumor is that the guy left her when he found out about the pregnancy. That was just over a year ago. Only guy she's dated since you, I believe, assuming the gossip mill's still working fine."

Ryder clenched his teeth. "Best oiled machine in town."

Now there were two men in Shadow Point he wanted to get his hands on. "What kind of jerk does something like that to a woman? To his child?"

"Not one worth having around," West said. "She's better off without him."

Folks had probably said the same thing after she'd kicked Ryder out. They wouldn't have been wrong then, either.

He grabbed his key, badge and sidearm, then headed into the sunset. There'd be plenty of time to fixate on all the ways he'd ruined his life during the three-hour drive back to Shadow Point. Right now, he needed to get moving.

IT WAS AFTER ten when Kara put on her second pot of coffee. It had been twelve hours since her hasty exit from Memorial Park with Casey, and Kara's nerves were still in bundles. Casey, on the other hand, was sound asleep in the nursery. Kara was glad for her, but personally, she couldn't shake the sensation she was being watched.

She'd locked all the doors and shut the windows the moment they'd gotten home. She'd even pulled the curtains in an effort to stop the heebie-jeebies crawling over her skin. Nothing had worked. On any other night, she'd have poured a glass of sweet tea and sat on the porch swing to unwind from her troubles. Tonight, she was a prisoner in her home. A very hot home.

The central air was set to seventy-seven, the lowest she could afford to keep it on her public teacher's salary, and she was dressed accordingly. A worn-out pair of cotton shorts and a pre-pregnancy tank top. The perfect pajamas for nights like these. Though hers were being tested at every seam by the added pounds of stubborn baby weight, she wouldn't complain. Those pounds were hard earned and well worth the prize.

Kara poured a cup of fresh coffee and sank onto a

kitchen chair. This wasn't supposed to be her life. If things had turned out the way she'd planned, she wouldn't be shaking the willies right now over some man in the park. She'd be sharing a late-night snack with Ryder Garrett, and laughing as he told her all the ways he could keep that man from ever looking her way again. And he'd mean it. Kara smiled against the rim of her cup. She'd never been afraid of anything when Ryder was in her life.

Let it go, she chastised herself. *You shouldn't want him.* Ryder had chosen a life of compulsion, danger and near madness over her. Based on that alone, she shouldn't love him anymore, but all these years later she still couldn't go twenty-four hours without thinking of him. Ridiculous. Especially since he'd left town and never looked back.

The sound of a car door drew Kara's attention back to the moment, and she was irrationally glad to have something else to think about. Even the possibility of an unwanted guest. Kara padded across the living room carpet for a peek between the curtains. There was no movement on the street or in her driveway. Whoever had arrived or gone in the car had already done so, and the neighborhood had settled back into the hazy calm of a sweltering summer night. She checked the door and window locks again for good measure, moving methodically around the first floor, then up to the second.

It was nothing. Just a neighbor coming or going. No reason to overthink this.

The tug of sleep pulled at her muscles and eyelids as she tested the final window. She rubbed the fine hairs on her forearms, smoothing them where they stood at attention, sent on alert by the goose bumps covering her skin. She'd reported her weird exchange at the park

to the local sheriff, a man who had nearly become her brother-in-law once. What more could she do? Thankfully, he hadn't judged her for her paranoia. Instead, he'd promised to look into it and to add a night patrol to her street. She really couldn't ask for more, especially considering nothing had actually happened. Kara had dealt with pushy men all her life, ones who leered at her and said crude things. She imagined all women had, but it was the first time she'd been confronted so blatantly with her baby present. Maybe that was what had upset her so much. The idea her baby was there. That he'd wanted to touch her. *Is her daddy at work?* Was that his creepy way of asking if Kara was involved with anyone since her ring finger was bare?

Kara moved to Casey's room for another look at her sweet princess. She needed a nice vision to replace the man's face burned into her mind. He'd had a slightly crazed expression like the one Ryder had worn at his worst, during the sleepless weeks of obsession over a fugitive named Timothy Sand. Ryder was barely human in those days, distant and monosyllabic. Like an addict or a man coming slowly unhinged. If only. Had either of those things been the problem, she could've gotten him help, sheltered him through the storm, but Ryder's problems were of his choosing, and no one could've put him on another path, not even her.

Kara stopped the still-turning mobile that dangled high above Casey's slack face. Baby drool edged from her droopy bottom lip, perhaps a sign of a first tooth on its way. One sweet dimpled arm lay across the stuffed dolly that had once belonged to Kara. Kara had gotten Rainy Rosie and her little yellow raincoat in an Easter basket during fourth grade and kept her in a memory

box for years before Casey was born. Now, Rosie was gnawed on endlessly by her precious daughter. Kara suppressed a chuckle and slid back into the hallway, tugging the door nearly closed behind her.

The trip back downstairs seemed endless, like a dream hallway that grew longer with every step. Maybe tonight was a good night to sleep in the nursery. She'd fallen asleep in the glider many times before. She could bring a glass of water and a book. Let sleep take her at will.

Kara flipped the light switches and tugged the lamp chains one by one as she shut the house down for the night. Coffeepot off. She poured a glass of water and tucked a worn paperback under one bent arm, then grabbed the baby monitor from the counter. She liked her plan more and more by the second. Locked inside the nursery, she and Casey would be together, and they would be safe. Tomorrow was a new day, and tonight's fears would likely seem as silly as they really were.

She checked the door lock once more and peeked through the front window for the last time. Breath caught in her throat as a tiny movement registered across the street. The glass of water jostled in her trembling hand. Kara shut her eyes and whispered, "It's nothing, there's nothing there, it's okay, you're okay." She reopened her lids and gave the darkened street another cautious look.

Slowly, the shadow of a man peeled away from a broad oak tree and started a path in her direction.

Chapter Two

Kara's pulse pounded in her ears. She pressed a hand to her constricting chest and willed herself to think. The man at the park had been big. He'd had at least fifty pounds on her, and she was out of shape. If he managed to get through the door, no one would see. At least at the park there were a hundred witnesses. Here, alone in her darkened house… Every self-defense move she'd ever learned was gone. Vanished. She could only think of how to escape, keep Casey safe and get away if the man tried to force his way inside.

Heavy footfalls clomped up her porch steps, vibrating through her soul. Where was that extra patrolman West had promised her? *West!* Kara pulled the phone from her pocket and dialed the personal number he'd left with her earlier.

She prayed softly against the phone receiver as the knocking began.

Pick up. Pick up. Pick up. She pressed her back against the warm wooden door for strength and willed West to answer his darn phone.

The knocks behind her came lightly at first, cautiously, and grew steadily more insistent. Her interior lights were already off. Maybe whoever was on her porch

would assume no one was home and go away. The nagging possibility she was being paranoid began to creep in. She hadn't gotten a clean look at the man crossing her street. It could be anyone. Maybe she was overreacting. Then again, whoever was out there at this hour was probably up to no good. Man from the park, or someone else. Didn't matter. It was far too late for visiting. Besides, who could it even be? No man had climbed her steps in a year. Figurative or otherwise.

Pick up. Pick up. Pick up. The call connected and Kara gasped. Tears of relief blurred her vision.

"Garrett," West answered, a bubble of laughter in his voice. Country music mingled with sounds of a crowd in the background.

"West?" she whispered, cupping her hands protectively around the phone. Not wanting to be heard by the man outside her door. "There's someone on my porch and I'm freaking out."

The background sounds grew silent. "Kara?" West's voice was sharp now, followed by the distinct snick of a closing door. "What's going on?"

She swallowed a yelp as the knocking grew into pounding against her spine. "Someone's here." The quiver troubling her limbs infiltrated her voice.

Kara swung her attention to the stairwell. She could be upstairs in twenty seconds, and at the backdoor with Casey in thirty more. Could the man on her porch break down the door in less time than that? What if he predicted her move and was at the back door when she got there?

"Sit tight," West said with utter Garrett-like confidence. "I'm sending someone to you. Give me five minutes to route him your way."

"Okay." Her darting gaze landed on the hearth. "I might hit him with a fireplace poker."

"Tell you what. Anyone comes through that door without an invitation, and you've got my support in doing whatever you want to him," he huffed. "He's not responding."

"Your deputy?" Kara squeaked. Could the man on her porch have taken out the patrolling deputy?

The knocking stalled, and a new kind of fear clawed through her. At least while he was knocking, she knew where he was. A shadow fell over her front window and the silhouette of a man came into view. "Kara?"

The voice of a ghost permeated her glass. It twisted her core and squeezed her lungs. A strangled noise rose from her parted lips.

"Oh, my goodness." Slowly, she moved away from the door, eyes wide, jaw heavy.

"What?" West barked.

"Kara? Open up," the voice continued, more pleading than stern despite the sharp edge to his words.

She turned the deadbolt and opened the door with bated breath.

"Kara!" West hollered through the forgotten phone in her hand.

"It's you," she breathed.

Ryder Garrett, the ghost of love lost, stood before her in an arch of porch lighting. Hat in hands, he dipped his chin in greeting. "Hello, Kara."

RYDER REACHED FOR her phone and spoke briefly to his brother in acronyms and grunts before returning the phone to Kara.

Kara batted dazed eyes at Ryder before inviting him

into their formerly shared home. He accepted with a nod and tried not to wonder what her expression meant, exactly.

She worked her mouth closed, still openly staring at him.

He tried not to return the favor, which wasn't easy. Kara was striking. He hadn't blown her out of proportion in his mind. She really was the kind of woman who could walk down the street and cause a ten-truck pileup. Her pale blue eyes were lined in thick, curled lashes. Her cheeks and lips were naturally pink, though at the moment they were both slightly white from shock. He ached to kiss the line of freckles spilled over her nose. The ones she tried desperately to hide with makeup when they'd gone out for special occasions. He curled his fingers at his side, reminding himself not to touch her. He couldn't do that anymore. It was a privilege he'd lost long ago.

"What are you doing here?" she asked, finally snapping back to life. She twisted the deadbolt and turned the lock on her doorknob before checking the window.

Did she really think any of that was necessary with him there?

He scanned the vaguely familiar room. Unlike Kara, the home was much different than he remembered. A giant mirror graced the wall above the fireplace where his massive mounted trout had once hung. Their engagement photos and candid snapshots had been replaced with selfies of Kara and an infant. He shook his head. The moment was surreal. It was his home, but it wasn't. She was his girl, but she wasn't. And the baby. Well, she hadn't existed to him until three hours ago.

Kara cleared her throat. "Well?"

Ryder forced a comforting smile. "I heard you had a

bad experience at the park today." *Ignore my poor manners for showing up at this hour, unannounced.* He'd dialed her number a dozen times on his drive back to town, but couldn't bring himself to hit Call. What would he have said? What if she'd told him not to come?

Her nose wrinkled. "West told you about the park? Why?"

"He was worried. Thought I might be, too."

"Why?" she repeated. A flash of emotion passed over her stunned expression.

"Maybe you could tell me more about what happened today." He inched toward the kitchen. "We can sit down. Go over the details."

"Okay." She ghosted in front of him. Flipping on lights and starting up the coffee maker. "Coffee?"

"Sure."

Kara kept her back to him as she prepped the mugs. Her head shook infinitesimally, and he was thankful not to know what she was thinking.

He didn't mind the view, either. Being back in this place with her was a lot for him to process. He hadn't anticipated the intensity of it. The sight of their old things. The sound of her grandma's too-loudly-ticking wall clock, and the scents of that sugar-and-spice candle she loved so much. He smiled. In all the years they'd been together, Kara never let their—*her*—personal supply run out. One year for Christmas he'd bought her a case of those candles to be mischievous, but she'd been so pleased that they'd made love right there under the tree. His attention drifted to the exact spot, and heat rose in his chest.

The coffee maker chugged steam into the air, drawing his attention back to the kitchen.

Ryder blew out a long breath and refocused on Kara, but that didn't help clean up his thoughts. And never mind the fact that Kara was wearing a tank top and shorts set that clung distractingly to her new, curvier...everything.

She spun on him suddenly. A frown creased her brow.

He jerked his gaze to her eyes. "What?" Caught ogling. *Real nice.* A true gentleman.

She shook her head again. "West told you that some creep harassed me this morning, and you what? Drove straight here from wherever you live now?"

He nodded slowly. "Cincinnati." That almost summed it up. That and the fact that he believed her harasser to be a murdering psychopath, but there was no reason to say so until he was sure. For the moment, Ryder was enjoying this strange trip into his past. It was nice being there with her. Nostalgic.

Unfortunately, once Kara learned it was probably him who'd put her and her baby in danger, she'd want to cold-cock him with that coffeepot.

She made her way to the table, two mugs in hand. The faint scent of cinnamon drifted in the bitter steam. He'd almost forgotten the way she added the spice to her grounds.

"Thanks." He took a seat and waited while she did the same. "Can you tell me everything you told West about the man, plus anything you might've forgotten to mention, but thought of later?"

"Sure, but it's probably nothing. I only called because the park was so busy, and I knew I'd never forgive myself if the guy tried to take one of those other children and I hadn't spoken up."

Ryder's shoulders relaxed by a fraction. "You think he

was a child abductor?" Timothy Sand was many awful things, but pedophile wasn't one of them. Maybe he'd been wrong about this.

"I don't know. He leered at me pretty good," she said, looking fairly ill.

"What made you think the man might try to take a child? Did he try to take your baby?"

"No." Kara sipped her coffee. "He asked if he could hold her, but I'd already told him we needed to leave. It was really weird. Then, he put his hand on the stroller for a minute when I tried to go, but he relented, and he never threatened us. I just had this feeling." She fisted a hand against her gut. "You know?"

He did. Instinct had told her that man was dangerous, so he probably was. "Start from the beginning."

She set her cup down and stared into it. Slowly, her lids slid shut, and she began to recount the exchange in unbelievable detail. A hat had hidden the man's hair and shaded his eyes, but she was certain they were both brown. He was clean-shaven, and she'd noticed acne scars along his cheeks. There was a tattoo on his left wrist. A single black heart.

"Observant." Pride bloomed in Ryder's chest. They used to test one another about the little details around them. She'd enjoyed the game more than he did because despite his flashy badge, she'd usually won. She claimed being a kindergarten teacher made paying attention to the details especially necessary.

Kara opened her eyes and lanced him with her careful stare. "I'm glad you're here, Ryder. You look good, and I'm glad to see you this way again."

He didn't have to ask what she meant by "this way again." He knew. *Healthy. Rested. Fed*. The last time

she'd seen him, he was a shell of himself, obsessed with the one that had literally gotten away. He didn't eat or sleep in those days, and he was pretty light on the showers and speech. He'd spent every hour fixated on Timothy Sand and his capture. Ryder raised his mug and blew across the fog of steam. "Thanks. I took your advice. Got some help."

Agency-mandated help, but still.

He'd lost control and laid a fist into the new kid who'd brought Sand in but failed to keep him in jail because of the flimsy case he'd prepared. Ryder had been temporarily relieved of his badge and sidearm after that. It was the lowest point of his career. The lowest point of his life had been two months earlier, when Kara told him to pull it together or leave.

The suspension eventually opened his eyes to how far he'd fallen down the rabbit hole. Mandatory sessions with an in-house therapist had helped him get his life back together. By that time, it was too late to come home to Kara. His mind was clear, and he finally understood how much he'd hurt her. She deserved better than that.

"You ever catch that guy?" she asked. "What was his name—Timothy Rand?"

"Sand," Ryder corrected. "Timothy Sand. No. I never did."

She twisted her mouth into a sad smile. As if to say, *It was all for nothing, then*. A broken engagement. Two broken hearts.

Ryder cleared his thickening throat. "How about you? You're stunning as ever. Motherhood's been good to you, I see."

"Thanks." She dropped her attention away from him, and a blush darkened her cheeks. When she dragged her

gaze back to his, she smiled. "She might be the best thing that's ever happened to me. I never expected I'd be a single mother, but she's worth it, and I know we'll be okay."

Kara was strong. He'd never let the kindergarten-teacher front fool him. She could command armies if needed. "And the father?" Ryder forced the last word through his teeth. No one who abandoned his woman and unborn child deserved a title like that. But what else could he call him. Whoever he was.

"Gone." She pulled in and released a long, steady breath. There was no remorse in her face, no anger. She was a better person than Ryder. The man hadn't done a thing to him, and he wanted to punch his face.

"Does he check in from time to time or…"

"No," she interrupted. "Like I said. He's gone."

"I'm sorry to hear that." And he was. Because if the guy was here, he could hit him.

"Thanks."

West had it right on this one. Kara was better off without a man who'd leave her like that. Ryder settled back in his chair, stretching booted feet beneath the table. He and Kara were about as caught up as they could get without unloading the massive elephant from his pocket. He set his phone on the table and flipped quickly through the photos he'd downloaded after speaking with West tonight. "I've got a photo of a fugitive I'd like you to look at."

Kara stiffened. He could almost see the lightbulb flicking on as fear bleached her freckled cheeks. "You think the man who talked to me is a federal fugitive?"

"It might be nothing." He forced a lazy smile. "Maybe your guy was a run-of-the-mill weirdo."

She lifted crossed fingers in a show of sarcasm.

"Let's find out."

Kara raised her chin in agreement. "Okay." She opened her hand to him. "Let's see it, then."

Ryder turned the little screen to face her. "Do you recognize him?" The photo of Sand was nearly two years old, and the most recent surveillance the US Marshals had. He wore a bushy beard and full head of hair in the picture, nothing like the description she'd just given him.

"That's him."

Ryder's gaze jumped to hers. "You sure?" His heart pumped strong and hard against his ribs. "This is the man who bothered you today? You said he was clean-shaven and wore a hat. How can you tell with the big beard and wild hair?" He even had sunglasses in the gas station photo.

Kara set one pale pink fingernail on the grainy image. "There."

Ryder turned the screen to him for a closer look.

The photo showed Timothy crossing the parking lot, legs extended in midstep, tucking cash into his wallet. One wrist in full view of the camera, with a small black spot marking him for the marshal.

She leveled Ryder with a no-nonsense look. "I'm willing to bet you'll see that's a heart if you blow up the image. Now, it's your turn."

Ryder stared at the photo. Sand didn't have a tattoo. Did he? If so, he'd gotten it since the last time Ryder had laid eyes on him, and he hadn't noticed it in this photo until now. Because he hadn't expected it, the spot had seemed to him like nothing more than a digital blemish, but Kara's description and the placement of that mark were too coincidental.

Ice rolled through Ryder's veins. Timothy Sand was in Shadow Point, and he knew who Kara was.

"You want to tell me exactly who that man is?" she asked, arms folded on the table. "And why a federal fugitive whom you're hunting sought me out in a park bursting with people?"

Ryder pulled in a deep steadying breath. "I can only guess at how to answer that last question."

"And the first?"

Ryder dropped the phone between them. "This man is Timothy Sand."

Chapter Three

Kara's eyes bulged. Her heart lodged in her throat. "No," she said, unwilling to allow the vile statement to be true. "He *can't* be." She pressed her pointed finger against the tabletop. "No."

Ryder rubbed his mouth and lightly stubbled cheeks, a look of apologetic desperation in his eyes. "Kara," he began.

She shook her head, cutting off whatever he'd planned to say. "Unless the next words out of your mouth are going to be 'Just kidding,' then keep 'em to yourself." Her traitorous lip quivered and tears stung her tired eyes. There had been far too much drama today. Too many men. They were ruining the peaceful, predictable, nearly perfect life she adored. She and Casey were supposed to be safe in Shadow Point. Supported by the community. Surrounded by a tight network of moms she'd met in Lamaze and Stroller Fit classes. Things were going really well, and now…her gaze fell on Ryder's handsome, bunched up face. "You can't come strutting back into my life after years of doing who-knows-what and mess it all up. I won't allow it."

His jaw dropped. The startling blue of his eyes seemed

to darken in disbelief. "What do you mean? *Who-knows-what?* What do you think I've been doing?"

She crossed her arms in a show of defiance, but fear was already sliding over her, jarring her composure. "I can't do this." She dropped her tone and petulant posture. "Not anymore. I put you and your Sand obsession out on the curb. You can't just pop back up. My heart can't take it." She rubbed her chest. She shouldn't have to worry about protecting her infant from a fugitive, and she shouldn't have to endure the pain of watching Ryder walk away again when his business in Shadow Point was done.

Her arms found their way back around her middle, uselessly trying to hold herself together while a tornado of emotions spun in her scrambled head. How stupid of her to feel heartbroken all over again. The sight of Ryder Garrett shouldn't do this to her. It wasn't right. Wasn't fair. She bit into her lip and forced herself to think rationally. Ryder wasn't back for her. He was back for Sand. He'd landed on her doorstep dragging the same baggage he'd left with. Only this time everything was worse. The fugitive was in town. And she had a baby to think about.

She narrowed her eyes at Ryder, measuring what to say next. She should never have let his clear expression and sensible words fool her. He wasn't reformed. Ryder was still a junkie. He might not be hooked on anything illegal, but his drug of choice was every bit as lethal.

RYDER WATCHED HELPLESSLY as Kara's wide eyes brimmed with tears. Never one for a big show of emotion, she shoved away from the table and turned her back on him. He followed her to the living room on instinct. "Kara." This was 100 percent his fault. He'd somehow allowed

the monster he'd chased for so long to wind up on her doorstep. Whether or not Sand had made a personal appearance at her home, he'd found her at the park, and that meant he knew her routine. He'd likely been watching since the first day he was set free. "I'm sorry."

She stopped midstep and turned on her toes to face him. A solitary tear rolled over her cheek, but she made no move to catch it. Instead, her stubborn chin inched higher. "Why?" she snapped.

"Why what?" Ryder froze, mentally flailing. "Why is Sand here? Bothering you? I don't know, but I promise you, I *will* stop him this time."

She puffed out her cheeks, sending air into her bangs and setting them to flutter. "*Why* are you sorry?" She dragged the question into long, pointed words.

Ryder rocked back on his heels. A boulder of regret settled in the hollow of his chest, flattening his lungs and strangling his breath. He slid his fingers into the front pockets of his jeans. When he'd followed her to the living room, he'd intended to hold her, to cradle and comfort her, but the look on her face said he'd likely lose a hand for trying, and he'd better start talking or he was going back to the curb, fugitive or not. "I'm sorry for everything." He cringed at the lame answer. He knew it wasn't what she wanted, but it was true anyway.

"Keep talking."

"All right." Might as well start with the most obvious and pertinent reason. "I'm sorry my position as a US marshal has upset your life and possibly endangered you and your baby."

Her eyebrows rose in unison. A perfect expression of *You think?*

She turned to pace the room, aimlessly righting top-

pled piles of plastic toys and stacks of small pink blankets. "Anything else?" she prompted, suddenly abusing a frilly pillow.

"Yeah, but I don't think this is the right time to talk about that." In other words, he didn't know where to begin, and he'd rather not. He'd imagined contacting her a thousand times, even rehearsed in the shower what he would say to her, and, embarrassingly, once to his therapist at work. It hadn't been his intent to talk about Kara, but there was only so long he could discuss punching his coworker in the face.

Kara snapped upright, dropping the little pillow onto the couch. "Now's not good for you, huh?" She nodded slowly, baiting him. "Well, a better time, then." She glided around the coffee table straightening magazines. "I wonder when that will be?" She tapped her chin thoughtfully. "Maybe two or three years from now when you turn up without notice again? Will that work for you?" She smiled, tight and bright. "I can't imagine what the reason will be next time. Maybe a crime boss on the run will be posing as my daughter's preschool teacher."

Ryder's lips twitched. He'd always gotten a kick out of Kara's fury. Not that she was usually wrong in her anger. She was patient and forgiving to a fault, but she was also stretching for five foot four, and her long wavy blond hair and big cartoon princess eyes made it all the worse. Angry Kara was a fluffy bunny baring her teeth, and the sight of her tiny face turning six shades of pissed usually ended their fights. He'd laugh, apologize and drag her into his arms, because what kind of jerk upsets a bunny?

Kara's forced smile fell. She pressed her palms against the narrow curve of her waist, emphasizing her full

breasts and testing the integrity of her tank top. "Something funny?"

He pulled his eyes back above her collar where they belonged. "What?"

"Why is the fugitive you were chasing three years ago bothering *me* now? To hurt you? That seems silly. If he thinks we're still a couple, he should brush up on his stalking skills."

"I imagine that's what he's doing now. I think you're right. He's looking to hurt me, and now he's free to do it."

Kara's knees buckled. She planted onto their old couch with a sharp exhale and covered her lips with narrow fingers. "He asked me about the daddy."

"What did you say?" A bubble of hope rose in Ryder's chest. "Did you tell him the father's name? Make sure he knew she wasn't mine?" Maybe Kara and her baby were safer than he'd thought. Sand was sure to leave Kara alone if he knew she wasn't in Ryder's life anymore. He'd have to move on. Find another angle.

Kara stretched her eyes wide. "I didn't tell him anything. He asked if her daddy was at work, then he said he must be missing her. I just said no. I don't engage with people like that, and I never give out personal details. I made it crystal clear that my level of interest in talking with him was zero, and I left."

Ryder swore, then pinched his lips tight. He ran a heavy hand through his hair and curled his fingers knuckle-deep into the strands. Kara had done the right thing for any other situation, but she'd likely only kindled Sand's interest today. They were engaged when Ryder started to pursue him. Sand had no reason to think they weren't married now and raising a family.

"S-so," Kara stuttered. "Sand is definitely coming

after me now because he thinks we got married and had a baby."

Ryder took a seat at her side and swooped an arm around her shoulders like he had hundreds of times before. "Come here."

She leaned into him, covering her face with one hand and rolling against his side. He inhaled the soft, familiar scent of her, soaked in her warmth and longed to be her hero once again. The man she'd fallen in love with when he saved her goofy kite from a tree. Her class had finger painted terrible kites to look like butterflies and rainbows. An errant wind had blown Kara's into a tree. If it hadn't been for that damn kite and Ryder's affinity for tree climbing, they might never have met. But they did, and they were happy.

He missed being there for her. Opening jars and carrying things her short little arms couldn't manage. He missed driving her places in his truck so she could perform a one-woman karaoke concert in the passenger seat. More than that, he desperately missed *her*.

Kara pulled her legs onto the couch, hugging her knees to her chest and pulling away from him. She folded herself into a little bundle, and Ryder longed to toss her in his truck and rush her to safety.

But she had a baby now. And a life here without him. He couldn't carry her away.

He had to stay and protect her. He needed to fix the mess he'd inadvertently caused. "Hey." He set a careful hand on her back and rubbed the pad of his thumb against her shoulder blade. "I know you don't have any reason to believe this, but I'm not the same as I was before. My head's clear. My priorities are straight. I've never been better at what I do, or knowing who I am. I

can catch Sand this time, and when I do, I've got enough evidence to form a pretty strong case against him for his first murder."

She rolled her head against her knee until her face came into view. Her lashes were wet with tears. "Yeah?"

"Yeah." He curled a swath of her hair around his finger and tucked it behind her ear, keeping his eyes fixed on hers, begging her to see the truth. He could and would protect her at any cost.

Kara nodded. "Okay."

"Good," he whispered, emotion choking the word. He opened his arms and she fell right in, collapsing against his chest and curling into the curve of his side. Kara believed him. Despite everything they'd been through, and despite seeing him at his worst, she trusted him to protect her and her baby. That meant something. His heart swelled with joy and hope for a different future. "I won't let Timothy Sand hurt you," he said, stroking her soft vanilla-scented hair. "That's a promise."

SQUEALING TIRES BURNED a hole in the comfortable silence and Kara's limbs went rigid.

She yelped as Ryder swiftly shoved her aside. He leapt away from the couch before the raucous sound had ended. "What is it?" She jumped onto her feet a split second behind him, but Ryder was faster, already out her front door and jogging down the street. A pair of glowing red taillights were barely visible in the distance.

Kara shut the door and locked it. She grabbed the baby monitor from the counter and found a place at the front window where she could watch whatever happened next. Should she call West? Or make a run for the nursery to collect her baby?

Outside, Ryder strode confidently through the night, gun in one hand, cell phone in the other.

Maybe he would call West.

He stopped at a large SUV parked catty-corner from her home and holstered his weapon. He turned in a small circle before lifting something from the vehicle's windshield.

Kara strained to see what it was.

Ryder made another call and headed back in her direction, moving slowly at first, then breaking into a jog.

As he passed beneath the motion light over her driveway, the mysterious object came terrifyingly into view.

Someone had left Ryder a badly charred matchbook.

Chapter Four

Kara unlocked the door and stepped away as Ryder turned the knob. He walked back inside unbidden, a sadly appropriate metaphor for their relationship. All he had to do was show up, and she let him in. He dropped a black duffel bag onto her floor, apparently planning to stay awhile. She shook her head, silently scolding herself for the naive flutter of excitement. Ryder Garrett might offer protection from whatever he'd gotten her into, but he was dangerous for her heart. Just seeing his face had quickened her pulse, and the way she'd felt while briefly in his arms tonight had brought an unwelcome rush of nostalgia.

Nice as it was to think things could be different, she couldn't allow Ryder's presence to shift her world in unfair ways. And she couldn't afford to let her foolish heart distract her from the real reason Ryder had shown up at all.

"Well?" she asked, wrapping goose-pimpled arms around her middle and eyeballing the charred matchbook in his hand.

He rubbed the sleeve of his black jacket across his forehead. "Can I borrow a baggie?"

Kara glared at him before marching into the kitchen.

Ryder followed, tapping away at his phone screen with the thumb of one hand, while carrying the ruined matchbook, reverently, in the other. The crazed look on his face tilted her stomach.

"Is that from him?" she asked, as if the answer wasn't obvious.

"I believe so, yes."

She swung the pantry door open and tried not to vomit. Kara had been afraid of many things in her life, but never *for* her life. Certainly not for the life of her daughter. Her gut clenched more tightly at the thought.

"Here." She thrust an empty sandwich baggie in his direction, half terrified, wholly pissed. "Will this work?"

"It's fine."

"Are you sure?" she snapped. "Because as far as I know, it's only meant to hold the innocuous parts of my lunch. Not the charred remains of a serial arsonist's blatant threat."

Ryder dropped the matchbook into the baggie and zipped it shut. "Don't sell him short. He's also a murderer."

Kara's jaw dropped.

Ryder grimaced. "Sorry. I just can't believe this is happening."

That makes two of us.

When Kara had woken this morning, her biggest concern was fitting back into her pre-pregnancy wardrobe before school started next month. She'd feared having to buy more clothes on an already tight budget and leaving her baby for the first time since seeing her sweet face in the delivery room.

Now, thanks to some evil twist of fate, she and Casey were on a lunatic's radar when the man he truly wanted

was in her kitchen unpacking what looked like an overnight bag.

Cruel fate had to keep twisting that knife a little deeper. Taking Ryder from her, then returning him only because his criminal obsession had visited. Now, to require that he stay with her, in the home they'd once shared. Kara rubbed the heated skin above her heart, unable to soothe the deep ache.

"Ryder." She placed a hand on his shoulder as he unearthed a small fingerprint kit and gloves from a compartment beside a change of clothes.

Her hand slid off as he set up a makeshift workstation on her countertop, unhearing, then adjusted a lamp to shine on the area. The efficiency of his quick movements was all too familiar. Kara recognized the stiff posture and focused expression as he entered what she'd grudgingly called "marshal mode." A chill slithered down her spine, sending a mass of ugly memories to the surface. The gut-churning recollections of watching helplessly while her fiancé became consumed rolled her stomach.

"Ryder," she repeated, using her teacher voice this time.

His face jerked in her direction, and a look of shock raised his furrowed brows. Had he already forgotten she was there?

"Yeah?" he asked, seeming to return to himself. His ruddy cheeks and clear eyes were an improvement over the last time she'd interrupted him like this.

A bud of hope grew in her heart. Maybe Ryder was telling the truth. Maybe he was better now. Much as she wanted to believe it, she had more than herself to worry about. She had to think of Casey's best interest and not her own desperate heart.

Kara moved forward, pressing into his personal space and leveling him with her business stare. "Stop."

He dropped his hands to his sides and turned to face her fully, leaving the project to wait. For a moment, he looked frightened, as if whatever she said next could have the power to break him.

Somewhere deep down, Kara thought that might be true. After all, Ryder had loved her once, just not enough, and never more than his fixation on a man who didn't know he'd existed.

Kara pushed hurt feelings and pride aside. Everything that had happened between them was in the past. Right now she needed to know why Timothy Sand had approached her and how to keep Casey safe.

Right now, Kara needed a partner.

She lifted her brows at him. Ryder wouldn't want to answer her next demand, but he had to. The moment his job had put her daughter in danger, Kara earned the right to know exactly what she was dealing with.

She tipped her chin upward and squared her shoulders. "I need to know everything there is to know about Timothy Sand."

RYDER TRIED HIS best not to argue. He needed to at least attempt to pull prints from the matchbook, but she was right. He also needed to help Kara understand the things he'd never told her before. When they'd been in love, he'd worked hard to shield her from his work. It didn't involve her, and Ryder had wanted to protect her. Kara was sweet-natured and kind. The sort of woman everyone loved at first sight. It didn't make sense to ruin that with stories of fugitive apprehensions or prisoner transports. She didn't need to know all the awful reasons people

lived in witness protection, or why serving federal arrest warrants wasn't as simple as what was portrayed on TV.

He'd intentionally kept the details of Timothy Sand's crimes out of their pillow talk and dinnertime conversations because Kara was too good to hear that mess. She was good and true. Timothy Sand was something evil.

Ryder poured two fresh cups of coffee and sent another round of messages to his team in Cincinnati on his way to the table where Kara waited. He'd protected her before. The gruesome details had had nothing to do with her. But things had changed.

He settled into the chair across from her at the small dinette, hating everything he had to say next almost as much as the man it was about. Timothy Sand had given him no choice but to reveal the sequence of events that had nearly driven Ryder insane.

"Just say it," Kara blurted. "I can take it. I just need to know. No more secrets or you're not staying."

Ryder patted the table with one heavy palm. He was staying whether she liked it or not. It might be in a sleeping bag on the porch, but he wasn't leaving. Not until he could take her with him, which would hopefully be in the morning.

"Timothy Sand is an arsonist," he said. Kara knew that much, of course. She tipped her head sarcastically, as if to say, "No kidding." "He set fire to the home of his in-laws after his wife ran there for refuge."

She sat back then, obviously feeling the weight of his words. Her lips pressed into a thin white line. Domestic violence was a personal villain of Kara's. An ex-boyfriend in high school had hit her after she didn't "act right" in his opinion. She didn't talk about the details often, but she'd made it her mission that day to shed light

on people like him and expose abusive men for what they were: criminals.

Ryder had been very careful to make sure she knew he wasn't like that guy. He'd have gladly stepped in front of a train to protect her. Still would. And anyone who wouldn't didn't deserve her time.

"And?" she prompted, coming back to life after the initial jolt.

"He'd been charged with multiple counts of domestic violence over the years. Eventually, his wife had enough and left him. You know the statistics on that." Leaving an abuser often escalated the abuse. Timothy was no better than the average aggressive asshole. No. He was much worse.

Ryder wrapped his hands around the nearly forgotten mug of coffee. "He followed her to her family's home where she went to hide. Then he killed her, her parents and her younger siblings with a hunting knife."

Kara covered her mouth with one small palm.

Ryder's face heated with residual anger, and he felt the disgust rise inside him. He hadn't captured Sand when he had the chance and now that monster was after Kara.

The look on Kara's face was so heartbreaking Ryder considered ending the story there. He hated being the cause of that expression. The one that said, *How can you deal with this every day? It's unthinkable. Vile. Horrific. Disgusting. What kind of person chooses this work? Chooses to expose themselves to these things without end?*

All legitimate questions, but what most people didn't understand was that there were days when everything was golden and the bad guy paid for his crimes because of people like Ryder. Days when a family was released

from their personal hell because a fugitive was captured. A killer put in jail. Those days made all the bad ones worthwhile.

"Timothy Sand burned the house down around their bodies, making it harder to identify them and the causes of their deaths, but there will always be a few things that can't stay hidden."

"The sun, the moon and the truth," she said.

Ryder nearly smiled. It was nice to know she remembered his family's favorite saying. Four brothers and a father, all lawmen. All who believed in justice and vowed to serve as best they could to make it happen.

"Sand was caught, eventually. He had no remorse. Probably blamed his wife for running and the family for giving her shelter. He's still wanted for the original charges plus multiple counts of murder and unlawful flight to avoid prosecution when his path crossed mine."

Kara listened intently. "'Multiple counts of murder to avoid prosecution,'" she repeated. "Does that mean he killed again, while you were chasing him?"

Ryder nodded.

"And that was when you got hooked. Trying to stop him."

"Yes." *Hooked.* She'd always used that word as if Ryder had been on drugs. Though, in hindsight, it wasn't the worst analogy. He'd been just as addicted, just as sick.

"That was the beginning," he admitted. "After a while, I made some progress tracking him, and things got worse. I followed him to a small town in Ohio."

Kara crossed her legs and leaned closer. "You were gone two weeks. I remember."

"I had him." *Almost.* Ryder swallowed hard, forcing his shameful gaze back to Kara's sincere one. He'd

driven through the night to get there, then followed the leads right to Timothy Sand. Within forty-eight hours, he knew everything he needed to bring him in. "I walked the town. Talked to the locals and uncovered his one mistake. He'd used his real name with a convenience store clerk, Jennifer Sayers." Ryder's lids fell shut. When he reopened them, he focused on the details of his old kitchen instead of the beauty before him. "Jennifer was young, happy and pretty enough that he'd forgotten himself, forgotten the alias. That slip was all I'd needed to get my hands on him."

But he hadn't.

Instead, Ryder had lurked in the shadows, building his case and waiting for the right time to make his arrest. "Three days after I'd started following him there, about a week after I'd received the notice that someone fitting his description was in that town, I went to the docks where he worked under an alias and waited for him to return from lunch. There were plenty of witnesses on hand, and he had nowhere to run without going for a swim. He took a bus to work, so there was no getaway car. Just a marshal and a fugitive. It should have been a textbook capture, but Timothy never showed. Instead, he went into town during his lunch and burned down the home of Jennifer Sayers."

Kara gasped.

Ryder pressed on. "Somehow, he'd known I was there. Knew she'd told me about him. And he went to punish her." Ryder pressed angry fingers to his temples. "She had an infant and three other children with her in the home."

Shock twisted Kara's sad expression into something caught between pity and horror.

Ryder couldn't blame her. He'd felt those things and more when he'd gotten the news, until eventually he'd felt nothing. In fact, the aftermath of that fateful day had nearly killed him. Thankfully, punching his colleague six months later had resulted in him getting some help. All those weeks of Marshals-mandated counseling should have been a joke, but it became his lifeline.

"That was when I began to unravel," he admitted. He dragged his gaze back to hers, hating what his hesitation had done to the lives of Jenifer Sayers and her family. To Kara's. To his. "For me, that was the beginning of the end."

Kara set her fingers over his hand on the table and warmth spread through him. "Hey."

Ryder raised reluctant eyes to hers. "I'm so sorry."

Kara nodded once. "I wish I had known."

"I couldn't say it out loud," he whispered. "When I came home to my happy life. My fiancée. Planning our wedding." He swallowed long and slow. "Everything Jennifer had lost because I didn't act faster..."

Kara's fingers curled under Ryder's palm. "If he's in Shadow Point, I know you'll find him. You can get him this time."

Ryder forced a painful lump of emotion deep into his chest. "I will."

"Okay," she said. "Should I guess from the duffel bag that you'll be staying here while you're in town?"

He glanced at the couch. "If it's all right with you, I'd rather not leave you alone. Tomorrow I'll find a better place for you and your baby until Sand is captured."

Her panicked gaze jumped to the baggie with the charred matchbook. "You don't think I'm safe here? You

think that guy might burn my house down?" Kara was on her feet then, hands waving helplessly in front of her.

Ryder met her there in an instant, and he wrapped her in his arms. The fear on her face ripped at his already shredded heart, and he did the only thing he could in that moment. *Be there for her.* Shockingly, she let him. "I'll protect you, Kara," he vowed. "You and your baby. We'll move you someplace safe tomorrow, but right now there's work to do."

Kara wriggled free, wiping her eyes and staring anywhere except at Ryder. "Right. I'll go pack my things and a bag for Casey so we're ready."

Ryder nodded, already back to the island and setting up to check the matchbook for fingerprints. "I'll call and make arrangements for the move."

The baggie fell from his fingertips then, caught by the counter beneath his hands. He turned to gape at Kara as she hustled toward the steps to the second floor. "What is your daughter's name?" he asked, projecting his voice so Kara was sure to hear.

Her cheeks went crimson. Her feet slowed on the carpeted stairs. "Casey," she repeated, a pained look in her eye, before hurrying out of sight.

Ryder Casey Garrett worked to reinflate his lungs.

He'd been gone far too long to be the baby's father, but maybe Kara hadn't written him off as completely as he'd imagined. Maybe there was still hope there.

Chapter Five

Ryder watched, dumbfounded, as Kara disappeared up the steps.

The buzzing of a new message on his phone pulled him back to the task at hand. West was waiting for photos of prints taken from the matchbook. He'd promised Ryder access to the county's lab and anything else he needed while he was in town pursuing Sand.

Ryder didn't have to work hard to get prints. It was as if someone had deliberately pinched the book between a thumb and forefinger, intentionally leaving clear and blatant marks. He didn't need the prints to know Sand was in town. Kara had confirmed that with the photo, but physical proof would allow Ryder to stay and hunt him. His caseload was too full to take a side trip on a hunch. These prints were a permission slip to stay. Without them, he'd be unemployed because he'd sooner quit the marshal service than leave Kara and Casey alone in a town with a killer.

The knots in his already twisted stomach pulled tighter.

Sand knew who Kara was *and* where she lived.

Ryder snapped the digital photos, then sent them to his

brother, jaw clenched and teeth locked. The sonofagun had crossed a line, and he wasn't getting away with it.

"Everything okay?" Kara reappeared in a baggy T-shirt and pajama shorts. She lined a row of neatly packed bags beside the door. Some were familiar pieces she'd once taken on their trips together. Others were new, smaller and covered in pink polka dots.

He tried not to think about why she'd changed her clothes or the fact that she'd caught him ogling her more than once despite the awful circumstances surrounding them. Hell, he wanted to stare a little longer, memorize every curve of her body and freckle on her nose, but it wasn't time to think about what he wanted. It was time to focus on what Kara needed, which was safe passage out of there with her baby.

He rubbed his neck and forced a casual tone. "Yeah." He took another look at the pink dotted bags. *Casey's* bags. He tried hard to reconcile the fact at hand with his childish dream that one day they'd have reason to meet again and things between them would be okay. That somehow, their previous life together had only been interrupted, not utterly railroaded. Nevertheless, the truth was everywhere. Ryder had spent three years healing, and Kara had spent the time moving on without him.

As she should have.

He dragged his attention from the tiny luggage to Kara. "You're all packed?"

Her eyes had already been on him, watching as he struggled with the reality of her life in progress. "Am I bringing too much?"

Ryder released a windy sigh. "You're a mom."

"Every day."

Ryder's gut clenched. Kara was supposed to have *his*

babies. Be *his* wife. Her firsts were supposed to be his as well.

But he'd ruined that. He'd give anything for a do-over with her, setting things right this time, but not at the expense of her happiness, and based on the photographs weighing down every flat surface, of a blissful Kara and her beautiful baby girl, she was happy.

A mix of emotions swam over her face before she turned on her toes and swept past him. She opened a cupboard door and unloaded empty bottles, canisters of formula and boxes of baby cereal into a purple bag on the counter.

A few moments later, she looked up, crossed her arms and stared hard. "I'm going to assume you smell something bad and that ugly frown doesn't have anything to do with me being a mother."

Ryder slid a hand across his forehead, smoothing the angry lines that had gathered there. "No. It looks good on you."

"Sure," she nodded, mocking. "I'm three years older and twenty pounds heavier than the last time you saw me. I haven't slept in four months, and I answered the door in worn-out running gear. Meanwhile you look…" She waved one hand aimlessly before dropping it back to her side. She groaned and went back to packing baby food.

Ryder drifted closer, unable to help himself. "I wasn't kidding or being polite or whatever you think. You really do look amazing."

She turned to face him, squaring her shoulders and locking him in her gaze. Challenging him.

He tugged the ends of blond waves hanging loosely at her elbows. "Your hair's even longer than I remember, thicker. You're tanner. You look happy." The final word

nearly choked him. She was happier after three years without him, even after that other loser she'd been with had left her, than she'd been with him.

He dropped his gaze and stepped away, his breath stolen by the sickening thought. Ryder had no business standing so close to her. No right to interject his desires into her perfectly happy life. He'd done a good enough job of screwing things up three years ago. Right now, he needed to focus on keeping her safe and getting his hands on Timothy Sand before he came at her again.

"I sent prints from the matchbook to West for testing, but I'm positive they'll come back as Sand's."

Kara relented her position, deflated, turned back to the purple bag and tugged the zipper across the top. "I've packed enough for Casey and me to be gone a week. Will that be enough?"

Ryder couldn't let it go this time. "You named her Casey," he said, still mystified. "Why?"

"It's a good name."

"It's my middle name," he said.

Kara stared into his eyes again, a long beat of silence stretching between them. "I know."

Dammit. How could he focus on the job when all he could think about was Kara and what her life was like now? What had it been like for her during those three years he'd missed? Had she thought of him? Was that why she named her baby Casey?

He took a step toward her again. "Kara."

She rolled big blue eyes up at him. "I should probably get some sleep."

Ryder leaned forward. "Please wait."

She didn't move.

He leaned closer still, testing the boundary that must

be there and inhaling her sweet scent. She looked so comfortable in her pj's, standing with him in their old home. Everything about the moment was so pleasantly normal that he nearly kissed her.

Except she wasn't his to kiss anymore, and nothing about their sudden reunion was normal.

His heart ached as she turned, and he caught her hand in his for one brief squeeze. She'd found happiness without him, and he needed to let her have it.

Find Sand. Go home. That was what he was there for, not to muck up Kara's life any more than he already had. "Good night, Kara."

KARA MOVED SLOWLY up the steps, forcing herself not to look back or run ahead. The grip Ryder Garrett had on her heart, *had always had on her heart*, was unfair, and darn it, she was mad at him for showing up like this and bringing a killer to her doorstep.

But there was no denying the way he looked at her. As if he didn't see how time had changed her, or didn't care.

She slid under her covers and let the memories come. Good ones this time. The sweet press of his mouth on hers. The taste of his lips. *Of his skin.* All the days she'd spent lost in Ryder's blue eyes and the nights she'd spent wrapped in his arms.

Sleep took her fast despite the danger lurking outside, and Kara woke to the sound of Casey's cry at six sharp. She sat upright with a bolt as the night rushed back to her. Her pajamas clung to the sheen of sweat still moist on her skin. Courtesy of falling asleep thinking of Ryder's body on hers. She plucked the soft cotton shirt away from her chest and peeled long strands of hair off her neck, cheeks and shoulders. Kara ran a hand through tangled

waves and sighed. She was a mess. *Doesn't matter*, she chided herself. *He's only here to catch his criminal and leave. He didn't come for you.*

Casey cried again, and Kara flung the sheet away from her body. She padded into the nursery and lifted her baby from the crib for a long snuggle. Casey quieted at the first sight of her mama's face. Kara sat in the nearby rocker for several minutes, giving herself time to cool off, then danced Casey back to the master bedroom, where Kara could freshen up before making an appearance downstairs.

She dropped a Tiffany blue sundress over her head and let her hair fall over both shoulders, then followed with mascara and a swipe of lip gloss, plus a good hair brushing. She'd have preferred a shower and shampoo, but Casey's need for breakfast trumped Kara's need to look pretty, so she descended the stairs with Casey in her arms.

Ryder did a double take when she entered the room. He looked ten years younger sitting on her floor in his old basketball shorts and Shadow Point Football T-shirt, surrounded by scattered papers. His ball cap was on backward and one long arm was looped around a bent knee. "Good morning."

Kara smiled. "You look like you're studying for finals. What is all that?"

He hoisted himself off the floor and loped in her direction. "I wish I was still in school. I'd do a lot of things differently."

"Oh, yeah?" She hoped that she was one of those things. That he'd have chosen her over Timothy Sand.

He stopped just inches from her, reaching out to stroke Casey's cheek. "Good morning."

The weight of his presence seemed to press the air from her lungs all over again.

Kara cleared her throat. "Ryder, this is Casey. Casey, Ryder." She angled herself then, giving Ryder a perfect view of her daughter's beautiful face.

"She's gorgeous."

"Yeah."

Ryder lifted pained eyes to Kara. "She looks just like you."

"Thanks." Kara fought a blush, but lost the battle. "Do you want to hold her?"

"No." He leaned away. Panic lifted his brows, and color bled from his cheeks. "I can't. I've never. So, I shouldn't."

Kara stepped closer, pushing Casey in Ryder's direction. "Go on."

"Uh." He cocked his head and shifted his gaze from Casey to Kara and back.

She smiled, watching the gamut of emotions race over his big, strong, US marshal face. "You can do it. She won't bite."

Ryder flicked his attention back to Kara. "You're taunting me."

"Yeah."

A smile twitched on his lips. "If I drop her, it's your fault."

Kara transferred her tiny princess into Ryder's capable arms.

Casey's pink blankie draped over his elbow, and her wide blue eyes focused intently on his.

Ryder's jaw went slack. His lips parted, and his shoulders dropped away from his ears.

Caught in Casey's spell. Her daughter had that effect on people.

"You won't drop her," Kara said. Her heart swelled with pride at the beautiful little human she'd made, the one she was raising on her own, the one who was all hers. For the tiniest moment, she wondered what it would be like to share her. She lifted her eyes to Ryder, recalling the amazing, funny, loving protector he had once been, and a wave of longing rolled through her, stealing her breath.

"How do you know?" Ryder asked.

Kara righted her thoughts and dropped a kiss against Casey's soft blond curls, then trailed the backs of her fingers over Ryder's stubble-coated cheek. "Because you're a born protector."

RYDER'S CHEST PUFFED with pride and heated with pleasure at Kara's words, *at her touch*. Her stamp of validation made him feel ten feet tall and unstoppable, but the baby in his arms made him feel curiously weak. As if his heart had been exposed and was suddenly, perilously endangered. By everything.

Was that what Kara felt like all the time now? Did caring for a tiny human do this to a person?

He turned his gaze back to Kara with renewed interest and increased respect. He hadn't thought either was possible. Then he remembered the question in need of an immediate answer. He looked into the tiny angel's gaze once more and felt his bones soften. "Casey," he whispered. Kara had named her daughter after him.

Kara returned a moment later carrying a bottle and tiny stuffed doll wearing a yellow raincoat. She gathered the baby into her arms and laid the doll on Casey's belly,

then smoothly maneuvered the bottle into her daughter's eager mouth. "What?" she asked, glancing at him as she got situated.

"Why'd you name her Casey? Don't tell me it's a good name again. It's my name. Why?"

Kara returned her attention to the baby in her arms, hungrily gulping her breakfast.

Ryder swallowed hard. "I need to know."

"Being alone and pregnant was tough," she started softly. "I guess you're the strongest person I know and I missed—"

The doorbell rang, interrupting Kara's words, and a fresh blush colored her cheeks.

Ryder grabbed his sidearm from the floor near his paperwork and shot Kara a pointed look. "Hold that thought. And stay back."

Kara hurried into the next room while he checked the window. "It's West." Ryder swung the door wide and welcomed his little brother with a strong hug.

"It's been a long time, Ry," West said, patting Ryder's back and squeezing him hard.

"Indeed."

The men stepped apart and looked one another over with keen eyes.

West rubbed his chin. "It's good to see you, but I wish it wasn't like this."

"That makes three of us." He cast a wayward look over his shoulder in the direction Kara had run.

"How was the reunion?" West asked, his voice low and pointed.

"Better than I'd expected," Ryder admitted. "Her daughter's in danger because of me, and she still let me live."

"She's either the definition of grace under pressure, or she's making plans to turn you over to Sand."

"The definition of grace, huh?" Kara strolled back into view. Her speed increased with each step until she nearly reached a jog. She lashed her free arm around West's neck and kissed his cheek. "I've missed you so much." She stepped back and beamed. "How are you?"

"Good." West's smile was wide and genuine. "Really good."

Kara's smile stretched impossibly wider. "I read all about your wedding in the paper. There were pictures by that local photographer."

"Marissa," West said. "Blake's wife."

Ryder had three brothers. All incurable playboys, and all recently married. Happy as he was for each of them, it hadn't escaped Ryder's mind that *he* was the first to be engaged. *He* was the one never interested in sampling from some bizarre woman-buffet. Ryder had only ever had eyes for one woman, and she was standing before him now, completely unattainable. And that was all on him.

West's gaze slid to the pink bundle in Kara's arms. "Well, hello," he cooed, slipping into a weird-sounding baby voice. "Who is this?"

"This is my daughter, Casey," Kara said.

West tented his brows. "Casey?"

Kara nodded, color staining her cheeks once more. "That's right." She kept her gaze on Casey while West shot Ryder a smug smile.

"May I?" West asked, nodding toward the infant.

"Sure."

Ryder drifted closer to Kara without thinking and set his palm against the small of her back.

She leaned casually into his touch as West pulled Casey into his arms.

"How soon can we move?" Ryder asked. Things had been too quiet for too long, and his gut said it wouldn't last.

"We're ready," West answered. "I've got two deputies waiting out front to escort us to the new location."

Kara set her hand on Ryder's stomach and rested her head against him, either terrified by the reality of being taken into protective custody with her infant or of the monster making the move necessary, Ryder couldn't be sure.

What he did know was that the heat of her gentle touch had burned a hole in his already aching heart. It wasn't a touch between friends. It was intimate and powerful. He jerked his face toward her, peering down as she looked up. And for the breadth of a heartbeat, there was no denying the emotion in those big blues. In the next moment, her attention was on West and Casey. Her hand at her side.

The doorbell rang, and the trio started. The front porch was empty, yet someone pushed the button over and over, rattling Ryder and launching Kara toward West.

"Back door," she said, hurriedly collecting Casey from his arms.

Ryder was already halfway there, gun drawn and motioning West to follow. It could only be Sand. Who else would push the bell maniacally, as if it was tied direct to Ryder's last nerve. Who else would approach the back door, at this very moment, while two deputies sat out front and the county sheriff stood inside.

Ryder's hands ached from the grip on his gun, but that was nothing compared to the invisible vise around his

heart. It was infuriating enough that Sand had come to Shadow Point to taunt him and threaten Kara and Casey. Now he had the nerve to walk up to her door and ring the bell that Ryder had once installed? To darken the doorstep of the porch where Ryder had once proposed? Where Kara had said yes?

Hell. No.

The brothers moved into position against the rear wall. West nodded, then swung the back door wide.

Ryder darted outside. He cleared the porch, the yard and the alley beyond, where Kara stored the trash bins.

"Ry?" Kara's trembling voice pulled him back to her like the snap of an outstretched rubber band.

She stood in the open kitchen doorway, Casey cradled in one arm, a piece of paper shaking in the grip of her free hand.

West met Ryder on the steps, pushing Kara back inside and locking the door behind them.

"What is it?" Ryder eased into her space. He wrapped a protective arm around her and worked to free the paper from her fingers.

"Us," she whispered.

A pair of photos were printed on copy paper. In the first image, Kara held Casey on one hip, and in the second image, Ryder curled Kara against his chest. The look on his face was pained and fiercely protective. The caption scrawled beneath simply said:

What a lovely family you have there, Marshal. Would be a shame to see it all go up in flames.

Chapter Six

The fine hairs along Kara's neck and arms stood at attention as Ryder pulled his SUV away from the curb with her and everything she cared about stuffed inside. He'd practically thrown her and Casey into the back seat the minute he'd seen the photo and read the note. *What a lovely family you have there, Marshal. Would be a shame to see it all go up in flames.* Her teeth chattered despite the sticky hot temperature. She curled her arms across her chest for warmth.

A killer had walked onto her porch and rung her doorbell.

He'd stood outside watching them. Photographing them.

West glanced at Ryder from his position in the passenger seat. "Tech services is working on a current photo of Sand for the media, and they say they will be able to tell which printer printed the photo once they get a look at it."

"Do we care about the printer?" Kara asked, still shocked by the boldness of Timothy Sand. Weren't there more important questions to ask? Like what else Sand had been up to right underneath their noses?

Ryder glanced at her in the rearview mirror. "We can

use the information about the printer to help track Sand's steps, and that's a good thing."

Kara certainly hoped so. She wasn't sure her heart could take much more fear and anxiety. Timothy Sand needed to be stopped. Today.

She set one hand on Casey's car seat, then turned her face toward the morning sun. She tried not to think of how dangerous things could get moving forward or about all the things she'd had to leave behind. The hand-me-down rocker where she'd nursed Casey for the first three months. Her grandmother's afghan. The porch swing where Ryder had proposed. She couldn't take it all with her, but everything she left behind was at risk of being burned to the ground, courtesy of Timothy Sand's fixation on hurting Ryder.

Kara watched as each car, street and friendly face flashed by outside the tinted glass. She searched for signs of danger but found only beauty. Growing fields of corn and sunflowers stood tall and proud beside big red barns and small white houses. Distant forest-covered mountains lined the horizon, but sadly, all the beauty in the world couldn't overpower the tumbling sickness of knowing a crazed arsonist was after her.

Beside her, Casey played contentedly with the plastic teething rings hanging from her car seat. For her, this was just another ride in the car. A quick trip to a new place with love and snuggles on the other side.

Meanwhile, Kara's worst nightmare was unfolding.

West caught Kara's eye in the rearview mirror as Ryder hooked a right through the center of town. "You doing okay?"

Considering the facts at hand? "No."

Cole, the youngest Garrett brother and current Cade

County deputy, drove behind them in a faded red pickup, trying to look inconspicuous without his cruiser. Unfortunately, three cars tailing one another through Shadow Point at this hour was conspicuous regardless. It was barely after seven, and shops in town wouldn't open for two hours. Sheriff's cruisers or not, their little caravan might as well have been a Fourth of July parade for all the attention it was getting from people walking their dogs, collecting mail from their boxes or rocking on their front porches.

Kara tried to smile at West's reflection, but couldn't manage the task. Her muscles and insides were knotted tight with fear. "Where are we going?" she asked. It hadn't occurred to her to ask before, but suddenly the destination mattered very much. Would they be safe? Would there be neighbors? *Witnesses?* Would there be collateral damage if Sand caught up with them?

She shivered hard at the thought, then rubbed rough hands against the gooseflesh of her arms. Each Garrett man was a force of nature. If they thought it would take three of them and an extra deputy to get her out of town safely… Timothy Sand must be the devil.

Kara's fingers curled tighter over the side of Casey's car seat. Sand had been close enough to do the same just yesterday. He'd gripped the stroller and looked at her as if she'd made him angry and not the other way around. It had seemed so strange at the time, but now she understood. He was angry. He'd probably hoped to find Ryder with her at the park.

West twisted at the waist and hung an elbow over the seat for a better look at her. "Our granddad's cabin. You know it?"

A rush of heat coursed over her skin and nostalgia

kicked around in her stomach. Kara's gaze jumped to the rearview mirror, where it met with Ryder's steely blue eyes. "Yeah," she said as flatly as possible. How could she forget the place? She'd lost her virginity in that cabin.

West turned back with a nod, attention fixed through the window once more. "I always loved it up there, but I haven't made the trip in years."

Ryder followed the other deputy into the parking lot outside the sheriff's department and chose a space around back. "I want to talk with tech services before we leave town. West's working with them to get Sand's photo on the news and in the local papers. I'd like your stamp of approval on the sketch we share."

"Okay," Kara agreed, thankful to be at the sheriff's department where Casey was sure to be safe.

She pulled Casey's car seat out of the vehicle with Casey strapped safely inside and followed West through the open door. Ryder entered last, keeping a close distance. Always protecting. Always watching.

The sheriff's department bustled with noise and energy, conversations and ringing phones. A vast contrast to the near-silent ride over. From her position near the door, Kara could see all six local deputies, plus folks in jackets with white letters spelling *Crime Scene*.

West and Ryder moved into the midst of the action and the other lawmen began to circle up. Only a few people, still talking on their phones, hung back.

"Kara?" Ryder's voice carried over the white noise around them. He waved a hand, summoning her.

The room watched with expectant faces as she carried Casey's car seat closer.

"What do you think of this rendering?" Ryder asked, turning a photo of the man from the park to face her.

"This sketch is based off our most recent photos and an age simulation software."

Her heart rate sputtered, then jolted into a sprint at the sight of him. She immediately recalled the determined set of his jaw. The tenor of his voice, and his hand on Casey's stroller. Unable to find her voice again, she nodded to make sure Ryder understood. Even without a clear view of the man's eyes, she'd recognize that long jaw, narrow chin and broad cheekbones anywhere. She'd never forget them for the rest of her life because now she knew he was the man who wanted to take everything from her. All to spite Ryder, a man who didn't love her anymore. Maybe instead of putting Sand's face on the news, they should hold a press conference announcing the three-year-old breakup. Kara wasn't Ryder's wife. Casey wasn't his daughter. They weren't a family. Sand should keep marching, out of Shadow Point, back to Cincinnati, where he could harass whoever Ryder was involved with today instead of haunting his past.

Ryder's frown deepened. He stuffed two fingertips between his lips and whistled loudly enough to call horses from the next county. "Listen up," he announced to the stilling room. "This is Timothy Sand. We want his face on every television station, every local newscast, relevant website and blog. Push it across social media. Get it out there. Offer a reward. Take every resulting call seriously. When something shakes out, get in touch with West or me immediately. I want this whole town looking for him, maybe even all of Cade County."

The room burst back to life. Men and women hurried to their desks and tapped wildly against the screens of their phones.

Kara concentrated on her breathing, forcing back the panic that threatened to pull her apart.

What a lovely family you have there, Marshal. The killer's words scratched against her mind. *Would be a shame to see it all go up in flames.* He'd tucked the photo neatly into her window frame as if it was a flyer for a new restaurant and not a threat to burn her baby alive.

Kara counted her breaths, deepening the inhalations. She tried to swallow, but her tongue seemed to have doubled in size. Her mouth was dry. Her eyes wet. Her lips quivered. *Keep it together,* she begged internally.

Casey fussed in her seat, no doubt feeling the intensity of the awful day.

Kara unlatched the five-point safety harness and lifted the little girl into her arms. "Hello, pretty," she cooed, nuzzling her daughter with her nose. "I wish I could think of somewhere out of town to send you until this nightmare is over. Someplace safe. With someone I trust."

But the truth of the matter was that when it came to safety and protection, there was no one better than the Garretts, and they were all in Shadow Point. She pressed Casey's head against her shoulder and bounced gently on her toes, hoping to either entertain her so she wouldn't cry or lull her back to sleep. Kara didn't care which. Once again, she felt a debt of gratitude for the busy sheriff's department. The cabin where they were headed was remote and not easy to find, but there was safety in numbers and something to be said about a room full of men and women licensed to carry a gun. *And trained to fire it.* Kara couldn't think of a safer place for Casey.

She jiggled her baby gently and hummed a happy tune. She left the car seat near the far wall of windows

and made a loop around the room's edge, watching the familiar and not familiar faces chatter and design plans to accomplish various goals. Contacting local news networks. Spreading the information online. Surveilling her empty home around the clock in the hopes of catching Sand on the property in search of her.

In the moments she dared a look in Ryder's direction, he was always looking back, as if he'd never let her out of his sight. She recalled his vulnerability at her kitchen table the night before, when he'd told her his story about Timothy Sand. Her heart broke all over again for the lives Sand had taken. The families he'd left permanent holes in. For everyone he'd killed and those he'd left behind.

Kara hummed and bounced Casey, but her attempts at comfort were rejected. Instead, the baby squirmed and fussed against Kara's chest. The strange room with all the new noises had to be the cause, but what could Kara do? Certainly not leave. Instead, she shushed her daughter and planted kisses in her hair, singing softly for only her to hear.

They passed Ryder as he spoke with West. Ryder's eyes were alight with hope and his lips were parted in an almost smile. He was impossibly more handsome than she'd remembered. Ryder clapped West on the shoulder, and her heart stuttered.

The sound reverberated off the walls of her mind, slamming her into a memory of those same strong, confident hands on her body. Those hands had taken her places she'd never been before or since, and she longed for one more trip.

"Kara?" Ryder stood before her.

Kara's muscles tensed with humiliation, caught reliving her most intimate memories in such a public place.

And under the most awful of circumstances. What was wrong with her?

"You okay?" He tipped forward for a closer look at her burning face. "Can I get you some water?"

"Yes. Water." She adjusted Casey on her hip, trying desperately to collect herself.

Casey complained. A slobber-covered fist cracked against Kara's cheek.

"Yuck." A bubble of laughter lifted from Kara's chest as she wiped Casey's drippy fingers on her sundress and kissed her daughter's chubby cheeks until she squealed with delight.

Ryder returned with a pointed paper cup. "I couldn't find a normal glass."

"Thank you." Kara gulped the icy drink and wished for more. What she needed was a cold shower and plane tickets to someplace Timothy Sand couldn't find her.

Casey whined again.

This time, Ryder reached for her. "May I?"

"Uh."

"You look like you could use a few minutes," he said. "This is a lot to take in, and I managed not to drop her last time, so…"

"Okay."

"If you want to freshen up or get a snack from the break room, there's time. I'd like to hang around long enough to see Sand's photo make it onto the morning news shows before we leave civilization."

The alarm on her face must've been evident because Ryder smiled. "We'll have everything we need. Don't worry. I've done this before." His brow furrowed suddenly, and his comforting smile faded.

It wasn't hard to imagine the guilt he was feeling. He

had done this before. As unintentionally three years ago as it was today, Ryder had put Jennifer Sayers and her family in the psychotic path of Timothy Sand.

That family hadn't made it out alive.

Kara handed Casey over. "Thank you. I only need a minute."

Ryder lifted Casey into the air, and she went silent, gaping down at her mother from the space above Ryder's head.

"Careful," Kara urged, slipping against his side to peer up at her baby.

He brought her back to his opposite hip. The mischievous expression on his lips had vanished, replaced by something dark and meaningful. "You're going to be okay," he vowed. "Both of you."

The deep, convincing promise in his voice was enough to weaken her knees. He used to profess his love to her in that voice. Kara's eyes stung with repressed emotion and unshed tears. The stress of the moment had caught up to her fully, and a fearful tremble worked through her limbs. She and her baby were at the sheriff's department, preparing to flee town in an effort not to be killed by a psychopath. The only bright spot in it all was that she got to see Ryder again and that he was well. But what would become of her when he left again? Why did it hurt so much, even three years later, to know his presence wouldn't last? The whirl of emotion got the best of her and a small sound escaped her lips.

Ryder wrapped his free arm around her, strong and steady as ever. "Come here." He curled her against him, cradling Casey on one side and Kara to his chest. "I know you're scared," he said. "What's happening right now is unthinkable, but it won't last. I've got the county's very

best on this case. It's going to be okay," he vowed, "and I will get Sand."

Kara lifted her chin for a better look at the man saying exactly the right words for her frightened heart to hear. Ryder's lips were far closer than she'd expected, and her mouth parted instinctively. The room seemed to fade around them as her gaze rose to meet his. She could kiss him. *He would let me*, she thought. The look in his eyes left no room for doubt about that, but what would it mean? Only a knife through her heart when this was over. A moment of comfort today was not worth the inevitable rivers of tears that would be shed later.

She untangled herself from him, dropped her attention to the floor and forced back the flood of waiting tears. "I just need a minute," she said, waving a hand toward the restroom across the way.

Ryder dipped his chin sharply. The arm he'd secured around Kara curled against Casey's back then, letting her walk away. He turned back to the room's center and the bustling lawmen.

Kara started for the ladies' room, but Casey's abandoned car seat caught her eye. Maybe Rainy Rosie would help make her smile.

The doll wasn't in the seat. She checked through the giant hobo bag on her shoulder. No Rosie. She'd surely remembered to bring her, hadn't she?

Kara moved to the window and looked into the lot, trying to focus her thoughts. She'd been so overcome by the need to pack as many memories as she could, in case Timothy Sand decided to burn her house down, that she'd left Rosie on the sofa. She could picture her there now. She felt the wilting drop of her shoulders as she slumped forward, exhausted. Mentally. Physically.

Emotionally. Hopefully Rosie would be safe until they returned. Hopefully her home would be safe.

She hung her head and turned for the ladies' room, where she could cry out her infinite and multiple frustrations in peace.

Two steps later, an earsplitting boom exploded behind her, knocking her from her feet.

The building shook and glass shattered.

People screamed and scattered, running and shouting as a plume of dust rolled through the sheriff's department and debris fell from the ceiling.

Somewhere in the darkness Ryder screamed her name.

Casey released a sharp gut-wrenching wail that tossed Kara onto her feet and in the direction of the sound.

Her lungs filled with dirt as she raced and fumbled blindly through the smoke-filled building. "Casey!" Kara coughed and hacked against her arm, straining to see her daughter in the thick smoky room. "Casey!"

Kara's ears rang, snuffing out the sounds of panic around her and hastening her footfalls in the general direction where Ryder had last been. Casey's cries had ended. Ryder's voice was gone.

Where were they? What had happened? A barrage of awful, deadly images rampaged through Kara's mind as she swatted and kicked her way through the nearly invisible world around her. As she made slow, bumbling progress toward the exit, bodies bumped against one another and rushed blindly, tripping over toppled desk items and sliding in sheets of broken glass.

Outside, the explosions continued. Booming and echoing from every direction.

What the hell was happening?

Her head beat with pain and the steady whooshing in her ears.

"Casey!" The scream seemed to launch from her very soul.

Where had Ryder and her baby gone? Were they rolled in a heap on the floor? Were they one of the things she'd kicked and hobbled over, unseeing? Kara turned in every direction, begging her eyes to reveal Ryder and Casey, but there was just debris, dust and smoke.

When she looked up once more, the crush of escapees had vanished ahead of her, leaving Kara in the broken building alone. She hoped. "Casey! Ryder!" *Please don't be here. Please don't be hurt. Or worse.*

Her gaze lifted to the bright spot several yards away. Sunlight beyond the open door. The place where everyone had filed outside. She needed to get there, find Ryder and her baby or get help to find them inside the building.

Kara stopped as the deep guttural groan of bending metal rumbled her bones and turned her eyes upward. A series of clicks and snaps echoed overhead, and a portion of the ceiling gave way with a resounding, thunderous crack.

The scream in her throat was extinguished as her body crumbled, crushed beneath an excruciating weight. Kara's world dimmed to black as she sent up a final fervent prayer that somehow Casey had gotten out of this alive. That somehow Ryder had protected her baby.

Chapter Seven

Strong hands wrapped Kara's biceps, pulling her onto her feet. "Can you walk?" Ryder's voice cut through the ringing in her ears. "I can carry you."

She shook her hazy head and shuffled along beside him through piles of plaster and insulation at her feet. "What happened?" she croaked, keenly aware of pain raging in her skull.

The sheriff's department was in utter disarray. The front windows were broken, and shards of glass cluttered the floor. A giant dust cloud loomed in the air, thinner now, but evoked memories of the explosion. She'd been looking out the window near Casey's car seat. Rainy Rosie was missing. Then, she'd turned away toward the ladies' room.

"Casey!" She pulled against Ryder's hand, scanning the floor in a frenzied panic. Her baby had been in his arms when the blast went off, but where was she now? Why wasn't Ryder looking for her? "Casey!" Fire scorched up Kara's windpipe, morphing her screams into deep, throaty hacks. Her eyes and nose burned from smoke still trapped in her throat and lungs.

"She's okay." Ryder struggled to find a new hold on

Kara's squirming arms. "She's with West. She's fine. He's fine. I went to find you. He took her outside."

"Where?" She coughed, straining to see West in the mass of distant bodies lining the parking lot. "Where?" she repeated, forcing more demand into her quavering voice.

"There." He extended an arm to the thickest part of the grouping.

Kara squinted against the blast of sunlight as they stepped through the door and into the parking lot. "I don't see her."

"Cole," Ryder barked. He waved a hand overhead, and his youngest brother lifted his chin in acknowledgment. Cole had gone to medical school before deciding to be a lawman. She still had trouble understanding why. All Ryder had to say about it when they were together was that the law was in the Garrett blood. "Over here."

Ryder set his hands on her cheeks, gently bringing her gaze to his. "Look for his hat. West is getting things back in order. Casey is with him. You need to stay here while Cole looks you over." He cupped her face in his palms, leveling her with a heartbroken stare. "Casey's fine." His voice was low and careful. "We weren't near any of the blasts. Nod if you understand."

Kara blinked through tears of relief, praying his words were true and needing to see for herself that they were. Where her baby was concerned, she wouldn't take chances.

Ryder released her. He lifted a finger toward the people once more.

This time, Kara looked for the broad brimmed sheriff's hat, its peak standing just above the crowd. A moment later, the group shifted, parting and reassembling

into smaller factions, revealing Casey on West's hip. He gave orders to the deputies and other bystanders, motioning with his free hand, holding Casey in place with the other. As if it was perfectly normal to run the show with an infant attached to his side.

Her pulse lowered a bit. "Okay." She nodded, and pain split the top of her head. Casey was okay, but Kara definitely wasn't. "I think the ceiling fell on me."

"Drywall," Ryder said, looking half ill. "The blast shook the building and an older section of the ceiling gave way." He rubbed his forehead with force. "I thought you were dead."

Kara lifted careful fingers to her scalp and the warmth of fresh blood coated her fingertips. "I'm not dead." She stepped away, but Ryder caught her again. This time, she shot him a warning look. "I want to see her, Ryder. Let go."

"Cole!" Ryder yelled, authority tightening the word. "Get over here."

Kara took another step and his grip tightened. "I will take you with me," she threatened.

Ryder released her, lifting open palms into the air. "She's fine. You're not. You need to stay here and let Cole look at you. You were just in an explosion," he nearly shouted.

"So was she!"

A few faces turned in Kara's direction.

She didn't care.

"Your hair has blood and dirt streaked through it," Ryder snapped. "Your face is scratched up and filthy. At least take five minutes to get your bearings before you march over there and collapse or something."

Kara glanced down at herself. She was a mess. He

wasn't lying. The blood on her fingertips came into view then. She swept her attention back to Casey on West's hip. She wanted to hold her, kiss her, tell her everything was okay.

"Five minutes," Ryder asked.

She swung her gaze to him. "What happened in there?"

Ryder's expression was remorseful. He was making her mad, but she could see the regret in his eyes. He blamed himself for what had happened.

What *had* happened?

"You were near the window." He locked his jaw and lifted his gaze over her shoulder.

Cole Garrett jogged swiftly in her direction, toting a red tackle box with a white cross on top. Behind him, and all around the building, dumpsters roared in flames. The largest fire was just outside the window where she'd been standing.

A sob broke in her throat, and she wrapped her arms around Ryder's sturdy core.

He closed his arms over her and held her tight.

Kara's will to be strong faltered in his embrace. She'd grown tougher in his absence and had eventually become Casey's refuge, but in that moment, her strength was testing its limits. Ryder's arms had once been her safe haven. A place where she could be vulnerable. Somewhere harm couldn't find her. And she needed that now more than ever.

The wailing cry of emergency vehicles broke into her awareness.

Kara pulled back with a start, remembering how many people had been inside when the explosion occurred. "Is anyone hurt?"

"You," Cole said, flashing a light into her eyes. "Everyone else was in an office or gathered with Ryder by the far wall, going over strategy protocols and sorting details for the news reports."

"Was it Sand?" she croaked.

Ryder's Adam's apple bobbed long and slow, but he didn't answer. The look on his face said it all. *This was Sand.* And that alone said so much more.

RYDER KEPT AN eye on Kara as a line of unnecessary ambulances roared to a stop in the parking lot and along the street. Despite the extensive property damage, the only person in need of medical attention was Kara, and she could barely hold still while Cole checked the gash on her head and tested her for a concussion.

The fire trucks arrived next, spilling men in traditional yellow gear onto the pavement.

Uncle Henry was the first EMT to make his way from the bus to Ryder's side. The others went to check the unharmed crowd.

"Everyone's okay," Cole said, addressing Henry as he crossed the final few yards between them. "Except this one." He dabbed an alcohol-soaked pad against her head, and she winced. "She's going to need stitches."

Kara shot Cole a threatening look. "I need to see my daughter."

"Take it easy," Cole said, his face sliding from all-business to slightly playful. "I'll send big brother this way. She's all yours Uncle Henry. Strap an oxygen mask over her mouth, would ya?"

Ryder bristled and fought the urge to trip his cocky brother before he said anything so curt to her again. Cole and Kara had always had a playful banter, but this wasn't

the time for it, and it wasn't fair that Cole could fall back into step with her so easily after so long. He settled for glaring as Cole walked away.

Henry greeted Kara with a warm hug, then quickly got to work. To Kara's apparent dismay, he took Cole's advice and snapped an oxygen mask over her face. "This will help with the breathing. You probably took in a lot of smoke and dirt. Were you unconscious at any point?"

"Yes," Kara answered with a deep inhalation, seeming suddenly thankful for the cumbersome mask.

Henry opened his medical kit. "How long was she out, Ryder?"

"Two minutes. Maybe less. I saw her go down, then I passed her baby off to West and shoved them out the door. I went to her from there. Took thirty seconds to pull the drywall away. She was out when I got ahold of her." Two minutes. The words sounded insignificant, but it was the length of two lifetimes. Pulling the drywall away and not knowing what he'd find beneath had been the worst moments of his life. He'd imagined the worst. The bloody, gory, irreparable worst. He rubbed the spot on his chest where it ached with fear again at the memory.

Henry gave her a careful exam, then cleaned and sutured her head. The cut wasn't as bad as all the blood had made it seem. She was finished after only two stitches.

Kara tried to leave again, but Henry held her fast.

"Almost done," he'd promised multiple times, examining every infinitesimal cut and bruise he could find. Several minutes passed before he relented his cause. "I think that'll do it. Come see me if you feel nauseous, light-headed or get any double vision." He handed Kara a two-pack of pain relievers, then cracked open a small bottle of water for her.

Satisfied, he slid smoothly from medic to uncle mode, swinging his face to Ryder. "What the hell happened here?"

"Arson."

He nearly laughed at the ridiculous answer. *Arson.* The word was far too tiny to describe the destruction and chaos swirling around them now. A sheriff's department temporarily out of service. Firefighters circling the building. Every deputy and the sheriff of Cade County displaced into a parking lot surrounded by local onlookers wondering what on earth had happened in their quiet little town.

Kara seized her moment and stripped the oxygen mask off her head. "Thank you." She handed it back to Henry. "I'm going to check on Casey."

Ryder trailed behind her, waving his uncle off. His brothers could fill Uncle Henry in on the details, whatever they turned out to be. He wasn't letting Kara out of his sight again. The moment he'd turned his back on her inside, all hell had broken lose.

Kara kicked into a sloppy jog as she neared West and her baby girl. A tear rolled over her cheek, glistening in the sunlight. "Casey," she cooed. "Come here, sugar." She scooped the little nugget off West's hip and hugged her tight.

West tipped his head, urging Ryder closer. A fireman stood with a clipboard and grimace before him. "Chief Michaels was going over some preliminary findings. You want to jump in on this?"

Kara moved into position at West's side, as if West had been speaking to her.

Ryder fought the quirk of his lips. "What do you

know?" He crossed his arms to keep his hands off Kara, and focused on the fire chief.

The chief looked at his clipboard. "The fires in the dumpsters were primed with kindling and ignited with Molotov cocktails. The receptacles closest to the building also had M-80s inside. Those were the blasts that continued after the initial eruption."

"All of the dumpsters?" Kara asked, drawing the chief's attention. "Could one man have done this on his own?"

An excellent question. Ryder looked to the chief, his gut twisting at the thought of someone like Sand with an accomplice.

"If it was well planned, maybe even rehearsed, yes. But for one man to pull this off, the execution would have had to be perfect."

Ryder groaned. Perfectionism was one of Sand's more infuriating qualities. It was nearly impossible to get ahead of a criminal who planned ahead and had contingencies in place for everything. He shuddered as sickness coiled through his gut at the thought of other potential traps Sand might have set in other locations where he suspected Ryder might take Kara. "We need to be on the lookout for other setups like this. He didn't have time to do this while we were in the building. He must've set up sometime earlier and waited for us to show up in the blast range. There could be more like this all over town."

West and the chief nodded. Ryder could count on them to send search teams into the community.

Meanwhile, Ryder scanned the fringe for signs of his nemesis. He needed a watertight plan to get Kara and her daughter to safety without Sand seeing. It wouldn't be easy. Ryder could practically feel Sand's menacing eyes

on them now. He repositioned himself at Kara's back and placed a hand on her shoulder. He needed to move her before something else exploded.

Kara or her daughter might not be so lucky the next time.

Chapter Eight

Ryder took advantage of the chaos before it settled and loaded Kara into the back of a panel van driven by the crime scene crew. Cole tagged along just in case.

They waited there, unseen for nearly an hour before the van pulled away with a number of other vehicles. *If Sand was watching. If he'd noticed they were missing.* He'd be hard pressed to guess where they'd gone, and he couldn't follow every exiting vehicle at once.

Ryder made a show of leaving alone, followed by West in the sheriff's cruiser. They needed to examine the perimeter of Kara's home. They knew Sand had been there this morning, at least long enough to take the picture he'd left for them on her kitchen window, and he wasn't a ghost, so he had to have left trace evidence of some kind. Footprints. Fingerprints. *Something.* At least, that was Ryder's prayer as he drove slowly back through town. They would also search for more of Sand's little booby traps. More fires waiting to happen.

Ryder checked the clock on his dashboard, already wishing he was back with Kara and her baby.

If all went as planned, the ladies would be at his mom and dad's home in time for dinner. It would make for a long day, but at least it would be a safe one. Ryder had

sent Kara and her daughter back to the crime scene offices in the panel van, where they would pass the time until the workday ended, then they would ride in a crime scene team member's SUV to the Garrett homestead, which was on one guy's way home. Anyone watching would see nothing unusual, except the pit stop to deliver the women. Then again, Sand would never see that stop because the Garretts lived on a narrow country road that would make it impossible for anyone to tail the SUV. If the SUV's driver suspected someone was following him, he would go on to the Cade County jail, where a solitary confinement cell would be waiting to protect Kara and Casey until Ryder could arrive, corner and capture their stalker. If Sand was brave and stupid enough to try an ambush, he'd meet the business end of a department-issued Glock.

A few minutes later, West rocked his cruiser to a stop in Kara's drive and lumbered out.

Ryder followed suit. He gave the home a long appreciative look by the light of day before joining his brother on the little walkway to the only window where the photo could have been taken. Flower beds lined the walk and rosebushes flanked the porch. A small, hand-painted sign hung between two red rockers beside the door, with the words *Life is better on the porch* painted in Kara's curly script. A tall, narrow sign beside the steps read *WELCOME* in big block letters. His finger curled at his sides as he moved into place outside the window where Sand had stood watching them. Trees and thick masses of red roses obstructed the view from anywhere besides that specific space on the walkway. Sand had been right there, separated from Ryder by a thin pane of glass, and Ryder had had no idea.

West dropped into a squat, scanning the ground for clues. "Don't look so grim, brother."

Ryder responded with a scoff, trailing his gaze over the blooming flower bed and tidy cobblestones. "I'm not sure how else to look right now."

West stretched back to his full height and clapped him on the back. "It's not over yet."

"Damn right." He shook his head in disgust. "This won't be over until Sand is behind bars where he can't hurt anyone else ever again."

West narrowed sharp eyes on Ryder and smiled. "We both know that's not what I meant."

Ryder's gut gave a squeeze, and he turned away. A future with Kara Noble and her sweet baby girl wasn't in the cards for him. The best he could hope for now was nailing Sand to the wall like he should've before, and if he was really lucky, Kara might someday forgive him for all the trouble he'd caused her.

KARA HELD FAST to Casey as the SUV clamored to a stop behind the Garrett homestead.

Mr. Garrett greeted Kara's driver, shotgun in hand. Square-jawed and ruggedly handsome like his sons, the retired sheriff was a patriot and born protector. Her heart kicked at the sight of him. To know Mr. Garrett was to understand his boys. Their instinctual and profound quests for justice were the stuff of storybooks. *Unfortunately*, Kara thought, recalling the awful stories Ryder had shared with her about the murders Sand had committed while Ryder had been in pursuit of him, *not every fairy tale has a happy ending.*

Cole climbed down to talk with his dad.

Kara opened her door and stepped into the sunlight,

examining the beauty around her. The intoxicating scents of fresh-cut grass, hay and horses rushed up to greet her. The Garrett farm was gorgeous, well loved and frequented by a large and proud family. Memories of backyard barbecues, birthdays and holidays around the gathering-room fireplace raced into mind. If breaking up with Ryder had been the hardest thing she'd ever done, then cutting ties with his family had been a close second.

The back door opened and Mrs. Garrett barreled out. Her graying hair was swept into a bun, and flyaway strands fluttered at her temples as she made a run for Kara, arms wide. "Baby girl," she cooed, wrapping her in a warm embrace. In that moment, in her arms, Kara was safe. The world was as it should be. And Ryder was inside, setting their plans for an evening of handholding and kissing under the stars.

Mrs. Garrett kissed Kara's cheeks and stroked Casey's soft curls. "I'm so glad you're home."

Emotion clogged Kara's throat as the weight of the day nearly overcame her once more. "Thank you for having me," she whispered, not trusting her voice to be any louder without cracking.

Mrs. Garrett released her and reality returned with a smack. A chill rushed against Kara's chest in her absence, despite the blazing summer temperatures.

She couldn't help wondering if this would've been her life sooner if she'd have married Ryder. Aside from the shotgun at his hip, Mr. Garrett seemed completely at ease, as if this was just another day in the life of a lawman. Was this what Mrs. Garrett's life had been like for twenty years while her husband was the local sheriff? Was this what Ryder's brothers' wives went through? Weekly? Daily? How could they do it?

Casey wriggled in her arms, letting out a soft warning. She was tired, overstimulated, ready for a bottle and probably needed a dry diaper.

"It's okay," Kara cooed.

Casey blinked. Her fussing stilled and a warm, toothless smile broke over her face.

And then she knew. The women in the Garrett men's lives did whatever it took because they loved them. Kara would do anything for Casey. Even trade her life to protect her daughter's. That was the kind of love the Garrett men had found, and as unreasonable as it was for Kara to think so, she was sure Ryder would do the same for her. Regardless of the wreck their relationship had become and all the time that had been lost between them.

"This way." Mrs. Garrett turned her toward the house by her shoulders. "Let's go inside and get all caught up now. I've already put on a roast, potatoes, carrots and fixed a salad. And there's sweet tea on the counter."

"You shouldn't have," Kara said, settling into step at her side.

"Nonsense. It's been too long for you and me, and you've got someone here to introduce me to." She pulled the back door open and smiled at the sleepy baby in Kara's arms. "Who is this?"

"Casey." Kara managed to maintain eye contact with Ryder's mother, despite the obvious desperation in that word. How sad was it that she'd named her child after the ex she'd never stopped pining for?

Mrs. Garrett gave a knowing smile. "Seems we have more to talk about than I thought."

The sound of crunching gravel stopped their progress. A vehicle was approaching on the long, winding drive,

and Kara's muscles went rigid with fear as she waited for it to roll into sight.

Before she had a good view, Mr. Garrett waved a hand overhead and smiled.

Her shoulders relaxed. Mr. Garrett knew the visitor. She was safe.

Mrs. Garrett bounced on her toes as Ryder's truck rolled to a stop beside the family home. She clapped her hands and darted back off the porch and across the lawn toward her son.

The driver of the SUV Kara had arrived in shook Mr. Garrett's hand, then climbed back into his truck. Cole hugged his dad, saluted Ryder's truck, then joined the crime scene guy on a return trip down the lane. Kara lifted a hand to wave goodbye. She'd forgotten to thank them for her safe passage.

Ryder and his parents joined her on the porch and ushered her inside.

The cozy kitchen smelled like brown gravy, apple pie and brewing coffee. The scents wafted tantalizingly through the air, resurrecting a forgotten hunger in Kara's empty belly. She hadn't eaten today, and while she knew she should have, fear had made it impossible. The most she'd managed to consume at the crime scene department was some orange juice while she cleaned up her face and hair. She'd need a shower and shampoo to get all the bits of drywall debris from the strands.

Ryder poured Kara a cup of coffee, then took the seat beside her. His hair was disheveled, as if he'd run his fingers through it too many times, and there was weariness in his eyes. Something hadn't gone as planned at her house. She could only hope it was still standing and not in a pile of ashes.

"Thanks." She wasn't ready to ask.

He examined her and Casey with careful eyes. "You okay?"

"Yeah."

Mrs. Garrett dragged a high chair to the island and pulled Casey from Kara's arms. "I'll take this one," she said, giving the baby a little wiggle. "Well, hello, Casey!" She made a silly face, then kissed her chubby cheeks and deposited her into the seat. "I told West that I was smart to buy baby things for my house," she said to Casey in a high-pitched voice. She fished infant toys from a quilted bag hanging on the back of the high chair. "Every good and decent grandma has her own baby things." She lined bulbous plastic farm animals on the tray for Casey to chew or knock down.

"Grandma Garrett had a farm," she sang, "E-I-E-I-O."

"She hates being a grandma," her husband dead-panned.

Kara smiled, warmth blooming in her chest. "I see that." Kara's parents hadn't seen Casey since her delivery, and while she hoped to travel to Oregon to see them for the holidays, that was a long time from now, and Casey wouldn't know them then. The idea of having a local grandma like Kara had had was heartwarming. Some of her very best memories were made at her grandma's side.

She blew across the bitter tendrils of steam rising from her cup, gathering her courage before forcing the nagging question from her lips. "How'd it go at my place?" She braced herself, half afraid to know the answer.

He gave his head a firm shake. "Nothing."

Kara nodded. They were no closer to catching Sand

now than they were yesterday when they didn't even know he was in town.

Mr. Garrett leaned his elbows on the island. "Care to fill me in on why this is happening? I got the wiki version from your brothers, and I already know all about Sand. What I don't understand is what he's doing here."

Ryder rocked onto one hip and removed a wallet from his back pocket. He slid a folded newspaper article from beneath a leather flap. "I attend the Sayers Vigil in Ohio every year. Jennifer's family invites everyone to the town square. Folks who knew her or her children share stories about them. Others take the podium as experts on the topics of stalking, domestic violence and mental health awareness." He slid the newspaper to his dad. Red ink circled part of the crowd. "This year, I thought I saw Sand there."

Kara moved to stand behind Mr. Garrett. She examined the grainy image over his shoulder. "I can't tell if that's him."

"It's him," Ryder said. "I wasn't sure at the time, but I know it now. The image was taken from quite a distance, and it's grainy, but I was there." He tapped a finger just outside the photo. "I tried to find him in the crowd, but he'd disappeared. I thought it was my imagination. That somehow being there, in that town, seeing photos of the lost family had conjured old ghosts. Until West called last night to tell me what had happened to you. It didn't make sense for Sand to risk attending the Sayerses' vigil."

Mr. Garrett gave a sad smile. "He wasn't there for them, Ry. He was there for you."

RYDER CARRIED HIS dad's words with him throughout the evening, running all over town with West and two mar-

shals who'd come to help locate Sand. As usual, the efforts were futile, and Ryder returned to his parents' home with no news to share.

If there was a bright side to an otherwise terrible day, it was that the sheriff's department had cleaned up well. The windows had been replaced, and an electrician had deemed the facility safe for business. The drywaller couldn't repair the ceiling until Monday, but that didn't matter. Everyone was back in their places and working hard to find Sand before he could do any more damage to their town.

His chest tightened at the sight of Kara and his mother on the old porch swing. Casey was fast asleep in Kara's arms.

Ryder climbed the steps slowly, taking in the lovely view. "Evening, ladies." He kissed his mom's cheek and stroked the fluffy yellow curls on Casey's head. "How are y'all holding up?"

His mom rose to hug him around the neck. "We're just fine, but it looks like you could use some rest." She turned to face Kara. "How about I put on some hot tea and take this little one off your hands so the grown-ups can talk?"

Kara's gaze jumped from Ryder to his mother. "Oh, no. You don't have to. She'll wake and fuss. You're already doing too much."

"Nonsense," Mrs. Garrett reached for the baby. "She can sleep in the nursery where all my grandbabies stay when they visit."

Kara flushed.

His mom must've read the emotion on her face because she leaned forward, cuddling Casey to her chest and whispered, "You'll always be part of this family.

Your little one, too." With that, she carried Casey inside, leaving Kara and Ryder alone on the dark porch.

He lowered himself onto the swing beside Kara. "She's right, you know? They're still your family. They adopted you the moment you showed up for dinner with me five years ago."

"I've missed them," she said.

Ryder considered his response. He could stay focused on the case, or he could make sure Kara knew she was his top priority, like he should have before. "I've missed *you*," he said finally.

She swung her face away from him.

Three years too late, he thought as she wrapped her arms around her middle. He was too late, but at least he'd finally told her.

She flicked an uncharacteristically shy look in his direction. "I've missed you, too," she said. "Every day."

Ryder's jaw sank open. "What?" He stared hard into her big blue eyes, willing her to say it one more time.

"Every day."

His arms were around her then, pulling her close. He buried his face in her hair and inhaled the sweet scent of her. The thrill of his heart pounding against hers enveloped him, and when he thought he couldn't take any more, she hugged him back.

Not just a hug. Kara melted into him. "I'm scared, Ryder."

"I know," he whispered, "but you don't have to be. Sand is on his way out of Shadow Point, and I'm going to be his escort." He brushed soft hair off her shoulder, wishing the moment could last, and that Timothy Sand's wretched name wasn't part of it.

She wiggled her head against his chest, peering up

at him in the night. "Are we putting your family at risk by staying here?"

"No." Ryder cleared his throat. "When you're here, Dad's on duty. Every Garrett has gone all-in on this case, from Dad and me to West and Cole, even Blake." His oldest brother, Blake, was a federal agent living in town, and Blake liked nothing better than capturing guys like Sand. "Plus, there are two more marshals in town now," he added. "They trailed Sand to a fleabag hotel on the outskirts of town before he vanished. He'll be too busy staying clear of them to find you tonight."

Kara shifted positions on the swing, releasing his torso and tucking her feet beneath her on the soft cushion. She leaned her weight against his side, setting her gaze on the horizon.

Ryder planted his boots against the floor and swung them gently, absorbing the moment, with its lilac-scented air, bullfrog-and-cricket chorus and firefly light show. "You know," he said, unwilling to miss another opportunity to say the things that had weighed on him for so long. "I was wrong to lose myself in the work like I did. I was too young and too green to know it would swallow me whole if I let it. You didn't deserve that."

"Can I ask you something?" she said, her voice more timid than he'd heard it before.

"Anything." His nerves bundled as he waited. Would she want to know why he'd chosen chasing Sand over being her husband? Why he'd given up a future with her to follow a psychopath? Because no answer would ever be good enough. And there was no sense to be made of it.

"Are you disappointed in me?" she asked.

"What?" He cocked his head back for a look into

her eyes, but she kept her attention on the distant field. "Why would I be?"

"Oh, I don't know." She sighed. "Maybe for letting a man into my life who I knew wasn't the one my heart truly wanted. It sounds dumb, but I feel like I let you down that way. I was selfishly trying to fill the void you'd left, and I should've known no one else could."

Ryder bristled. "I could never be disappointed in you," he said, mad all over again at the moron who'd left her and Casey to figure things out on their own. "What were you supposed to do? Your fiancé lost his damn mind and moved out to chase a killer. Your wedding was canceled. Your world changed irreparably because of me. I'd never blame you for anything you did to get through that."

An ugly thought wound through his mind then, and the words were on his lips in seconds. "But I am jealous. I've got no right to be, but I am."

"Of what?" She turned to him with a frown that seemed to say he was crazy for being jealous.

"Of knowing you found love somewhere else," he said. "Knowing you let another man into your heart…" *Into your bed.* "I thought you'd gotten married, had a baby, done all the things we'd planned to do together, with someone else…" *A jerk who'd walked away.* He grimaced, feeling the unreasonable clench of his jaw. "You had every right, and I have no business saying so, but I hate that guy."

Kara laughed, her expression moving swiftly to something light and peaceful.

Ryder scanned her curiously. He'd expected her to read him his rights.

"I kind of hate that guy, too," she said. "But the truth is nothing has ever felt right since you left." A tear fell

onto her cheek, and Ryder wiped it away. "I had to let you go because you'd chosen the hunt over me. Over us."

The words were a punch to his gut, but he deserved that.

"It feels like the worst days of my life are happening all over again," she said, "except this time everything's worse. This time my baby and I are in danger while you're hunting this lunatic."

"It's not like that," Ryder said, reaching for her hand. "I'm not the same man I was then, and I wouldn't even be chasing Sand right now if he hadn't come for you."

A fat tear rolled onto Kara's cheek. "Why'd you do it before?"

Ryder hung his head, feeling the leaden weight of her question on his shoulders. There was no good answer for what he'd done or for the pain he'd caused. Youthful ignorance seemed like an excuse, but that was what it had boiled down to. "I thought catching Sand would prove something. Make me a better man. A stronger protector. Save the world." He gave a low and humorless laugh. "I reached rock bottom that first year without you, and it took a while, but I got help, turned myself around and made Sand a side project instead of my purpose in life. I even turned the case over to a colleague while I left town to relocate a family in WitSec. Sand burned down another home while I was gone. My stupid colleague presented a case weaker than Grandma's coffee, and Sand got off with a scolding and some probation. Now, he's free again and here we are."

"Your dad's right, then. He's come for you," she said.

Ryder gave a sad smile. "Yeah." He set a hand along her jaw, curling his fingers against her warm skin. "I

swear I never dreamed he'd go after you. I had no idea he knew you existed."

"I know."

"It doesn't make sense for him to go after the woman who kicked me out of her life. He has to know by now. He seems to know everything."

"Maybe he just wanted to go back to where it all started with you?" Kara offered.

"Maybe." Ryder felt his brows furrow. Everything that had mattered in his adult life had started with Kara, and he wanted her at his side for everything else that mattered, too, but how could he ask her for anything when he'd ruined what they'd had in the past. And he was still hurting her now?

"I will fix this," he said, wishing she could see it was true. "I won't let Sand get near you, and I swear I will never do anything to hurt you again."

Kara's emotion-filled gaze slipped from his eyes to his lips. "Promise me," she said, curving featherlight fingers against the back of his head and pulling him nearer.

"I promise," he vowed.

Then, he covered her mouth with his.

Chapter Nine

Ryder's cell phone interrupted the moment he'd been waiting impatiently for these last three years. He pulled back, apologetically, taking his time to remove his hands from Kara's perfect cheeks. "Don't move."

Kara blushed, but nodded.

His heart hammered as he dug his phone from his pocket, cursing whoever had ruined the moment. West's face glowed across the screen. "This had better be good, brother," Ryder said.

"I know you've been at it all day," West began, "but I need boots on the ground near the old bank building, and frankly, we're running low on boots."

Ryder heard him out and stuffed the phone back into his pocket.

"What?" Kara asked, already on edge. "Did something else happen?"

"No, but I've got to go." He heaved a long breath and dragged one palm over his face. This was exactly the kind of thing that had broken them up before. "The barista at the coffee shop across from the sheriff's department made a call to dispatch on her way home a few minutes ago. She said there was a man at the coffee shop when the fires broke out earlier, and he stuck by the win-

dows watching the fallout to the very end. She didn't get a good look at his face, but she saw the car he got into when he left. She just saw that car again parked alone in an alley down by the bank."

"You think Sand is at the bank?" Kara asked. "Why?"

"It's probably nothing." Ryder reached for her hand and cupped it in his. "No one was in the car, and we don't know it was Sand she saw earlier. Someone still needs to check it out. Run the plates. See who it belongs to."

Kara nodded. "Okay. I'll come with you."

"I don't think so."

"Why? You said you're just going to call in the plate number, and we still have plenty to talk about, like how long Casey and I are supposed to hide from Sand while you hunt him down and bring him in."

Ryder considered her request. In any other circumstance, he would've said absolutely not, but this seemed like a good opportunity to show her he really had changed. He could go check out a car's plate without spending the night on the streets searching for Timothy Sand. And to be honest, he wasn't ready to say goodbye again.

Kara watched him. Her lips pressed into a thin line.

"Okay." Ryder pushed onto his feet and extended a hand. "Come on, then. Let's get this done so we can come home and kiss good-night."

THE DRIVE TO the bank was short. Kara had been quiet, but his phone had been busy. Cole was en route to the bank, but he was still ten minutes out. Everyone else was tied up, already chasing tips and leads that had come in following the evening newscast.

"Look," Kara said. "There."

The barista had been right. There was a car in the alley beside the bank, but Sand wasn't a bank robber, so Ryder wasn't concerned. He radioed the plate in to dispatch and turned back to Kara. "See? Easy."

She was pale in the moonlight streaming through the windshield. "What if this is an ambush?"

Ryder shook his head. "He has no idea the barista noticed him earlier, or that she saw the car he got into, or that she drives past the bank on her way home. Wait here while I peek in the windows. Due diligence," he explained, "then let's get out of here." He lifted her hand to his lips and left a kiss there before climbing out from behind the wheel.

Ryder shut Kara inside the truck, then went in for a closer look at the car. It was locked. No one inside. Nothing notable on the seats.

"Ry?" Kara called. Her voice carried through his windshield in the silent alley. She pointed toward the brick building opposite the bank.

Ryder followed her troubled gaze to a rear entrance. He crossed the alley for a better look at the door in question.

He swore under his breath. The door was ajar.

Behind him, the soft snick of his closing truck door drew his attention to Kara, hurrying across the alley to his side. "Are you going in there?"

"You're supposed to stay in the tuck." He scanned the alley before sending texts to West and Cole. "Cole will be here any minute," he told her, reading their responses aloud. "West is contacting the store manager." He squinted at the next incoming message from West, then backed up to stare at the darkened building. "This is a camping store?"

"Yeah," Kara whispered, a quiver in her voice. "The drugstore closed last year."

Tension knotted in Ryder's gut. It couldn't be a co-incidence that he'd wound up there while following a lead on Sand.

Kara shivered at his side, one small hand wrapped around his elbow. "What should we do?"

"We should wait in the truck until Cole gets here."

Kara's safety was Ryder's top priority. He pressed a hand against her back and forced his feet away from the store.

They'd barely taken a full step before a harrowing thud echoed through the partially open door, followed by a series of muffled grunts and ugly, strangled sounds.

Kara gasped. Her wide, questioning eyes turned to Ryder.

"Get in the car," he told Kara. "Lock the doors." He removed his gun from the holster. "I need to make sure no one is hurt."

Kara shook her head. "No way."

"Go," Ryder demanded, lowering his voice. "Cole is on his way. I need to be sure the building is clear and some poor stock boy isn't in danger."

"No," she repeated. "The man who wants to kill me is probably in there, and you want me to wait alone in a dark alley while you go inside? What if he slips out another exit and comes for me?"

Ryder ground his teeth. Kara was right, but if someone was hurt inside the building, he couldn't walk away. He also couldn't leave her alone in the alley. *Where the hell was Cole?*

The guttural scream of a man in pain split the air and stood the hair on Ryder's arms at attention. He sent one

more text, this time to dispatch, requesting an ambulance, then turned to Kara. "Stay close."

She gripped the material of his shirt and moved in close to his back.

Ryder pulled the door open, senses on high alert.

Inside, security lighting glowed eerily over the store's central merchandise, casting heavy shadows over the perimeter and much of the store. Large taxidermy displays of mounted animals loomed around them and looked down from balconies, making it seem like a hundred glass eyes were watching. The choking sounds of distress came again, and Kara's fingers tightened in the material of his shirt.

Ryder moved swiftly through the darkened racks of clothing and camping gear, toward a massive hunting knife display, wishing for all the world he'd left Kara at home. He didn't want to think about the reason a man like Sand would break into a store like this or what he'd find on the other side of the ghastly noises.

There were too many places to hide. Too many unknowns, and yet what could he do besides hope whoever he heard struggling for air would survive whatever Sand had likely done to him or her?

Ryder stopped short as the outline of a man's broad shoulders came into view. Only a tall narrow display of designer oars stood between them.

Ryder raised a palm, signaling Kara to slow, then directing her, silently, to wait as he continued on. With Kara safely tucked into the shadow of the wall, Ryder aimed his weapon. "US marshal. Hands where I can see them."

The figure raised both palms. The strangled gurgling sound came again. Louder now.

Instinct moved Ryder more quickly toward the man. Something was wrong. This wasn't Sand. Sand never would've obeyed so easily. *Unless this was a trap.* He lowered his gun, shocked as the silhouette came clearly into view. The man seemed to be tied upright with a hammock fixed tightly around his torso and the oar display. Ryder hustled closer, and the man's bloodied face and throat came into view. His uniform identified him as the night watchman. His eyes were wide with panic, held open by adrenaline and fear. Blood rolled in steady lines around the metal of a serrated hunting blade shoved through the side of his throat.

Ryder unfastened the man and lowered him to the floor carefully. He pressed hunting socks from a nearby display to either side of the blade, hoping to stanch the blood flow and knowing it wouldn't help. This man needed a surgeon, not a failing marshal. "Help is on the way," he assured the man, who was still reaching for a hold on Ryder's arms. "My brother's a medic and a deputy. He'll be here any second, and ambulances are on the way." Ryder sent texts to Cole and dispatch, his blood pressure rising with every keystroke.

The watchman continued to clutch at Ryder's sleeve and wave a trembling hand near his shoulder. Ryder followed the direction of his wild gaze to a stack of boxes behind him. Lighter fluid.

KARA STRAINED TO see what was happening. Ryder had called for the intruder to freeze. To put his hands up, then nothing more. For a few moments she could see both men, then they seemed to have disappeared. Had they run? Were they on the floor?

She inched through the shadows, too terrified to stay

put, not knowing what might happen. What might have *already* happened. Her heart hammered with indecision. How far could she stray from where Ryder had left her? Where the hell was Cole?

The rough palm of one broad hand clamped over her mouth, and her frame went rigid.

A thick arm wrapped her in its iron grip, smashing her ribs. A hunting knife was clutched in her assailant's long fingers. "Your marshal has a bad habit of ruining things for me," he said, as the sounds of a police siren registered outside the door. "Now, come on. Before the cavalry arrives."

Kara didn't have to see his face. She knew that voice. The man from the park. Timothy Sand. She dug her feet into the concrete floor beneath her, hoping to stall him long enough for Cole to arrive or Ryder to come back for her, but Sand was too strong, and the tip of his blade dug precariously against her shirt.

"If you struggle, I will kill you," he promised, rancid breath streaming over her cheek. "Casey deserves better than to be an orphan, don't you think?"

The word struck ice through her veins. *Orphan.* For the first time since becoming Casey's mother, it was her own life that seemed unbearably fragile. She nodded slowly.

"Good." He edged her toward the elevator. One floor later, he guided her to the balcony, where a display of toboggans and mannequins in ski gear looked out over the floor below.

A pair of paramedics raced through the first-floor entrance, shuttling a gurney in the direction Ryder had disappeared. Cole followed on their heels.

A sudden blinding flood of fluorescent lighting

snapped on overhead, and Sand started. His left hand loosened over her mouth, and the knife in his right sliced swiftly through the thin material of her shirt and tender flesh below.

"Ahh," she cried, the pain searing through her.

"Freeze!" Ryder yelled from his position below. His seething voice boomed through the cavernous store. "You've got nowhere to go, Sand." He raised his gun. "Release her and step away now, and you might still get out of this alive."

Cole rushed to Ryder's side, matching his stance, gun drawn.

Behind them West ran toward the elevator.

Sand sighed into the hair at her ear. "I guess I have to go for now. Next time, you won't be this lucky." He released her without warning, his hands flowing instantly to her back. And he pushed.

Kara's feet fumbled, and her arms flailed as she was propelled off the display's end and into the open air. She screamed again as the floor came rushing toward her. Thoughts of her precious baby girl flickered in her mind.

Casey would be an orphan.

The sounds of gunfire burst around her; the fall seemed impossibly long. Her ears rang and her tummy lurched.

Ryder was in motion. Did he think he could catch her?

Their bodies collided as he dove at her, tackling into her before she met the unforgiving floor with a bone-jarring thud. Air rushed from her lungs as they tumbled over the camping display, through a tent and over bedrolls and sleeping bags before bursting apart.

Cole slid on his knees to their side. "Are you both

okay? Is anything broken?" His eyes jumped from Kara's face to Ryder's. "That was insane!"

Ryder grunted, sucking in air. He forced himself onto his side with a wince. "Kara?"

"I'm okay," she sobbed, rolling to face him. Tears rolled hot and thick over her cheeks and his shirt. "Thank you."

Ryder enveloped her in his life-saving embrace. "I should never have brought you here."

THE GENTLE CLINKING of silverware and shifting of plates grew louder with each aching step toward the Garretts' bustling kitchen. Kara had had the worst night of her life, but it was time to put on a brave face for Casey, even if her ribs were bruised and so was most of the rest of her body. The cut on her side hadn't even required stitches, just some medical tape and a good cleaning.

However injured Ryder was, he didn't let on. At least nothing was broken.

Casey squealed in delight at the sight of her mama, and kicked her tiny feet beneath the high chair tray.

"Hello, gorgeous," Kara said, kissing her baby's head, cheeks and chubby, dimpled fists.

Mr. and Mrs. Garrett flanked the high chair at a small dinette in the nook. "Good morning," they said in near unison.

Mrs. Garrett wiped a dollop of rice cereal from the high chair tray. "Help yourselves when you're ready."

A spread of breakfast foods lined the countertop.

Cole and West were seated at the island, dressed in matching khaki-and-brown uniforms, plates piled high from the extensive buffet.

Beyond the open back door, their oldest brother,

Blake, paced with a cell phone pressed to his ear. His navy T-shirt and jeans seemed oddly casual for an FBI agent, but she supposed he wasn't really on duty, and a suit was overkill for any reason in Shadow Point. He lifted a hand in silent greeting when he saw her watching. Apparently, stopping Sand had become an official all-Garretts-on-deck situation.

Kara returned the wave, then busied herself freeing Casey from the high chair. She felt the weight of a dozen Garrett eyes on her as she wiped Casey's hands and face, trying not to get any breakfast on her pretty sundress or booties.

Ryder moseyed toward the coffeepot, fatigue in his eyes. "Any sightings since last night?"

West shook his head. "Nothing viable. The deputies have followed up on everything we had."

"At least everyone made it out alive," Mrs. Garrett said, her cheeks going pale with the words. "Tell me the security guard lived."

"He did," Cole answered, wiping his mouth on a napkin. "Ryder saved his life. If he'd waited to get him down or put pressure on the wound, he wouldn't have made it to the hospital. The knife missed his carotid. He was damn lucky."

Ryder sipped his coffee. He didn't seem to think *lucky* was the right word. "We stopped Sand from making off with ten cases of lighter fluid. That's something."

The back door slapped shut as Blake walked inside. "Tech traced the photo from the printer to the drug store on Maple about forty minutes before they closed last night, which supports the theory he set the kindling and M-80s in place earlier. Then delivered the photo to move you to the station."

Kara cuddled Casey closer and moved toward the brothers. "So, he set it all up, knowing you'd take me there?"

West nodded. "I'm not surprised. Sand has been running from the law long enough to know how we operate."

Kara felt her mouth downturn. "Great."

"It's not a bad thing," West said. "Sand knows our protocols and he'll expect us to follow them."

"And you're going to change things up?" she guessed.

Cole frowned. "No. We're going to do exactly what he expects us to do so he thinks he has the upper hand, and when he shows up feeling overly confident, we'll be waiting to arrest him."

Kara cast her gaze around the room, suddenly uncomfortable. "When he shows up where? Here?"

"No." Ryder returned to her side with a plate of food, concern lining his brow. "Right now, Sand doesn't know where you are, but he'll be looking. That means we have the upper hand. There's a deputy stationed outside your house and tech added surveillance cameras to the utility poles near the sheriff's department in case he goes there looking."

Blake swiveled his cell phone to face her. A black-and-white image of a car from the alley outside the camping store centered the screen. "Footage collected from the drug store confirmed that he's driving the older-model white sedan you saw last night. We're circling the wagons, and it'll squeeze him out."

Kara didn't share Blake's confidence or enthusiasm about their progress so far. Maybe he'd feel differently if Sand had thrown him off a second-story balcony. "Why didn't the car come up as stolen when Ryder called in the plates?"

"The owner is on vacation," West answered. "When I spoke to him, he was shocked to hear it wasn't in his garage."

Ryder rubbed her back. "Every criminal makes a mistake eventually, and Sand's mistake was coming here."

The Garretts lifted their coffee mugs in unison. A toast to Ryder's words.

Kara leaned against his side, hoping to absorb even the smallest measure of his confidence, but the moment was cut short by the sounds of multiple dings and buzzes.

The Garrett brothers lifted their cell phones and swiped the screens.

"Turn on the news," Ryder called.

Cole flashed to the little television lodged in the corner of the kitchen.

Mrs. Garrett went for the larger flat screen in the family room. "Which channel?"

"Any," Ryder said through gritted teeth.

Both televisions settled on the same distant image of a burning cornfield. Different news anchors reported from the foreground. A woman cornered the little screen in the kitchen. A balding man in glasses was on the television in the family room. Behind them blazed a ring of fire twenty feet across and nearly as high.

A trio of scarecrows were arranged in the center.

Kara covered her mouth as the helicopter covering the scene on the kitchen television circled lower, making the figures more visible. A large cardboard star had been cut out and staked through the first scarecrow's chest. *US MARSHAL* was scratched across it in thick, heavy lines.

Two other scarecrows lay on the ground at the base of the first's support post.

"That guy's you," Cole said to Ryder, "but what's that

supposed to mean?" He marched up to the television and pointed at the other two prone figures.

West joined Cole a foot from the screen, hip cocked, both hands gripping his waist. "Is that us on the ground?"

Cole hacked a deep, throaty noise. "Think again, Sand."

Blake swore under his breath and shot Ryder a pointed look. Ryder nodded, short and quick.

Kara watched Ryder for an explanation. He and Blake had seen something there the other brothers hadn't.

Mr. Garrett set his steaming coffee mug aside and crossed the room to the television. He studied the scene with clear, discerning eyes. "Must've taken some time to do this. It's precise." He waved his pointer finger in a circle, indicating the line of fire. "He had to have wet down the field to stop the flames from spreading in this weather. A drought, really. We haven't had a lick of rain in more than a month. I sure hope Farmer Mays has good insurance. That's going to ruin his crop."

Kara turned back to the image, mesmerized. "Is this meant for us?" she asked the room. Her heart hammered and her tummy ached. "Is this his big move?"

Ryder gave a stiff dip of his chin. "It's a threat."

"Was anyone hurt?"

"No. He wants us to react."

Kara breathed easier, knowing no one had been hurt in Sand's attempt to get to them. "He wants you to go to the scene?" she guessed. "All of you, or just you?" she asked Ryder.

He locked eyes with her then. "He wants me out of hiding. I suppose if your entire detail went to the scene and left you alone, he wouldn't complain, either." Ryder turned to his parents. "We won't spend another night

here, and you should consider visiting Aunt Linda in Lexington. It won't take him long to get your address from someone in town."

His mom barked a laugh. His dad ignored him completely.

Kara imagined the Garretts would rather go down fighting. Their sons had gotten the disposition honestly.

Before she could beg Mr. and Mrs. Garrett to reconsider, something small and yellow caught her eye in the blazing cornfield. "Oh, no. Look." She gripped Ryder's arm with one hand and tucked Casey more tightly against her with the other. The little yellow figure came more clearly into view as the helicopter swooped in. "It's Rosie," she whispered.

Ryder turned angry eyes on Kara. "The doll?" His gaze slid to Casey, then to his brothers.

"Who?" Cole asked.

"She was mine when I was young," Kara said. "I gave her to Casey when she was born, and I forgot her at my house when we left yesterday."

Recollection was written on West's face.

Ryder swore.

Kara let her desperate gaze drift from face-to-face through the room. "That doll in the yellow raincoat belongs to Casey. The figures on the ground aren't other lawmen. They're me and my daughter."

Chapter Ten

Ryder turned his back to the television as his brothers broke into action, scraping plates into the sink and pressing cell phones to their ears. Pain and regret tugged Ryder's heart as he pulled Kara and Casey against him. He'd known Sand wouldn't stay quiet for long, but he'd hoped they could at least finish breakfast before all hell broke loose.

Kara wound her arms around his middle and rested her cheek against his chest. Her heart pounded furiously against him and there was a distinct shudder to her breaths.

"This will be okay," he promised, lowering his lips to her ear. "No one was hurt. That field is on the other side of town. We're safe here, and we have time to plot out the best course of action."

She rocked her head back, bringing her chin to rest where her cheek had been. She rolled frightened blue eyes up at him. Her fingers curled into the fabric of his shirt.

"I mean it," he said. "And you should eat. It's looking like a busy day."

Kara gave a soft groan, then pulled away.

Casey tried to take Ryder's shirt with her, her tiny fin-

gers tugging the fabric of his sleeve. Her little arm out-stretched as Kara shifted away, but didn't offer release.

Ryder reached for her then. "How about I hold her while you eat?" he asked Kara.

Burning cornfields and making scarecrows into bi-zarre voodoo dolls were behaviors way outside Sand's norm, and Ryder had no idea what would come next. Kara needed to eat and rest now because here, in the safety and shelter of his family home, surrounded by lawmen, retired and otherwise, she was still safe. This was the time to fill her belly and prepare for whatever awaited them.

She turned Casey over to Ryder with a quick kiss, then wrapped her arms around her middle. "I don't think I can eat," she said, "but I should probably get dressed."

He cuddled Casey into his arms and kissed Kara's forehead. "We can take some fruit and muffins with us. In case you get hungry later." Or they were forced into hiding somewhere they wouldn't have easy access to anything worth digesting.

Casey released his shirtsleeve in favor of gnawing her fist.

Kara marched woodenly up the staircase, eyes glued on Casey until she disappeared onto the next floor.

The kitchen stilled in her absence.

His brothers stared, no longer rapt in their phones.

"What?"

Silence.

Casey pulled her tiny hand from her mouth and slapped it against Ryder's cheek. A string of slobber stretched between them.

"Nothing," West said flatly. "Just looking. That's all."

Cole chuckled. "You just got slapped by a baby."

Blake only shook his head and went back to tapping hard on his phone screen.

Ryder's phone buzzed, and he struggled to free it from his pocket.

"Here." His mom came to take Casey.

If Ryder wanted any time to get to know Kara's baby, he'd have to carve it out when his mom wasn't around.

"I have an idea," his mom said, gathering the infant into her arms. "What if I take Casey and Kara to Aunt Susie's farm across the river while you boys handle things here?"

"I don't know," Ryder said, immediately missing the weight and warmth of Casey in his arms. "That's a big property. We don't have enough manpower to guard it and look for Sand at the same time."

"No," Blake said, butting into the conversation. "Mom's idea is a good one. It's smart to go to Susie's. Sand wouldn't know to look for her there. Susie isn't even our real aunt. There's no logical link for him to follow. Dad can go with them and keep a tight perimeter around the house only. Mom can keep Kara and Casey inside."

Their mom dropped a floppy sunhat on Casey's head. "She has her own disguise." She tugged the brim low on the baby's head. "No one will recognize her now." She beamed into the baby's face. "Look at this angel. The hat matches her booties. I'm fit to die."

"Well, don't do that," Cole said, "you're on babysitting duty."

West stuffed his brown sheriff's hat onto his big head and went for the back door. "My guy at Kara's house said there was no movement all night, so Sand must've been there and taken the doll before my deputy arrived."

That left a narrow window. Ryder wondered idly if

Sand might've been at Kara's yesterday while he and West had searched the ground outside for footprints.

He pinched the bridge of his nose and tried to stay focused. All the bad that had come from Ryder's last run-in with Sand didn't compare to the amount of potential damage that could be done now. He'd barely gotten Kara back, *if* he'd gotten her back. They hadn't talked about reuniting officially. She'd just said that she still loved him, and he'd reciprocated. There had been a kiss after that, but Ryder had no doubt that Kara would walk away in a heartbeat if she thought he wasn't good for Casey.

Ryder knew he would be. He'd be everything he could for both of them.

He watched his mother sing softly to Kara's daughter. His mom looked truly happy, but Casey looked so fragile.

Could he protect Kara *and* Casey? Could he capture Sand before he hurt someone else this time? He drifted closer to his mother and the sweet baby girl in her arms. "We'll get him," he told his mother, setting a hand on her back.

"I know."

The sound of Kara's footfalls came from the steps, and Ryder turned to see her.

She'd traded the pajamas for a pair of cutoff shorts, a faded red T-shirt and running shoes. "Ready," she said, a look of determination on her brow.

He tried not to imagine running the palms of his hands up her long tan legs and turning those shorts inside out.

"I want to go to my house," she said. "Sand took Rainy Rosie off the couch, so I know he was inside. I want to salvage whatever I can before he burns the place down. Assuming that was what the fire in the cornfield meant." She had a brave face in place. "I'm okay with

Casey going away for the day. I heard you talking while I changed."

Ryder frowned. "You heard that? And you don't mind parting from her?"

She gave a sad smile. "Old house. Thin walls. Honestly, I'd prefer Casey wasn't with us while we run home. It's probably best if Casey lay low." Her voice cracked on the final sentence, her bravado a nearly convincing facade. "If Sand is watching, he'll assume Casey's with me. With us. She'll be safer with your folks, and I can't live knowing I've put her in any more danger today."

"Okay," Ryder said. "I'll take you home to get whatever you want. Mom and Dad will take Casey to Aunt Susie's for the day." He scanned the room for anyone in disagreement.

Kara walked to his mom's side and took Casey into her arms. "I love you," she whispered. "I'll see you soon, so be good for Mrs. Garrett and try not to worry. Ryder and his family are going to protect us."

Ryder struggled to swallow the brick of emotion growing larger in his throat. Whatever happened, he couldn't let Casey or Kara get hurt. His heart had become irrevocably tied to them. He'd never stopped loving Kara, so it made sense that he'd fallen so easily into his old thought patterns and instincts with her, but Casey was new, and his desire to guard and protect her was something completely *other*. Nothing so sweet and fragile should have ever come to be in Sand's path.

His brothers moved in on him then, phones in hand, delivering reports and updates from their contacts in the field.

"No activity," West reported. "It's quiet at Kara's and

at the station. I've got two plain-clothed deputies at the fire, too. So far, no signs of Sand."

Blake hooked an elbow on the island behind him. "That's smart. Arsonists are known for watching their fires burn. We might still find him there, enjoying the spectacle."

Ryder agreed. "Okay. Good. Meanwhile, Kara and I will go to her place. Get what she needs and get out. We'll meet Mom, Dad and Casey at Aunt Susie's afterward."

Kara swayed slowly to his side, a sleeping baby in her arms. Casey's little head rested on her mama's chest, rising and falling with Kara's every breath.

Ryder's mom hooked a giant purse over her shoulder and palmed the keys to his SUV. The sadness in her eyes was enough to break his heart. "Take your father's truck instead. Leave your SUV in the barn for now. Sand will be looking for that. We'll take my Ford to Susie's."

Reluctantly, Kara shifted her baby into Mrs. Garrett's arms. "Protect her," she whispered.

His mom's eyes glossed with emotion he'd never seen before. "With my life," she pledged.

THE RIDE TO Kara's home from the Garretts' homestead had never seemed longer. To make matters worse, Kara's mind was split with worry for Casey and fear for the town. She sent up continual prayers for her daughter's safe passage to the farm across the river, adding a round of pleas for herself and Ryder in between.

Kara wanted Casey to grow up with a loving mother at her side, not a horror story about a monster who came to town and killed her. She wanted to grow old watching Casey grow up, maybe even Casey's children, too. Kara wanted to watch them change the world, and if

she was really lucky, she hoped Ryder would want to do that with her.

The truck came to a stop in her driveway, and Ryder climbed out with one hand on his weapon. "Two minutes," he said before closing his door and locking her inside the vehicle. He walked the length of her house, then vanished around the back.

Kara checked the clock on the dash, then scanned the scene beyond her window. Two minutes later, Ryder reappeared with a stiff nod.

She jumped out, too anxious to sit still any longer. "All clear?"

"Outside, yeah," he said with a flick of his gaze to the small black Mustang across the street. "West's deputy's here. He'll keep watch from the front. Once we go inside, you need to wait in the foyer, door locked behind you, while I check the house."

Kara nodded.

She followed his instructions inside, until he returned to her once more, this time looking somewhat at ease. "All clear. Where was Rosie when you left yesterday?"

"On the couch."

Kara hefted a plastic tote from her hall closet and dumped the contents onto the floor. If she was lucky, those things would still be there when she came back, *not burned*. And hopefully that would be soon.

If Sand burned her house down, it wouldn't matter about the mess.

"I'm going to put a few things in here to store at your folks' house, if that's okay. Nothing I need. Stuff I don't want to lose. Just in case."

Ryder's solemn expression made it clear that he un-

derstood and, apparently, he agreed that losing her house in this mess was a possibility.

She turned away then, leaving Ryder to peer through the front windows while she collected a second round of favorite things from her home. She started with the framed photos from the fireplace mantel. "Where do you think he is?" Did he really think there was a chance Sand was outside now? Wouldn't the deputy stationed out front have seen him? Her mouth dried further. He'd walked right up to the back door while deputies sat out front before.

"I don't know." Ryder dropped the edge of her curtain and stepped back from the window facing the small side yard. "I hate that he's out there plotting his next move, and I'm playing defense. I should be chasing him and not the other way around."

Kara set the plastic tote on the couch. Déjà vu pricked and snapped against her skin. It wasn't the first time she'd stood helplessly by while Ryder longed to be somewhere else—*chasing Timothy Sand*, specifically—but it felt just as abysmal. She told herself not to feel betrayed. They'd shared a kiss last night. Nothing more. Emotions had been running high, and chemistry had never been one of their problems. He certainly didn't owe her a happily-ever-after because of it.

Ryder released a long, labored breath and turned arresting blue eyes on her. "I'd thought chasing Sand was long behind me."

Kara moved into him, letting Ryder's strong arms form a protective cocoon around her.

"Then again," he said, "I'd thought a lot of things were behind me."

Kara fought to keep the emotion away from her ex-

pression as the same old worry came to mind. Could Ryder really put her and Casey first, whatever might come?

"How are you holding up?" he asked.

"Not well," she admitted, refocusing on the bigger issue. "I feel like we're playing Sand's game without knowing any of the rules."

"Doesn't matter what his rules are. He's in our town now, and he's going to wish he hadn't come here."

Kara hoped he was right. "What do you think the fire in the field meant?" The answer seemed obvious. Sand planned to burn them or maybe just burn the world down around them, but Ryder had studied Sand for years, and she suspected he saw something more this morning when the fire flared through the television screens.

Ryder watched her for a long beat before speaking. "I think it was retaliation. He didn't like having his face plastered all over the news yesterday, so he returned the gesture with me in the form of a scarecrow. I put his image out there to let everyone know I'm after him."

"And he did the same." Kara's pulse quickened. "You think he was publicly announcing his intentions like you did."

"I do." Ryder's voice was low then, fierce. "I won't let him take you and Casey from me." His warm breath tickled her face as he planted kisses along her forehead, cheeks and chin. His sweet words melted her heart and loosened her knees until she was sure she couldn't stay upright without his help.

Slowly, Ryder pressed his mouth to hers, kissing her fully and deeply until the world fell away. His lips made promises she knew he couldn't keep. Not while they were

being hunted. But hopefully he'd make good on them very soon.

She stepped back in a daze, enjoying the flood of desire rolling through her core. "I should get busy."

He loosened his grip, but didn't let go. His heated gaze raked over her body, obviously thinking the same thing she had been. There was a bedroom just up the steps. A couch behind them. Floor all around. Kara knew firsthand about the toe-curling, earth-stopping pleasures that came after a look like that, and she was tempted to ask for them.

Until the blazing cornfield crept back into her mind, and a chill slid down her spine.

Kara stumbled back to collect herself, then lifted her tote and moved to the next room in search of irreplaceable items. "I'll hurry," she called over her shoulder.

In the kitchen, she braced the bag against one hip and plucked the fabric of her shirt away from her chest, trying to settle down. It was time to be real. Last night's confession of love didn't come with promises. Just kisses. He could easily go straight back to Ohio when this was over and leave her heartbroken. The only thing she could afford to think about right now was Casey.

Head in the game, Kara treated the house like a grid and worked methodically from room to room, tossing treasured books, photo albums and keepsakes into the tote for their salvation. When she reached her bedroom, she made a direct path to the bedside drawer.

Her feet slowed as the nightstand came into view. The top drawer, where she kept her most private memories, was pulled slightly open. "Ryder?" she called.

Had he and West searched the house when they came by yesterday? He'd told her there was no new evidence of

Sand's visit outside the home, but had he and West been in her room? Had they seen the drawer full of Ryder's old love letters and the stacks of accompanying photos? He hadn't said so, but maybe he thought it would embarrass her. It might have at the time, but after her confession on the porch swing, the collection would've made more sense. She'd never had the heart to let anything of his go.

Regardless. The drawer had been shut when she last stood in her bedroom.

"Yeah?" Ryder's voice echoed up the stairwell, accompanied by quick-falling footsteps.

Kara moved closer, curling her fingers around the drawer's handle. "When you and West were here yesterday," she began, tugging the drawer wide before Ryder made it into the room. "Did you—" Her gaze landed on the blackened contents and her heart jerked into a sprint. She stumbled back on a sharp intake of air, bumping her legs against the bed.

"What?" He strode through the open doorway.

Kara jumped.

"What's wrong?"

She turned her eyes to the nightstand. A partially burned book of matches lay inside the drawer atop the love letters, engagement photos and a million other things Kara had clung to in Ryder's absence. Someone had painstakingly scorched the edges of everything. Melting and curling the photos' corners, singeing and charring the paper, without letting any of it be completely destroyed.

Ryder swore. He dragged his phone from his pocket and pressed it to his ear.

Kara scooted onto her bed, pressing her back against the headboard and clutching her knees to her chest.

Somewhere in the back of her mind, she'd created a false image of Sand rushing into and out of her home, grabbing Rainy Rosie, the first thing he saw. Her gaze returned to the letters and she held herself more tightly. This was...meticulous. He'd taken his time. What else had he touched? Infected? How long had he spent invading the privacy of her life? Her stomach knotted impossibly tighter.

Ryder's voice carried on beside her, conveying the findings to West, then speaking with what she assumed was another marshal.

The landline rang beside her, and her hand shot out to answer on instinct. "Hello." Her voice quavered, still unsteady from the shock of the ruined keepsakes.

"Mrs. Garrett?" a familiar voice asked. The voice, she realized with a drop of her stomach, was the one from the park and the camping store. "No, no, no," he corrected himself. "Sorry about that. I've learned I was wrong. It seems you are the *almost*-Mrs. Garrett."

Kara made a strangled sound, suddenly unable to breathe.

"Kara?" Ryder dove onto the bed beside her, dropping his cell phone on the pillow. He mouthed, "Is this him?"

Kara wobbled her head, still straining for air as fear clutched her windpipe.

Ryder took the receiver from her shaking hand and held it on his open palm, pressing the speaker option with his fingertip.

"Speechless?" Sand taunted. "I've had that effect on a number of people." He chuckled darkly. "I've lost track of how many. But I didn't call to talk about me. I wanted to talk about you, and that little princess of yours. She looks so lovely today, doesn't she? In her little sundress

with the matching booties and bonnet." He clucked his tongue. "It's good that you dressed her for the weather. I'm afraid it's going to be a scorcher."

The sound of a striking match sizzled through the line, and Kara's body jolted forward, heart seizing.

"No!" she screamed. Her breath coming back to her in a powerful rush. "Don't hurt my baby," she cried.

Ryder jerked the phone from her hand. "Sand!"

"Don't touch her," Kara grappled Ryder's shoulder, lunging closer to the receiver, ready to pledge her soul in exchange for Casey's safety.

But it was too late. The line was already dead.

Chapter Eleven

Kara launched from the bed, her limbs weak and clumsy with shock. "We have to go." She swung her arm out for Ryder, but her hand collided with the tote she'd so carefully packed instead. Keepsakes and treasured memories scattered across her bedroom floor with a crash. "Oh!" she squeaked, jumping wide and tangling her feet in an attempt not to step on the beloved contents.

Ryder's long arm snaked out to catch her as her knees weakened. His lean frame was beside her in seconds, pulling her against him. "Stop." His voice was low and even, but his grip was firm.

She stood, shell-shocked, as a fist of emotion punched through her chest, and the world tilted. "Come on. Hurry!" Kara tried to take another step forward, but Ryder wouldn't be moved.

His sinewy arms tightened around her middle. "Kara," he said coolly. "Wait."

"Wait for what?" she snapped, jerking herself free. "For him to kill her?" Bile flooded her tongue, rejecting the words. A bead of sweat broke on her forehead.

"No." Ryder shook his head slowly, purposefully. "But we can't just run off and lead him straight to her."

Kara considered the notion. "He's already there," she

croaked through a constricting throat. "He saw her hat and booties."

"We don't know that," Ryder said, "and we can't take a liar's word."

Kara worked to relax her stance. "Then, what?"

"Well, first, we can't get overemotional and react to his stimuli. That's how he wins. He sets up the scene he wants to unfold, then waits while we rush in and act it out for him, and we can't afford to do that."

Kara's limbs had stilled, but her heart and lungs worked double-time beneath her rib cage, pinching and aching with each wild thump. "I think he's got her, Ryder. He's got my baby girl."

"My parents would have called."

"What if they *can't*." Horror and nausea pulled at her core. "I sent Casey away to keep her safe, and now she's the one in danger." The words were whispers, barely audible against the ringing in her ears. "He knew what Casey was wearing."

He struck a match.

Kara clamped a hand over her mouth. "I'm going to be sick." She raced to the adjoining bathroom and retched until it hurt to breathe.

Ryder lowered to his knees beside her. He pulled her hair away from her face and offered a wet washcloth for her thrumming head. "I've already spoken with West. I was on the phone with him when I heard Sand on your line. He had just checked on Casey. Mom and Aunt Susie are playing peek-a-boo with her in the den. It's in the center of the house with multiple exit options from that point. Dad's got it covered. Casey's okay." He cupped her face in his confident hands, bringing their gazes to

meet. "There's no one at Susie's farm who shouldn't be, and West is on his way for added cover. Just in case."

Kara wanted his words to be true, but what if he was wrong? "He has to be near. He saw her."

Ryder nodded. "I think it's most likely that he was watching my folks' home and saw her there before we all left. My parents' place is well fortified and monitored by a security company, but it's also the obvious place for us to have hidden. It wouldn't have taken Sand long to find us there."

"What if he followed them?" she asked, her voice shaky, her tummy sick. "What if he's lying in wait at Susie's? Maybe your dad just hasn't seen him yet."

"I don't think so." He hooked a swath of hair behind her ear and leveled her with calm, confident eyes. "When we split up with my folks, Sand could only go one way. We know he chose to follow us because he called us here. He couldn't have known we'd come here unless he'd followed."

Kara slumped into a seated position, leaning against her bathtub for support. "So, he didn't follow your parents? He doesn't know where they are?"

"I don't think so, no."

She pressed the washcloth to her eyes. "And, he's here somewhere?" Her stomach churned painfully once more. "Watching us?"

Ryder didn't answer. He didn't have to. He'd already said as much, and the look on his face said so much more. The set of his jaw and color of his skin. The fists clenched tightly against the bathroom floor.

Kara released a long breath and set the washcloth aside. Sand wasn't with her daughter.

Casey was safe.

"Feeling better?"

"Yeah." Kara pulled herself up by the sink and rinsed her mouth out. If Casey was okay, then she would be, too. "What do we do next?"

Ryder strode back to the bedroom and refilled the toppled tote. "We collect your things as planned and take them away from here."

Kara moved to the nightstand and stared at her ruined letters. "I can't take them. Can I?"

"Not those," he said. "Those are evidence now."

Her bottom lip trembled, but she nodded in heartbreaking acceptance. Her lovely treasures would soon be read by tech support, by strangers and by his brothers. She turned her eyes to Ryder.

"I'll write you more letters." He looped a strong arm around her shoulder and pulled her near. "You don't want those memories anymore. When we're finished with Sand, I'm making it my mission to eradicate everything he's tainted. He can have the letters. Those are pieces of the past. We'll make better memories in the future."

Her heart swelled with hope and regret. The everpresent tornado of emotion continued to churn and twist inside her. "People are going to read those," she said.

Ryder gave a sad smile. "I know. It doesn't matter. Everything in those letters was true. Is true," he corrected. "And anyone who can't relate to those kinds of feelings, the love, the desire—" he rested his forehead on hers "—those people should be damn jealous." He kissed her head and hefted the refilled tote into the sharp V of his side, securing it with his free arm. "Right now, we should go. I'll look out for Sand, and we'll sneak over the river to Aunt Susie's so you can see Casey's okay."

Kara squeezed him tight before setting him free.

"Thank you." She looked beyond him to the silence outside her room. "Maybe you should lead the way."

RYDER PASSED HER the tote and removed his sidearm before descending the stairs.

The house was still. No signs of an unwelcome guest.

Ryder repeated his perimeter sweeps inside and out before escorting Kara to the truck.

He folded himself behind the wheel and connected his phone to the truck's Bluetooth. "Call Mom."

"Calling Mom," the truck answered as he reversed onto the road. Hearing that Casey was safe, directly from his mother, would put Kara's mind at ease, and she desperately needed that.

Kara's skin was pale and her gaze was jumpy, as she searched endlessly outside the window. Her knee bobbed and her fingers worked a thread from her shirt until he thought the entire garment would unravel.

Ryder locked stares with the undercover deputy in the black Mustang, dipping his chin only slightly in acknowledgment, unwilling to give the man away if Sand was watching. West would fill him in on what they'd found in Kara's room. Ryder needed to get Kara out of there and check on Casey.

He turned back to the road with a grimace. He and West had been on Kara's property after the fire at the sheriff's department, looking for booby traps and trace evidence of Sand's presence, and they'd left before the lookout had arrived. Their haste had given Sand time to sneak inside, steal the doll and ruin Kara's letters.

The ringing stopped and the call went to voice mail.

Kara's muscles stiffened visibly. Her cheeks flushed,

and she cracked the window, sucking in deep breaths of free-flowing air.

Ryder redialed his mother several times before changing tactics. "Call Dad." Surely his father would answer. Ryder knew they were okay, logically, but the fact that his mother hadn't jumped on her phone was a point of concern. Hearing his dad clear things up would put his mind at ease and help Kara to relax on the long drive to Aunt Susie's across the river.

"Calling Dad," the truck agreed.

The call went to voice mail.

Kara jerked her face in his direction. "Call Susie," she told him. Desperation dripped from her words. "Maybe cell service is bad there. Try her landline."

Ryder grimaced. "I don't know Aunt Susie's number."

"What?" Tears welled in her wide blue eyes. "Then call West again," she demanded. "Call West."

"I just called West."

"Calling West," the truck agreed.

Ryder stifled a groan and checked the rearview one more time for a tail, then took the final turn out of Kara's neighborhood, through the main entrance that dipped dramatically through a historic brick-lined tunnel.

His truck hugged the hilly residential road, ducking quickly under the old railroad tracks by way of an arched cutout in the grassy hillside. The stubby passage was lined in elaborate landscaping and flagged with hand-carved signs announcing guests' arrival to Deer Hollow, a quaint, family-centric allotment perfect for raising children. None of the other neighborhoods they'd looked at three years ago had come close to appealing to the family man in him like this one had, and he'd been elated

to know Kara loved it, too. She especially loved the entrance tunnel and sidewalks throughout the area.

Ryder breathed easier the moment his truck emerged from the tunnel without encountering any sort of ambush that Sand might have considered setting within. Still, Ryder couldn't shake the feeling Sand had called to rush them outside for something. So, what was it? Why had he called? Not just to scare them. That wasn't a big enough goal for someone like him.

Ryder checked his rearview once more. This time, an object appeared in the air, and Ryder slowed the truck to a stop, craning for a look at what was heading his way.

"What's wrong?" Kara asked. "Why are we stopping?"

"Garrett," West finally answered the call as the thing landed in the bed of his borrowed truck with a loud crash and an explosion of flames.

Kara screamed, twisting in her seat and staring wide-eyed through the rear window. Her chest rose and fell in sprinting puffs, and Ryder felt the familiar coil of rage rise up inside him.

FIRE WHOOSHED INTO the air, licking the glass between the cab and the bed. Smoke roiled into the air, obscuring the world around them.

He jammed the truck into Park and jumped onto the street, muscles tensed to spring. Adrenaline charged through his limbs as he surveilled the scene, staring into the veil of dark smoke. His fingers locked instinctually over the butt of his sidearm, waiting to spot his target.

"Out!" Ryder hollered, stealing a look at Kara, who was still frozen with fear inside the cab.

The flames in the truck bed burned low and dirty. A

distraction. From what? He couldn't begin to guess, but it would be bad, and he needed backup.

Kara leapt from her seat, stumbling against her open door and asking a thousand questions he couldn't answer. *What was that? Where did it come from? What do we do? Is it Sand? Where is he?*

Ryder yanked opened the crew cab door, then unhinged the fire extinguisher he'd tossed inside before leaving his family farm. A must-have, he'd thought, for hunting an arsonist.

"Ryder?" West barked through the truck's speaker. "Where are you?"

"Outside Kara's neighborhood." He pulled the trigger on the extinguisher and aimed at the dancing flames.

A white chemical cloud lifted into the air, mingling with smoke from the suffocated flames.

Ryder scanned the scene in search of the only person who would do something like this.

Kara coughed her way to his side. "Are you okay?"

Another thump! Another round of broken glass and a fresh blast of flames.

"Dammit!" Ryder snuffed the fire and turned to the truck. "West! We're on Oakvale. He's tossing bottle bombs, and I can't see anything but this damn smoke."

"Already on the way," his brother answered.

A third bottle exploded into flames in the truck's bed. The hovering fog of chemicals from the extinguisher and smoke from the pint-size Molotov cocktails stung his nose and eyes.

Kara screamed and clutched him tighter.

Ryder's fury heated to a boil. "Sand!" he yelled into the smoke-filled air, his voice wild with rage. "Come out, you cowardly sonofabitch!"

Beyond the smoke and flame, a figure stood on the railroad tracks over the tunnel, another flaming bottle in one hand.

Kara gripped Ryder's elbow. "Sand."

"Change of plans," Ryder muttered. He handed the extinguisher to Kara and pulled his gun. "Pull this trigger, and keep your eyes on him. If he disappears get in the truck and lock the doors. Otherwise, keep the chemicals coming." He wiggled the extinguisher.

She nodded, unsure. "I'll try."

That was all he needed. Ryder turned with purpose toward the hill to the railroad tracks and bolted forward.

West's voice continued to make demands through his truck speakers. "Where are you? What is going on?"

Ryder crouched as he jogged, using the thinning smoke as cover for his approach, hoping to maintain the element of surprise as long as possible. The acrid air stung his lungs as he climbed the hill behind the Deer Hollow sign.

Another bottle hit Ryder's truck with the same crash and whoosh as the others. Kara kept the dry chemical cure going, rejuvenating the white cloud around her until she became nearly invisible behind it.

Ryder's feet slid on loose pebbles in the dried grass as he reached the abandoned tracks. The area was foggy, drenched in the pollution of too many homemade bombs and the effects of an active extinguisher. The ground was littered with ripped clothes and empty bottles. No Timothy Sand.

He'd lured Ryder there. The phone call had been meant to push him out of the neighborhood and through the tunnel. For what? To toss mini bottle bombs at his truck? To infuriate him and scare the daylights out of

Kara? Was this just a game of cat and mouse now? An itch at the back of his mind turned his face toward the white cloud behind him. Could Sand have gotten to Kara while Ryder had been coming for him? Was that what this was for? Had Ryder done exactly what Sand wanted, all the while trying not to?

Ryder braced his arms, gun extended into the haze. He stepped carefully, putting the full extent of his training to work. His senses were on high alert. Muscles tensed to spring. Turning back for Kara might be exactly what Sand wanted him to do.

Ryder's thoughts circled uselessly, trying to guess the intentions of a madman.

The sickening sound of a lighting match struck at Ryder's heart, and he spun in search of the source.

Back on the road, the telltale slam of his truck door said that Kara had gotten inside.

That meant she was safe.

It also meant that Sand must have vanished from her view.

The chemicals thinned, revealing the taillights on his dad's truck as it rolled forward, away from the scene of the ambush.

Good girl, he thought. *Lead him away. Make him think I'm with you.*

"You're fast," a familiar voice taunted.

Sand's form took shape as the remnants of smoke drifted away. He had another burning bottle in his hand.

"Drop it, Sand."

"Gladly." He launched the bottle at Ryder's head.

The flame scorched his hand and face as he attempted to deflect the crudely made bomb. The bottle landed and

bounced on the ground without breaking, but the fire raced to consume the spilled fuel.

Skin burning and temper flaring, Ryder was forced to stop and stomp the flames along the old railroad track, kicking mounds of gravel and dirt onto the fire until it was satisfactorily snuffed out. To let it burn would have been to ignite the town in this seemingly endless drought.

Ryder whipped his head up then, spinning in a tight circle to hunt Sand, who was already down the hill and fleeing at full speed toward a small red sedan.

"Stop!" Ryder gave chase, easily closing the distance Sand had created. He'd gotten older and heavier while Ryder had gotten fitter and more fine-tuned.

The blessed sounds of emergency vehicle sirens cried in the distance.

West was on the way. Along with a fire truck and possibly an ambulance. Another good thing. The firemen would need to deal with the abandoned bomb-making materials on the railroad tracks.

Ryder's feet hit the street as Sand reached the car. "Freeze, Sand!" Ryder hollered. He braced his arms and leveled his Glock in line with Sand's back. A torso shot would bring him down so that Ryder could bring him in.

The growling of a massive engine drew Ryder's eyes to the road behind them. His dad's truck raced forward, practically out of control and seemingly straight for Timothy Sand. Kara's determined face was at work behind the wheel. Ryder jumped back. She looked as crazy as any mother whose infant's life had been threatened one too many times in a day, and for a moment he wondered if she planned to run Sand down.

Sand turned and ran. He passed the sedan and slowed, looking angrily over his shoulder. If that wasn't his ride,

then where was he going? Surely he didn't expect to beat Ryder at a footrace.

Ryder dashed forward. "Hands where I can see them," he demanded, a sense of cautious victory playing in his chest. He hoped Kara would slow when she saw Ryder had Sand cornered, but the engine only growled louder.

The big black truck tore a path between him and the arsonist with a screech of burning rubber, instantly blocking his view of Sand. Kara slammed the beast to a hard, rocking stop, already screaming, "Get in!" Her voice burst through the open windows.

She didn't have to ask twice. Something was undeniably wrong. It was written in the terror on her face. Whatever she needed Ryder for, she'd decided it was more important than capturing Sand, and that made the matter unimaginable.

Ryder bounced onto the bench seat, eyes fixed on the fleeing lunatic visible outside the windshield. "Chase him," he said. "Don't hit him, but don't let him get away!"

Before he could close the door behind him, the red sedan exploded in a teeth-rattling eruption. The truck rocked under the force. Ryder's ears rang and his vision blurred. The car he'd expected Sand to get into and race away in had blown three feet off the ground before plummeting back to earth in a flaming disaster. A wave of heat rushed out to meet them like an angry apparition, sweeping over the windshield and hovering above the ground outside.

Kara panted behind the wheel, then shifted into Reverse and tore away from the scene, separating Ryder from Sand yet again.

She shifted roughly into Park at a safer distance and sobbed outright. "West told me," she cried. "Sand bought

explosives from a demolition website last week. The team tracing his financials found a record of the purchase today. They're looking at everything he's been doing since his probation ended, trying to guess his plan, and they found that. West said to be careful, but you were already alone with him, and I just…" She set her forehead on the steering wheel and cried.

Ryder sorted the words, thankful the team was making progress in tracing Sand's recent activity and especially glad that those strides had saved his life. *Kara* had saved his life.

A funny thing occurred to him then. "You weren't going to run him over?"

She rocked her forehead against the wheel until her puffy eyes came into view. "No," she half laughed, half scoffed. "I was coming for you. I thought I was too late."

Ryder turned to stare at the flaming car. The place Sand had last been seen. "I thought I had him."

Before he'd disappeared into the smoke and vanished.

Chapter Twelve

Emergency vehicles flooded the scene, dividing and conquering. Crime scene crews gingerly packed the bottle-bomb materials found on the train tracks. Deputies fanned out across the area searching for clues and examining the path Sand had taken to the exploding car. Firemen contained the fire, soaking the grass with water and applying a thick layer of chemicals to stanch the beating flames. Marshals tracked Sand's escape route through Kara's neighborhood, but he was long gone.

Ryder was the first marshal to give up. He dragged himself back into the chaos, past the charred sedan, past the place where he'd almost become a pile of ashes, back to Kara.

He'd gone after the arsonist once the car had finished exploding and settled into low flames, but Sand's trail had gone cold. The other marshals arrived later and stayed behind to canvass for sightings. Ryder needed to get back to Kara.

Kara stood in a tight triangle with Cole and Uncle Henry outside the doors of an ambulance. Their heads tilted inward, arms crossed tightly over their chests. Kara had begged him not to give chase until he'd had his burns looked at, but Ryder hadn't felt them then. All he'd been

able to think of was getting his hands on Sand. He'd been so close that he could almost feel his fingers tightening the handcuffs around Sand's wrists.

Kara's face was the first to lift from the huddle. Her gaze found Ryder immediately. Deep lines cut across her forehead and gathered between her brows as she watched him draw nearer. "You shouldn't have left on your own again."

Ryder disagreed. No one else had been there to follow Sand, and someone had to. Time was everything, and there was none to spare.

"You look like hell," Uncle Henry said in lieu of "Hello."

Ryder hadn't exactly taken time to look in a mirror yet, but judging by the missing skin on his hand and searing pain in his face with every whisper of wind, he believed him.

"He just ran off like that," Kara complained, waving a hand as if to showcase his injuries. "The minute the worst of the explosion settled, he was out of the truck and racing into the smoke."

Ryder had raced into the thicket of trees outside his old neighborhood and across a small stream on the other side. He'd hoped to catch a glimpse of Sand, or at least find a clue about the direction in which he'd fled, but there was nothing. No tracks in the parched earth. No broken limbs or thudding footfalls. "I thought I could at least see which way he went or what kind of vehicle he was driving."

Uncle Henry moved cautiously toward him, a pile of unopened bandages in one hand and some kind of plastic bottle in the other. "I need to clean those wounds."

Cole and Kara locked him in serious stares.

Ryder didn't have the energy left to argue, and the burns were starting to hurt. "We can't reach Mom and Dad. Someone needs to check on Casey." The thought had sickened him every step of his way through the old neighborhood in search of Sand. "We don't know where Sand went, and Mom and Dad weren't answering their phones when we tried calling them earlier."

Kara set a small hand on his elbow. "West's spoken with them. They're okay."

He slumped against the silver bumper of Uncle Henry's bus and rolled his shoulders. Injured, angry and shaken to his core, Ryder wanted nothing more than to get back out there and search for Sand. But it was time to step back and evaluate how this day had gone so wrong.

He'd been so certain he had Sand right where he'd wanted him, that he'd run full speed toward a car bomb and had had no idea. Ryder had been so focused on catching Sand that he hadn't stopped to wonder *why Sand had indulged in all the theatrics*. Why would Sand call Kara's landline? Why would he lead them into a purposeless ambush of tiny bottle bombs just to run away and jump into his car? Why would a clever criminal ever intentionally let him know what he was driving?

He wouldn't, and he didn't. It wasn't his car. It had been a trap, and Ryder had walked, no, *he'd run*, right into it.

Timothy Sand had plans stacked ten deep, and Ryder just kept signing up to be his puppet.

"Ow!" He jerked away from Uncle Henry. "Dammit!"

Henry slapped his hand away. "Be still." He ripped the packaging on a sterile bandage, then placed the clean white square gently against Ryder's jaw. "These are second-degree burns. You're going to need to keep them

clean and covered for a couple weeks at least, maybe more than three. Depends."

He leveled Ryder with a no-nonsense stare. "What happened here?"

Ryder grimaced. "Arson."

Uncle Henry shook his head slowly. "That's what you said last time. You're going to tell me this is arson on your chin?"

"Might be a bit of chemical burns, too," Ryder admitted. "He threw a Molotov cocktail at my head. I blocked it with my hand."

Uncle Henry gave a sour look. "And your face. Let me see your hands."

Ryder lifted the one he'd used to thwart the attack.

Uncle Henry repeated the careful cleaning and bandaging process he'd performed on Ryder's jaw and cheek.

Cole lifted a palm in goodbye. "I was just here for muscle in case you tried to get away without having those burns treated. Now I'm going to help canvass Kara's neighborhood. See what turns up."

Ryder waited impatiently for Uncle Henry to stop fussing with him, then dragged himself back onto his feet and winced at the pain. "Thanks."

"Don't mention it. Though if you need me again tomorrow, I might start charging you a frequent-flier rate."

Ryder walked away, waving a hand overhead. "I've got calls to make." First to his parents, then to his team. He needed to check on Casey before he did anything else.

Behind him, Uncle Henry delivered verbal instructions for the care and treatment of Ryder's burns. "Everything you need is in the bag," he said. "Call me if he gives you any trouble."

Ryder climbed behind the wheel of his dad's truck,

aching to scream until the hills fell down around him. Kara wasn't his caregiver. He didn't need a nurse, or a bagful of pills and bandages. He needed Sand hogtied and tossed in the back of the burnt-up pickup.

KARA FASTENED HER safety belt, then jammed the bag of medical supplies into the glove box. It'd been more than an hour since she'd saved Ryder from being blown to pieces by the car bomb, but her heart still raced like it was happening again and again.

"Call Mom," Ryder said, shifting into Drive. His tone and expression were hard, challenging. His gaze was distant.

Kara had seen him look like that before. In fact, during the days preceding their breakup, Ryder had rarely looked any other way.

She watched him carefully as the phone rang, searching for signs he would be okay. Hoping for some measure of kindness or normalcy to return to him. She'd barely gotten him back, and she was losing him all over again. Fear and pain came clutching at her heart and clawing their ways into her mind.

You will never be enough for him.

There will always be another fugitive, another cause, another chase.

Casey deserves better than a man who's only half in.

"Ryder?" His mom's voice jumped through the speakers. "Are you okay? Your father and brothers have barely told me anything. Where are you? What can I do?"

He narrowed his eyes and repositioned his white-knuckled grip on the steering wheel. "We're on our way to you. How's Casey?"

Kara whipped her gaze to Ryder's stoic face. He was

worried about Casey? Not thinking about Sand? She stared at the nearest speaker, waiting for an answer.

Why hadn't his mother answered him yet?

Her heart rate sprinted impossibly faster. The only solace she'd had since the bottle bombs began coming was that knowing Sand was near her meant he wasn't near her baby.

A sudden sigh blew through the speakers. "Casey's wonderful, adorable and perfect," she answered. "How are *you*?"

Kara deflated. Casey was okay.

"I'm pissed," Ryder answered.

"Are you hurt?"

Ryder clenched and worked his jaw but didn't answer.

For a moment, Kara considered reaching for his hand the way he always reached for hers when she was in distress. The lethal expression on his face warned her off. Something more than worry was going on inside his head, and Kara didn't want to think about the truth of that.

"We called earlier," Ryder snapped. "You didn't answer. Dad didn't answer. Why?"

"I don't know," she said. "The reception's not great here unless we're near the house or the road, but we took Casey to see the stables when we got here. She loved the horses. Was that when you called?"

Ryder looked thoroughly disgusted. "I thought something happened to you."

"No," she said with finality. "*We're* fine. *You* were hurt."

"Hi, Mrs. Garrett," Kara said, addressing his mother before Ryder said something rude that he would regret.

No matter his mood, she owed his parents everything for keeping her baby safe. "Casey's doing okay?"

"Yes." Mrs. Garrett's voice was sweet but strained, and in that moment, Kara understood. Her earlier pause had nothing to do with a problem on her end and everything to do with fear for her baby: Ryder, the twenty-eight-year-old US marshal. He'd been in danger and he was hurt; so was his mother's heart by association. "I borrowed a swimsuit from Susie's granddaughter for Casey, and she's been splashing her little hands in a basin of water for a long while now. Cries when we take it away. She'll be happy until lunchtime."

The bud of a smile crested Kara's lips. Casey wasn't even wearing that dress and booties anymore.

Sand really couldn't see her. He wasn't magical. He was one man who could only be one place at a time.

And he wasn't with her baby.

RYDER CROSSED THE bridge over the river and forced his thoughts away from Sand. Obsessing was how he'd lost everything the first time around. He wouldn't let that happen again.

"Hey," he said, reaching for Kara's hand on the seat between them. "You okay?"

She chewed her bottom lip, staring intently through the passenger window. "No," she said flatly. She swiveled occasionally as if she'd seen something significant pass by. "I keep thinking I see him."

Ryder knew that feeling well.

He checked his rearview for signs of a tail, then pressed the gas pedal a little harder beneath the toe of his boot.

Kara shifted nervous blue eyes to him, then back to

her window. "I hate that he's brought Casey into this. She's a baby, and he knows by now that she isn't yours, so what's his point?"

Ryder ignored the punch to his chest. Casey wasn't his, but he wanted her to be. "He wants to punish me."

How could Kara ever allow Ryder to be in her baby's life when he'd put her in danger before they'd even met? The invisible fist twisted against his sternum, stealing his air and delivering a powerful realization. Ryder didn't want to just be *in* Casey's life, like a neighbor or a family friend. He wanted to be *part* of her life. *Part of her family.* The revelation would have been enough to knock him down if he wasn't already seated.

"How can anyone want to hurt a baby?" Kara continued, still watching for signs of Sand at every turn.

Ryder cleared his throat and squeezed her hand. Oxygen seemed to return to his lungs when she opened her palm to him and twined their fingers. "His games are about hurting me. Not you. You're going to be okay," Ryder said.

He willed the words to be true, but even as he spoke them, they rang false in his mind.

"Really?" Kara's voice hitched an octave. "He murdered his ex-wife's entire family, the Sayers family, and I don't even know how many others. He hurt their children. What makes you think he won't hurt mine?"

Ryder flinched. Jennifer Sayers had answered his questions and helped Ryder locate Sand. She should have been the hero of that story, but instead she'd been murdered for her good deeds, and Ryder would never shake the feeling it was partially his fault she and her family were gone.

"Sand is a psychopath," he said, rubbing a heavy hand

against his aching eyes. "He's cold-blooded, but he's never killed anyone who didn't cross him first." Sand was meticulous and calculating, but never erratic. "His ex-wife ran from him. Her family hid her from him. Jennifer Sayers helped me find him. You and Casey have done nothing to him."

Kara pulled her hand free and waved it in the air. "I haven't wronged him? I called West and filed a report after he scared me at the park. I went to the sheriff's department and gave the media his current description. Was that any less than what he punished Jennifer Sayers and her entire family for?"

The truth hit Ryder and splintered like a thousand ice slivers down his spine. He wasn't alone on Sand's hit list, and Kara wasn't just a means to rattle Ryder. Kara had earned herself a place on that list, too.

And little Casey had everything to lose.

Chapter Thirteen

Kara unbuckled her seat belt and powered her window down as the truck rolled along an unfamiliar dirt driveway. Aunt Susie's small Craftsman-style home sprouted from behind a grove of apple trees. The world there was painfully still. No vehicles in sight. No signs of Mr. or Mrs. Garrett, Casey or Aunt Susie. Not even a dog raced over the land to bark at the newcomers.

"It's so quiet," Kara said, fear climbing over her skin. "What if something's wrong?"

Ryder opened his mouth to speak, but the sound of an approaching engine spun her in her seat.

A whoosh of relief flew from her lungs at the sight of Mr. Garrett on a four-wheeler behind them. A shotgun rode across the vehicle's handlebars, secured in a custom rack.

She tapped anxious fingers on the door at her side as Ryder pulled the truck around back. His dad passed them, angling his four-wheeler through the grass and parking outside a massive structure at the rear of the property. He dismounted his ride, then opened a set of barn doors tall and wide enough to guide an airplane inside. Kara's hand slid eagerly into position around the handle.

Ryder parked his dad's torched-up truck beside his mom's Ford.

Kara was out and moving toward Mr. Garrett before Ryder settled the engine.

"She's in the house," Mr. Garrett said as she drew nearer, but his eyes were fixed over her shoulder on his injured son.

Kara broke into a sprint, headed for the home's back door. She knocked hastily before dashing inside, unwilling to stay away a moment longer for the sake of manners. "Hello?"

A portly gray-haired woman peeped her head through an interior doorway. "Kara Noble?"

Kara's headed bobbed wildly. "Yes. I'm so sorry. I didn't mean to be rude, I'm just…" Her voice cracked, and a bolt of emotion struck through her. "Is Casey here?"

The woman stepped fully into sight then, a shotgun in her left hand. She extended her right. "Of course. It's nice to meet you. I'm Aunt Susie. Your little angel is right through here."

Kara shook Aunt Susie's hand, then followed on her heels. They wound through the open archways of several small rooms, all delightfully warm and welcoming, before arriving at their destination.

Mrs. Garrett sat in a rocking chair with a sleeping Casey cradled against her chest. A beach towel speckled with rubber ducks was draped neatly over them both. "Wore herself out," she said proudly. "This one loves the water."

"May I?" Kara asked, moving in close and reaching for her daughter. She turned Casey's limp body around and cuddled her against her heart, then collapsed onto the nearby couch in sheer bliss.

Kara stroked her daughter's hair and lowered her nose to inhale the sweet scent of her skin. She kissed each of Casey's tiny dimpled fingers before pressing her perfect palm against her cheek. Kara's eyelids slid shut, and she felt peaceful and complete. In that moment, there was no danger outside, no spectators inside, only her and Casey. Nothing else mattered and things were right again with the world.

The back door opened and shut again, jarring Kara's eyes open.

"Don't shoot," Mr. Garrett said playfully, his hands raised in mock surrender.

Aunt Susie lowered her rifle.

Ryder moved into the room with a deep frown. "Cole says there was a report of someone fitting Sand's description in my parents' neighborhood this morning. A jogger stopped by the sheriff's department to let us know he saw him three hours ago. As if that is somehow helpful now." Anger scorched a path over Ryder's cheeks. "Not sure how I'm supposed to catch him three hours ago, but at least we can confirm the theory Sand only had Casey in his sights while we were all together. Once we split up, he had to make a choice. He chose us."

"He got away again," Kara said. "Are we sure he didn't follow us here?" She whispered the words, but inside her head she was screaming. Could Sand be out there? Lurking just beyond the walls of Aunt Susie's cozy home? If no one knew where he was, how could anyone be sure he hadn't circled around and followed them there? "We could've led him right here."

Ryder lowered his lean frame onto the couch at her side, his pain and fatigue as evident as his disappointment. "He didn't follow us. I was very careful."

Mr. Garrett moved to the armchair across from them. "What's your next move?"

"I don't know." Ryder dropped his head back and stared at the ceiling, as if the answers were written there. "He's escalating," he said. "He used to be satisfied taunting me. Today, he tried to kill me." Ryder lifted his face. His bandages were dark and needed to be changed. "He's planned it all out. He bought the explosives a week ago." Ryder leaned forward, bracing both elbows against his thighs and gripping his head in one hand. "He didn't come here to continue our game. He came to end it."

Mrs. Garrett stood on shaky legs and moved toward the kitchen. "I'm going to pour some sweet tea and fix a snack."

Mr. Garrett kept his eyes on Ryder. "Your murder is the agenda now."

"Apparently."

"Well, that changes things for the worse. Did you hear about the online money trail your team is following?"

"Yeah," Ryder frowned. "He bought C-4. We just saw it in action."

His dad glanced from Ryder to Kara. "According to West, Sand also bought enough incendiaries and propellants to light up Kentucky, and we're going on thirty-three days with no rain."

Ryder clenched and released his good fist. "I'm worried he's had some kind of mental break. The escalation feels sudden and extreme."

Kara waited to catch Ryder's eye. "He could've been planning this a long while. Maybe the whole time he was on probation. Maybe longer. What's sudden to you might have been a slow unraveling for him." She planted a kiss on her baby's face and tried to stay calm. She'd

nearly seen Ryder blown to bits today, and the image of him running toward the bomb hadn't stopped replaying in her mind. What would have happened if West hadn't warned her? If she hadn't gotten to him soon enough? Would Sand have left town, satisfied, or would he have kept coming for her and Casey until they were all reduced to smoke and ashes? She couldn't bear to think of it. "Maybe I should take Casey away for a while. Hop on a plane and just go. Sand might be easier to find if he's looking for two people who've left the continent. I've always wanted to visit Timbuktu."

Mr. Garrett snorted. "You'll have to buy three tickets. I don't think you'll be able to separate my wife from your baby."

As if on cue, Mrs. Garrett returned with a tray and a smile. Five glasses and a pitcher of sweet tea sat beside a big plate of cubed cheese, fruit and crackers. Crisp wedges of vegetables were piled along the plates' sides. "Help yourselves."

Mr. Garrett patted his middle, quickly moving toward the tray. "Nervous cooker. She loves us with food."

Ryder sucked down a glass of tea without stopping, wiped the back of one hand across his brow then poured a second glass.

"Are you okay?" Kara asked. She'd never seen Ryder look so wrecked. "You should take the pills Henry gave you for pain. I put them in the glove box."

"I will." He rocked onto one hip and freed his cell phone. "It's Cole." He hit the speaker button and palmed the device, making it easier for the entire room to hear. "Garrett."

"Hey," Cole began. "Where are you?"

"With Mom and Dad."

Kara glanced at their blessed hostess. Ryder's gaze was on her, too. He'd intentionally omitted her name.

Aunt Susie watched silently from the room's corner, shotgun within reaching distance. Her gray hair was wound into a tight bun at the nape of her neck, and her clothes were neat as a pin, but something about her quiet disposition assured she could handle herself, whatever came.

Ryder dropped his attention back to the phone. "What do you have?"

"I got a call from a local gas station attendant who thinks Sand was in there thirty minutes ago. She sent some stills from the station's surveillance footage of a man fitting his description, but he's got a ball cap pulled low over his forehead in the picture, and his shoulders are hunched. Hard to say for sure if it's him. Even his exact height and build are hard to determine in the photos. I think it's worth checking out."

"What's he driving?" Ryder asked.

"Looks like a late-model hatchback. Possibly foreign. I'm headed over there now to interview the clerk and see the video footage firsthand. I thought you might want to meet me there."

"Give me thirty minutes," Ryder said, pushing back onto his feet. "We're going to need to relocate the clerk when we finish. Put her up somewhere outside the county for a few nights. I'll alert my team we've got an immediate witness in need of concealment."

His gravelly voice and ruddy cheeks broke Kara's heart. Jennifer Sayers was a clerk who'd helped him, too, once, and look how that had turned out.

He stuffed the phone back into his pocket and reached for Kara. "Walk me out?"

She let him pull her up, careful not to disturb Casey. Much as she hated to risk waking the baby, she refused to miss the chance to say goodbye to Ryder.

He shook his dad's hand, then kissed his mother and Aunt Susie on their cheeks. "I'll be in touch when I know something."

His mom nodded bravely. "Be careful."

Inside the giant barn, Ryder turned to face Kara. "I know more about Sand's agenda now," he said, motioning to his burned face with his bandaged hand. "After what happened today, there's no doubt he'll kill me if I let him. I won't let him."

Kara did her best to maintain a strong front like his mother had, but she was new to this, and her composure was all but gone at the thought of losing him.

Ryder lifted his hand to cradle her chin and pierced her with sincere eyes. "I will come back to you."

"Promise."

He lowered his gaze to her lips. "Always."

Ryder wound his injured hand behind her back and pulled her closer with his forearm, until their bodies aligned, toes to waist.

Casey snored gently between them, completely unaffected by the dangers of her world.

Ryder kissed Casey's head. He traced her round cheek with careful fingertips, then raised his eyes to her mother. "I will protect her."

Kara blinked tear-filled eyes. "Kiss me goodbye?" she asked softly.

A pleased moan rumbled in his chest, and he planted a powerful kiss on Kara's mouth.

Her limbs went light and her head went fuzzy. It was

the kind of kiss she wanted to wake up and fall asleep to every day for the rest of her life.

He released her too soon and onto unsteady feet. "That wasn't goodbye."

She lifted her fingertips to still-tingling lips and watched as his truck's taillights disappeared down the driveway. She wanted desperately to believe that Ryder would choose her over Timothy Sand if it came down to that again. Not just for her and Casey, but for Ryder. The last time, his obsession had left him broken. This time it could get him killed.

WEST AND COLE were already at the gas station when Ryder arrived. The clerk was young and happy. She seemed genuinely thrilled to be useful in the search for Timothy Sand, and it broke Ryder's heart. She had no clue what that report could cost her.

"Thank you," Ryder said when she finished. "Two members of my team will be here shortly to escort you to your home. You'll have some time to pack your things and make a few calls, then you'll be escorted outside the county and kept safe until we find the arsonist you saw in here today."

Her proud expression turned to shock. "Am I in danger?"

Ryder nodded. "Yes. This man knows exactly who he's seen or spoken with, and he will know who helped us catch up with him." He fought to ignore the boulder of emotion resting on his windpipe. "We can keep you safe if you follow the marshals' instructions. Witness protection is a service we take seriously and do very well."

Her eyes widened, and color bled from her skin. "Witness protection?"

Cole shot Ryder an ugly look, then reached for the girl. "Come on. He means well, but he's intense."

The clerk toddled along behind him, dumbfounded and tossing stray looks over her shoulder to Ryder as they exited the building.

West clapped him on the back. "Well, that girl will never sleep again."

Ryder stretched his neck. "What else can I do? Where's the line?" he asked. "What is the right amount of advice and honesty that makes folks pay attention, but won't scare them half to death? This *is* scary. And it's life or death."

West shrugged. "I don't know. I'm just saying she's calling her therapist right now. That's all."

Ryder shook his hands out hard at the wrists, trying to dislodge the tension that seemed to encase his body like iron. "What are you doing over there?" He moved toward West and the mess he had spread on the countertop.

West turned a wad of messy papers toward him. "Credit card receipts."

"He wouldn't pay with a credit card," Ryder scoffed. "He hasn't held a job for more than a few months in over a decade, and credit cards are traceable. He's not stupid, and this isn't his first rodeo."

West pressed a receipt against Ryder's chest. "Oh, yeah?"

Ryder lifted the paper into view. The signature was nothing but a scribble and a long flat line. "What's it say?"

"Credit card fraud. That card belongs to Mr. Bradly Perkins, a man who happened to file a report this afternoon about his late-model hatchback that was stolen last night from the Hitchin' Post Saloon. His wallet was

in the glove box. When I got the report this morning, I figured Mr. Perkins could get in line for the department's attention. Killer arsonist on the loose and all. I didn't have a spare officer to search for his car, which I assumed was probably still parked at his friend's house or along the street somewhere. Mr. Perkins was nursing a heavy hangover when he called. I told him we'd get to it as soon as we were able. Then I started thinking, we don't get a lot of car thefts around here, and I wondered if anyone in Cade County might be in need of a new ride and a stolen identity. Guess who came to mind."

A small smile curled Ryder's mouth. He freed his phone from his pocket and swiped the screen to life. "You're a genius, brother."

"Yeah, but you can call me Sheriff."

Ryder pressed the phone to his ear.

Ten minutes later, tech support had provided the most recent activity on Mr. Bradly Perkins's stolen Mastercard.

Ryder scrolled carefully through the text message, searching for a clue to Sand's whereabouts. He read one line twice, and a smile broke across his lips. "Gotcha."

West angled around for a better look at the little screen. "Well, looky there. Mr. Perkins checked into a hotel around lunchtime today. Wonder if that was before or after he filed the report?"

"Can't say," Ryder mused. "Could be a trap."

"Could be the break we need." West tidied his mess, then stopped to speak with Cole and the clerk on his way out.

Ryder hoped West was right because Ryder sure didn't want to be this time.

A black SUV pulled into the lot at Cole's side. Two US Marshals climbed out, ready to protect the girl.

She turned the lights out and flipped the sign in the window to Closed before returning to the somber-faced men trading supportive nods with Ryder. They would take care of her. Ryder didn't have to worry. He could put everything he had into the much larger problem at hand. Like a plan to capture Sand when he returned to the hotel. Ryder needed to set up an ambush and bring Sand in without anyone else getting hurt. Or killed.

West and Cole pointed their cruisers onto the road, and Ryder shifted into Drive behind them. Next stop: the Lucky A Hotel.

THE GARRETTS PULLED into the restaurant parking lot beside the hotel and fell into formation on the pavement. Ryder took point, flanked by his brothers.

A blast of icy air poured over his shoulders as he entered the main office through a side door. Cole and West stood outside, keeping watch for signs of Sand.

A cranky-looking redhead glared at Ryder from behind the desk. Her pointed gaze fell to the shiny star hanging from a beaded metal chain around his neck. "Yeah?"

He forced a tight smile, recalling his mother's theory that it was easier to catch bees with honey than vinegar. "Hello, ma'am. I'm US Marshal Ryder Garrett. I'd like to ask you a couple questions about a man staying here."

"Pft." She turned her face away, returning her attention to the daytime talk show playing on her rabbit-eared TV.

He strode to the desk, pressing forward until his toes hit the cheap wooden veneer. "Excuse me?"

She rolled her eyes. "I ain't allowed to give out information on our guests. That's invasion of privacy."

Ryder clenched his jaw until he thought his teeth would snap. "Please don't misunderstand. I have reason to believe a very dangerous man is staying at your hotel. My need to apprehend him supersedes your need to protect his privacy."

She didn't look convinced. "I think you need a warrant."

"I don't…" He raised his palms in exasperation, then marched around the desk and bumped her out of the way. A few keystrokes and mouse clicks later, Ryder had what he'd come for. "Thank you." He gave her a limp salute on his way out.

The woman tapped frantically on her phone, a fierce scowl on her face as she watched him leave.

"Come on," he told his brothers as the door swung shut behind him. "Room 117."

They moved swiftly along the hotel's exterior wall, making their way to Sand's room.

West checked his phone and snorted. "Dispatch says there's someone at this hotel harassing staff and posing as a marshal."

Ryder shot him a sour look, then pointed to a white hatchback up ahead.

Cole ducked to the car's side and set his palm to the hood. "Still warm."

"Television's on," West reported, standing just outside the room in question.

A thrill of victory ignited Ryder's cache of adrenaline. He circled a finger in the air, instructing his brothers to cover all the exit points, then pulled out his cell phone and called his team. They needed backup to contain the

situation and a bomb-sniffing dog to evaluate the perimeter before Ryder kicked the door down.

Timothy Sand was about to get a brand-new jail cell with free rent for life.

Chapter Fourteen

Room 117 was surrounded. Just twenty minutes after Ryder's call, every spare lawman in Cade County was in place, including four tightly wound Garretts ready to put Timothy Sand behind bars.

"One," Ryder mouthed, taking position in front of the door.

A plain-clothed deputy had walked a bomb-sniffing dog past the door twice, playing the role of bored animal-owner, allowing the canine time to scent for explosives.

"Two." To Ryder's surprise, the door wasn't booby trapped.

He waited one beat longer, then kicked the door down, three years of frustration fueling his aggression. He marched inside, gun drawn. "US marshal." He moved swiftly room to room, clearing the messy space with a pack of reinforcements behind him.

Two additional marshals had made the trip to Shadow Point from Cincinnati following the car bomb, and they'd arrived in time to join the capture team. A stroke of much-needed luck after losing the other two to protect the clerk.

Unfortunately, this was no longer a corner-and-capture mission.

This was another miss.

"Clear," he said one final time, feeling his hopeful heart turn slowly to stone. Ryder holstered his sidearm and let loose a slew of swears, forcing himself not to topple something or kick the wall.

Behind him, the explosives dog barked, commanding the room's attention and directing it to a set of empty duffel bags and suitcases stacked inside the closet.

Blake pulled free of the cluster of lawmen, his FBI badge gleaming under the cheap fluorescent lights, and went to get a closer look.

The marshals descended on a small round table covered in photographs and newspaper articles.

An entourage of men and women in a mix of plain clothes and uniforms gathered outside the open door, speaking to other hotel guests and making guesses as to how Timothy Sand had made another clever escape.

Ryder imagined screaming, swearing and pounding something until the excess energy, anger and adrenaline were spilled from him, but there was no time for that. No time to waste on outbursts and tantrums. It was time to double down. Make his own plan and get his priorities in order.

West appeared in his periphery, breaking through the crowded room in a straight line to Ryder's side. "You okay?"

"Yep."

"You sure, cause you look like you're about to lose your mind."

"Yep."

West gave him a long once-over, cocked hip, tipped head, scrutinizing eyes. "My guys are going to canvass the area. See if anyone saw Sand today, which way he

went, anything like that." He glanced over his shoulder at Blake, who was frowning into empty bags and suitcases. "Looks like he was holding a lot of nasty materials in here. Nasty, *flammable* materials. I'm hoping he used all the C-4 in the car. I don't want to think about what else he has in mind."

Ryder rubbed his brows. "Any use hoping that was his big play, and he botched my murder, so he's out of moves?"

Blake shook his head. "Nah."

"Garrett." A marshal Ryder knew as Jim Riggs waved from the table covered in newspaper clippings and photographs.

The Garrett brothers circled him at the little table.

Ryder was sure Jim had only meant to get *his* attention, but calling out for "Garrett" in Shadow Point rarely turned up fewer than two or three responders. "What've you got?" Ryder asked, staring at piles of sorted photos.

The marshal looked from brother to brother as the Garretts closed in around him. "I know y'all are brothers, but I don't think I've ever seen four people look so much alike."

"Jim?" Ryder pushed, redirecting the man's commentary. "You found something you want me to see?"

"Sorry. It's just really weird," he muttered under his breath. "Here." He turned a stack of papers to face the Garretts. "These are all articles and photos of you from the last three years. Everything's date-stamped, like he was chronicling your life, and he's stalked your career pretty tightly, too, especially the last twelve months."

Ryder lifted the nearest stack of evidence and flipped through the unnerving pages.

"I sorted all the piles by date," Jim said. "You've got the most recent. They get older moving left to right."

West chose the pile closest to him and thumbed through the photos. He let out a long, slow whistle. "This is all from those first days when you left town. You looked like hell. He tracked your fall from grace damn closely. Probably wore it like a feather in his cap."

Ryder examined the collection in his hand. "I can't let him take all the credit."

Ryder had chosen to chase the monster at the expense of everything else.

Not this time.

Ryder cringed at first sight of the final photo in his stack. A snapshot of him taken in the last forty-eight hours, since his return to Shadow Point. Sand had drawn a big sad face on his lips and put neat X's over his eyes. The repetitive arch and curve of pen-drawn flames bordered the page's edge. He stood outside the sheriff's department in the photo.

Cole walked away. "This guy's sick." He appraised the room for a long beat before he began running his hands along the hanging photos. "He left plenty of his crazy out in the open. Let's see what he's hiding." He moved on to peering inside the vents with a flashlight.

West lifted another stack of papers. "And here we have a detailed account of your more recent rise to fame."

Jim snorted.

Ryder grunted. He was hardly famous, but he knew what West saw. "I was only standing in."

West turned an article in Ryder's direction, misplaced pride all over his face. "You led Ohio's most successful drug task force in the state's history? Last fall?"

Ryder shrugged. "They needed a warm body. I was

between witness relocations, and I run a steady ninety-eight-point-six. I qualified."

"Sure," West said. "No big deal." He made a crazy face and turned back to the stacks of papers. "You've got to call home more."

Ryder didn't deserve any accolades for his work as a lawman. He'd been stalked for three years without a single clue it was happening. That took an amazing lack of skills. Sand had been in Cincinnati with him. Bought copies of the local newspaper detailing his career drama. Hell, he'd probably even watched Ryder drive haplessly to work every day. *At the US Marshals office.* All while he took his picture.

Cole gave up on the vents and knelt beside the bed, gloved hands searching busily between the mattress and box springs. "Bingo." When he stood, he had a notebook in his hand.

Ryder moved to his side. "What's that? Is it Sand's?"

Cole lifted and dropped a noncommittal shoulder. "Someone doodled a stick figure with X's on his eyes and flames on his head. Big star on his chest. Put it right here on the cover." He held the notebook up beside Ryder's head.

Blake laughed.

Ryder snatched the notebook from him. He turned the pages slowly, mesmerized and horrified by the heavy-handed scrawls. "It's all nonsense. It says, 'Stop following me. Let me live. Stop following me. Go away. Go away. Go away.'" He frowned at the little book, wishing he could throw it through the window. "Is this a joke? A planted thing to make me chase my tail some more?"

Another clue that meant nothing, led nowhere. Just like all the others.

Cole craned his neck and read over Ryder's shoulder. "I didn't think that guy could get any creepier. I was wrong."

West reached for the book. "May I?" He looked stricken as he turned the pages. "Those words and phrases sound like pleas. They aren't aggressive like the photographs, though that spectacular rendering on the cover is a little worrisome." He flipped back to the stick-figure marshal. "I'd say the nut is coming fully unhinged. But we already knew that. What do you think about me asking my wife to weigh in on this? Unofficially." His jaw went rigid, his eyes, hard. "She's a clinical psychologist with some recent and very personal experience in handling stalkers."

"Yeah," Ryder agreed. "If she's willing. I'll take whatever edge I can get. This is new territory for me." West's wife, Tina, had undergone a horrible ordeal when her stalker stole her baby and tried to force Tina into a weird mommy-and-daddy relationship with him. She'd been lucky to get out with her life. West had played a major role in that, but he didn't like to talk about it.

Ryder nudged West with his elbow and nodded his appreciation. He was lucky to have brothers like his most days. But especially this one.

Blake turned his phone's camera on the notebook as West flipped the pages. "This can't be good," he said. "The guy stalks you for three years, then fills his creepy little notebook with pleas for someone to stop following him?" He raised an eyebrow.

It didn't make any sense to Ryder, either, but Sand had never been sane to start with. "Being on the run wears on a person," he said. "I see it in the witnesses I relocate. They've sometimes been underground for ages before

they come forward and ask for protection. Hiding always seems to chip away at their sanity. Makes them paranoid and constantly on edge. The life he had while I was chasing him couldn't have been easy, especially for someone already so messed up, but this last year should have been better. The marshal's office caught him, tried him and let him go with a temporary ankle bracelet." Ryder felt his muscles tighten. Sand had killed entire families, but he'd avoided jail time, and now he got to walk free.

Blake scrolled through the photos of the notebook on his phone. "I can't say I feel sorry for a flame-throwing murderer, but I wouldn't mind helping end the man's life on the run. Maybe tuck him into a tidy little cell at the local penitentiary for a hundred or so years."

"That's the goal," Ryder said. He checked his watch for the tenth time. Hours had passed since he'd left Kara and Casey at Aunt Susie's, and Kara was probably thinking the worst.

He scanned the room, deliberating. He could stay and help tear the hotel apart looking for Sand, the little cockroach, maybe hunt for clues, go door-to-door canvassing with the deputies, or sit tight and pore over the stalker-grade surveillance photos on the table until he lost his mind, or he could go to Kara.

He was done with choosing work over family.

Ryder had a lady and a baby to protect, and the former was probably worried sick. Kara and Casey might not be Ryder's by marriage or blood, but his heart had laid a heavy claim to them, and his mind was working on how to make it official. "Let me know what else you find. I'm going to get Dad on the road with the girls. Wherever Sand is, he's got his hands full trying not to be identified by the horde of lawmen on his tail and most

of Shadow Point on the lookout. This is the perfect time to move Kara and Casey to the next location. I'll meet them there."

"Cabin?" Blake asked.

Ryder gave a stiff dip of his chin.

"That's good." Blake said. "Off the grid. Virtually unused. And not easy to get to. Wherever Sand is, he left his car out front. He might see you pull out of here, but he can only follow you so far before his legs get tired."

Ryder said his goodbyes, then jumped in the truck, eager to arrive physically where his heart had been all day.

KARA SAT ON the small front porch of an old log cabin in the mountains near the national park. The land had been in the Garrett family since before the park was anything more than the local hunting grounds. The cabin had been built by their ancestors' hands. Somehow it wasn't a hard stretch of her imagination to see any of the Garrett men living in the rustic home today.

Mr. Garrett sat a few feet away, perched on the steps, shotgun balanced across his thighs as he whittled something from a fallen branch he'd cracked over one knee and busted into a wedge the size of a coffee mug. "Someone's coming," he said, setting the knife and piece of wood aside, then taking up his rifle. "Better see who it is."

Apparently his superhuman hearing didn't come with an ability to see the future.

Kara stilled, but Casey didn't notice. Snuggled warmly against her mama's chest and tummy, Casey's tiny mouth moved in sweet little circles as she dreamed of an invisible bottle, no doubt. For a moment, Kara wondered if

she should wait inside the cabin until the guest arrived, or maybe even prepare to run. Mr. Garrett had promised her they weren't followed, but she wasn't feeling very secure anywhere today.

Rifle in hand, Mr. Garrett moved silently along the path covered with twigs and leaves that he called a road. He stopped at the crest of the hill and raised his arm to whatever he saw beyond.

Kara had no idea what it meant. A greeting? A warning? Hopefully it wasn't her signal to run. Though, if she had to flee, she knew what she'd do. It was the only thing she could think of since arriving at the cabin with her baby.

First, Kara would run behind the cabin and over the hill. If she kept moving down the slope long enough, eventually she'd come to the river that ran along the docks at the edge of town. Then, she could follow the racing water back to civilization. She knew better than to try to make it back on her own by wandering in the woods. Everything looked exactly the same on the mountain. Brown mud and twigs and tree trunks. A thick green canopy overhead. Fallen leaves from seasons long past clung to the earthen floor.

Mr. Garrett moved again, this time into the tree line, an expectant look on his brow.

Ryder's SUV rocked into view, bouncing over the pitted remnants of a long-forgotten road. She was somehow thankful he'd left his dad's truck with the burnt-up bed behind.

Her heart leaped at the sight of him climbing down from behind the wheel. She ached to run to him, to embrace him and to cry relieved tears of joy and thankfulness, but she contained herself, determined to keep her

escalated emotions in check. She settled for allowing her smile to spread widely and enjoyed the relief as her limbs grew lighter with the knowledge that Ryder was okay.

He was better than okay. He was there.

Mr. Garrett hugged his son, then climbed into the driver's seat of Ryder's SUV. "Take good care of that baby," he said, shifting into reverse gear.

Kara lifted one hand in goodbye, surprised to see him go so soon. "Okay." The word came too late, and his tail-lights were already gone, rolling back from sight, down the long, questionable road to the busy town below.

Her attention jumped to the handsome US marshal moving confidently in her direction.

"Sorry it took me so long," Ryder said. His voice was so low and thick she couldn't help wondering if there was a much deeper meaning there.

"Were you able to finish whatever you wanted to get done?"

"No." He moved closer, watching her and Casey with a soft smile. "Everyone's got a job to do. They all have my number if anything comes up." He gripped her hips and leaned into her with a warm, contented smile.

"You just left?" she asked, warmth blooming in her chest. He'd chosen her and Casey when he'd just gotten a huge break in this case? She felt her lips curling into a broad, hopeful smile. "That's not at all like the marshal I was engaged to once." That man had been the last one to leave every crime scene involving Timothy Sand, and he'd brought all that he could home with him, so he could keep working until dawn.

"That man died of a broken heart," he said, tucking hair behind her ear and letting his fingertips trail over her neck.

Kara shivered. "If everyone has a job to do, how did you manage to get back here? What about your job?"

"Well," he began, his loving smile turning wolfish. "My main priority is taking care of you. So, unless you have an objection, I was thinking I'd like to get started."

"No." She smiled, enjoying this side of him, the side who could be both marshal and family man. "No objections here."

Ryder kissed her cheek, then looked at the sleeping baby snuggled between them. "How's Casey?" he asked, cupping the top of her little head in his hand, then planting a kiss on her as well.

"Tired," Kara admitted, easily speaking for the both of them. "Why don't I put her down? I set up her playpen in the small bedroom, and I made coffee."

Ryder followed her into the cabin and to the room where the playpen stood.

"Okay." Kara crept away from the makeshift crib, and looked to Ryder for a plan of action. "Coffee?"

Ryder shook his head. His brilliant blue eyes were dark with want and his hands took no time in finding purchase on her hips and hauling her close. "I don't ever want to lose you again," he said. His Adam's apple bobbed long and slow.

Kara's heart seemed to swell and stretch with a thousand things she wanted to say, but could never properly articulate. "Good because I don't want to let you go again. I shouldn't have let you go before."

Ryder dropped his forehead against hers in what looked to be a sigh of relief. "And Casey?" he asked. "I've put her in so much danger."

Kara rocked her body against his, arching her back and rolling onto her toes. She brushed her lips seductively

across his, turning his words of worry into a deep guttural moan. "We forgive you," she whispered.

Ryder curled his strong arms around her back and pressed her more firmly against the lean, muscled length of him. He lowered his mouth over hers, and warmth flooded through her on contact. His kiss curled her toes, made her gasp and set her world on fire.

Her palm grazed the bandage at his jaw, and she pulled back, afraid to hurt him. "Is it painful?" she asked. "To kiss me?"

"All I ever want to do is kiss you," he said. "It's going to take more than that little burn to keep me from it."

Kara smiled. Her roaming fingertips found the hem of his shirt and peeled it over the top of his head before moving to the waistband of his pants. "How's your hand?"

His eyes widened for a moment, before his lids drooped slightly and his expression went dark and lust-driven. Kara had missed that look even more than she realized. Her skin snapped and tingled with excitement and memories of what she could expect to come next.

"My hand's excellent," he said with a grin. Then, he had her shirt off and lying with his on the floor a second later. The heated skin of his torso pressed to hers, scorched a path of desire through her middle.

"I need you," she whispered breathlessly into his ear, catching the perfect lobe between her lips. Kara wanted Ryder every way she could have him, and she never wanted to let him go once he agreed.

Ryder swept her feet out from under her and carried her to the bedroom across the hall. He lowered her onto the bed and hovered over her, watching her squirm at first, then trailing hot kisses across her collarbone and

into the valley between her breasts. His unbandaged hand found the button at the top of her shorts, and he raised his heated gaze to hers in question.

Kara's hand fell immediately on his, eager to get their bodies back together as soon as possible and preferably without the clothes. "Do you need help?" She smiled, certain that removing her pants with one hand would take far longer than she could stand to wait.

Ryder's dark eyes caught hers with a mischievous twinkle. "I don't, but you might when I'm finished with you."

"Hell." She flopped against the bed and let her hands fall overhead in delicious anticipation.

Ryder dragged her zipper low and slow, continuing his delivery of hot wet kisses until Kara was sure she would soon need help saying thank-you.

Chapter Fifteen

Casey's cries pulled Kara from bed an hour later, far sooner than she was ready to leave Ryder's side. She padded to the next room and scooped her princess from the playpen. Casey's complaints quickly turned to coos of love and playfulness. Kara reveled in the simple joy of moments like these.

She swayed gently, instinctually, to the music of her infant's sweet sounds, and embracing the utter joy still flowing through her heart at the day's satisfying turn of events. Kara had fully anticipated Ryder standing guard at the windows all night while she sat silent in rigid fear. She hadn't even considered he might be as ready as she was to make their reunion official. And she had to admit, making love to her personal hero sounded worlds better than sitting silently anywhere. Her smile grew, and she pressed her lips to Casey's head. Kara had everything she wanted inside these cabin walls, and despite the monster lurking beyond, she was happy.

She turned in search of somewhere to snuggle and rock her baby, and started as she saw Ryder leaning, shirtless and motionless, against the doorjamb. The top button on his jeans was still undone, begging her fingers to slide them off one more time.

He watched her closely, smiling warmly and thoroughly melting Kara's heart.

"You're great with her," he said. "I've seen mothers with babies before, but you and her? Something else entirely."

Kara felt a welcome blush on her cheeks. There was no higher compliment, really. "She's been my world for a long time now. She was my best friend even before she was born."

Ryder moved into the room and wrapped them in his arms. "I'm so sorry I wasn't here to see you pregnant, to watch you glow and to comfort you when you were scared or lonely." He pressed his cheek against the top of Kara's head. "And I hate that I wasn't in that delivery room to meet your baby with you." His warm voice was thick with regret. "I've missed way too much."

Kara pulled back to look into his glossy eyes. The love and admiration so evident in his words were just as clear in his emotional stare. Ryder didn't resent her for being with another man, nor for trying to move on or even for having a baby with someone so poorly chosen that he'd left her. Ryder only hated that he'd missed so much.

She ran a palm over his chest before raising it to his cheek. She wasn't normally prone to believing in fairy tales, but it occurred to her then that this was probably what people meant when they used the term *soul mates*. Because nothing else mattered. Not the past. Not the future. Only that they would be together. Everything else was irrelevant. And now they had a sweet baby girl to make their story all the more enchanting.

Ryder's phone buzzed in the pocket of his jeans, and he loosened his grip on them to check the screen. "West," he said, snapping into business mode. He kissed Kara's

nose and backed away to take the call, leaning against the nearest wall instead of walking out the door.

Kara appreciated that more than she could say. She basked in the feel of his eyes on her as she changed Casey's diaper and carried her into the kitchen for a bottle.

Ryder followed, copping a feel as she strode by.

Kara jumped and laughed, enjoying the little break from reality more than she should. The knowledge that playtime would soon end, possibly in catastrophe, niggled, ever present in the back of her mind. But all she could do was take the passing seconds as they came, and pray she was wrong about the catastrophe.

Kara unloaded the makings of a bottle onto the kitchen counter and began to mix the formula for Casey's next meal.

The house had been dusty from disuse when Kara had arrived with Mr. Garrett, but she'd put her nervous energy to use on the details. Now, everything smelled like lemons and evergreens. She'd scrubbed the place down and opened the windows, bringing the gorgeous summer day inside. She'd removed sheets from the furniture. Swept the floors. Wiped the counters. Then, moved on to the bedroom where everything she'd needed to turn the simple mattress and headboard into a cozy cabin bed had been carefully stowed in plastic bins and stacked in a closet. As a blessed bonus for her efforts, the coffee maker was in good working order.

"Nah," Ryder answered West's unheard question. His blue eyes sought hers, and she couldn't miss the impish glint. "I've brought her here before."

Kara smiled.

She and Ryder had come to the cabin to celebrate the

one-month anniversary of their first date. He'd told her they were going to look at the stars, but in reality, they'd spent the night exploring one another.

It was her first time, and it had been one worth having. She'd always cherished the memory. No regrets about any bumbling high school sweetheart or a groping college frat boy. Just Kara, Ryder and his heartrending touch.

Ryder had been the town playboy, like his brothers before and after him. He'd sworn the rumors weren't true, but his experience was hard to deny once he'd gotten his hands on her. The temptation to give herself to a man had never even registered until Ryder. From the moment she'd first realized she loved him, Kara had needed him like she needed oxygen, and the three years they'd spent apart had been as unfulfilling and uncomfortable as having never taken a full breath.

"I guess I'm going to need a shirt," he said, tucking the cell phone safely away and moving in her direction, completely unaware of the lovely memories she'd been reliving.

She pushed her bottom lip out and grazed the backs of her fingertips over the smooth angles and planes of his chest. "Are you leaving?" A pang of fear pinched in her chest.

"No." He gave her a confident, cocky smile. "Company's coming."

KARA WAITED IMPATIENTLY while Ryder dressed and went to keep watch for Tina, West's wife. According to Ryder, Tina was a clinical psychologist they'd brought into the loop on Sand, hoping she'd see something in the evidence that they couldn't, like a pattern that might help

them figure out Sand's next move. After reviewing the files, she'd requested an audience with Ryder and Kara.

Kara's tummy twisted as she imagined what a therapist would think of this man, and she was only slightly certain she wanted to know what horrible thing was going to happen next.

Ryder met Tina at the crest of the hill, the way his dad had met him, but instead of taking her truck and leaving, Ryder walked her to the porch and extended his hand to introduce her. "This is Kara Noble. Kara, my sister-in-law." He shot Tina a goofy smile. "Tina Garrett. Man, that never gets less weird."

She snorted. "Yeah? Have you ever been around when someone calls Rita 'Mrs. Cole Garrett?'"

Kara laughed with Ryder at that one. Little Cole Garrett was forever burned in everyone's minds as the baby brother of three rowdy troublemakers. He was Cole the middle school baseball star, and nobody thought of him as a veteran or a medic or a deputy, and certainly not a devoted, respectable husband. But there he was. All those things and still goofy as a three-legged pig.

Kara shook Tina's hand. "It's nice to meet you. This is my daughter, Casey."

Tina's smile softened and her face lit up with the tender, doe-eyed look of a mother. "I love her." She moved closer, stroking Casey's hair and lifting her small fingers. "My Lily will be two soon, and little West is five and a half months this week." Her eyes brightened. "We should get together sometimes. The kids should be friends. Maybe playmates one day."

Kara smiled. West had *two* children. It was hard to believe, and then it wasn't. He wasn't the same man she'd known three years ago. He was better. Happier.

She glanced at Ryder, wanting more than anything to have a family with him one day. "I'd like that."

"Perfect." Tina clasped her hands to her chest, then grinned at Ryder as he moved toward the cabin door. "Hopefully we'll all be seeing a lot more of one another once this mess is resolved."

Ryder held the door and ushered the women inside. "I was surrounded by brothers for twenty-seven years, then I got hit with three sisters in the last eighteen months. And all of you are meddlesome."

Tina's smile widened. "So, that's a yes? We will be seeing more of you three, together, once this is over?"

Ryder rolled his eyes and went to pour coffee.

Kara blushed stupidly and took up a deep interest in Casey's hair. "Thank you for coming," she said.

"Did you have any trouble finding the place?" Ryder asked. "It's not easy for a reason."

Tina tipped her head left then right. "Not really. I made a couple of passes on the main road before I turned off. I wasn't sure there was really a road where I was told to turn. West had to draw me a map since it isn't on any."

Ryder set two mugs of coffee on the table, for Tina and Kara. "Was there anyone else on the road?"

"Was I followed?" Tina smiled. "I don't think so. I tried my best to be careful."

Ryder's expression hardened.

Tina either didn't notice, or she pretended not to.

Kara didn't like it. If Ryder was worried, she was downright terrified.

Tina twisted her mug on the wooden tabletop. "I could've called, but I'm not a fan of phones and texting is too impersonal for something so deeply personal. I wanted to give you my thoughts on Timothy Sand, and

be available when I finish in case you have any follow-up questions."

"All right." Ryder gripped the back of the empty chair beside Kara, unable or unwilling to sit still. He locked his elbows and leaned into the wood. "Hit me."

Tina moved her gaze from Ryder to Kara. "I've been reading up on arsonists this evening. I haven't worked with one in years, and I wanted to be sure I gave you the most accurate information I could. Forgive me if some of this is redundant. I'm sure you've done your own research." She released her mug in favor of folding her hands on the table in front of her. The sleeves of her tan cardigan matched beautifully with her cream tank top, khaki slacks and nude heels. She didn't look anything like a woman who'd marry the town sheriff, a man who preferred night fishing to restaurant dining, but this was clearly an example of opposites attracting each other. The most noticeable things about Tina were her warm smile and sincere blue eyes. Kara had known her for ten minutes and she already adored her. "You may know this, but there are six main reasons for a fire starting."

Ryder nodded.

"No," Kara said. "I don't."

"Vandalism." Tina lifted one manicured fingernail. "Excitement. Revenge." She raised another finger, then another, ticking off the reasons. "Crime concealment. Profit. And extremism." Her lips pressed into a firm line as she finished. "I think we can easily count out vandalism, profit and extremism."

Ryder crossed his arms and widened his stance, sliding effortlessly into marshal mode.

Kara worked to steady her breathing. Fear jumped all over her as she just thought of the man who'd led Ryder

to the red sedan and tried to blow him up. Her hand went to his, needing to feel their connection.

Tina shifted in her seat. "I looked at all the case notes, the timelines and the revelations. Granted, I did it in a hurry because I think time is as valuable as accuracy at the moment, but there's a lot going on with this man."

"Like what?" Ryder asked, almost before she'd finished the statement. "Specifically."

"Well, for starters, I think the first fire he set was simply meant to be a crime concealment. He'd murdered his wife and her family, and he tried hastily to cover his tracks. He killed them first. Burned the house down afterward."

Kara looked to Ryder to see if he agreed.

He didn't speak, but he also didn't argue.

"The second fire," Tina said, "was revenge. Sand followed Jennifer Sayers home to punish her for aiding you to find him. He burned her home down for revenge."

"Different motives," Kara said, letting the criminal's variation in reasoning settle in. "Is that common?"

"No. But many pyromaniacs don't realize they are pyromaniacs until they're presented with the opportunity to set a fire and watch it consume something. I think the first fire was an act of desperation that happened to introduce him to his illness. Now he knows he likes fire, and the ones he's been setting in Shadow Point so far, bomb excluded of course, seem to be for the thrill of it. Sure, he's trying to get your attention—" she looked to Ryder "—but he could do that in lots of other ways. For example, I understand that he brought you here from another state just by having the right kind

of conversation with the right person from your past. He's very clever."

"Manipulative," Ryder added with unnecessary snap. "Calculating."

"Yes," Tina agreed. "So, we know he doesn't need to start fires to get you to pay attention. He lights the fires because he likes it. Which moves him into the excitement category. The thrill and anticipation of striking the match is a strong motivation all by itself. Couple that with his desire for revenge against the marshal he blames for keeping him on the run, never letting him rest and possibly for forcing him to kill the Sayers family, and this is a recipe for disaster."

Shock and anger warred on Ryder's face. "You think he blames me for what he did to that family?"

"I think he can enjoy lighting the fires, but has incredible internal guilt over the murders. Especially the Sayers family because they weren't personal to him. Not like his wife and former in-laws."

"All of that is crazy," Ryder said. "He can't blame me for those murders."

"Because you already blame yourself?" Tina asked.

Ryder's face reddened. "I haven't chased him in a year. I'm not keeping him on the run." His words were clipped and impatient. "I wasn't even the marshal who arrested him or got him assigned to house arrest. I'm not in the picture," he barked. "Or I wasn't until he dragged me back here."

His words pierced Kara's heart. He made it sound as if he regretted returning here. She knew it wasn't what he'd meant, but it stung, nonetheless, especially after she'd let her hope rise and soar all day. Silly images of

her with Casey and Ryder at the park, or in the backyard as a family, had wormed their way into her mind, as if they were possible, inevitable, guaranteed.

But nothing was guaranteed. Including her surviving this nightmare.

Tina watched Ryder carefully as he composed himself after nearly losing his temper. She took a tentative sip of her coffee, and pretended to smile at Casey, while letting her gaze slide sneakily back to Ryder several times. "I have a few more opinions," she said. "This is where my interpretation of the evidence gets dicey, and like I said, he's not my patient, so take this under consideration and nothing more."

"Go on," Ryder grouched.

"I think that in addition to his new thrill of setting fires and the pursuit of revenge against you, he's possibly dealing with a serious psychological issue."

Ryder made a deep, throaty noise. "No kidding."

"I've read his notebooks," Tina said. "He's definitely got something else going on as well. Possibly schizophrenia. Again, I'm only going on the information which was available to me, and I can't be sure without an interview of the patient, but the scribbles in his notebook suggest he may be hearing voices or that he believes he's following some kind of orders. It looks like he might have had a psychotic breakdown about six months ago when the note keeping began."

Ryder went still. His arms fell slack at his sides.

Kara raced backward through the loads of disturbing information she'd been given in the last few days, but she had no idea what Tina meant, or why Ryder had reacted that way. "What happened six months ago?" Kara

asked, interrupting a stare-down between Tina and her brother-in-law.

Ryder lowered his eyes to Kara. "There was a vigil for Sand's ex-wife and her family around that time. The local church puts it on every year. It's nothing like the one for the Sayers. Not a rally or a call to action. Nothing like that. It's just a time of remembrance."

Tina formed a sad smile. "I think Sand wanted to attend, but couldn't because you were always there. You attended faithfully every year." She set her giant purse on the table and removed a folder from the contents. Tina opened the folder and selected a photo. "This is a copy of one of the pictures left at the hotel." She placed a fingertip beside Ryder's face among a two-dimensional crowd. Little red X's were scratched over his eyes. "It's a photo of the event covered by his hometown paper," she said. "You'd stopped hounding him, but you were still mucking up his life. The vigil is important to him. It's where it all started." She took another paper from her bag and turned it to face them. This was a newspaper clipping. "The morning after the vigil, Ryder was in the local paper for a commendation on a national case."

Kara lifted the newspaper clipping in awe. She'd had no idea how well Ryder had been doing. Come to think of it, he'd come back to her today instead of staying at the hotel room where Sand had vanished again. Pride lifted her chest. He really was better. Had his priorities right. Wanted her and Casey in his life. He hadn't acted like the obsessed man he'd once been during any part of this investigation, and the truth of it overtook her. Ryder was exactly who he said he was, a formerly broken man who had healed.

"I think Sand got some satisfaction while your life

was spiraling," Tina said. "But watching your more recent successes go public when he couldn't even attend his wife's vigil without risk of capture and arrest, *by you*, might've pushed him over the edge."

Tina slid an apologetic look from Ryder to Kara. "I think that's why he targeted Kara. She was almost your wife once. That's close enough for him to make his point."

"Which is?" Ryder asked.

Tina eyeballed him. "How would you like to be kept from her?"

Ryder's hands landed protectively on Kara's shoulders as he moved behind her to stand. "That's not going to happen again."

Chapter Sixteen

Two long days dragged on with no visitors at the cabin, although Ryder's phone rarely stopped buzzing and dinging with texts and messages. Kara's nerves twisted into a fine point and jabbed at her heart and lungs. Her imagination grew darker and more detailed. Thoughts of a thousand ways Sand could appear and hurt them haunted her nights and days. Despite the busyness of Ryder's cell phone, it was always a new clue, but never a fresh sighting. Sand had turned to smoke.

For Kara, time alone with Casey and Ryder was both perfect and terrifying. Ryder left several times throughout the day, scouting the area, looking for signs a person had been in the woods nearby. His trips weren't long, but they left Kara on the brink of panic every time. What if Sand was out there and Ryder never came back? What if Sand was out there waiting to ambush her and Casey the moment they were alone?

Ryder took them on short hikes after dinner each night, never far from the cabin, but the change of scenery was always welcome. They walked a set of abandoned railroad tracks covered in leaves and forgotten by time. Ryder said the line had once been a direct route to

Shadow Valley, a town now covered by water inside the national park, submerged long ago to manage flooding.

He'd led her through a pair of derelict passenger cars from the 1930s, dragging his hands over the dilapidated structures and telling her stories from his childhood. He and his brothers had staged elaborate games of cops and robbers, using the cars as hideouts, shelters and occasionally army barracks.

The cars had given Kara the chills, sitting at odd angles, the tracks beneath them half-sunken in the earth. Their once-shiny metal walls were scored with mud, their floors drowned in leaves. The wide viewing windows were empty, the glass long gone. Kara could almost see the ghosts of past travelers seated on the faded and cracked vinyl seats or standing single file down the center, awaiting a stop that would never come.

Ryder had smiled as they passed the cars on their way back to the cabin, but Kara was glad to put them behind her.

At night, she curled on the couch beside him.

"Any news?" she asked, leaning her head against his strong arm.

"No." Ryder's frame was tense.

She felt the muscle of his biceps clench beneath her ear as he answered. "No?" Kara straightened and twisted for a better look at his face.

His gaze jumped from window to window as it did most nights when the forest grew inconceivably still. "I don't know what he's waiting for. Where he is. I keep thinking something big is coming. This quiet can't last."

"Can't it?" she asked. "Can't he have given up and left town?" Kara's heart pleaded for it to be true. "He avoided his wife's vigil every year because he didn't

want to risk going to jail. And he must know he can't accomplish whatever it is he wanted to do with a dozen lawmen looking for him around the clock. His face is plastered on every news spot in the county." She raised her brows. "Maybe he gave up. Went home."

"Maybe." Ryder wrapped a protective arm over her shoulders and settled her back against his side, tucking her in close and holding her tight.

It was impossible not to hear the "No" in his answer.

"What's the latest news, then?" she pushed. Something had him on edge all day, and he hadn't come out with it on his own. She was tired of waiting. "What does West say? Or Blake?"

Ryder released a long, tired breath. "West thinks it's not too late to put you and Casey on a plane to Timbuktu while I go after Sand full force until he's locked up somewhere he can't ever hurt you."

"And Blake?" Kara asked. Ryder likely got feedback, requested and otherwise, from everyone out there looking for Sand, but the feedback that mattered most would come from his brothers.

"Blake thinks we should stay at his place, and keep a SWAT team on standby until Sand loses his patience and makes a move."

Kara hated both options for different reasons, but living on a mountain was going to be a problem when winter came, or Casey started school in five years. "What do you think?"

"I'm leaning toward Timbuktu," Ryder said with another deep exhale. "We've been in this strange stalemate too long, and I don't like it. I'm going to have to do something to put things in motion again, but my first priority is keeping you and Casey safe."

"Okay." Kara ran a palm over his arm.

"Okay?" he parroted, a note of surprise in his voice. "Timbuktu? Just like that?"

"I mean, I'd rather go to Paris, but I trust your judgement." She traced the dips and grooves of his torso with one finger. Counting abs. Admiring pecs. "I just got you back. It's hard to think of leaving. But it's even harder to think of Sand getting his hands on Casey." An involuntary shiver rocked down her spine. "That's…not something I can live with."

Ryder trapped her roaming hand in his and twined their fingers. "You don't have to go to Timbuktu. If you're willing, I can ask the marshal's service to treat you like a witness until this is over." He dropped their joined hands against his thigh. "I should've looked into that immediately."

"Hey." She turned her face up to his. "We're okay. You've kept us safe, and if you want us to go, we'll go. We trust you to protect us. Whatever comes."

"Tomorrow," he said. "We'll move you both off the mountain after breakfast, so I can get back out there and help end this. I put in the paperwork for your temporary relocation this afternoon. I didn't know how to tell you."

Kara could hear sacrifice in his words. She could feel it in his touch. Ryder wanted to be her sole protector, but he also needed to hunt this monster. He couldn't do both.

He repositioned his arms around her, tipping her back and lowering her onto the couch. He covered her body with his, slowly, intentionally. Ryder was saying goodbye.

"Will you come for us after you catch him? Bring us back to you." A renegade tear slid from the corner of her eye and over her temple. Kara had no doubt that the mar-

shals would keep her and Casey safe. She worried about what would happen to Ryder. "You have to be careful, too. You're not invincible, and Sand is crazy."

He kissed her eyelids, pulling back after each gentle press of his lips, as if he was memorizing the details of her face. "I promise."

A knot of emotion tightened in her throat. "Is this what you were thinking about all day? Sending me away?" He'd been quieter than normal, distant. She'd thought for sure he'd been withholding bad news. That maybe Sand had hurt someone else in the name of hurting Ryder. She'd never expected that he'd been worried about asking her to go with the marshals. She knew he wouldn't ask unless it was for the best.

He pinned her with sincere blue eyes. "No. I've been thinking of how I might convince you to stay with me when this is over."

A small smile budded on her lips. "You weren't trying to figure out a way to deliver bad news or ask me to leave without upsetting me?"

Ryder bunched his brows together. "Not unless wanting to make you mine, officially, upsets you." He leaned on one elbow and stroked the spot on her finger where his engagement ring had once lived.

A ragged gasp tore from her lips. Her thumb still went to that spot sometimes, wishing things had been different.

"I know it's only been a few days since I showed up without an invitation, and hauling the absolute worst kind of trouble. I put you in danger. Put Casey in danger."

"You've been thinking about marriage?" The words were soft on her tongue, floating away from her in small whispers.

For a moment, his expression fell.

Was she wrong? Had she made an obnoxious, embarrassing leap? He'd only touched her ring finger, and she'd blurted the word *marriage*. Heat rolled over her cheeks. "Sorry. I didn't mean to assume. You touched my finger, and I am so stupid." She raised a hand to shield her humiliated face. "Can we pretend I didn't say that?"

Ryder sniffed hard. Emotion glossed his eyes. "You aren't wrong."

She straightened with a snap. "What?"

He smiled. "But that has to wait."

"For what?" She knew the answer. *Sand.* Everything had suddenly become all about Sand.

"Hey." Ryder kissed her hand and slid onto his knees in front of the couch. "You deserve a proposal without *him* looming in the background."

Kara scooted to the edge of the couch and locked her wrists around his neck, her ankles around his back. "I would marry you anytime. Anywhere. And no one could ever put a smudge on that." She kissed his square jawline. His sexy dimpled chin. "Sand came here to take me away from you, but he's brought you back to me instead. And I'm never letting go."

Ryder's lids drooped. His gaze fell to her lips.

Kara's insides heated and flipped. "If I'm leaving in the morning, you might want to send me off properly."

Ryder pulled her off the couch and flipped her onto the floor with ease. "Tomorrow, I'm getting you away from here, and I'm going to overturn every stone in Cade County until I find Timothy Sand. When I'm done, I'm going to beg you to marry me."

Kara pulled his face down to hers. "And what about right now?"

Ryder planted a slow, bone-melting kiss on her lips, then let his hands and mouth wander. Her heart pounded recklessly from the effects of his skilled touch. Her mind was limp with endorphins and bliss before he paused to check on her well-being. "You okay?" he asked with a proud grin.

She nodded, breathless. "Take off your clothes."

Ryder's eyes darkened. "You first."

COOL AIR SWEPT over Kara's chest. She reached for Ryder on the floor beside her, but he was gone. The slow glow of daybreak flickered on the horizon outside the cabin's living room window.

"Ryder?" she asked softly, rising onto her elbows and pulling on her discarded shirt.

The room around her was still. Only the sound of Casey's steady breathing carried to Kara's ears through the baby monitor at her side.

She wiped the sleep from her eyes and finished dressing.

It wasn't unusual for Ryder to slip away and check on things. It was odd, though, that he hadn't woken her to watch the sunrise. She'd enjoyed those precious moments yesterday with him at her side.

Kara cleaned up the pillows and blankets tossed haphazardly on the floor.

Ryder's clothes were gone. She could discount a trip to the bathroom. He must've gone outside.

She inched toward the front window, wondering what time it was and how long she'd been asleep. She didn't feel rested. Granted, she'd enjoyed quite a workout before nodding off.

Beyond the glass, the haze of dawn hovered strangely

in the air. Normally, the fog hung like clouds in the trees where the cabin's yard turned to cliffs, and clung to the ground near the porch, but it was different this morning.

An unpleasant scent set her intuition on edge. She knew in the next heartbeat that the smell filtering beneath the door, stinging her nose and scratching her throat, was smoke.

Fear shot through her as she turned for another look outside. It wasn't dawn. Wasn't fog. There was a fire burning on the horizon and the smoke was crawling its way into the cabin.

Kara grabbed her phone and dialed Ryder.

The line connected instantly, but he didn't bother with formalities. "I'm right out front."

She darted into the night to wait for him.

A moment later, his silhouette emerged from the thin gray smoke. "He found us."

Kara covered her face with both hands, begging herself not to scream. There would be time for screaming later. Right now, they needed to get out of there. "Can we make it off the mountain?" She nodded to Mr. Garrett's truck.

Or were the fires burning across the only access road they had?

"We're going to try," Ryder said. "I walked as far as I could to get an idea of where the fire originated, but I can't tell. Smoke's too thick. I had to turn back. Good news is the flames are still far away, and I've got an army headed in our direction. The fire department will take care of the fire, rescue teams will meet us en route off this mountain."

A tiny bubble of relief rose in her chest. The fire wasn't close yet, and help was on the way. "Do we have

enough volunteer firefighters to handle this? It seems really big, and the drought…"

Ryder didn't bother looking at the orange glow burning through the smoke. "West's already spoken with every volunteer in four counties. It'll take some men longer than others to get here, but they're coming, and we're going to need all the hands we can get. If we're lucky, the winds won't change and take the fire into town."

Kara forced images of burning homes from her mind. "I'll get Casey."

Ryder nodded. "I'm going to keep walking the perimeter. Just in case."

Air pressed from her lungs as she interpreted the thing he didn't say. *In case Sand is already here.*

Kara hurried to the room where Casey slept. The moan of the swinging front door stopped her short of lifting her baby into her arms. She froze, arms extended, body tipped forward, waiting.

The sound of creaking floorboards followed. Someone was in the front room, and it wasn't Ryder. He would've called out to her or been at her side by now.

"Knock, knock," a hoarse voice echoed through the cabin. "Anyone home?"

Kara scooped Casey into her arms and grabbed an extra blanket. She snuggled her baby tight and bounced her gently in an effort to keep her asleep. She knew that voice too well.

Sand.

She sent up a silent prayer that he'd sneaked past Ryder, and that Ryder was unharmed out there in the smoke and growing forest fire.

She unscrewed the lid from her water bottle left beside

the rocking chair and dumped it over the spare baby blanket, saturating as much of the thin material as possible.

"Dear," the voice rasped, "it seems you are home after all. Taking a bath?" he asked.

Kara stopped, her eyes darting over the room, as if he might actually be present with her somehow.

The baby monitor glowed beside the playpen.

Her stomach dropped, and her pulse raced. *Be calm. Be calm. Think*, she begged herself.

The curtain billowed beside an open window, and Kara tiptoed closer to push the screen wide. She kissed Casey's head, then climbed onto the narrow ledge, baby fussing quietly in her arms.

She let the curtain fall behind her, then jumped lithely onto her feet in the forest behind the cabin. A small, two-or three-foot drop, but it had felt like multiple stories. Casey's eyes blinked and rolled, trying to wake, but not yet ready.

"Shh." Kara arranged the dampened blanket like a shield covering Casey's head and shoulders against the growing cloud of smoke.

The ominous orange glow had risen higher in the sky, illuminating the mountain in eerie shades of red and casting shadows over the little cabin.

"Ah, ah, ah," the voice sounded at her ear. The man from the park, *Timothy Sand*, stood behind her, inside the bedroom window where she'd been just seconds before.

"Ryder!" Kara screamed and leapt away from the cabin. "Ryder!"

She ran until her sides began to ache from the smoke inhalation. Her ankle turned, and she stumbled over the edge of the mountain, barely staying upright with the help of a nearby tree. She looked for Ryder in the thick-

ening cloud, but there was no one and nothing. Even Sand had vanished from view.

Casey whined, all but forgotten in her mother's trembling arms.

"Shh," she cooed, watching the baby's heavy lids attempt to pull open. Her button nose wrinkled and her tiny mouth pulled down into a deep frown. "Nonono. Shh. Shh. Shh." Kara turned in a frantic circle, squinting against the thickening smoke that stung her eyes and muddied up the already dark forest around her. Even the moon couldn't be seen through the suffocating, acrid air.

"Kara!" Ryder's angry voice echoed through the hills.

She spun in search of him, babying her tender ankle.

A twig snapped nearby, and Kara began to run again, no longer sure which way the cabin had been, only that it was up the hill, and she was fumbling quickly down it, toward the river that would lead her to town. Panic clutched her like a vise, insisting she stop moving, stay, hide, but she had a plan, and she was sticking to it, twisted ankle, burning throat and all. Another few yards and the air began to clear. She sipped thirstily at the untainted oxygen, clearing her lungs and attempting to unscramble her thoughts.

Her ringing cell phone nearly sent her out of her skin, and she groped for it in her pocket. "Ryder?" His face lit her screen.

"Where are you? Are you okay?" he asked, racing through the words.

"I'm down the mountain," she said. A cough ripped through her words. "He's here." She stopped again, unable to continue speaking. The winds shifted, pushing a wall of smoke in her direction and bringing the licking flames into view. The fire crawled branch to branch high

overhead, it rode on embers through the air, and it landed in a blanket of dried and fallen leaves at her feet, igniting small flames. Her head grew fuzzy as she stomped the leaves. Her face grew slick with sweat.

"Where's Casey?" Ryder asked, a mix of fear and hope in his voice.

"With me." She coughed. "I can't breathe." She turned away from the reaching inferno, unsteady on her feet. One ankle throbbing. Her chest, eyes, nose and throat aching.

"I'm coming," Ryder vowed. "West and the others are almost here. Firefighters are in place. Sit down. Get your head below the smoke and let me come to you," he instructed. "I will find you."

"Okay."

"Tell me what you can see," he said.

A rough hand landed on her shoulder, gripping her tight, aggressive and unforgiving. The sting of serrated metal cut through her tender flesh at her throat. "Hello, Mrs. Garrett," Timothy Sand whispered into her ear. His body pressed against her back. "You're a hard woman to catch up with."

"Kara?" Ryder asked. "Kara?" He barked her name, and it echoed through the hot and glowing world around her.

Her phone fell into the leaves at her feet as Sand dug his fingers into her hair and yanked her down the mountain.

Chapter Seventeen

Kara whimpered, fighting screams of pain as Timothy Sand dragged her over the smoky hillside. Her scalp burned and ached as more strands ripped free in his relentless grip.

Casey cried in her arms, but Kara couldn't find focus beyond the pain to coo or comfort her. The best she could offer was not to scream while holding Casey tightly to her chest.

Screaming would only make Kara cough again, make her dizzy again. And she suspected Sand wouldn't have a problem shoving the blade he held at her throat as deep as necessary if she gave him a reason. So she stayed as quiet as possible, trying not to frighten Casey or make her baby cry any louder. She could picture her tiny infant lungs filling with the ghastly smoke already.

Instead, Kara dragged her twisted foot against the ground behind them, leaving a trail, she hoped, like Hansel and Gretel, for her hero to find.

The path would have been obvious in normal conditions, but the fast-moving fire and wall of darkening smoke made it hard for her to see. Hopefully Ryder wouldn't miss it.

Scarlet and amber flames licked the night sky above

the smoke, changing the beautiful summer forest into the wicked, twisted setting of a Grimm's fairy tale.

Kara clung to the hope that none of this would stop Ryder. He was raised in these woods, trained to track and hunt. He would find her as long as she kept dragging that foot.

Sand stopped abruptly and the knife dug deeper into the tender flesh of her throat. "Here," he said, swinging her around to face the other direction.

The decrepit passenger cars came into view. "No," she gasped. *Anywhere but there. Anywhere but the abandoned tombs of a forgotten train.* Despite the growing fires, a ghastly chill overcame her as Sand shoved her inside.

Kara stumbled on her useless ankle, nearly dropping her infant as she tumbled painfully onto the first seat.

Sand loomed over her, glaring down with soot-stained cheeks and bits of ash clinging in his hair. "Put her down."

Kara gripped Casey tighter, her impending death registering like a hard slap to the face. "No."

He ground his teeth and leaned in close, positioning the tip of his broad hunting knife against her temple. His hot stinky breath washed over her face. "Then I'll kill you now and take her with me."

Kara bit back a thousand venomous retorts. There was no way she was letting him take her baby. "Okay," she agreed. "Put your knife away." She waited while he lowered the blade, then she laid Casey on the seat beside her.

"Good girl." Sand shoved the knife into the holster on his belt and moved behind Kara. "Now, give me your hands."

She pulled them back. "Why?" Her stomach lurched

and churned as she awaited the answer. Would he cut her again? Burn her? Tie her up? The last possibility scared her most. How could she escape with her hands tied behind her back? She couldn't carry Casey, and she wouldn't leave without her. She batted stinging eyes and searched the dense smoke outside the missing windows. *Ryder, where are you?*

Sand snarled. He grabbed her, apparently done waiting for her compliance, and twisted her arms roughly toward him. He tied her wrists to the rusted metal rod along the seatback, dragging her hands carelessly across the sharp and broken edges. "You were supposed to be married," he complained. "It's not the same if you aren't married."

She didn't have to ask what that meant. Tina had speculated that the final straw for Sand was probably the fact that Ryder kept him from his dead wife's vigil. A woman who was dead because *he* killed her.

"Then let us go," Kara begged. A new idea forming. "I'm not his wife. She's not his baby." The words sent a spear of raw pain through her gut. Kara wanted a future with Ryder, but more than that, she wanted Casey to have a future. "Let us go and find whatever woman he loves in Ohio. He moved there when he left here three years ago, and he didn't come back until you showed up. He's not here for me," she cried. "He's here for you."

Sand moved back in front of her where she could see him, a look of amusement on his face. "He may have come for me, but he got you first." His sick, demented face turned red with delight. "A few hours ago. On the cabin floor, I believe."

Bile flooded Kara's mouth.

Sand had been outside the cabin while she and Ryder made love. "You were watching." Her skin crawled and

she fought the urge to puke. How long had he known they were there? How long had they thought they were safe, but it was just more of his game?

"It was hard not to watch," he said. "Impossible to deny your love." He turned the corners of his mouth in disgust. "I could sit back and wait for you to marry, but I think ruining things for him a second time seems the stronger move."

"How did you find us?" Kara asked, biding her time and praying for just a little more.

Keep him talking, she thought. *Ryder is looking for us. A rescue team is coming.*

Just. Don't. Die.

Sand sucked his teeth and frowned impossibly deeper. "I was worried I wouldn't find you when you left town after the car bomb, but I wasn't in a hurry. Nowhere to go, you know?" He dug into one of the pockets of his camouflaged cargo pants and liberated a squeeze bottle of lighter fluid. "I went back to the sheriff's department after things settled down at my hotel room. Had to borrow a new car." He shrugged. "I saw a fancy lady talking with the sheriff about me. He had photos of me and a pile of papers. He gave it all to her. I thought she was a reporter or a fed." He twisted the bottle's little red cone cap with his teeth, then spit it onto the floor. "He walked her to her car after that, and he kissed her right on the mouth."

Tina.

"She had her hands on his chest—" Sand put a hand over his heart "—like this, and there it was. A wedding ring." He turned the lighter fluid over and sprayed it up Kara's legs, then squeezed a line of it on her lap and over her torso.

She braced herself, fighting the urge to scream. Casey's cries were already moving from general complaint to serious demand, and she didn't want to make them worse. Kara wiggled away from her baby, pressing herself against the mud-streaked wall and putting as much space as possible between her lighter-fluid-soaked clothing and Casey. With any luck, the flames wouldn't jump to her when Sand struck the match.

She promised herself not to scream when it happened. She didn't want Casey to hear it, and somehow recall the dying screams of her mother being burned alive.

The empty bottle made an ugly gurgle, and he tossed it aside, pulling another from his pocket. "That's when it hit me," he said. "If I couldn't find one Garrett's wife, I'd just use another one to get to the first. So, I followed Mrs. Sheriff home. Or, I thought I did." Sand cast his gaze into the blowing gray smoke beyond the train car.

The wind had changed direction, putting them in the path of destruction.

Kara coughed against the onslaught of smoke.

Sand's eyes were distant, unmoved by the fast-moving wall of fire in the distance. He was somewhere else. Not with her inside the dilapidated train car, on a mountaintop he'd set on fire.

"You followed her here," Kara guessed, choking on the acrid air. *Keep him talking. If he's talking, then he isn't killing you or touching Casey.*

He dragged his attention back to her. "When she turned her fancy car into the trees, I thought she was crazy." He shook his head, then seemed to recall his mission to burn down Kentucky. He went back to spraying the pungent liquid over every seat along the aisle. "I parked my car

and followed her. It was easy. I walked alongside her, slipping between the trees right to your door."

Kara tugged and twisted her arms behind her, testing the strength of her bindings. The material was rough and narrow like twine, but wrapped several times around each wrist, making it impossible to break. She pulled the binding tight between her wrists, separating her hands as much as possible to protect them, then she dragged the twine across the edges of jagged metal, attempting to saw herself free. The ragged edge of rusted metal cut into her skin as she worked, drenching her palms in hot, sticky blood.

Sweat rolled over her forehead and dripped into her eyes as the fire drew near and the temperature rose dramatically around her.

Casey thrashed and kicked at her blankets, demanding to be held, and desperately needing water and fresh air.

Sand continued to pull little bottles from his giant cargo pockets and cover everything in sight with lighter fluid. He moved backward through the open door, doodling destruction and dropping the empty bottles in his wake. With two fresh bottles, he stepped outside, spraying the door and ground before moving out of sight.

Breath caught in Kara's throat. He'd left her there for a reason. Next would be the match. She imagined the flames erupting, circling the car, sealing her fate. All while she couldn't even hold her baby to say goodbye.

As if Casey could feel Kara's desperation, her cries grew relentlessly fevered.

"Shut her up!" Sand called through the open door, having made a full circle around the car. His eyes were wild, his expression feral as he emptied the final con-

tainers. He jerked his head left, then right, turning side to side in search of something. "Shut up!"

All Kara heard was the cry of her terrified infant and the growing roar of a fire chewing through the forest to meet them. She recalled the soaring embers, landing in leaves and igniting the forest floor. She didn't want to think about what one floating ember could do to the train car, or to her.

Sand pressed his palms against his ears.

Kara worked more doggedly at the twine between her wrists.

"Shut. Her. Up!" Sand screamed, his face morphing into something animalistic in the haze of smoke. "Do it now, or I will." His hunting knife was back in hand.

"Shh," Kara cooed, but the efforts were swallowed by Casey's desperation. "I need to hold her," Kara said. "She's too upset. She won't calm down on her own now." Kara had only let Casey get this upset once before. She was three days old, and Kara could barely move following her C-section. The healing had been harder and slower than the nurses at the hospital had promised, and the extra-strength pain killers weren't doing much to help her manage the pain. She was exhausted, hurting, depressed and alone. And Kara had let Casey cry while she sobbed along with her in her own bed, too unsteady to trust her legs to carry her to the nursery. She'd fallen asleep despite her infant's wails, and she'd woken feeling like another woman, but she'd vowed never to put Casey through that again. Every day since then, she'd paid close attention to her baby's needs and met them, often before Casey had thought to complain. "I have to hold her," she repeated, louder this time. "She needs to know I'm still here."

Sand's face was red, his hands smashed tight to his ears.

Kara tipped her face nearer Casey's ear. "You are my sunshine," she sang in a raspy, quavering voice, trying to draw her baby's attention, but it was too late. Casey was in a spiral, and she wouldn't recover without her touch.

If her hands were free, Kara could hold her. If her hands were free, she had a chance of escaping with Casey.

She had to get them out of there before Sand struck a match.

Casey's cries grew strange and labored. Her face turned frighteningly red with heat and frustration. Her fingers were curled into little fists in the air. It seemed impossible that she could withstand the smoke much longer without the worst kind of consequences.

"Please," Kara begged.

Sand stalked forward, up the angled step and into the train car with menace on his brow. He unleashed a rectangular silver lighter from his pocket and opened the lid with the flick of one thumb.

"Stop," Kara begged. "Don't do this. You don't have to do this."

"I do," he said, eyes locked on her screaming baby. "I really, really do."

Kara threw herself over Casey, shielding her despite her lighter fluid-soaked clothes. Anything was better than letting Sand get his hands on her. "No." She tightened her jaw and dragged her bindings over the jagged metal once more, lining the thinnest section of material against the sharpest point of the bar. She leaned her weight into the efforts, desperate to finish the job. "You will not touch my baby."

Sand barked a laugh. He flicked the lighter shut then open, his thumb petting the tiny wheel that would call a flame to life at his command. "I'm trying to decide if Marshal Garrett would be more upset knowing the baby watched you die, or if it would be worse for him to know you watched her die. Before you die. So, who. Goes. First?"

He flipped the lid back and forth a few more times, rubbing the little gear with his thumb, never letting the fire erupt.

"He's going to kill you for this," Kara seethed, not caring if it was completely true, only that Sand knew he would pay soundly for whatever he did next.

"I think I'll start with the baby," he decided.

Kara curled her fists into tight knots.

Sand stepped closer. "Get out of the way." He grabbed Kara's hip and tried to swing her away from Casey, but Kara fought.

She kicked him in the knees and shins, still hung up by her bound wrists and one narrowing portion of twine.

He stumbled back with a roar, grabbing his kneecap and snarling. "You bitch!" He bared his teeth and raised his hands, coming at her as if he planned to strangle her.

But Kara had had enough.

She set her jaw, planted her feet against the floor of the forsaken passenger car and lunged at him. The remaining threads of twine sliced through her already bleeding skin and ripped her left thumb out of its socket.

The force of her momentum snapped the final binding and set her free.

His eyes went wide with shock as she collided with him, knocking him through the door backward and roll-

ing them both against the water-starved earth, soaked in lighter fluid.

Kara screamed as her ankle gave a deafening crack.

Sand rolled her off him and reclaimed his fallen lighter. He held it toward the train car where Casey still screamed in terror, desperate for her mother, for help, anything but the thick gray smoke swallowing the train car and the lunatic wielding a lighter outside.

"No!" Kara slapped his arm, unable to reach the lighter as intended.

The resounding strike of his hand against her cheek sent stars through her vision. Her ears began to ring. Her back hit the earth with a thud, expelling the air from her lungs in one fell whoosh. She blinked her way back from a near blackout, pressing one palm to her scorching cheek, and forcing herself onto her knees. "Please!" she cried. "Don't hurt my baby."

Sand's expression went flat. His body motionless. He slid wild eyes toward the suddenly silent train car.

Kara listened harder. The unstoppable soul-twisting wails of her infant had stopped. Smoke filled the car until there seemed to be no car at all. There was only fire, smoke and Sand.

"No!" She lurched forward and vomited.

The soft snick of the lighter in his hand turned her crying eyes upward. The flame danced, reflected in Sand's dark eyes. "Say goodbye, Mommy."

Behind him Ryder's silhouette moved into view, cutting a path through the suffocating smoke. Kara blinked through the haze.

Ryder raised his gun in unison with Sand's lighter. Before Sand could toss the flame that would engulf the train car and steal her daughter's precious life, Ryder

brought him down with the butt of his gun. Sand collapsed like a ragdoll at Kara's feet.

The lighter and its deadly flame fell in slow motion toward the lighter-fluid-saturated leaves.

Chapter Eighteen

A wall of flames shot into existence, climbing the tree-tops and enveloping the train car.

"Casey!" Kara's clothes were alight with fire, flames racing over the lines of fluid Sand had sprayed on her and eating up the twigs and leaves along the ground.

For a moment, the sudden wave of heat stole her breath. Then, the excruciating pain took over, sending a long piercing scream from her core.

Ryder dove through the smoke and flames. A crushing blow smashed the air from her lungs as he covered her body with his and sent them into a united spiral over the hillside. He clung impossibly tighter to her with every beat of unforgiving earth.

They rolled to a stop several yards away, landing in a spot with clearer air and flameless leaves. The fire on her clothes had gone out, but the pain remained. On her skin. In her heart.

"Casey!" Kara bawled. She'd survived being set on fire, survived the serial arsonist's capture, and if there were miracles like those available for her today, then there had to be one more for Casey. Kara's aching mother's heart wouldn't survive the alternative. "Casey!" She pushed onto her feet as Ryder rolled off her. Another

scream tore from her throat. "My ankle," she croaked, then attempted to hobble toward her daughter.

Ryder wound strong arms around her back and hoisted her upright. "Your wrists and throat are cut. You're bleeding. Covered in burns." He scooped her feet off the ground. His eyes were wild with fear and worry. "Uncle Henry's at the cabin. Tell me all your injuries. How long have you been bleeding?"

"Stop." Kara struggled against his iron grip, but he locked her in tight. "Go back to the train," she cried. "Get Casey! She stopped crying. I think she's..." Fat tears of fear and grief stole Kara's words. Her arms reached uselessly toward the passenger car now completely concealed in flame.

Ryder carried her away, giving the site a wide berth.

"Casey's fine. You're not. Stop fighting."

"No," she sobbed, unable to make sense of his words. "My baby." Kara clamped shaking hands over her mouth as he continued to move away from Casey. Blood smeared across her lips and chin. Why wouldn't he listen? Maybe he didn't know? "She was in the train car." Kara's words fell like stones from her lips. Heavy. Impossible.

"She's okay," Ryder said again. "Control your breaths. The smoke gets thicker up here."

Kara tried to obey. Tried to think beyond the fear.

The fire seemed to have retreated, leaving a path of charred wilderness in its wake.

Somehow, the forest had burst into a flurry of activity. Firefighters, lawmen, strangers in oxygen masks and coveralls had appeared everywhere. Where was her baby? How could she possibly have survived this? Outside the now-smoldering train car, two men in US Mar-

shals jackets stood over a lifeless figure, doused in the white chemicals of a fire extinguisher.

"They don't have her," Kara demanded, punching Ryder's shoulder and thrusting against his chest. "Go back!"

Casey's sharp cry broke through the air, and Kara froze.

The sound came again, not from the abandoned car, but from far away, maybe as high up the mountain as the cabin. "Casey?" she whispered, daring to dream.

She turned her face in search of the sound. "I don't understand," she choked out, coughing roughly and fighting another wave of nausea.

"She's fine," he promised. "At the ambulance with Cole and Uncle Henry."

"How?"

"Cole stole her through the open window of the train car, after you lobbed yourself at a killer."

Kara's heart lifted and fresh tears sprung to her eyes. "What?"

"I had Sand in my sights. It would have been a clean shot until you knocked him on his ass and went tumbling through the train car door."

"You saw that?" she asked, her ears still tuned closely to the beloved screams of her baby.

"Everyone saw that." He swept his gaze through the space around them. "I told you West and his deputies were already on their way and the fire trucks were dispatched. My team, Blake and his men, were all en route. I met them at the crest of the hill while you went for Casey, but when I went for you, you were gone."

"He was in the cabin," she said, the awful memory of him in the bedroom window behind her flashing back to mind.

"Lucky for me you're smart. You left the world's most obvious trail behind you."

"I thought you wouldn't be able to find it in the smoke. I thought you wouldn't come."

"Baby," he said, slowing to look into her eyes, "I will always come for you."

Kara kissed Ryder's cheek. She pulled herself closer to him and held on tight, the burn of her thighs and stomach returning with each jostle and jolt as he climbed the hillside with her in his arms.

Back on the mountaintop, the red lights of emergency vehicles swam over the charred remains of the Garrett family cabin. Firefighters on four-wheelers, carrying backpacks of water, worked to squelch the glowing embers that threatened to start the flames all over again.

Many of the firefighters wore different-colored uniforms emblazoned with a half-dozen town names. West really had rallied men and women from all over.

But the best sight of all was her baby.

Cole stood awkwardly, bobbing a screaming Casey beside Uncle Henry's ambulance. She'd been cleaned up and wrapped in a white hospital-issue blanket. Uncle Henry pressed a stethoscope to her heart while she wailed.

Cole's head jerked up suddenly, eyes locked on Ryder as he crossed the final few yards to Cole's side. "You're both okay?" Cole asked. He looked them over with a mix of awe and joy.

"No," Ryder rasped, letting loose on a smoke-induced cough. "She's hurt her ankle, her wrists and throat are bleeding, and the sonofabitch set her on fire."

Uncle Henry swung the ambulance doors wide, his eyes stretching with shock. "Heavens. Put her down in

the bus." He watched Kara carefully. "Your baby is just fine. Dehydrated and pissed off, but she's going to be all right. We've given her oxygen and cleaned her up nicely." He checked her wrist and neck wounds as he spoke, following her into the ambulance, stethoscope already pressed to her chest.

Kara stiffened as Ryder climbed back outside. "Don't leave."

He collected Casey from Cole, then returned with a fierce expression on his brow. "Never."

Uncle Henry started an IV line.

Cole shut the ambulance doors and gave them a pat.

The ambulance rumbled to life, and Kara's world grew hazy.

Ryder spoke softly to Casey, kissing her hands and face.

Kara imagined the glimmer of a tear on his cheek as her eyes pulled shut with fatigue and possibly the effects of whatever was in that IV bag.

FALL LEAVES FLUTTERED to the ground at Kara's feet, thrown from the gorgeous gold-and-scarlet covered trees. Trick-or-treat night had always been her favorite as a child, and though it had previously lost a little interest for her as an adult, seeing Casey bundled in her puffy white marshmallow costume had put trick-or-treat back at the top of Kara's list.

Ryder pointed his camera at them again. "Get her belly," he said, a big smile on his face. "That always cracks her up."

Kara poked the puffy costume at its center. "I can't get anywhere near her belly. You're going to have to make do with that look of general glee she has going."

"Fine." He lowered the camera and exchanged it for Casey, pulling the nearly eight-month-old baby to his face for a snuggle. "Who's the most beautiful princess in the world?"

Kara snapped a photo, capturing another of her favorite moments forever. Her heart warmed at the sight of them together.

"What?" he asked, tucking Casey back into her stroller.

"Nothing."

Ryder rounded the front of the stroller and ran his palms over Kara's hips before catching her in the curves of her waist.

"I'm just really happy," she said. "Happy you're home. Happy to be alive." Happy her burns had all healed with minimal scarring, and that the snap of her ankle had only been a fracture, not something that had required surgery. Most of all, she was happy her baby girl had no lasting effects from that horrible night in the burning forest.

The Garretts had lost their cabin, a piece of their history, to Timothy Sand, but they'd all assured her countless times that they much preferred the things they got to keep. Everyone they loved had made it out alive, and Ryder had proposed before she'd even left the hospital. Then, he did it again at his parents' house where everyone could see. Apparently, his brothers had started a new tradition in his family. If the whole clan wasn't present, it didn't happen.

Ryder kissed her cheek. "I love you," he said, in the same tone of awe he seemed to use since she'd said yes from her hospital bed. He raised her hand in his, heavy with the most beautiful ring she'd ever seen, and he kissed the puckered skin along her wrist. Ironically, she'd done more damage to herself, attempting to free

her hands from Sand's twine than he had by dousing her in lighter fluid. The burns on her legs and torso were all but invisible, even to her knowing eyes, but the scars at her wrists would forever remind her of just how strong and resilient her new family really was.

"I love you, too." Her skin warmed with the truth of it.

Sand had done his best to take everything from Kara, but he'd actually given her more than she thought was possible. Until he'd shown up at the park, Kara had thought a life alone with Casey was all she needed. She hadn't dared to dream of what her days could be with Ryder back at her side. For that, she was almost thankful the fugitive had returned. She only hated that Sand hadn't lived to see their engagement announced in the paper. He hadn't survived the burns and smoke inhalation he'd suffered after dropping his lighter and igniting the circle around the train car where he'd fallen.

"We're going to be late again," she whispered. A bad habit she and Ryder had developed since he'd moved back in. It was hard to get anywhere on time when she couldn't keep her hands off him. With that thought, she turned her lips to his ear. "Maybe after the Halloween party we can go home and celebrate some more."

He rolled his forehead against hers and gave a deep throaty moan. "You're making it hard for me not to turn around right now."

Kara smiled. "We've got an announcement to make. Remember? Everyone has to hear about our little day trip today, or it didn't happen."

Ryder's smile broadened. He straightened to his full height and looked down at her with deep pride in his eyes, hands clutching the thick, goofy costume material

at her sides. "When we get home, I'm peeling this big candy wrapper off of you nice and slow."

"Why?" she teased, striking a pose in her giant chocolate bar costume. "I say we leave it on."

Ryder barked a belly laugh, and Casey joined in from her seat in the stroller, clapping her dimpled hands and laughing, gleeful at the sound of his joy.

Kara took position at the stroller's helm and began to move toward Blake and Marissa's house a few blocks away. Ryder looked positively good enough to eat in his big ole graham cracker costume, and she wasn't kidding about that private after-party.

He kept pace with her, one arm around her back, waving at their neighbors, passing treats out to tiny knights, pirates and cheerleaders. "I'm seeing a lot of dressed-up folks tonight, but I dare someone to say my family isn't the best-looking s'mores ingredients they've ever seen."

Kara leaned against him, letting his perfect words sink in, her heart swelling impossibly further. She and Casey and Ryder were a family.

Other couples and hordes of kids streamed around them on the leaf-speckled streets illuminated by lamplights and echoing with peals of laughter.

"I think this is my favorite day so far," Kara said, straightening to guide the stroller through another group of costumed families.

Ryder kissed her head. "I think you say that every day."

"I do." She beamed. And it was true every time.

"Just make sure you say *that* next weekend."

"We'll see," she teased.

The six short days until the wedding felt more like six end-to-end eternities, and if brides were supposed

to be nervous, then Kara was doing it wrong. The Garretts had stepped in to handle everything while she recovered in the early weeks after being released from the hospital. She'd had crutches for her ankle, and cream for her burns, but the Garretts had circled around her and Casey as if they were invalids, only asking what she wanted, then disappearing to get it done. She'd felt guilty at first for all the help, knowing she was capable of finding ways to do more. If it had been just her and Casey, she'd argued, then she would have had to do it all herself. The Garretts dismissed the argument. It didn't matter to them what might have been, only that she and Casey weren't alone now. They had family, and families got things done.

When she'd met Mrs. Garrett and Ryder's brothers' wives for lunch to make wedding plans, she'd seen it on their faces. They were happy to be a part of her life. They wanted to be there for this big day and all the others that followed. That was when it had finally sunk in. She had three sisters now, a set of parents living in town and cousins for Casey to grow up with.

"Here we are." Ryder smiled at the adorable display on Blake and Marissa's front porch.

A giant cauldron overflowed with candy on the top step. A happy ghost stood behind it with a sign instructing local ghouls and goblins to help themselves to two pieces each. A small print notation warned that the candy was monitored by a federal agent and taking more than two pieces constituted theft.

Kara snorted. "He must be a hit with the neighbors."

"Lucky for him everyone loves Marissa. If they didn't this place would be covered in toilet paper." Ryder rushed

forward to swing the garden gate open at the side of the little bungalow.

There was no room for doubt as to where the party was: a trail of jack-o'-lanterns led them up the winding cobblestone walk all the way to the backyard.

West greeted them with open arms. He stood near the gate, watching a toddler in a pink princess dress waddle around a display of pumpkins and cornstalks. "Finally," he said. "Do you know how many times Mom has asked when you were coming?"

"Sorry, man," Ryder said, straight-faced. "Kara took forever to get dressed."

Kara shoved him, her cheeks heated with the thinly veiled implication. "We're sorry we're late," she said. "We let Casey finish her nap before we tried to dress her in that marshmallow."

West stood back then, taking in the sight of them together. He hooked his thumbs in the thick overall straps of his fishing waders. He shot a twisted grin at his brother. "What are you supposed to be? A two-by-four?"

"I'm a graham cracker," Ryder said, reaching out to flip the wide brim of West's bait-lined hat. "What are you? A fisherman? How original."

Tina made her way to West's side then, dressed as a fish, a baby sheriff in her arms. "Oh! You're here!" She hugged Ryder, then Kara. "I'm so glad to see you. Mrs. Garrett is about to explode from anticipation. Did you make it to the courthouse?"

Ryder held up a finger. "Hang on now. Your husband put on some waders, called it a costume, then made you come here as a fish?"

West slid an arm around Tina's waist. "She's a striped bass, and my best catch yet."

"Yet?" Tina asked, her perfect eyebrows arched high. "You're lucky I wasn't the one who got away."

West kissed her, successfully stanching her protest. Kara smiled as Tina took the bait.

Blake appeared then, a look of concentration on his face as he strode through the thick crowd of Garretts filling his little backyard. Marissa followed closely behind.

Kara tried not to laugh at his costume. If Ryder thought West's was unoriginal, Blake's FBI badge and jacket over a T-shirt with jeans won the contest for not-even-a-costume. "Hey." She leaned forward for a hug when he arrived. "This is one heck of a party, Blake. Everything looks amazing. Food smells great. Music is perfect." She giggled as the *Ghostbusters* theme song began.

"Marissa and her sister," he said, a bag of suckers clenched in one hand. "They love this stuff. How's the candy situation looking out front?"

"Not as bad as that costume," Ryder said.

Blake shot him a droll look.

A loud squeal broke through the white noise, and West stepped to the side. "Here she comes."

Mr. and Mrs. Garrett, and Cole and Rita rushed across the lawn in single file toward them.

Mrs. Garrett was dressed as a life-size Raggedy Ann doll, complete with painted red cheeks and freckles. "Look at you," she cooed, dragging her happy gaze from Ryder, to Kara, to Casey. "How did it go?" she asked. "Did you have any trouble?"

"No." Ryder pulled Kara closer. "Casey's biological father had no problem signing off on her adoption. The lawyer drew up the papers, we signed and they'll be filed for us on the Monday after the wedding."

"More Garretts," she said in a hungry, theatrical voice,

her fingers wiggling happily in front of her. "That's the best news I've heard all day."

"Agreed," Mr. Garrett said with a wide smile.

Blake raised his bag of suckers overhead. "To more Garretts."

"More Garretts," the little crowd echoed.

Tina shook her head. "There are so many things I could say about this family." Her psychologist's mind was clearly working as she smiled and laughed.

"No doubt," West agreed as Cole and Rita ran off. "Come on. Those two are about to bob for apples again." He rolled his eyes. "She lets him win, but he doesn't care."

Kara exchanged a pointed look with Tina and Mrs. Garrett, who burst into laughter.

"What?" Mr. Garrett freed Casey the Babbling Marshmallow from her stroller and lifted her into his strong grandpa arms.

"Nothing," the women said.

What the men didn't know wouldn't hurt them.

Ryder grabbed Kara's hands and pulled her into the mix of relatives and friends. He spun her against him as the "Monster Mash" began. He twined their fingers and kissed her lips beneath the crisscrossed strands of orange-and-purple twinkle lights. "Marry me," he whispered.

"Yeah." She stretched onto her toes and kissed him longer, deeper.

"I bet my mom would keep Casey for the night," he murmured against her lips.

Kara giggled.

Ryder pulled back an inch, holding her torso tight to

his. "I'll make the arrangements and swipe a bottle of wine from the buffet."

Her eyes and smile widened. "What do I do?"

Ryder gave her a sharp wink. "Don't take off that costume."

Kara covered her mouth with one hand and let the heat rise over her cheeks as she watched the big graham cracker steal wine and kiss his mom goodbye. He was back at her side in a flash, tugging her through the rear gate and along the quiet trail back to their neighborhood.

"I think this should be our new tradition," he said, stopping to kiss her again beneath an ancient oak tree.

Kara closed her eyes and let the kiss carry her away.

* * * * *